I'LL TAKE MANHATTAN

JUDITH KRANTZ

CROWN PUBLISHERS, INC.   NEW YORK

Published by Crown Publishers, Inc., 225 Park Avenue South, New York, New York 10003
CROWN is a trademark of Crown Publishers, Inc.
Manufactured in the United States of America
Library of Congress Cataloging-in-Publication Data
Krantz, Judith.
I'll take Manhattan.
I. Title.
PS3561.R264I44   813'.54   85-22403
ISBN 0-517-56110-7
10 9 8 7 6 5 4 3 2 1
First Edition

*For Steve, who knows why I keep dedicating books to him.
With all my love, always.*

I am grateful to these friends who generously told me things I needed to know.

> *Helen Gurley Brown of* Cosmopolitan
> *Alexandra Mayes Birnbaum of* Good Food
> *Amy Gross of* Vogue
> *Cathy Black of* USA Today
> *Mark Miller of Hearst Magazines*
> *Ellen Levine of* Woman's Day

I'LL TAKE MANHATTAN

M

axi Amberville, with characteristic impatience and a lifelong disregard for regulations, sprang out of her seat in the moving Concorde that was taxiing to a stop, and raced along the narrow aisle toward the forward exit. Her fellow passengers sat in the aloof tranquility of those who have paid twice the price of a first-class ticket to travel from Paris to New York and felt no further pressure to hurry. As she flew by a few eyebrows were elegantly raised at the sight of such an unpardonably pretty girl in an undignified rush.

"What's taking so long?" she demanded of the stewardesses.

"We have not yet arrived, Madame."

"Arrived? Of course we've arrived. Damn these things—they spend more time on the ground than in the air." Maxi quivered in fury and every inch of her body, packed with nervous energy and intensity of purpose, expressed disapproval of Air France.

"If Madame will please return to her seat?"

"The hell I will. I'm in a hurry." Maxi stood her ground, feet planted in the flat boots she always wore for travel. Her short, dark hair was ruffled in seven different directions, here standing straight up and there covering part of her forehead with thick bangs that fell over her indignant face. She would have been riveting in a room full of beautiful women, for she made mere beauty seem not only irrelevant but uninteresting. In the subdued daylight of the cabin she was as alight with anticipation as if she were about to enter a ballroom. Maxi was wearing an old, tightly belted cognac-colored suede jacket and well-worn jeans tucked into her boots, a shoulder bag slung like a Sam Browne belt from one shoulder to the opposite hip, and as she pushed her bangs back impatiently she revealed the thick blaze of white hair with which she had been

1

born, a streak that sprang out of her hairline over her right eye.

The Concorde whispered to its final stop and the stewardess, with dignified disdain, observed Maxi as she stomped through the exit door before it was fully open, clutching an American passport in her free hand.

Maxi came to a full halt at the closest Immigration booth and thrust her passport at the inspector. He opened it to her picture, studied it casually, and then looked at it intently.

"Maxime Emma Amberville?" he asked.

"Right. Isn't it a god-awful photo? Look, I'm in a hurry. Could you just stamp that thing and let me get out of here?"

The inspector looked at her with noncommittal scrutiny. He calmly punched up some keys on his computer.

"Who," he asked her finally, "is Maxime Emma Amberville Cipriani Brady Kirkgordon?"

"I know. I know. An unwieldy name at best. But it's not against the law."

"What I mean, miss, is why don't you have your full name on this passport?"

"My old passport expired during the summer and I renewed it at the Embassy in Paris . . . you can see that it's new."

"Did you change your name legally?"

"Legally?" Maxi said, offended. "All of my divorces were perfectly legal. I prefer my maiden name so I returned to it. Do you want to hear the whole story of my life? Everyone on that blasted plane is going to get ahead of me. Now I'll have to wait at customs!"

"The baggage isn't off the plane yet," he remarked reasonably.

"That's the whole point! I don't *have* any baggage. If we weren't haggling about my lurid past I'd be in a taxi right now. Oh, bloody, *bloody* hell!" she complained, ardent in her fury.

The inspector continued to study the passport. The photograph didn't manage to convey her quality of electric vitality and as accustomed as he was to bad pictures he had not, for a brief moment, been convinced that the snapshot was legitimate. It showed mostly bangs and a neutrally smiling mouth, but the woman standing wrathfully in front of him, her hair looking like the feathers of an outraged bird, had a boldness, an audacity, that would have forced him to notice her, as if a flare had been sent up in front of his nose. What's more she didn't look old enough to have had more than one husband, much less three, in spite of the date of her birth, twenty-nine years ago.

Reluctantly the inspector stamped her passport with the day's date, August 15, 1984, and gave it back to her, but not before he'd made a special illegible notation on the back of her customs declaration.

Moving with the tadpole agility of the born New Yorker Maxi slapped her shoulder bag down on a customs table and looked around impatiently for an inspector. At this early hour they were still gathered in one corner of the big room finishing their morning coffee, not anxious to start the day's work. Several of the customs men caught sight of Maxi at the same time and each of them put down his mug of coffee abruptly. One of them, young and red-headed, broke from the pack and started off toward Maxi.

"What's your hurry, O'Casey?" asked another inspector, catching him by the arm.

"Who's in a hurry?" he asked, shaking off the arm. "This pigeon just happens to be mine," he announced, walking quickly toward Maxi, outdistancing the closest of his fellows by several yards, in his determination.

"Welcome to New York," he said. "The Countess of Kirkgordon, unless my eyes deceive me."

"Oh, cut out the countess nonsense, O'Casey. You know I dumped poor Laddie a while ago." Maxi looked at him with a trace of unease, her hands on her hips. Just her bad luck to fall into the hands of cocky, freckled, far-from-unattractive Joseph O'Casey who fancied himself some kind of throwback to Sherlock Holmes. There should be a law about civil servants like him molesting decent citizens.

"How could I have forgotten?" he marveled. "You got divorced just before you came through with a major new wardrobe from Saint Laurent. . . . You never were much of a seamstress, Miss Amberville—those labels you sewed on from Saks were very unprofessional. Will you never learn that we study the European fashion lines as soon as they're photographed?"

"Good for you, O'Casey." Maxi gave him a solemn nod of

approval. "I'll keep it in mind. Meanwhile, could you do me a favor and check out my shoulder bag? I'm in a desperate hurry today."

"The last time you were in a hurry it was a question of twenty bottles of Shalimar, the two-hundred-dollar size, and the time before that it was a new Patek Polo, the one you were wearing in plain sight on your wrist, thinking no doubt of the story of the purloined letter. It was carved out of solid gold and worth eight thousand dollars, no less. And then, let's see now, it wasn't too long ago that there was that little problem of a Fendi mink, the one dyed pink, that you told me was a fun fur from a flea market worth under three hundred dollars. Fifteen thousand bucks in Milan if I remember correctly." He smiled, pleased with himself. There was nothing like a memory for details.

"The Shalimar was a *gift*," Maxi objected, "for a friend. I don't even wear perfume."

"You're supposed to include gifts, it says so right here on the declaration," O'Casey said blankly.

Maxi looked up at him. There was no mercy in those Irish eyes. They were smiling, all right, but not harmlessly.

"O'Casey," she admitted, "you're perfectly right. I am a habitual smuggler. I have always been a smuggler and I'll probably always be a smuggler. I don't know why I do it and I wish I could stop. It's a neurosis. I'm sick. I need help. I'll *get* help, when I have a chance. But I swear to you that this time—this one single time—I haven't got anything with me. I'm just here on business and I have to get into the city fast. I should be there now, for pity's sake. Search my bag and let me through." She spoke imploringly. "Please."

O'Casey studied her intently. She was so pretty, this chance-taking dame, that he felt his toes curling right down into the soles of his shoes at the mere sight of her face. As for the rest of her, for like all customs inspectors he was trained in the meaning of body language, it betrayed nothing at the moment. God knows what she must be bringing in to be able to stand there so innocently.

"Can't do it, Miss Amberville," he said, shaking his head in regret. "Immigration knows about your record, he noted it right there on the declaration, and there is no way I can just wave you on. We'll have to do a body search."

4

"At least look through my bag, damn it!" Maxi demanded, no longer the supplicant.

"Obviously it wouldn't be there. It's got to be on you, whatever it is," O'Casey replied. "You'll have to wait till a female inspector comes on duty. There should be one here in an hour or two and I'll make sure she attends to you first."

"A body search? You're not serious!" Maxi cried in unpremeditated astonishment. Twenty-nine years of having her own way in almost everything had created a conviction that ordinary rules just did not apply to her life. And certainly nobody did anything to Maxi Amberville without her permission. Never. Never *ever!*

"I'm perfectly serious," O'Casey said calmly, with a hint of a grin on his lips. Maxi looked at him incredulously. He really meant it, this power-mad bastard. But every man has his price, even Joe O'Casey.

"Joe," she said, giving a deep sigh, "we've known each other for years, right? And I have never been a bad citizen, have I? The United States Treasury is much richer from my fines than if I'd just paid the duty."

"That's what I've told you, every time I've caught you, but you just won't listen."

"I've never brought in drugs or unpasteurized cheese or a salami with foot-and-mouth disease—Joe—can we make a deal?" Her voice traipsed the range from cajolery to delicate, yet unmistakable down-and-dirty.

"I don't take bribes," he snapped.

"I know," she sighed, "I know only too well. But that's your problem, Joe. You're neurotically honest. No, I want to make a trade."

"What kind of nonsense are you giving me, Miss Amberville?"

"Call me Maxi. I am suggesting the straightforward, honest surrender of a body in exchange for an unnecessary body search."

"A body?" he repeated blankly, although he had a clear notion of her intention and the very possibility of such an extravagant bounty was enough to make him forget the uniform he wore.

"A body, my very own, duty-free, welcoming, warm, and all of it, every inch, for you, Joe O'Casey," Maxi said, casually running one of her fingertips down between two of his fingers without taking her eyes off him. She gave him a look that Cleopatra had invented but Maxi had perfected. The man cracked. She could tell from the way he blushed so deeply that his freckles almost disappeared. "Eight tonight, at P.J. Clarke's?" she asked, almost casually.

He nodded speechlessly. Dreamily he put a chalk mark on her bag and waved her on.

"I'm always on time," Maxi flung over her shoulder as she took flight, "so don't keep me waiting."

Two minutes later she began to relax as she sat back in the long blue limousine that had been waiting for her, driven by her chauffeur Elie Franc, known as the canniest and swiftest in the city. There was no point in telling him to hurry for nothing on wheels could overtake Elie except a traffic cop and he was too smart to fall into their traps.

With a quick glance at her watch Maxi saw that, in spite of the impossible sluggishness at which airlines and arrival procedures operated, she would manage to reach her destination on time. Only yesterday morning she had been in Brittany, at Quiberon, subjecting herself to the hot seawater bubble-bath regime that was indicated after an unusually hectic summer, when she had received a telephone call from her brother Toby, telling her to get back to New York in a hurry for an unexpected board meeting of Amberville Publications.

Their father, Zachary Amberville, the founder of Amberville Publications, had died suddenly, as the result of an accident, just over a year ago. The company he had left behind was one of the giants of the American magazine business and board meetings were normally planned well in advance.

"Something about this rush makes me nervous, Goldilocks," Toby had said. "I smell trouble. I heard about it by chance. How come we weren't notified? Can you make it on such short notice?"

"Absolutely. As soon as I shower off the salt I can get the plane from Lorient back to Paris, spend the night and catch the Concorde while you people are still sleeping in New York. No problem," she'd answered. And indeed, except for the hitch almost imposed by O'Casey, she would have been early rather than just barely on time.

Now for the first time since the Concorde had landed, Maxi noticed that even though the day was cool for late August it was getting warmer minute by minute. As she took off her jacket she became conscious of something rubbing against her waist, under the belt of her jeans. With a perplexed look she fished inside and drew out a thin platinum chain that she had clasped there not more than six hours before in her favorite suite at the Paris Ritz. Dangling from the chain was an immense black pearl crowned by two plumes of diamonds from Van Cleef and Arpels. Well, bless my soul, Maxi thought as she hung the jewel around her neck. It was glowingly baroque, prodigally opulent and outrageously conspicuous. How could she have forgotten it so totally? Still, a penny saved is a penny earned, she gloated with the triumphant pleasure of someone who has won by cheating at Monopoly.

E lie slammed to a stop in front of the new Amberville Building at Fifty-fourth and Madison. Maxi didn't wait for him to come around and open the door. Again consulting her watch, she jumped out of the limo and tore through the four-story-tall glass atrium, not noticing the dozens of trees that had each cost the price of a small car, not glancing at any of the hundreds of pots of hanging orchids and ferns. Botany was not on Maxi's mind as she commandeered the express elevator up to the executive floor and her objective, the boardroom of the empire her father had started in 1947 with one small trade magazine. She pushed the heavy doors apart and stood stock still, surveying the assembled company with both hands on her hips, her booted legs spread two feet apart, a stance which she had often assumed since she had learned to stand upright. Frequently enough the world was up to something not entirely to Maxi's liking to justify a basic skepticism.

"Just why are we here?" she demanded of the group of senior editors, publishers, and business managers in the instant of silence that preceded their exclamations of surprise and greeting. But they were as ignorant as she and many of them had rushed into the city from interrupted summer vacations to attend the meeting. The difference was that they had been summoned back officially while Maxi had found out accidentally. Maxi had missed many an editorial board meeting, to all of which she was routinely invited, but it was unheard of that she should not have been informed.

A tiny, exquisite, white-haired man detached himself from the others and came toward her.

"Pavka!" Maxi exclaimed in delight, embracing Pavka Mayer, Artistic Director of all of the ten Amberville magazines.

"What's going on? Where's my mother and Toby?"

"I wish I knew. I don't appreciate rushed trips from Santa Fe, to say nothing of missing last night's opera. Your mother still hasn't arrived," Pavka replied.

He had known and loved Maxi since her birth, understanding that her complicated life was dedicated to extracting the greatest amount of fun that could still be found on the planet Earth. He had watched her as she grew up, and she reminded him of a miner panning for gold, moving feverishly from one claim to another, here hitting an ounce or two of ore, there finding only worthless pebbles and passing quickly on, but forever searching for that vein of pure gold—pure *fun*—that major strike which, so far as he knew, still eluded her. But she believed that it existed, and Pavka Mayer was sure that if anyone were to find it, Maxi would be that person.

"I find this all very strange," Maxi murmured.

"I too. But tell me, what have you been up to all summer, little girl?" he asked.

"Ah, all the usual—breaking hearts, cutting capers, playboy bashing, not playing by any fair rules, getting up to speed, keeping up with the golden lads. You know about them, Pavka darling; my normal summer games, sometimes winning on the swing and losing on the roundabout, a spot of seduction here and there . . . nothing serious."

Pavka inspected her in one experienced art director's glance. As well as he knew her he was always slightly amazed—and as if he had sustained a small electric shock—by her actual physical presence, for Maxi was, somehow, more real than other people, more *there*. She was only of medium height, somewhere around five feet six inches tall, and her beautifully boned body did not take up a lot of real room, yet she created a vibrating space around herself through sheer mesmerizing energy. Maxi was formed like a great courtesan of the Belle Epoque with a tiny waist, excellent deep breasts and sumptuous hips, yet she was not oppressively voluptuous and the masuline, piratical swagger of her garments only made her all the more feminine. Her surpassingly green eyes, the precise color of Imperial Jade—fresh, brilliant and pure—were unshadowed by any trouble.

Pavka knew that no photograph would ever capture the essence of Maxi because she lacked the ruthless bone structure that a woman needed for photography, but he never tired of looking at her dark straight eyebrows that were always raised in faint surprise over her wickedly undeviating gaze. Her delicately molded nose would have been classic if it hadn't turned up slightly at the tip, giving her a look of witty alertness, and the white streak in her hair only made her forever-tousled, capriciously falling mass of short thick hair seem darker by contrast. Yet to Pavka her mouth was her most compelling feature. Her lower lip was tenderly curved into a hint of a smile and her upper lip was unabashedly, undeniably bow-shaped, with a tiny beauty spot to the left of its deeply indented center, the mouth of a trueborn sorceress, he said to himself with the well-earned judgment of a man who had successfully loved women for more than fifty years.

Pavka was still admiring Maxi when the boardroom doors opened again and Toby Amberville walked in. Maxi ran toward him.

"Toby," she said softly just before she reached him and he stopped in mid-stride and opened his arms to her, pulling her close. For a long, quiet minute she remained clasped to him, lifting up her face to his bent head so that they could rub noses. "What's going on, Toby?" Maxi whispered to him.

"I don't know. I haven't been able to reach Mother for the last several days. It's a mystery, but I guess we're about to find out. You're looking great, babe," he added as he released her.

"Says who?" Maxi whispered.

"I do. I smell it in your hair. Your cheeks feel sunburned, high mountain sun, not Southampton. And you've put on weight, about three-quarters of a pound, give or take an ounce, right here on your butt. Very cozy." He pushed her gently away and she watched from the hallway as he continued on into the room, her older brother, by barely two years, a brother who could tell more about her from touching her palms or listening to her say three words, than anyone else in the world.

Toby Amberville was a tall, seemingly tireless man with an absorbed inward-listening manner that made him look older than his thirty-one years. At first glance he didn't have any particular physical feature in common with Maxi yet there was a similarity in the way in which they both fully occupied the space in which they found themselves. Toby's mouth, tender and full, seemed to contradict the strength of his chin, the obstinate determination that made him intimidating to many people, in spite of his easy laugh and his robust, healthy handsomeness. He had amber-brown eyes around which lines were beginning to show, lines which, to a casual observer would have been the sign of a man who squinted, a man who was possibly nearsighted and refused, out of vanity, to wear glasses.

Maxi hung back to scrutinize him as he walked easily and confidently ahead, sitting down in the chair that had been left empty for him by decree of his father since his twenty-first birthday, a chair that waited for him at each editorial board meeting, a chair he occupied more and more rarely, as the advance of his disease of retinitis pigmentosa made his eyesight increasingly limited. Was his tunnel vision still relatively stable? Maxi wondered. It was never easy to know what Toby saw or didn't see since one of the characteristics of his disease was that his vision varied from hour to hour, depending on the set of conditions in which he found himself, the distance and angle from which he looked at something, the brightness or dullness of the light, and a dozen other variables that had a maddening inconsistency so that at times he had moments of accurate seeing which only made the return of his condition of near-blindness more difficult to endure. But he *had* endured, he had made his peace with his condition as much as any man could, Maxi thought as she listened to him greet the various people in the room, immediately recognizing and turning to them at the sound of their voices. For a moment Maxi forgot why she was here in this large room, and lost herself in loving contemplation of her brother.

"Maxime." Her name was spoken in a voice that had a faint British accent, a silver voice whose beauty caused Maxi to shiver. Her mother's voice was the only one in the world that could make her jump and yet it sounded as if it had never been raised to give an order or ask a favor, much less express anger. It was a voice of such an assured and graceful pitch, of such cool, supple charm that it had obtained everything—or almost everything—that its possessor had ever wanted. Maxi turned to greet her mother, bracing herself.

"When did you get in, Maxime?" Lily Amberville asked betraying some surprise. "I thought you were still skiing in Peru. Or was it Chile?" She pushed her daughter's bangs to one side, a familiar caressing gesture that indicated permanent disapproval of the way Maxi wore her hair. Maxi felt a futile anger that she had stopped expressing years earlier. Why, she thought, can no one make me feel ugly except my mother?

Lily Amberville, who had lived the last three decades of her life in the aura of homage that surrounds a very few of the rich and powerful great beauties of the world, embraced her daughter with vice-regal dignity, an embrace to which Maxi submitted as she always had, with a mixture of resentment and longing.

"Hello, Mother, you're looking glorious," she said truthfully.

"I wish you'd let us know that you were coming," Lily replied, not returning or acknowledging the compliment. She almost seemed nervous, Maxi realized, although that wasn't a word she had ever thought of in relation to Lily. Nervous and a little tense.

"I think there's been some sort of mix-up, Mother. Nobody told me about today's meeting. I wouldn't have had any idea if Toby hadn't phoned. . . ."

"Obviously there's been some sort of communications problem—but hadn't we better sit down?" Lily Amberville said vaguely and drifted away, leaving Maxi standing in the doorway. Pavka Mayer came up to her.

"Sit next to me, you devil. How often do I get this opportunity?"

"'Devil'? You haven't seen me for two months," Maxi protested, laughing again. "For all you know, I may have reformed."

"Devil," Pavka insisted as she followed him into the room. How else, he thought, to describe the quintessence she distilled, a nimble, feisty, inquisitive, wide-awake ability to cause trouble, fascinating trouble that he couldn't and wouldn't do anything to change?

"Reformed? My Maxi?" he quizzed her. "May I assume that

the seven dwarfs gave you that amazing black pearl because you were so innocent, so untouchable, so pure, so much like Snow White?"

"There was only one of him, actually, and he was of a perfectly normal height," Maxi said, unblushingly, tucking the again-forgotten pearl quickly inside her blouse. It most certainly wasn't daytime jewelry.

Before she had settled into the chair next to Pavka a hand grasped her too firmly by the arm. She swung around, stiffening with displeasure. Her uncle, Cutter Dale Amberville, her father's younger brother, bent down and kissed her on her forehead. "Cutter," Maxi said coldly, "what are you doing here?"

"Lily asked me to come. I'm surprised to see you, as a matter of fact. I was convinced that you'd abandoned us for more interesting places. I'm so glad you're home, Maxime." His voice was warm and welcoming.

"Just where did you think I was, Cutter?" Only an effort at control kept the dislike she felt out of her voice.

"Everyone thought that you were skiing in Peru or Chile, somewhere quite unreachable. Something to do with helicopters and glaciers."

"Is that the reason that I wasn't notified of the meeting today?"

"Naturally, my dear. There didn't seem to be any point in trying. We didn't have a phone number. But I'm delighted to see I was wrong."

"You should never listen to rumors, Cutter. Toby knew where I was if you'd thought of making that most obvious inquiry. But apparently even he wasn't told. I find that very odd indeed. What's more, even if I'd been up the Amazon I don't like to be out of touch," she stated crisply.

"It must just be a simple mistake." Cutter Amberville smiled, a smile that reached the depths of his youthful blue eyes, a smile that redeemed his features from being impossibly distinguished, a smile so wide that it disarmingly revealed one crooked tooth and transformed his elegant head from that of an ambassador to that of a roustabout. He owed his fortune to the undeniable power of his smile and he had long forgotten the prep-school days when he used to practice it in front of a mirror, forcing warmth, and thus sincerity, to mount from his lips to his eyes by subtle alterations of his facial muscles.

Cutter Amberville had spent the last three years in Manhattan, returning in 1981 after an absence of more than twenty-five years punctuated only by a few brief visits. He had changed surprisingly little during all that time, never losing the spare fitness of the superb athlete he was. His still-blond hair was closely cut, his gaze a slash of blue, his manner never less than disarming. He was a compellingly alluring man who had bewitched many women, yet there was a darkness of some inner purpose in his manner, a hint of something hidden. He seemed to have little need for humor or for people whom he didn't find useful. During his entire lifetime Zachary Amberville had loved his brother deeply.

Cutter continued to beam down at Maxi with the unanswerable weapon of his smile. His hand still held her arm in a firm, even a protective way. Abruptly she jerked away, not caring if it looked rude, and popped herself down near Pavka. Cutter, unrebuffed, touched her hair with a small yet clearly intimate movement that made Maxi's nose twitch briefly in disgust. Just what the devil, she wondered, had brought Cutter to the meeting? He had never attended one before.

She watched as her mother, with the distinctive floating walk, the unshakable proud distinction of the ballerina she had once been, went to the head of the table. Lily sat down next to the chair that had remained empty since Zachary Amberville's death, a chair different from the others in the room, a worn, battered chair that achingly reminded everyone there of the laughing, daring, eager, gutsy, earthy man who had gone so suddenly.

She must not allow her tears to fall, Maxi told herself angrily. Every time she saw her father's chair she was so vividly aware of him that, try as she would, tears rushed to her eyes. God knows, she'd wept and wept during this last year for the father she had adored but she always tried to keep her outbursts private. People were always embarrassed by the outward expression of another's grief and such emotion had no place in a boardroom.

14

Holding her breath and concentrating fiercely, Maxi made herself retain her composure. Her eyes were bright but the tears did not fall. Safe now, from a public display of her deep loss, she watched as Cutter followed Lily. Just where was he planning to sit? Maxi asked herself. There didn't seem to be an extra chair for him. She watched, incredulously, as her mother made a gesture as precise as it was astonishing and with one slender hand indicated to Cutter that he should take the chair that had never been occupied by anyone but her husband.

How could she! How *dared* she let Cutter sit there? Maxi cried to herself, her heart thudding. Next to her she heard a muffled sound of disbelief escape Pavka's lips and all around the table there were hastily stifled sounds of shock. The atmosphere in the room quivered with the impact of this unexpected act of Lily's and people exchanged surreptitious, bewildered glances. However, Cutter seemed oblivious to them and sat down without any change in his expression.

Zachary Amberville had dominated his privately owned company, assisted by the group of people who were all in the room today. After his death his widow had started to appear at the board meetings that she had never attended during her husband's lifetime. She was now the majority shareholder of the company. Lily had been left seventy percent of the voting shares in the corporation; the other thirty percent had been divided among Maxi, Toby, and their younger brother, Justin.

Maxi and occasionally Toby had both tried to attend board meetings when they were in town. However, Maxi had never heard her mother express any opinion or take part in any decision, nor had she done so herself. The editors of each magazine, the publishers and the business managers, headed by Pavka Mayer, had continued to run the huge enterprise as they had done under Zachary, with devotion, competence, great expertise and no diminution of zeal.

There was a moment of silence. Since no one knew the agenda of this meeting, they waited for Lily Amberville to announce it to them. But Lily still said nothing, her eyes cast down toward the table. Maxi watched, dumbfounded, too amazed to take a breath, as Cutter pushed her father's chair a few inches out from the table, leaned back comfortably, perfectly at ease and took over the meeting.

"Mrs. Amberville has asked me to speak to you today," he began quietly. "First of all, she regrets that she had to bring some of you into the city on such short notice, but she has an announcement to make that she felt you should all know about as quickly as possible."

"What the devil . . . ?" Pavka said, in a low voice, turning to Maxi. She shook her head, tightened her lips and glared at Cutter. What had induced her mother to ask him to address the board? Why wasn't Lily speaking for herself, instead of this investment banker, this stranger to the group who had no right to be taking any part in the workings of Amberville Publications?

Cutter continued to sit calmly and speak in measured, authoritative tones.

"Mrs. Amberville has not, as you all know, made any changes in the structure of Amberville Publications in the last year since my brother's unexpected and tragic death. But she has made a serious study of the future of this company, of its ten magazines and its real estate. Now, I think the time has come to face the fact that although six of the magazines are undisputed leaders in their field, four of them are in trouble." He stopped to take a sip of water and Maxi's heart beat even more rapidly. Her devious uncle was giving himself the aura of a general. "I think," he had said, and all down the long table people were sitting without a sound, waiting for the announcement he had promised and had not yet made.

"We all know," Cutter continued, his manner leisurely, "that my brother took more pleasure in creating a magazine than in enjoying its success; more interest in curing the problems of a sick magazine than in exploiting to the maximum the potential of a well one. That was his great strength, but now that he is gone it has become a weakness. Only another Zachary Amberville could have the necessary stubbornness, the willingness to sustain years of losses, and, particularly, the faith in his own creativity, that is necessary to continue to pour the profits of our six successful magazines into the hungry mouths of our weak ones."

16

"Our," Maxi thought in outrage. *Since when,* Cutter, have you had a part of Amberville Publications? Since when do you have the right to say "our"? But she sat in antagonistic, apprehensive silence, waiting, her stomach sinking at his ominously dominating manner.

"Three of our newest magazines, *Wavelength, Garden,* and *Vacation,* have been losing money at a rate that is simply unacceptable. *Buttons and Bows* has a value that, for years, has been purely sentimental. . . ."

"Just a minute, Mr. Amberville," Pavka Mayer finally spoke, his voice slicing through Cutter's composed urbane tones. "I hear a businessman talking, not a magazine man. I know every detail of Zachary's future plans for *Wavelength* and *Garden* and *Vacation* and I can assure you that he didn't expect them to be showing profits yet. However, it's only a question of time before they do. As for *Buttons and Bows,* I feel . . ."

"Yes, what about *Buttons and Bows,* Cutter?" Maxi interrupted violently, suddenly finding herself on her feet. "You probably don't know, innocent as you are of the business, but Father always called it his baby. Why, he founded this whole damn company on it!"

"A luxury, my dear," Cutter answered, ignoring Pavka Mayer as if he hadn't spoken. "It was a luxury to keep a magazine going because it had been lucky for him a long time ago, a luxury your father could well afford."

"Then what the hell has changed?" Maxi cried. "If he could afford it, why can't *we* afford it? Who are you to tell us all what we can and can't afford?" She was shaking with pure, released anger.

"My dear Maxi, I'm speaking for your mother, not for myself. She *controls* Amberville—you seem to have forgotten that. Naturally it's a shock to you to have the brutal facts of business expressed by someone who is on the outside."

He looked at her expressionlessly yet he turned slightly toward her, focusing his words. "While your father was alive this corporation was a one-man show, as even you, my dear impetuous Maxi, would have to admit. But today Zachary Amberville isn't here to make the difficult decisions. Only your mother has that right, only your mother has that power. She feels that it is her duty to engage in sound business practice since we don't have the genius of your father to guide us. It's her duty to look at the profit-and-loss statement, to look at the bottom line."

"I look at the statement, Cutter. So do Toby and Justin. Last year our profits were many, many millions of dollars. You don't deny that, do you?" Maxi asked defiantly.

"Certainly not. But you aren't taking into account the fierce competition we face each month for our share of the magazine market. It's a little frivolous to ignore the fact that with one difficult, painful decision . . . one necessary decision, Maxi, that your mother has *decided to make,* Amberville's profits can be vastly increased."

"Frivolous! Wait a minute, Cutter, I refuse to allow that kind of . . ."

"Maxi, the word was ill-chosen. I apologize. But you are aware, are you not, that your mother is accountable to no one, to no one whomsoever?"

"I know that, but I tell you that Amberville is *not* in financial trouble," Maxi insisted, mutinously, stubbornly determined that nothing should change in the world her father had left.

Pavka Mayer, at her side, was gripped by an equally fierce resolution. As he had listened to Cutter Amberville's words he had been seized by memories of Zachary leading the editorial group with unfaltering courage and imagination over so many difficult periods in the magazine business. Zachary, his friend, who had never attempted to conceal his real motives or emotions as did his subtle brother; Zachary who had plunged into each meeting with a gusto that had made all his colleagues feel as if they were his equals, his companions in the challenges of publishing. Pavka knew far better than Maxi that Amberville Publications was in no difficulty but, unlike her, he didn't have the authority that stock ownership gave. He watched grimly as Cutter turned away from Maxi's protests as if she had become invisible and looked around the table, meeting the eyes of each member of the group briefly.

"Amberville Publications," he said, "is in a situation in which it is *intolerable* that certain, clearly predictable losses should be permitted to continue. Mrs. Amberville's decision is to *cease publication,* as quickly as possible, of the four magazines that have been losing money. She regrets the necessity of this decision but it is not open to discussion."

He leaned back easily, armored and impassive, knowing that the reaction to his words would, in spite of anything he had said, erupt in the room full of men and women, many of whom had just had their working lives demolished. Frightened and incredulous voices burst out all around him. Maxi had gone to Toby's side, whispering fiercely to him. Suddenly the room grew still as Lily Amberville, astonished at the opposition that came from all sides and finding herself, for one of the rare, almost unthinkable times in her life, on the defensive, held up both of her lovely hands, palms forward.

"Please! Please, there *is* something I realize I must say after all. I see now that I've done a disservice to Mr. Amberville in asking him to tell you this difficult news. I didn't anticipate . . . didn't quite understand how unsettling it would be . . . a business decision merely . . . but I should have tried to talk to each one of you separately. However, I'm afraid that was quite beyond my powers. Please don't blame Mr. Amberville for my decision and don't feel that he had no right to announce it to this group. I haven't even been able to tell my children the reason I asked him to speak for me until this minute . . . I . . ." Lily turned to Cutter imploringly and fell silent. He took her hand and again looked around the table with perfect self-possession, like a lion tamer in a cage establishing his supremacy.

Maxi watched them in a condition of incoherent insurrection. What possible excuse could Cutter have to speak for her mother? She remembered unwillingly, but unable to prevent the thought from surfacing, a night when she had been fifteen and Cutter had been on one of his rare visits to New York, staying in one of the guest rooms of her parents' house. She had been in bed, studying for an exam, when he had come into her room in his bathrobe, looking for something to read. He had asked her what she was working on and had approached her bed to inspect the textbook. Suddenly she had felt his hand darting under her pajama top, grasping her bare breast, fingering her nipple. She had pulled violently away, her mouth open in shock, ready to scream, and he had drawn back with a smiling, smooth, plausible apology. But Maxi

19

had known, in that instant, what he had wanted, and he had known that she knew. The attempt had never been repeated, but she could never be with him in the same room without remembering that split second of evil contact. Why was Cutter holding her mother's hand?

"Yesterday," he announced, looking directly at Maxi, his triumph so certain, so absolute, that it seemed emotionless, "Mrs. Amberville and I were married."

3

Zachary Anderson Amberville
had never looked anything like an Anderson, his mother, Sarah
Cutter Anderson, of Andover, Massachusetts, had been heard to
remark plaintively. The boy was obviously a throwback to one of
the French Huguenot Ambervilles who had come over to fight for
American independence with Lafayette, in the regiment of the
Marquis de Biron, and decided to settle in New England. Every
generation or so, a dark-haired, dark-eyed Amberville boy or girl
would be born who would grow to only medium height and who
would have a lamentable tendency toward a certain plumpness in
middle age, and her oldest son was one of them, she complained,
to mask the pride she felt in him which it would have been un-
becoming to express.

Her own Anderson ancestors were stern Swedes and the Cutters were . . . well, the Cutters *were* Andover. No money anymore,
of course, in either of the two branches of her family, but the Ambervilles hadn't done particularly well for themselves either, considering the head start they had had on the rest of the country.
They might all have been considered a bit stick-in-the-mud, determinedly provincial, except that Zack had as much dynamism, as
much ambition, as much get-up-and-go as you might hope to find
in one entire large family of recent immigrants.

He was born in 1923, several years after Sarah Anderson's
marriage to Henry Dale Amberville, the young editor of a small
country newspaper near Andover. By the time Zack was seven he
had his own paper route, delivering his father's paper every day at
dawn. He tried valiantly to expand his sales to include the *Saturday
Evening Post* but he had little luck, for the Depression had just

started to settle over the United States and people were beginning to cut back on every unnecessary expense.

The Ambervilles' second child was a daughter named Emily, who became known as Minnie Mouse and finally just Minnie. By the time their last child, Cutter, was born in 1934, the Depression had almost wiped out the small income of Henry Amberville's newspaper. Zack went to the local public school instead of to Andover, which generations of Ambervilles had attended, and after school he always managed to hunt up some kind of paying job: jerking sodas, delivering groceries, chopping wood, running errands for the town's shopkeepers. He didn't care what he did as long as he could contribute to the family funds. His summers were spent working at the newspaper for his father, learning the business, trying to sell ads and taking over many of the tasks his father now had to do single-handedly, since Henry Amberville had eliminated his tiny staff as the Depression grew worse.

Zachary was a brilliant student who had skipped fifth and eighth grades and his sophomore year of high school. In the spring of his senior year of high school, when he was just barely fifteen, he applied for a scholarship to a number of colleges. His dream was to go to Harvard, for in Cambridge he could have stayed close to his family. His sense of responsibility toward his parents, toward Minnie, and particularly toward his four-year-old brother, Cutter, was so strong that he proposed to go to work after high school and forget about college, but the Ambervilles would not permit this. "We can manage, Zachary, so long as we don't have to contribute to your tuition, but if you think that I'm going to see a son of mine do without a college education . . ." His father's voice trailed off in horror at the enormity of such an idea.

The only university that offered Zachary Amberville a full scholarship, including books, room and board, was Columbia, in Morningside Heights. Ambervilles and Cutters and Andersons and Dales had visited Manhattan, of course, throughout the centuries, but never had one of them actually spent more than a night in the city that they found, unanimously, too loud, too crowded, too expensive, too full of foreigners, too commercial, in fact, as one of them finally put it to everyone's satisfaction, "Not, in point of fact, really American at all."

At fifteen, Zachary Amberville, strongly built but still grow-ing, was a full two inches short of his final height of five-ten, and three years younger than most of his classmates, but he had the mind-set of someone not just bigger but also older. He had been independent for so many years, so driven by the need to take care of his family that he had an inner sense of authority that college freshmen almost never have. He inspired respect at first sight al-though he was, by nature, invariably rumpled, his black hair ruffled by his habit of running his hand through it and tugging on his white streak whenever he was temporarily puzzled by anything. He was carelessly dressed and obviously neither knew nor thought about how he looked. He was volatile, ready for any adventure, talkative, intensely curious about everyone and everything new, and had a belly laugh that could be heard from one end of the dorm to the other. He had never had a drink, never used profanity and never spent a night away from home, but there was a boldness and a largeness about this teenager that had nothing to do with the rules by which college boys usually judge each other. Zachary Am-berville had a good, wide mouth and a pleasingly big, blunt nose and most lively, easily amused, animated green eyes under thick quirky eyebrows. He wasn't handsome, this dark Amberville, but he had a quality that made others like him at first sight and follow him in his many enthusiasms.

Zachary Amberville fell in love with New York City at first sight. "'I'll take Manhattan, the Bronx and Staten Island too,'" he sang to himself as he studied in the stacks of the Low Library, the words of the immortal song that Rodgers and Hart had written in 1925, never far from his lips. I'll *take* Manhattan, oh yes I will, I'll *take* it and I'll *keep* it! he vowed to himself as he grabbed a subway downtown whenever he had a few free hours. He knew the city on foot from the Battery to Harlem, from river to river, he knew the bridges and the parks, the avenues and the sidestreets, and except for the museums, he knew it all, from the outside only, for the price of a subway ride and, once in a while, the best hot dog in the world bought at a pushcart on Delancey Street. Money for the subway, the hot dogs and all his other small needs came from his part-time job waiting on tables at the Lion's Den, the sandwich place on campus. Every extra penny he earned he sent back home, deciding that the luxury of abandoning the Lion's Den job to try out for the *Spectator,* the Columbia daily paper, was something he couldn't afford. In fact there was no element of reluctant choice in what he did. To assume responsibility for his family was a natural function of his personality.

Zachary Amberville had planned his future. When he graduated from Columbia he was going to get a job at the *New York Times* as a copyboy. Surely, he reasoned, as he spent his summers putting out a daily paper almost single-handedly, for his father's health was steadily failing, he would be able to persuade them to give him a job . . . he knew every aspect of the business, from printing through delivery. The Columbia School of Journalism, he judged, would be a waste of precious time and he couldn't afford it in any case.

He had taken the tour offered by the *New York Times,* managing to join groups of schoolchildren who were welcomed into the infernal lower depths of the *Times* building and given a glimpse of the great presses at work. From copyboy to reporter, from reporter to . . . there his imagination stopped, stunned by the richness and varieties of opportunity offered by the best newspaper ever published.

The world had other plans for the members of Columbia's class of 1941. The day after war was declared, eighteen-year-old Zachary Amberville, a full-fledged senior, joined the Marines. He could have waited to be drafted and probably, almost certainly, he would have been allowed to graduate, but he was too impatient to get the war over with and get back to the *New York Times.* "Tell me what street compares to Mott Street in July," he sang, roaring out loud above the sound of the engines of his Marine Corsair fighter plane as he flew countless missions in the Pacific; a hero, a Major by his twenty-first birthday, a Lieutenant Colonel by V-J Day, and, six months later, in Hawaii, a violently angry full Colonel.

"What the fuck do you mean, I can't go home yet? I should have been out on points months ago, sir. Sorry, sir."

"Colonel, I'm sorry, but the General needs you."

"Damn it, sir, what about 'first in, first out'? The General has dozens of other officers, what the hell does he need me for?"

"It seems you have unusual organizational abilities, Colonel."

"I'm a fighter pilot, sir, not a pencil pusher. Sorry, sir."

"I know how you feel, Colonel. I'll talk to the General again about you, but it doesn't look good. He said, 'Tell Amberville that if he wanted out so badly he should have joined the *Army* Air Force.'"

"That's a fucking insult, sir!"

"I know, Colonel, I know."

World War II had been over for ten months when Colonel Zachary Amberville finally got back to New York City. His father had died in 1943 but Sarah Amberville was living in the family home near Andover. Her husband's life insurance had been meager but her son's flight pay, sent home regularly and saved carefully, was still helping to bring up the younger children.

J. Press was the new civilian's first stop. He couldn't show up at the *Times* in his uniform and medals. It would look ridiculous. Copyboys had to dress like copyboys, he reasoned as he knotted his first personally chosen tie in more than five years; a red one with white polka dots that expressed the jubilation that danced in his eyes. He didn't want to look too Ivy League either, though God knows, the only suit J. Press offered that he could afford was a stiff and hairy tweed that would have been perfectly at home in the Harvard Yard if it had only fit him and been twenty years older. The only thing that looks good, brand new, Zachary Amberville reflected, studying his barely recognizable self in a full-length mirror, is a toothbrush.

"I don't understand," he said to the *Times* receptionist. "I simply do not understand."

"We have as many copyboys as we can possibly use and we have a waiting list," she repeated patiently.

"But I have years of newspaper experience. I've *run* a newspaper. All I'm asking for is an entry-level job—I didn't ask to be city editor."

"Look, Mr. Amberville, the *Times* promised all its copyboys when they went into the service that their jobs would be waiting for them when they got back. God knows they didn't all get back, but those who did were the first ones to be hired. Then there were the former servicemen who were graduated from journalism schools. In fact we have copyboys who *taught* at journalism schools. It's too bad you never graduated from college. Then, of course, the other former officers . . ."

"Any Marine Colonels?"

"We have a former General, Mr. Amberville, only one, but he *was* a General."

"Air Force?"

"How did you know?"

"It figured. Those fuckers. *Sorry*, Miss!"

"I'd be glad to put you on the waiting list?" she offered, suppressing a giggle.

"I don't have the time to wait. But thanks anyway." As he left the *Times* Building, Zachary Amberville passed an eager group of schoolchildren about to start the tour. He turned aside, and, for the first time in his life, bought a copy of the *Daily News* and opened it to the pages of want ads.

The Five Star Button Company had prospered mightily through a war in which metal and fabric and leather were rationed, yet buttons could be made out of almost any nonessential material. "Change Your Buttons, Change Your Look," had been their slogan and they sold many millions of buttons made of feathers and pompoms and sequins. They made a superior button, Mr. Nathan Landauer explained to Zachary, a button that you could count on, a button that you could be proud to wear.

"I'm sure of it, sir," Zachary answered, looking around the walls of the office on which cards hung, onto which models of hundreds of different buttons were pinned.

"It's just that the job seems a little, well, not exactly what I'd expect you to be looking for," Landauer continued, admiring the Marine Air Force Colonel's uniform, the four rows of medals, the military haircut.

"It's running a paper, isn't it, sir?"

"Yes . . . if you call a house organ for a button company a

'paper'—frankly I've never thought of it that way . . . just an extra service for our customers, Colonel, and a way to make our employees feel a part of one big family."

"But you publish it every month, you use a regular union printer in New Jersey, there's an office and a part-time secretary that goes with the job, and the salary is sixty-five dollars a week?"

"That's right."

"I'd like the job, sir. Very much."

"You've got it, Colonel."

"Call me Zack. I'll be back in an hour. Just going to change into something more comfortable. Change my buttons, change my luck." Nathan Landauer looked after him wistfully. Those were the best-looking buttons he'd seen in a long, long time. Nathan Junior, proud as he was of him, had spent three years in the Navy, as a simple seaman, and if he had a decent button on his uniform he'd never so much as showed it to his father.

"Nat," Zachary Amberville said to Nathan Landauer, Jr., between bites of pastrami on rye, "don't you want to do something more with your life than make buttons, even if it's more than a living? More than a very good living?"

"What else can I do? It's a family business and Pop expects me to take over for him when he retires in five years. I'm the only son in the family and he built that business up himself from absolutely nothing. It's the biggest button business on Seventh Avenue. I'm trapped, Zack. I just can't break his heart. He's a good guy."

"He's a great guy. But you're not trapped. You can run the business with one hand tied behind you, and with the other . . ."

"With the other?"

"You can become a partner in a magazine."

"Indian say, 'Never invest in show business.'"

"What's that got to do with it?"

"Didn't you see *Annie Get Your Gun?* Ethel Merman asks Chief Sitting Bull how he got so rich and he says, 'Indian never invest in show business' . . . magazines are show business as far as I'm concerned. I don't know fuckall about them."

"Do you know belts? Do you know about bows? Do you know

braid? Do you know hooks and eyes and fake flowers and snaps and crochet trim and . . ."

"You can't walk down Forty-sixth Street without picking up a notion about notions, Zack, it's all part of Seventh Avenue . . . a garment has to have something besides buttons on it even if Pop would never admit it. Yeah, sure I know a little, but so what?"

"*Trimming Trades Monthly.* A new magazine."

"You leave me less than overwhelmed. Condé Nast you're not, my friend."

"It could serve a need. Thousands of garment manufacturers in this country making thousands of different kinds of garments, and none of them knows what's new, what's happening, what's available in the trimming trades."

"Somehow they seem to struggle along all right without being up to date, haven't you noticed?"

"Sure, and they didn't need the wheel either until someone thought of it."

"*Trimming Trades Monthly* . . . would it have color photos of pretty girls wearing nothing but little knitted pussy wigs?"

"No, Nathan Junior, with your filthy Navy mind, it would not. It would have information, ads, stories about what's happening on Seventh Avenue, where the trimming trades are going, what the designers are using this month, maybe even next month, what's happening in Paris, how the various companies are doing, who's changing jobs, who's getting promoted, ads and more ads. In black and white, on medium-quality paper so the print doesn't come off on your hands, but nothing too fancy, and a large, handsome picture of your father on the first cover."

"And, as the sun sets slowly over the beautiful downtown garment center, I begin to see what you want, Colonel, sir. And here I've always thought you loved me as a fascinating lunch date."

"You'd own half."

"How much would it cost?"

"We'd need at least fifteen thousand dollars, before we could begin to make money, according to my best estimates. I don't think we'd pick up enough subscribers for—oh, at least six months to begin to make a profit and, of course, I'd have to quit my job at

Five Star to spend my time getting ads and writing the magazine, so I've included my salary in there."

"How much would you invest of this fifteen thousand dollars?"

"The idea and my salary. I wouldn't get paid until we made a profit."

"What would you live on?"

"There's plenty of room in your apartment, two can eat as cheaply as one, girls are willing to go Dutch, and I walk to work anyway."

"I'd put up *all* the money?"

"Who else?"

"You'd be editor?"

"Who else?"

"Christ, I know I'm an easy lay . . . but what am *I* supposed to get out of this? Besides half of the nonexistent profits?"

"You'd be publisher. Every magazine has one, God knows why. And you'd own half of the magazine, you'd be more than a button manufacturer, when you met a new girl and she asked you what you did for a living you could say, 'I'm a publisher, my pet.'"

"What if she asked the name of the magazine?"

"You'd be on your own . . . lie, say anything you like . . . and when you finally meet a girl who really loves you then you can tell her. But I can't change the name, Nat, it's got to tell you what the magazine's about or nobody will go for it."

"Playboy. I'll tell them it's called *Playboy,"* Nathan Junior said dreamily.

"That's a lousy name for a magazine, Nat. But suit yourself. Let's go visit your bank before it closes."

Trimming Trades Monthly broke even in four months and soon Zack Amberville was able to pay himself a salary of a hundred dollars a week. Since he still lived at Nathan Junior's he sent most of it back to his mother.

Minnie was in her first year at Dana Hall Junior College and Cutter, at fourteen, was going to Andover. Sarah Amberville had found a job in a gift shop and between her modest wages and Zachary's earnings they were able to send the younger children to the best of schools, in spite of the fact that neither of them had won scholarships. In fact Minnie was lucky to get into Dana Hall, hardly a center of intellectual ferment, but she was so pretty and droll and happy that nobody minded that she never could better her C average, try as she would. Cutter, on the other hand, had a good, if lazy mind, but he chose not to work too hard at his studies, chose it coldbloodedly, because boys who were too bright were always menaced by unpopularity and he wanted popularity above all.

Cutter Dale Amberville, even in his cradle, had shown that he was going to take after the Andersons. He had grown quickly into a tall, exceptionally blond boy with the Swedish blue eyes of his ancestors, a fine-looking youth with an evil, ugly worm living and growing in his heart. He had despised growing up on the edge of poverty. As long as he could remember he had known that he was one of the poor Cutters, the poor Andersons, the poor Dales and the poor Ambervilles, in a small community in which the four families were all cousins to some degree and in which these distinctions of wealth were closely calculated and never mentioned.

Cutter looked down on his father's choice of career. Why pour your heart into a newspaper which obviously would never make any money? What kind of man would make such a choice? But the disregard he felt for his father was mild compared to the absolute repudiation he felt toward his brother whenever he was forced to realize that he was being supported by Zachary. However, he considered himself too far removed from the ordinary to go out and get a job himself. He was related to all of the best families in town; it was unthinkable that he should find himself delivering their groceries or standing behind a counter making sodas for them. Nor had his mother ever suggested such a thing, for she wanted Cutter not to know the struggle that Zachary had shouldered.

Sarah Amberville never suspected how Cutter felt about his brother, never knew that Zachary had always seemed sickeningly, terrifyingly all-powerful to her youngest child. Cutter judged him with contempt, mixed with baseless fear. Zachary was a violent, insufferable, potentially dangerous wind who swept into the quiet house whenever he could find time and filled it with his boisterous, laughing, uncouth presence, immediately becoming the center of

30

his mother's and father's total attention. It seemed clear to Cutter that their pride in this almost-stranger, this loud, brash, bold brother who hadn't lived at home since he, Cutter, was five, left his parents no room to remember that he was alive, much less be interested in him.

Bitterly he would return, time and time again, to dozens of memories of his childhood, telling them to himself like a rosary. There had been the time when he was eight and had the leading role in the school play but all his parents could concentrate on was the fact that his brother had gone off to fight in the war. For the next four years, no matter how popular he was in school, no matter that he became a junior tennis champion of Massachusetts, his parents were constantly waiting, every minute of every day, for news of their other son, the war hero, the fighter pilot. And when the war was finally over had his mother finally turned to him? No. Never. Not once. What could a teenaged boy bring home to show his mother that would compare to a letter from Zachary telling her of the new magazine he was creating in New York? To a copy of the magazine itself?

Cutter Amberville had always been so sure that Zachary had sucked up for himself all that was worth having that he turned secretive and bitter, not giving his parents a chance to become involved in his life. The heavy, omnipotent shadow of his brother had, Cutter *knew*, deprived him of the love and attention that would rightfully have been his. He'd been shoved aside, to the margin of his parents' life, and he interpreted his brother's generosity as bones thrown to a dog. The more Zachary gave him the more he owed him and the more Cutter owed his brother the more he hated him, with a passionate, permanent hatred that was deeper than any love he would ever know, the hatred that only early, unspeakable *envy* of one sibling for another can inspire.

At Andover, Cutter said as little as he could about his family. He certainly never intended to admit that his fees were paid by a mother who worked and a brother who edited a magazine with a name of which he was ashamed. He concentrated on developing his personal popularity within the school, using flattery as his weapon of choice. He cultivated the ability to ask those subtle questions that put other boys in the best possible light and, at an age when self-centered boasting was the rule, he learned the power of the person who would listen and admire. The worm in his heart was his teacher. He was excellent at sports but his marks were deliberately average. Quickly he became an accomplished courtier who bothered to cultivate only the boys whose parents were both rich and powerful. His good looks were highly finished, with strong, natural distinction, and a bred-in-the-bone strength. His well-cut hair covered a long, strongly shaped skull; Cutter's blue eyes could hold those of others with a steady, sincere expression, and he had trained himself not to use too often that practiced smile that seemed so charmingly natural.

Zachary was proud of the serious, striking teenager, although he found curiously little to talk to him about on the rare occasions when they were together, for now his brother's school holidays and weekends were invariably spent visiting in some home where young Cutter Amberville was regarded as a most welcome guest.

One autumn Monday of 1948, Nathan Landauer, Jr., walked into the offices Zachary had rented, with a combination of fearful joy and deep embarrassment on his pleasant face.

"Zack, I met a girl," he mumbled. "At a football game, on Saturday. She was with some guy who knows your family in Andover, nobody she cared about, so I persuaded him to get lost."

"There are a million girls in New York and you've met half of them. . . . What's so special about her?" Zachary asked, putting his feet up on his desk.

"Everything. She's perfect. I even told her the name of the magazine, the real name, I mean."

"And she didn't fall down shrieking with humiliating laughter?"

"No, not exactly. She thought it was very interesting, not just interesting but odd, considering that I'm the publisher of *Trimming Trades* and you're the editor and she and I had never met before. She said you must have been keeping us apart on purpose. Were you, Zack? Why didn't you ever introduce us, anyway?"

"Introduce you?"

"To Minnie?"

"Minnie? What Minnie?"

"Minnie your sister. The most beautiful, the most adorable, the . . . how come you never told me about her—I thought I was your best friend."

"It never crossed my mind. She's just a kid—eighteen—and you're a dirty-minded former Naval person who doesn't think about anything but getting laid."

"I'm an *ex*-dirty-minded former Naval person. I've reformed. Listen, Zack, buy my half of *Trimming Trades.* I'll practically give it to you."

"Are you crazy? Why would you want to sell? It's making a hell of a lot of dough between the ads, the new subscriptions and the low cost of production."

"I know, but I don't believe in doing business with family . . . it's the classic way to lose a friend."

"Family? Hold on now. Aren't you taking a lot for granted? Doesn't Minnie have anything to say about this?"

"After the football game we had drinks. After drinks we had dinner. At dinner we decided to get married. In two weeks you'll be my brother-in-law." Nathan Junior looked every one of his twenty-five years as he entered into manhood.

"My God, you're serious, Seaman Landauer."

"Some things you know right away. I knew about Minnie right away and she knew about me. That's the advantage of all my experience."

"You two were simply made for each other. Minnie never needed experience." Zachary stood up and grabbed his former partner in a giant hug. "How much do you want for your half?"

"Pay me what you figure is fair. I'll lend you the money to buy it."

"Love doth make suckers of us all," Zack yelled and waltzed Nat around the office. "Congratulations, sucker!"

Owning a magazine, becoming the sole proprietor, unleashed in Zachary Amberville all the ambitions he had not quite dared to entertain before. He had been marked by the Depression more than he realized and a certain natural caution had always restrained a devouring desire to create, to risk, to rule.

Soon after the marriage of his sister Minnie he launched his second magazine, *Style*. From everything he had learned about the garment industry and fashion magazines he knew that there was a place for a magazine that would appeal to women who couldn't afford to buy the clothes shown in *Vogue* and *Harper's Bazaar,* who were obviously too old for *Mademoiselle,* yet were too sophisticated for *Glamour,* with its rosy-cheeked, just-out-of-college models.

He went to banks for the money to start *Style* and they lent it to him, on the basis of the balance sheet of *Trimming Trades Monthly.* The late 1940s and early 1950s were prosperous ones for publishing, as the country entered a postwar boom economy and Americans, hungry for the material things of life, bought magazines with the same greed as they bought new cars.

Style made money almost from its first issue. Zachary Amberville had an invaluable knack for discovering and promoting new talent, and *Style* owed much of its immediate success to the talents of an unknown illustrator, Pavka Mayer, whom Zack had first hired to do black-and-white sketches for *Trimming Trades.*

Pavka had come to the United States in 1936, at the age of eighteen, a Berliner whose family had been wise enough to leave Germany. He had spent the war in the Army, landing on Utah Beach on D-Day, officially a translator and unofficially, as the Army fought its way up to Paris, a procurer of milk, hard cider, and fresh meat in return for blankets, soap, and sugar. Even an occasional entire jeep had been known to disappear along the route of Pavka's barter service.

"Go to it, Pavka," Zachary Amberville had told the diminutive, dapper man who was only five years older than he was. "Use any photographers you want, any models, any quality paper, any printer. We have too much competition. We can't hold back, we simply have to give the reader more than anybody else."

Pavka worked hand-in-hand with the fashion editor, another unknown named Zelda Powers. Zachary had spotted her toiling away in a back room at Norman Norell's—for even the great Norell could not design without buttons—and he had been struck by

an immediate appreciation of her eccentric, brilliant, purely personal style. She was from Chicago, a passionate student of fashion
who would work at anything as long as it kept her near the world in
which clothes were created.

"Listen, Zelda, you don't know anything about being the editor of a fashion magazine," Zachary said to her. "That's why I want
you. Give me the kind of magazine no one else has ever put out.
The kind you'd want yourself. No imitations . . . strictly original.
Do anything, *anything* you want, so long as you keep the advertisers
happy and show their clothes the minimum amount of times you
have to. Remember who's in your audience—and give them
dreams they can *afford,* but give it to them your way."

Pavka and Powers, according to people who watched the progress of fashion magazines, were single-handedly responsible for the
unexpected emergence of *Style* as a force and a presence. But people who had met Zachary Amberville knew otherwise.

By 1951 Zachary had made his fifth million. The first one had
been due to *Trimming Trades* and *Style,* the others to *Style* and
particularly *Seven Days.* He founded the weekly in 1950 with the
large size and photo format of *Life* and *Look.* But with a difference.
He had made his own studies of the reading habits of the American
woman and he had become convinced that there wasn't a female so
high-minded that she wouldn't read a dozen movie magazines in
private if she were sure no one would see her doing it. He understood the deep appeal of gossip columns and the power of men, like
Walter Winchell, who seemed to take the public behind the
scenes. He realized that there would always be a society column in
every newspaper, no matter how much some people deplored it.

Average people, who were almost everybody, wanted to know
about non-average people, wanted to know *everything* about them,
Zachary told himself as he walked the streets of Manhattan. He
visualized a big shining weekly magazine with lots of color pictures;
not heavy with text and letters and editorials, not concerned with
farmers or football or Middle America, not anxious about the rest
of the world and its miseries, not slightly to the right like *Life* or
slightly to the left like *Look,* but completely apolitical and reso-

lutely unserious. A magazine that would tell you what had been going on in the last seven days in the lives of glamorous, exciting, famous people, and tell it for an American audience in a way they'd never been told before, in a way that was irreverent, that didn't keep any secrets that its libel lawyers didn't say it had to keep, that held no man or woman sacred, yet realized that movie stars and royalty were more interesting than anyone else even if the United States was a democracy. *Especially* because it was a democracy.

Zachary hired as many of the best writers in America as he could find to craft the short articles that accompanied the many photographs. "Don't give me literature," he told them, "give me a first-rate blazing read and give it to me with guts . . . we're not a nation of intellectuals, as you may have noticed. It's too bad, but facts are facts. I want it fascinating, I want it red-hot and I want it yesterday."

Pavka Mayer took over the art direction of *Seven Days* and made it so piss-elegant that no one who read it noticed that it hardly appealed to their finer instincts. The world's best photographers were delighted to buzz off to all the corners of the world for higher prices than were paid by *Life* or its European rival, *Paris Match*. *Seven Days* was a wild, runaway, classic hit that became a national addiction almost overnight.

Late in 1951 Zachary Amberville decided to visit London. He'd been working too hard and as each of his European bureaus opened he'd missed the excitement of hiring bureau chiefs and seeing them get under way. London was his most important foreign bureau, except for the Paris office of *Style*, so he planned to stop there first. His executive secretary suggested that it might even be a good idea, while he was in England, to get a haircut and have some suits made.

"That's not even a hint, honeybunch."

"It wasn't meant to be, Mr. Amberville, it's not suitable for a man of your position to look the way you do. You're not even thirty and you could be a very handsome man if you cared to be," Miss Briny said with determination.

"I'm clean, aren't I? And so's my shirt. Even my shoes are polished. What's your problem?"

"A secretary is only as distinguished as the man she works for. You're undermining my position in the Executive Secretaries' Lunch Club, Mr. Amberville. Everyone else's boss has his suits made to order on Savile Row, he goes to the St. Regis for a haircut at least every ten days, his shoes are made by Lobb but you . . . you don't even go to Barney's," she complained tartly. "You don't belong to any exclusive clubs, you eat a sandwich at your desk instead of going to the best restaurants, you're never photographed in nightclubs with beautiful girls—I just don't know how to *explain* you."

"Did you ever tell them what you make?"

"Overpaying your secretary isn't what makes a man chic," Miss Briny sniffed.

"Honeybunch, your values are screwed up. But I'll think about that haircut."

Zachary refused to justify his private life to his secretary. It was none of her business. The occupations of a well-known bachelor around town were his idea of nothing to do. He didn't have the time or the interest. He knew a number of women, damned attractive ones, but somehow he'd never fallen in love. Too selfish? Too preoccupied with his magazines? Too cynical? No, why try to kid himself, he was too fucking romantic. Somewhere in the back of his mind there was a dream girl, and if that wasn't pure corn, what was? She was gentle, pure, idealistic; hardly a type who flourished in Manhattan. She was as unreal as she was beautiful and one day he'd get her out of his mind and settle for a gorgeous, sensible broad with a sense of humor. He needed a wife, if only to protect him from his secretary.

4

Nobody in her noble family could claim to understand the Honorable Lily Davina Adamsfield but they were as proud of her as if she'd been a rare portrait by Leonardo da Vinci, passed with reverence from one generation to another, the family treasure. She was the only child of the nineteenth Baronet and second Viscount Evelyn Gilbert Basil Adamsfield and Viscountess Maxime Emma Adamsfield, born the Honorable Maxime Emma Hazel. Her many cousins, male and female, were perfectly upstanding, healthy and appropriate, and they did the expected things. They cared for the family estates, they hunted, fished, collected, gardened, took an interest in good works and married the obviously appropriate young members of their own world with whom they would have quite satisfactory and appropriate children.

Ah, but Lily! Like so many of her friends, she had started to go to dancing school at the age of four. Miss Vacani's was and is the proper institution to which little aristocratic girls, and junior members of the Royal Family, are routinely sent to learn to waltz and polka. Almost all of them pass through Miss Vacani's as routinely as they learn to mount a horse. But Lily turned out to be one of the very few, the unpredictable yet constant few, who become utterly possessed by the ballet training from the very first moment. There is nothing any parent can do to quench this passion, as they learn in time, often to their regret.

At eight Lily had auditioned for the Royal Ballet School which she attended after school three times a week. She grasped ballet to her as if it were a vocation, as if she had had a visitation.

"If we were Catholics," her mother had said to her father,

"that girl would be counting the days until she could enter a convent."

"She certainly isn't one for chatter," her father had grumbled. "You'd almost think she already belonged to one of those orders that take a vow of silence."

"Now darling, that's not entirely fair. Lily just has a problem expressing herself—she's never been an easy talker. Perhaps that's why dancing is so important to her," Lady Maxime had replied soothingly.

When she was eleven Lily was able to audition for and be accepted by the Royal Ballet Upper School where she could combine her academic and ballet studies. Her life was totally absorbed by her work and, racing from one class to another with her schoolmates, she never minded that she had to renounce all the traditional activities of other girls of her background. The only human contacts in her life besides her parents were with her teachers and her fellow students and even those were limited to a necessary minimum. Lily wasn't at the Royal to make friends with her rivals, for by the age of eight she had an almost adult understanding of the nature of the ferocious competition that rages in the world of ballet, a lifelong competition that is only interrupted when a dancer finally retires.

For years her greatest fear was that she might grow too tall to dance. If she had reached five feet seven and a half or, God help her, five feet eight, she would have outgrown her future. Her discussions with other dancers were limited to the obsessive issue of height and her second greatest fear, that she might "get an injury," a terrible, ever-present possibility they all shared equally.

When she had completed the Upper School Lily's teachers agreed that she had so much promise that she should study for yet another year at the school run by Sir Charles Forsythe, a great dancer and teacher who had been formed by Anthony Tudor and Frederick Aston. This additional year of training would give her the final polish that would enable her to audition most successfully for one of the great ballet companies of the world.

Lily Adamsfield had grown into a girl of exceptional beauty, with gray-blue-green eyes as changeable as opals; lunar eyes that she never stopped in front of a mirror to admire. They were there merely to be enlarged by the stylized black makeup that she wore on stage. Her lovely hands, her long fingers, existed only to extend those gestures of languor and fragility that require the strength of a stevedore to look effortless. She had tiny breasts, broad, well-defined shoulders, arms and legs that were almost too elongated in comparison to her torso but perfect for the demands of the ballet; no heaviness or extra flesh anywhere, a flat back and a neck of exceptional grace; a body that had no other function than to dance. Her naked feet, without toe shoes, looked a thousand years old.

It never occurred to Lily that she was missing the pleasures of being admired by young men, for the only males whom she thought about were her partners in class; the only criteria by which she judged them were their elevations, the number of their leaps, the security with which they gripped her waist when they lifted her. She came into occasional contact with boys of her own social world and she had difficulty in finding anything to say to them. Outside of the cloister of the world of dance she had a speaking voice that, for all its silver sweetness, was tremulous, even slightly timid.

When Lily wasn't dressed in her rehearsal clothes, the beloved, well-worn tights, leg warmers, leotards, and sweaters that turned her into a bundle of moving rags, she had no idea what to wear. Viscountess Adamsfield, a woman of taste, chose all her clothes for her. Lily had no conversational ability, no practice at banter, nothing to say about the world of sports, of films, of new cars or horses. Any boy of her own age who was attracted by her new-moon loveliness soon gave up trying to get her to respond, or at least to pay some attention to him, and wandered off in search of a girl with more animation.

However, her parents and Lily's many cousins had no concern about this strange swan they had nurtured. She was wonderfully different, what did it matter that she wouldn't have any quick, worldly success as an adolescent? She would, as a matter of course, be presented at Court. It would be simply *too* odd for her not to make that necessary curtsy, not to have her photograph taken by Lenare, not to enter the grown-up world, but Lily drew the line at a debut, a party, a season. She had no time for any of those rituals for she was destined for glory. Indeed all their world knew that the Adamsfields' youngest girl was going to become another Margot Fonteyn. Her devoted family was as convinced of Lily's future as Lily was herself.

She took no credit for the conformation of the body with which she had been born but she knew that without her unquestioning, willing slavery to the almost unendurably hard work of ballet, without her unswerving determination, the mere possession of a dancer's body would mean nothing. Her muscles and sinews and the articulations of her joints, the length of her limbs, were a lucky accident of birth. But the career of a prima ballerina was not made by a body alone, it depended on something else, something even more than talent, something in the spirit, and whatever that something was, she knew absolutely that she had it.

No one who observed the shy girl who used no makeup, who wore her long, fair hair falling carelessly around her face, who hesitated on entering a room, who avoided conversation, who walked with an unstudied, felicitous grace but kept her eyes fixed in the middle distance, could have guessed at the thirsty ambition that never was far from her thoughts. She was violently proud, viciously proud, and she carried this strong plant of pride within her as well concealed as if it were a newly conceived child.

"She's an exceptionally accomplished performer," the familiar voice said. "There's no doubt that they'll accept her at the Royal."

Lily, on her way out of the school building, and already late for dinner, hesitated in the corridor. Sir Charles was talking to someone behind his half-closed door. Who else, she asked herself in anguish, which other girl among her classmates, her competition, would have such an easy time getting into the Royal Ballet? She had been given the lion's share of leading female roles this past year, but evidently she must have a rival. Jane Broadhurst? Anita Hamilton? Were they good enough for Covent Garden? Both strong dancers, but *that* good? She stood perfectly still, waiting to hear more.

"She could try for other companies, too . . . even the New York City Center." Lily clenched her fists. The second voice was that of her ballet mistress, Alma Grey. "Or perhaps Copenhagen—they need new dancers there since Laura and the other two were lured away to New York."

The Royal Danish? Lily repeated to herself, unbelievingly. It simply was not possible. There was no one to whom such prizes should fall but her.

"Yes, Alma my dear," she heard Sir Charles say with finality, "there really isn't a first-rate company in the world that wouldn't jump at Lily. Fifteen years ago, even ten, I would have said she might be too tall, at five feet and seven inches, but now that's not a serious problem if she's stopped growing. My regret is that she should be as good as she is . . ."

"Ah," sighed the ballet mistress, "it's heartbreaking . . . to come so close, so very, very close. This year she almost . . . yes, Charles, yes . . . she almost crossed that barrier. I promise you that there were moments when I prayed for her, as I watched, and then . . . no, I said to myself, no, it just isn't going to happen. She has such beauty, and technically nothing is missing. Yet . . . somehow . . . that *other* thing, that thing we can't put a name to, that thing that the public recognizes immediately, that lifts them out of their seats, that something just is *not* there."

"I have often thought that it is a question, in some way, of personality," Sir Charles mused.

"As for me, I don't try to dissect it. I prefer to call it magic," Alma Grey replied.

"She can dance all the second roles, in any first-rate international company," Charles Forsythe said judiciously, "and principal roles in lesser companies."

"Prima ballerina? I disagree. Lily will never be a prima ballerina. My dear Charles, you have to admit that there are no *almost* prima ballerinas," Alma Grey said sharply.

"There are indisputable prima ballerinas and there are greater prima ballerinas who sometimes are given the 'Assoluta' to console them as they age, but I suppose that was wishful thinking. . . . There are no 'almost' prima ballerinas . . . with that I must reluctantly agree."

"A strange metier, Charles, when you get right down to it, an unnatural sort of thing, and desperately unfair, I often think. As hard as we teach, as hard as they work, no one can really be sure until they have *already* devoted their youth . . . oh, of course there are those exceptions, the ones you know about immediately, but Lily never was one of them."

"And just how many have you seen in your lifetime, my dear?"

"Only four, Charles, as you know perfectly well. I'm waiting for the fifth. There will always be another, one of these days."

"Perhaps next year? Or the year after?"

"One can hope."

Envious, Lily thought, fleeing into the street so blindly that she was almost hit by a taxi. Old, disgustingly old, dried out, vile, pitiful, ignorant and above all *envious,* pure pig envy of her youth, her talent, a talent neither of them had ever had, those two old people raving on about something they admitted they couldn't even find words to explain, faking crocodile tears, gloating to each other, presuming to judge her, only too thrilled to be able to say she wasn't good enough at the same time they had to admit, were literally forced to admit that any ballet company in the world would want her.

Envy. She'd known about envy since she started dancing, Lily raged as she walked home as quickly as possible. She knew well the envy of her classmates each time she was singled out, praised, given a principal role. Envy meant that she was the best, the infallible sign, the one emotion no one could conceal, the one tribute that reassured her absolutely. Envy was her ally. But it made her sick to find out that even Sir Charles and Alma Grey weren't immune . . . they were supposed to be teachers, guiding and caring, not competitive; beyond envy, but obviously that was too much to expect from human nature. They would go to their graves envying her, shriveled, wasted, wizened with *envy,* for what else could it be? They nauseated her, she could almost feel sorry for them if they weren't so completely revolting. She walked faster, almost running, trying to put the words she had overheard out of her mind. Why should she waste another minute thinking about something that couldn't possibly be true? She walked with her head high, her

43

shoulders back, with the *portée* of a prima ballerina, the finest way a human body can move.

"Lily, you're so late. Is everything all right?" Lady Maxime called from the drawing room.

"Of course it is, Mother. I'm sorry if I've kept you waiting . . . I won't be a minute."

Damn Miss Briny, Zachary Amberville thought, he should either have brought her along or not listened to her sartorial jitters. He stood, jacketless, in front of a heavy wooden table on which were piled, in constantly sliding heaps, bolt after bolt of the finest silks and cottons in the world, solids, checks, stripes, plaids, a bewilderment of shirtings. The Bespoke Department of Turnbull and Asser was no place for a man who hated to shop and didn't have a clear idea of what he was looking for in the first place. The polite young salesman had finally left him alone, to meditate on a choice, after an hour of making fruitless suggestions and draping various lengths of fabric over Zachary's shoulder. He had brought over smaller swatches in little booklets, dozens of them, but the more choice there was, the more difficult it was to decide on anything.

Pale blue? That seemed to be the only sensible and safe idea but Zachary refused to be reduced to ordering custom-made shirts in the same solid color he'd been buying for years. Nor could he just leave quietly, not after having taken up so much of the salesman's time. Resolutely he started to eliminate the materials he couldn't imagine himself wearing, putting those bolts to one side. One thing he had learned about the British this Saturday morning, he reflected, was that loud shirtings were highly considered. Never had he seen so many perfectly outrageous candy-ass contrasts in stripes, bold checks and plaids so aggressive that only a gangster could even consider them.

Engrossed, determined, he finally picked out four possible fabrics and, as the salesman had shown him, released them from the bolts, in long lengths, and swathed himself in them. He studied himself in the mirror and shook his head in dismay. There was almost no light, either electric or natural, in the small room, and all the quiet stripes he had picked out seemed almost identical. He looked as if he were wearing a Bedouin tent.

"Excuse me, but would you mind giving me some advice?" he said, in the direction of a female figure he had vaguely noticed sitting for some time on a little couch, while an older man with whom she had entered the shop was deep in conference with his salesman.

"Forgive me?" she said, startled, as if aroused from a dream.

"Advice. I've got to have a woman's advice. Would you mind getting up and taking a look? Tell me what you think about these stripes. Don't be polite . . . if you don't like them, say so. I'd come over, but if I do these bolts will unwind all over the floor. I'm anchored to this table and I've lost my salesman's attention."

"I'll fetch him for you."

"Don't bother, he's given up on me. I need a fresh eye."

Reluctantly, Lily Adamsfield rose and approached him. Odd manners, but what could you expect of an American?

Hell, she's awfully young. Well, that just isn't going to matter, Zachary thought in a flash of absolute certainty that left no room for doubt. In one glance at Lily he fell in love, in love with her oval face framed with thick, straight sheaths of fair hair, in love with her eyes, their gray depths holding glints of the misty sea, with her mouth, vividly sweet in form, with a trace of delicious sadness, meant to be kissed away. He fell in love forever. She was his girl. And so vulnerable. If he'd known that the girl of his dreams really existed he would have come for her long ago. Zachary let the shirtings fall from his shoulders and took Lily's hand in his.

"We'll go now and have lunch," he told her.

The Honorable Lily Davina Adamsfield, just eighteen, a queen of the nymphs in her Norman Hartnell dress of priceless lace, and Zachary Anderson Amberville were married a month later, in January of 1952, with the bewildered blessings of Viscount and Viscountess Adamsfield, at St. Margaret's Westminster, in front of four hundred and fifty people, including the future Queen Elizabeth and Prince Philip, Miss Briny, Pavka Mayer, the entire

Landauer family and Sarah Amberville. Only Cutter, who was in the middle of exams, was missing. Lily had seated Sir Charles, Alma Grey and all her fellow ballet students in the second row, directly behind the princess and her parents.

Let them have a good look, a really good, long look, she mused as she carefully arranged their placement, at how happy she was, even as she sacrificed her career, her never-to-be-questioned future as a prima ballerina. She would always dance. Dance was essential but she wouldn't perform. The difficult, dedicated, single-minded existence demanded of a prima ballerina couldn't be included in the triumphant life that lay so radiantly, so securely before her as the wife of this amazingly forceful American, a man who worshiped her, who believed in her absolutely.

As she had told her astonished mother, if she had to give nightly performances it wouldn't be fair to Zachary. Joining the New York City Center Ballet was out of the question now. "I'll have the best of both worlds . . . all I'm giving up is a title, two words, 'prima ballerina.' What if I'd wasted my life on being those two little words, Mother? I can't marry Zachary and lead the life I thought I wanted. I have to grow up, and choice is part of growing. Yes, it is a sacrifice, you're not wrong, but it's a sacrifice I want to make. A sacrifice I must make. It's not a waste, I promise you. All those years haven't gone for nothing—I've just outgrown that life. Believe me, Mother, I know what I'm doing."

He'd taught her to kiss, Zachary thought in the state of light-headed euphoria that he seemed to have entered into permanently from the day he first saw Lily. She hadn't known how to kiss, she had never been kissed, he'd bet everything he possessed that if he hadn't come to England he could have spent the rest of his life in the United States without finding a girl who looked like Lily and had never been kissed.

And now he had to teach her to make love. Oh Jesus, if only it were a year from now and they were all settled into the big house she would pick out for them on any New York street that pleased her, if only they were going up to bed in a familiar room filled with all the beautiful things she was going to buy, to a bed with sheets that didn't have the cold, immaculate, polished finish possessed by these sheets in the Bridal Suite at Claridge's. Friendly sheets, damn it, might help. Or even a French hotel. Claridge's was too majestically British. Tomorrow they'd be in Paris, but tomorrow wasn't tonight.

If only he were one of the Ambervilles from centuries past facing a traditional New England wedding night with a virgin bride, something that would have been the only possible and natural state of affairs, just what he had been brought up to expect. Tradition was what he needed. Some ordinary old-fashioned traditional values. Maybe next year he'd vote Republican.

He suddenly remembered his own first experience, with one of the student nurses from St. Luke's Hospital, whose residence window was opposite his dormitory windows in Columbia's Hamilton Hall. He'd been a fifteen-year-old freshman and she'd been young too, but not as young as he. Whatever her age, she'd known exactly where and when and particularly how. Know-how . . . that was all it took. Every girl he'd made love to since that memorable night had had some degree of know-how, and not a virgin among them.

But he hadn't fallen in love before. So, he was a sort of virgin too, a twenty-nine-year-old emotional virgin, a virgin Marine fighter pilot, a virgin owner of three magazines, a many-times-over-millionaire virgin, a virgin who had had dozens of women, more than he could count. "Stop thinking," Zachary said out loud to himself in his dressing room. "It ain't helping."

He was momentarily reassured by the first sight of Lily in front of the wood fire that was burning in their immense paneled bedroom. He never realized, when he took her in his arms and felt the chill of her skin, that she owed the supreme composure with which she stood so quietly in her white satin and lace peignoir to hundreds of rehearsals of *Giselle,* to muscle memory of *Coppelia,* to the nights on which she had danced Odette in *Swan Lake.* The posture developed for dancers during a hundred and fifty years of classical ballet will sustain any one of them in any situation for the raising of any curtain. But once Zachary and Lily lay together in the wide bed, once she had laid her peignoir on a chair and wore only a satin nightgown with thin shoulder straps, he became aware that in spite of the warmth of the room she was shivering.

"Come on, kid, this is all too damned silly," he announced, bundling her up, blankets and all, and carrying her over to sit in his lap in a deep chair in front of the fire. "I feel as if we should invite the room-service waiters and chambermaids in to watch . . . it's like those royal wedding nights I've read about in the old days where everyone stood around putting the poor bride and groom to bed, gaping and, no doubt, making bawdy jokes."

"Tell me a bawdy joke," Lily said, trying to smile.

"You probably wouldn't understand the ones I know. And I can never remember punch lines anyway. It's one of my failures in life, but it makes me a hell of a good audience because every joke's new to me."

"What are your other failures?" she asked seriously.

"I can't play golf, always lose money at the track, but I still love to bet, I can't remember vintage years of wine or even the difference between a Bordeaux and a Burgundy, I never got that job as a copyboy at the *New York Times*. . . ."

"I mean real failures, major ones, the kind you never recover from," she said, unsmiling.

"I don't think I've made any. And I don't intend to. Not ever."

"That's what I thought about you the day we met . . . you're not a man who fails at anything in life."

"Darling, you sound so fierce." He looked in astonishment at Lily, his mysterious, timorous, inexperienced bride, whose every gesture seemed at once a caress and a quest for nourishment, yet whose expression was suddenly intent in a way he'd never seen before.

"You don't really know me, Zachary. I am fierce," she said in a voice that was so naturally angelic that he simply laughed and kissed her lips. She responded with the still awkward willingness that he found so touching in her. He put his arms around Lily under the layers of blankets. She was warmer now, more relaxed, the shivering had stopped. He ran his blunt fingers over the column of her neck, touching with wonder the astonishing curve

48

where her neck met her shoulder. His hand ventured to her collar-bone, felt the strength, the power under the muscles of her slim shoulders. He could ring her upper arm with one of his large hands. There was a delicate tautness there that made him alarmingly aware of the difference in the stuff of which they were made. She was like steel covered with silk and he was just flesh, ordinary flesh.

Excitement flowed through his veins, moving like a forest fire that has been started by lightning in a dozen different places at once, but he kept himself under absolute control. There was only one single thing he knew about teaching Lily how to make love and that was to take it easy, to go as slowly and as tenderly as was humanly possible, or, if it weren't possible for a human, to become inhumanly controlled. Minutes passed, while Lily, her eyes tightly shut, became aware of Zachary's fingertips gliding with the faintest of pressure from her shoulder to her elbow. The strap of her night-gown was a thin roll of satin, and it slipped off a shoulder, exposing one of her small, saucer-shaped breasts with a tiny, flat nipple, of a pink so pale that it made almost no contrast to the whiteness of her skin. Zachary saw her breast by the light of the fire, caught his breath, squeezed his thighs together mercilessly, and kept his hand away from the ravishing little mound. She wasn't ready to be touched yet, he told himself, as he lightly brushed his lips along her neck, under her hair. Lily made no sound at all and sat motionless, almost weightless in his lap, but he could feel that she was holding herself together tightly, scarcely breathing.

"Relax my darling, my baby, I won't do anything you don't want me to do, there's no rush, we have all the time in the world," he whispered to her, but she gave no sign of hearing him. His fingers left her elbow and descended caressingly along her forearm, reached her wrist and then spread out to cover her hand with his. In a quick movement that surprised him she turned her palm toward his palm, grasped his hand and lifted it up so that it abruptly covered her breast. "No darling, no, you don't have to, it's all right," he said in a low voice and took his hand away. She was only doing what she imagined was expected of her, he thought. Mutely she kissed his mouth, pressing her cool lips on his, seeming more like a child in search of security than a woman. He ground his teeth together to keep himself from thrusting his tongue between her lips. In the last month he had taught her to kiss without keeping her lips tightly together but she had retreated from his tongue as often as she had accepted it, and he was unwilling to initiate anything she might not want, tonight of all nights.

Lily, with a quick shrug of her other shoulder, caused the second strap of her nightgown to fall away from her body. With the blankets still covering her legs she sat defiantly upright on Zachary's knees, naked from the waist, her eyes still closed but her torso entirely revealed, a torso in which the combination of the girlishness of her immature breasts and the almost boylike width of her shoulders created a furiously erotic counterpoint. From her breasts to her waist she could have been molded out of ivory, Zachary thought. He could count her ribs, he could see her heart beating, the veins of her chest made an eternally memorable design under her pale skin. Using the utmost deliberation he traveled the largest of the veins above her breasts with his index finger, careful not to wander between her breasts, not to risk boldness too soon. He had to cross one of his legs over the other to restrain his rearing penis from forcing itself out between his thighs, for no matter how he fought to keep them together, the thick tip had a life of its own and nothing could keep it from swelling upward.

Lily seemed to shudder. Was she still cold or was she finally impatient? he wondered, and he let himself touch the tip of a nipple with one finger, touch it lightly, just brushing it, watching to see if she had any reaction. She neither shrank back nor pressed forward, but it seemed to Zachary that the nipple had risen, that it was distinctly standing up from her breast, and when he touched her other nipple he saw, with joy, that it too responded to his caress. "Yes, yes, that's right, that's good, that feels good," he muttered between his teeth, willing himself not to frighten her now that she was just beginning to enjoy it. He teased her nipples for minutes more, tracing their small circles around and around, returning again and again to the points that were now distinctly firm, and finally he bent his head and took one of the hard buds into his mouth, circling it with his tongue for a long moment before he actually dared to suck on it. Lily seemed to tense herself when he started to suck and he stopped, thinking, with an emotion that was

50

almost reverence, that it was the first time a man's mouth had ever been on her body, on her private places, but finally with another sudden and resolute movement she pulled his head back toward her breast with one hand and with the other she cupped her breast and offered it to him, put it in his mouth and mumbled, "Don't stop."

Soon both nipples were wet, lapped and tugged into small islands of engorged tissue, and when Zachary saw how big they had grown he picked Lily up, her nightgown slithering down the length of her body as he crossed the room. He put her down on the bed carefully and lay down next to her, preserving a distance between them so that she would not feel his rigid penis that lay straight up over his stomach, jerking in violent impatience. He rose on one elbow and with his other hand he tentatively smoothed her tiny waist, her elegantly narrow hips, her supple, firm, supremely developed thighs, learning the shape of the kind of body he had never seen on any other woman. Naked, Lily was a divinity, he knew, like the statue of a goddess from some other civilization, some finer civilization. His reverence grew, painfully mixed with the most maddened desire he'd ever felt when he saw Lily's pubic hair, blond and slightly curly and so much thicker than he had ever expected, over the rise of her mound of Venus, the pubic hair of a woman, not a girl. She quivered slightly under his hand, turning her head from side to side, her eyes still closed, but just as she didn't push him away she didn't put out her hands to touch him. It was almost as if she were asleep, he thought, almost as if she wanted him to take her in a dream.

After Zachary had touched as much of Lily's proffered body as he could, for as long as he could endure the giving of caress after caress, without moving closer, he pulled her to him and put one arm under her head. He took his free hand and put one of his fingers into his own mouth and wet it thoroughly. With that gentle finger he carefully parted her pubic hair and found the concealed entrance to her vagina. Slowly, a fraction of an inch at a time, he worked his finger into the passageway, anxiously searching her face for signs of pain or fear. Her expression didn't change although her lips were again firmly pressed together, her jaw set.

Zachary wet his finger again and again, each time returning cautiously to the warm tunnel, finding no resistance even when his finger was up inside as far as it could go. He couldn't tell if she had become wet by herself or because of all the wetness he had brought to her, but he knew that the moment had come to enter her. He straddled Lily on his knees and elbows and carefully lowered himself so that just the rounded, engorged tip of his penis nuzzled at the mouth of her delicate opening. Then he pushed into her, at first less than an inch and then a half-inch more. Slowly, oh so slowly, he moved, the sweat standing out on his forehead, always scanning her face for the moment when he would have to withdraw, when it would hurt her too much, but she was expressionless, although her breath came more quickly. She didn't move, she lay under him unflinchingly and let him fill her. Finally, after long minutes, she had accepted his entire penis, it throbbed within her at its full length, and Zachary lowered himself so that his legs were outstretched on the mattress, while his elbows kept him from crushing her. He could feel his penis swelling, growing larger and larger, although he didn't move a muscle. The soft, hot, tight inside of her was too much for him. Without a single thrust he came, his spasms so wrenching, so strong, so impossible to control after the frustration of the last hour that he poured his sperm into her with a rush, a flood, that was so quick that it was pure animal release.

For a minute Zachary, lost in the pounding of his heartbeat, forgot Lily, but as soon as he recovered himself he rolled off her body and gathered her in his arms, covering her face with kisses of wild gratitude, a hail of kisses mingled with the tears he couldn't keep from shedding. He hadn't expected her to become aroused. In the days to come, gradually, and with infinite care, he would teach her to enjoy sex, but now he was astonished at her courage, infinitely moved by her refusal to allow her innate modesty to make him feel as if he were brutal, touched to the heart by her willingness to permit him to enter her without any other sign of the effort she was making than her closed eyes.

"Did I hurt you, darling?" he asked at last.

"No, of course not." She opened her eyes and smiled at him. How could he know that her body had been trained to accept pain, to welcome it, to embrace it? How could he understand that the new set of feelings she had just encountered were as nothing compared to breaking in a pair of toe shoes? For many hours each day, from the age of eight, she had lived with constant pain, pain she was trained to smile through, pain that a dancer, like any other athlete, considers an inevitable part of life.

Lily had expected something different of her wedding night, something rough and exciting and unknown, something far wilder than the sensations she had when a strong partner lifted her farther than she had ever been lifted before. She had expected a duel of two bodies that would leave them both sore, aching, sweating and exhausted, as after a great performance. Not this long, drawn-out cuddling, not the stealthy exploration of a body she had long ago stopped thinking of as anything but an instrument, a body about which she had not the slightest self-consciousness. Oh, but how much she had wanted and needed to be *taken,* used, overcome, relentlessly plunged head over heels into a world she had never known, a world she sometimes heard the other students giggling about, a world that had fascinated her even as she rejected it.

She couldn't *do* more than she had, Lily thought, she didn't know the right movements, the right positions to take, but surely her immobility must have indicated clearly that she would permit him anything? She could not endure feeling awkward, ill at ease with her muscles, yet there was no one to teach her except Zachary. He was the one with the experience, she thought, as she drifted into sleep. He was the one who had to make it important to her. She had done her best. Now it was up to him to make it wonderful, yes wonderful, even more wonderful than applause.

The Ambervilles returned to Manhattan after a ten-day honeymoon in Paris. Zachary had never been away from his offices such a length of time, almost six weeks from the day he first left for London, and aside from fleeting visits to his London and Paris bureaus, he hadn't made the tour of inspection he'd planned. But he was much too happy to care.

Every night for ten nights he had made love to Lily, every night he had spent hours, hushed, halcyon hours, hours that were, to him, like the slow exploration, inch by inch, of a new, moonlit countryside. She was like a melody, he thought, an exquisite melody in a minor key that no one else could hear.

53

Lily never refused him anything except for one night, when he had first brushed his mouth between her thighs. She'd tentatively put her hands over her pubic hair and then taken them away. He'd immediately understood that she wasn't ready for that final intimacy and he had made no further attempt. He was certain that one day soon he would, by virtue of his patience and his tenderness, find the way to make her feel pleasure of her own. It was not that she had any distaste for sex, Zachary assured himself, but just that she hadn't yet learned to let herself go. It was a question of time and of never allowing himself to forget what it must be like for an eighteen-year-old girl—scarcely more than a child—who suddenly finds herself married to a man of twenty-nine. The foreknowledge that Lily always opened herself to him each night enabled him to moderate any roughness, any haste, any gesture that might, he suspected, seem animal, too rough, too frightening to a girl of her sensibilities.

After that first night he found that he always needed to take her a second time; her very immobility aroused him as if it were the most potent aphrodisiac, and after he had reached that first satisfaction he was able to stay inside her for a far longer period, lying motionless, hearing her breathe, kissing her gently while his penis grew and grew harder without friction, with just the smallest rocking motion of his pelvis against hers at his climax, so as not to bruise that infinitely delicate, silently accepting creature who was his bride.

5

Cutter Amberville decided to go to college in California rather than spend four years at an Eastern school. He wanted to put as much distance between himself and his brother as he could, to leave behind that part of the world in which the name Amberville immediately caused people to ask him if he were related to Zachary. At Stanford, or "the Farm" as Berkeley students, from their traditionally intellectual perch within sight of San Francisco, mockingly refer to their elite and non-egalitarian rival, he found companionship that wasn't different from that which he'd nourished at Andover; rich boys, boys who had something he wanted.

At Stanford Cutter had to work harder at his studies than he had done at Andover but he soon learned the art of doing only the necessary minimum, leaving himself as much time as he could to continue in his chosen fields of excellence: tennis, squash, sailing, polo and skiing. They were indisputably a gentleman's sports, they were a rich man's sports; they required years of practice to do well; they inspired admiration and confidence when a young man was able to master all of them. They demanded skill, coordination, endurance and, particularly in the case of polo and skiing, an acknowledged willingness to put himself on the line as far as physical courage was concerned. There was no risk—no reasonable risk— that Cutter wouldn't take on a horse or on skis, since physical courage, he deduced, with the measure of calculation he so carefully hid, was usually accepted as shorthand for courage, pure and simple. His brother, his enemy, had never learned to do any sport with skill.

Not the least of Cutter's abilities were devoted to tennis and squash. While his other chosen sports demanded that he compete against an animal or the elements, racket sports were man-to-man competition. Winning took an effort, but it was nothing compared to the skill and the technique with which Cutter eventually learned to lose a few crucial games, brilliantly contested games with a few carefully chosen fathers of his friends; men who played exceptionally well for men of their age; men who were in investment banking, men who would, someday in the future, be in a position to give him a job in a business in which contacts often meant commissions. Losing at tennis, losing with good temper, convincingly and without arousing any suspicion that he wasn't trying his hardest, became one of Cutter Amberville's particular assets, as important as his good manners and his good looks, even more important than his unquestioned courage.

"Yesterday I went shopping with the first Mrs. Amberville," Zelda Powers said acidly to Pavka Mayer as they had a drink together before lunch.

"Ah? You sound as mean as you look, my love. After all, Zelda, you have to remember that she's very young and very British and has been protected almost from the day she was born, or so I gather from Zachary, by her total immersion in the ballet. If she doesn't know how to dress, except in a tutu, that shouldn't be a surprise to you."

"But the Honorable Lily does know how to dress . . . now." Zelda said with a rancorous, sideways look at Pavka.

"Bad taste? Or just dull, ordinary provincial taste? The British aren't famous for their skill in self-adornment."

"We went to Bergdorf's, we went to Saks, we went to Bonwit's, we went to every fine shop in New York because Zachary wouldn't allow me to take her wholesale, and she looked at all our best designers' dresses with as much interest as if I'd taken her to see an exhibition of earthworms," Zelda said viciously. "There was just nothing she could even be bothered to try on, nothing at all. And she really needed clothes, Pavka, because her mother didn't have enough warning of the wedding to buy her a complete trousseau nor did either of them have any idea of what young married women wear in New York. She was all done up in pastel tweed that

56

looked like a cross between Alice in Wonderland and a very young Crowned Head on a State Visit to somewhere unfriendly."

"But so very, very beautiful," Pavka said quietly.

"I don't deny that she's beautiful . . . I just wanted to be helpful . . . you know I'd do anything for Zachary. Anyway, as a last resort, I took her to Mainbocher and she perked up, showed some signs of animation and by the time we'd left she'd ordered thirty-seven different outfits, almost the entire collection. The first fittings are in a week."

"Well, what's wrong with that? It solves your problem, doesn't it?"

"It does something to my insides. Mainbocher at her age! Custom-made, *the* most expensive clothes in the entire United States . . . very quiet clothes, Pavka, very well-bred, absolutely perfect clothes that could be worn inside-out if you wanted to. The ladies who buy there are the richest women in New York, they're members of a particularly exclusive elite. You work your way *up* to Mainbocher, damn it! And I'll bet not one of them has ever ordered so many things in a single visit. That, that *teenager*—she didn't even ask what they cost . . . it just never occurred to her."

"So what? Zachary can afford it."

"It's not the money, it was her attitude I couldn't stand. Has he told you about the house he's buying? The only house in the whole town that she condescended to like?"

"He mentioned something about it but I didn't pay too much attention."

"She took me to see it. Pavka, you know what sort of a guy Zachary is. Simple, down to earth, couldn't care less about show? How do you think he's going to like living in a pale gray marble palace that takes up half a block, spread out over three stories, with a ballroom, my dear, and a huge garden at the back? For just two people? It's half the size of the Frick; it's not a home, it's an absolute mansion."

"He'll love it if it makes her happy," Pavka said, enjoying being the devil's advocate.

"But *why* should a kid like that need such a palace to make her happy, for God's sake? Who lives like that anymore? Just think of the renovations, the interior decorating, the staff to keep it up, someone to tell the staff what to do because she won't know, or want to be bothered. Think of the gardeners. Gardeners in New York! You really don't have the slightest idea of what it's going to cost, do you?"

"No. But we both know Zachary can afford it, a hundred times over. I don't believe in deciding how other people should spend their money, Zelda, and I don't think you do either . . . you never did before." He softened his words with a tender, well-placed pinch.

"You're trying to say I'm jealous, aren't you, Pavka, my darling?"

"Well?"

"Of course I am. I should be ashamed. But I'm not."

"Even Zelda Powers allows herself a perfectly normal female reaction. Careful, you may lose your uniquely original touch. This could mean bad news for the circulation department of *Style.*"

"Don't bet on it."

"I won't. And you must have another drink. I insist. I will even pay."

In the days when they were young bachelors, right after the end of the war, Nat Landauer and Zachary Amberville spent many an afternoon at the track with Barney Shore, an amiable, carrot-haired young man in his middle twenties who had been Nat's roommate at Syracuse. Just as Nat was destined to run the Five Star Button Company, Barney was the heir apparent to the family business, something he referred to casually as "the racks."

"Dress racks?" Zack asked him one day.

"Nah, magazine racks."

"You make them?"

"Nah, we fill them," Barney said dismissively, not anxious to abandon his study of the *Racing Form,* a devout exercise which never did him any more good than it did Zachary. It was not until he began to publish *Style* that Zachary understood the importance of an institution called Crescent, founded by Joe Shore, Barney's father, which, along with Curtis, Warner, Select and NICD was one of the major national distributors of magazines.

58

Without these powerful distributors the business of publishing magazines could not possibly exist. While Zachary owned only *Trimming Trades Monthly* he sold his copies by subscription, but when he created *Style* he signed a three-year national distribution contract with Joe Shore, which established a pattern for the future. For the first year of *Style's* existence he paid Crescent ten percent of the cover price of each copy sold, and for the second and third years, six percent. In return Crescent acted as *Style's* banker, paying him against the number of copies printed.

Joe Shore, deceptively mild-mannered man that he was, could make or break a magazine by deciding how many copies he would send on to the various local wholesalers, who would then deliver them to individual retailers, who eventually—and sooner rather than later, the magazine publisher prayed—would put them out on the racks in prominent positions.

Zachary Amberville had instantly appealed to tough, quiet Joe Shore, whose approval was not easily gained, but, once gained, was never lost for any act short of not living up to a business deal. Murder, arson, loitering with intent to litter; none of these offenses would change Joe Shore's mind about a man he liked who kept his word.

"Joe," Zachary said to him one day in 1953, as they were having lunch together, "I want you to meet Lily. Would you and Mrs. Shore, and Barney and that new girl he's seeing, have dinner with us a week from next Tuesday?"

"We'd like that, Zack. Wait a minute, did you say Tuesday?"

"Right. Not this coming Tuesday, a week from Tuesday."

"Any other night, Zack, with pleasure, but not Tuesday, not *any* Tuesday. My wife would kill me."

"A pussycat like you? I thought you had the ideal marriage."

"Zack, don't kid a kidder."

"Come on. What's Tuesday night?"

"Milton Berle. Tuesday at eight o'clock."

"So what?"

"How many stories have you done on Milton Berle in *Seven Days?*"

"I'm not sure. . . . I keep seeing the damn things and wondering why, but my television editor tells me to trust him. Since I doubled his salary to get him to move over from *Life* I've tried not to second-guess the guy. Personally I've never had the time to watch much television, and Lily isn't interested in it at all. Maybe," Zachary grinned, "it's just her language problem."

"Hopeless. You just don't know what you're missing." Joe Shore shook his head in wonder. "I bet you don't even have your own set yet."

"I looked at Barney's once and all I saw was a bunch of midgets. They've got to do better than that. Give me a movie or a Broadway show anytime. Coffee?"

Imagine, Zachary thought, as he walked back along the busy streets, Joe Shore, a man who had as much tangible power as any man he'd ever personally known, couldn't make a dinner date on any Tuesday night because of Milton Berle. Did Eisenhower and Mamie watch? Did Senator Joseph McCarthy watch, and Estes Kefauver? Personally he was too restless to sit still for long, except for an occasional ballgame. Whatever importance television had, it was as a competitor for the advertiser's dollar, and not one to worry about nearly as much as he did about other magazines. He stopped abruptly at the corner of Fifth Avenue and Fifty-second Street. Did the whole country come to a stop on Tuesday at eight? Probably it did and probably it came to a stop for Lucille Ball and Sid Caesar and "The Honeymooners" and who the fuck knew what other shows? He, Zachary Amberville, was a shortsighted, ignorant horse's ass who had almost made the fatal mistake of thinking that he could judge the American public by his own tastes. But not too big a horse's ass to learn when he'd been one and to do something about it. *Television Week?* Too businesslike. *This Week on Television?* Too long. *Television Weekly?* There was something overtly intellectual about that, it smacked of *Harper's* or *The Atlantic. Your T.V. Week?* Still too long. *T.V. Week.* That would do. He crossed the street, imagining the first issue clearly. A square book, eight by eight, on good-quality paper, crammed full of photos and text, and television schedules of course, with a large color picture of Milton Berle on the cover. As his pace quickened, Zachary Amberville returned to his office, already, although he did not yet realize it, worth tens of millions of dollars more than when he'd left for lunch.

Months before the plans for the redecorating of the great gray marble house on East Seventieth Street had been completed, Lily discovered she was pregnant. Her immediate reaction was fear: what would this do to her body? Then she smiled at herself. That was a typical dancer's reaction and she had given up her career for a normal life. This baby would be the proof, if one was needed, that she was free, her own woman, a double rejection of that hermetic little world she had put aside. She always did her barre exercises for an hour every morning in the large suite at the Waldorf Towers where the Ambervilles had settled temporarily, but she hadn't so much as been to the ballet since she'd come to Manhattan. The barre was a habit, a way of keeping in shape, nothing more.

Her marvelous new clothes! Her hands flew to her mouth in dismay. They wouldn't fit in a matter of weeks. Well, it simply couldn't be helped. She'd go to Mainbocher this afternoon and ask him to design a complete maternity wardrobe. Should she write her mother immediately, or even telephone? It wasn't a minute too soon for Mother to start looking for just the right nanny to come over from England and take charge. Doctor Wolfe had told her to watch her weight . . . a good doctor, she thought, but a silly remark. When in her life had she not watched her weight? Lily hugged herself in the beginnings of enjoyment. Inevitably her slight dancer's breasts would become voluptuous. How nice she'd look in a low-cut gown. She'd tell Mainbocher that she wanted deep necklines for evening; wonderful, wide-skirted dresses, tied under the breasts in the Empire style. She might as well enjoy having a bosom while it lasted, for of course she wouldn't nurse the child. Her cousins had all nursed their children and it had seemed to her to be a most appalling waste of time; hours and hours of sitting patiently, night and day, while some little thing used you as a human cow, a baby who couldn't possibly remember if it had been nursed or not and most certainly wouldn't be grateful one way or the other.

She made a mental note to tell her decorators where to put

the nursery. It should be so far from her bedroom that under no circumstances would she be disturbed by the noise the baby would make, day or night. A baby's crying was unquestionably the single most irritating sound in all of nature and she didn't intend to endure it, any more than she would buy dresses off the rack.

A mother at her age? Well, she might as well get it over with while she was young, as the Royals always did, especially since she had no choice. But it was rather a pity really since she had so recently come to Manhattan, so recently begun to realize what it was like to be able to have everything she wanted, when she wanted it, at the slightest tug of desire. Still, a baby didn't mean postponing any satisfactions for more than a few hours. She'd known in London that Zachary was tremendously rich, but Lily now understood that he was far, far richer than she could have imagined, and far, far more generous than any man she'd ever known. Her father had been rather stingy, now that she came to think of it, he believed that children should be brought up with strict discipline about pocket money. She'd never needed pocket money, since she'd had no interests to spend it on, but since she had given up ballet, there seemed to be a multitude of things she did rather like buying. The shops of Manhattan were irresistibly tempting, and it was quite . . . cozy . . . to know that there wasn't anything in any of them that she couldn't buy, nothing Zachary didn't want to give her.

"Wealthy"—a disgusting word. Rich. The only way to say it was flat out. Rich. *Very, very rich*. Perhaps, when the baby was presentable, she'd let *Style* photograph her for its pages. The Honorable Mrs. Zachary Amberville, and her child. No, not *Style*. It wasn't designed for the very rich. Perhaps that was why it sold so well. *Vogue* then, or, better yet, *Town & Country*. There was a certain cachet, now that she reflected on the subject, to making her first appearance in the society magazines everyone in New York read every month, as a young mother rather than just as another young bride.

Of course New York society was one vast joke. In London you were either in society or not in society. If you were a viscount's daughter you would always be a viscount's daughter, no matter whom you married. You had your relatives, you had your ancestors, you had your place in the constellation. A girl could marry a title or into county society—or even an American—but everybody would always remember who you had been before your marriage. It would take generations before it didn't matter, or perhaps it would always matter, perhaps people would say hundreds of years from now, "Oh yes, Lady Melinda . . . her great-great-grandmother was some banker's daughter before she married the Earl of wherever." Snobbish, fearfully snobbish, she supposed. Nevertheless that was simply the way it was.

But New York! So many of their "great ladies" were three—or at the most four—generations removed from robber barons, and robber barons were simply successful thieves. Of course they had their *Mayflower* descendants and that Society of the Cincinnati, descendants of officers in Washington's army. In other words, Lily mused, they were descendants of colonials who had rebelled against a rather good sort of king, not even two hundred years ago. Apparently it was considered fearfully impressive to be a member, although Zachary, who could have joined, had never bothered. As her mother had told her in the few weeks before the wedding, although fifty families considered themselves to be historically "Old New York," there were only a handful of them who could claim really good Old World ancestors. The Van Rensselaers, whose coat of arms came from the Prince of Orange, had no land left. The Livingstons however were alive and prospering and they went back to the noble Scottish House of Callenders; the Pells too had been aristocrats in England and the Duers and Rutherfords had pedigrees with which anyone could be satisfied. Ancestor worship had its place, Lily thought mockingly, but shouldn't the ancestors have a bit more patina on their graves? Only a few years before the American Revolution, Louis XIV of France had sold titles for six thousand six hundred livres, whatever that might be in today's money, leaving blank the space in which the newly noble Frenchman would write his name. So little really stood up to the inspection of more than a few centuries. Even the Adamsfields had only been squires until the 1300s. No, being a title snob was quite nasty, and beneath her.

However. However, she was going to live in Manhattan and sheer self-respect demanded that she receive proper consideration.

Once the baby was out of the way she'd meet the few really quite decent people, and know them. Invariably she'd be asked to join many charitable committees, or whatever they called good works here—it seemed to be a New York mania—and she'd pick several, choosing them very cautiously. It was so very unwise to make friends too quickly in a new place, her mother had always said. You spent the next ten years getting rid of them.

Lily stretched agreeably. The house, the superb antiques she was buying to fill it, endless new clothes, the reign over Manhattan that was hers for the taking, the servants, the trips they would make when New York grew too hot or too cold, the jewels that she was beginning to contemplate and compare at the great jewelers of Manhattan . . . it all seemed to merge into one comfortable and busy circle of pleasure. She must have been quite mad to have spent most of her life chained to a discipline that allowed for no pleasure except the fleeting enjoyment of an exceptional performance. Ballet dancers, especially prima ballerinas, were truly *slaves*, she reflected, shaking her head. Slaves to their own impossible set of standards, slaves to their teachers, slaves to their bodies; slaves, above all, to the public who, by possessing a ticket, demanded a perfection the price of which none of them could possibly understand. Dancers were like trained animals, brought out to go through the hoops and yet, unlike animals, they had chosen to be slaves. How fortunate she was to have escaped in time. For once she had become a prima ballerina, as of course she would have, it might have been far more difficult to abandon that obsessive life.

The phone rang, and Lily stirred, her reveries broken. "Oh. Yes, darling, I slept beautifully," she said to Zachary. "No, nothing particularly new, just another day of talking to upholsterers and decorators. . . . Don't be silly, dear, I *am* having fun." She supposed she could have called to tell him the minute she found out about the baby but it had slipped her mind. Well, tonight would be time enough. Of course he'd understand that soon they would have to stop going to bed together. Soon, quite soon. She put down the phone and then picked it up again. She'd phone Miss Varney, her saleslady at Mainbocher, and make an appointment for tomorrow. No . . . for this afternoon. Why wait?

"Not nurse *my son?* No, darling, I couldn't possibly have said that."

"Lily, darling, come on, don't you remember? I distinctly heard you telling Minnie that all the stuff about antibodies in mother's milk was some American fad and fresh air and a good nanny were what counted."

"Perhaps. I'm sure you're right. But what does it matter since I've changed my mind? Where is that nurse with my son? She should have been here five minutes ago. Zachary, could you please go and find her? I'm terrified the hospital and staff might give him a bottle of formula for their own convenience . . . they hate mothers who nurse. It makes more work for them."

While Zachary roamed the corridors of Doctors' Hospital looking for a nurse, any nurse, Lily fretted impatiently in her bed. Tobias had been born three days before, an easy birth, and as soon as she had seen him, with his little pointed cap of blond curls, his fat cheeks and perfect body, she realized that she had never loved before. Not her parents, not ballet, not Zachary, not herself. The last thing she had expected was to be taken by surprise by a wave of maternal emotion but she had spent the entire day after the birth weeping because her son was not by her side but in the nursery with the other babies. He *was* her, he was *part of her body,* how could they take him away as if he didn't belong to her? It was simply too late to arrange for "rooming-in," keeping the baby in her own room in a little crib, her doctor explained. Every other mother in the hospital it seemed had opted for rooming-in and they didn't have the necessary equipment for half of them. If only she'd asked for it a few months ago, he had said, as if, a few months ago, she could possibly have *known* her baby would be Tobias?

Of *course* she'd had a boy. All that nonsense that people talk about not caring about the sex of a child so long as it's healthy! Everyone knew in the heart of hearts that the first child should be a boy. Cavemen knew it and so had all humans since then.

"Here he is!" Zachary said, pushing open the door for the nurse, "and he sounds hungry. I tracked him down by the noise."

"He needs to cry, it's good for his lungs," Lily said, sounding as expert as her mother before her, holding her arms out greedily.

"Shall I leave you and Father alone with the baby?" the nurse asked.

"I don't need you now, thank you, nurse. Zachary, darling, would you mind? I'm rather new at this . . . I think I'd like a little privacy. Come back in, oh, an hour or so. He does enjoy taking his time."

"You're sure?" Zachary tried not to sound as deeply disappointed as he felt. "Won't you need anything?" He looked at her lovingly, propped up on half a dozen pillows, their silk cases thickly encrusted with fine old lace, as were the sheets and coverlet she had brought from home. Lily had never looked so angelic as she did at this minute with her hair spread over her shoulders. At her ears were the enormous sapphires set in diamonds he had just given her from Van Cleef and Arpels—sapphires for a boy. The box that had contained the necklace and the bracelets that completed the parure lay open on the table beside her and the jewels themselves were heaped near the lamp, captured dreams of a midsummer's night.

"If I do, darling, there's a perfectly good bell right here on the bed table and I'll ring it, I promise. Now go, both of you, before my son wakes everyone in the city."

While the argument over the influences of environment and heredity will rage forever, no one could possibly deny that Tobias Adamsfield Amberville was destined to grow up a monster. It was unthinkable that a child born to such an adoring father and a mother who regarded him as an extension of herself, a self to whom she denied nothing, could not be overindulged.

"It must be his Anderson blood," his grandmother, Sarah Amberville, remarked. "The Protestant work ethic, you know."

Lily, six months pregnant with her second child, laughed merrily. "He does precious little work yet, Sarah."

"Look at him digging up the garden so seriously and methodically. You'd think he was getting paid by the shovelful. He hasn't cried once since I've been visiting you, he goes quietly to bed when he's supposed to, and according to Nanny, he gives her no trouble at all. He eats all his vegetables, and even Zachary didn't do that. I hope your next baby will be as easy."

"The next baby is intended to be Tobias's playmate. It's bad for a child to be an only child, that's why I'm bothering to have one so quickly. Otherwise I'd be very happy just watching my son grow up."

Sarah Amberville said nothing. She still hadn't grown used to her daughter-in-law and she never would. Actually she was rather frightened of her because she knew that if she got on the wrong side of Lily she wouldn't get to see her grandson, or much of her son either for that matter. Minnie had been banished for months when she'd dared to comment on the fact that since perfectly good clothes for children were made in the United States it seemed a bit farfetched to have them sent from London, especially since Toby outgrew them so quickly.

"Look, he's coming back. He must be ready for lunch," she said to Lily.

"Wait till the gardener comes tomorrow," Lily chortled.

"Will he be surprised?"

"Tobias has just dug up all the tulips, every last one. They were due to bloom next week. The gardener planted four hundred bulbs last autumn."

"Dear, dear," Sarah Amberville murmured. She hadn't realized that Lily had known all along that Toby was harvesting tulips in full bud. She'd been sitting firmly on her hands for the last two hours, biting her lips and praying for courage to stay silent. Well, perhaps it was easy to find good gardeners in Manhattan. In Andover the problem didn't present itself. Being a grandmother wasn't somehow as much fun as she'd thought it would be. But what was?

Maxime Emma Amberville was about as unattractive a baby as Lily could imagine: something like a plucked chicken, without hair at all, a pair of bandy legs, and a heat rash that developed on the first day. She had colic, she screamed when she was hungry and she screamed when she wasn't hungry. She was apparently the most difficult child in the nursery as the supervisor of nurses confided in her.

"I hope you told that supervisor to go fuck herself," Zachary burst out when Lily reported the remark to him.

"Zachary! I most certainly did not. The poor woman was at her wits' end. I just assured her that the baby would be going home tomorrow. The thing I'm really worried about is Nanny. What if she leaves? She's so used to Tobias."

"Nanny is underworked and overpaid."

"I called the employment agency and hired a second nurse. They have a very well-recommended woman, a Miss Hemmings, who specializes in difficult cases. She'll be here when we leave the hospital, and take over immediately. Fortunately Maxime's room is not right next to Tobias's so she won't wake him."

"Jesus, Lily, the baby's got ordinary colic, not leprosy. I happen to think the kid's got a hell of a lot of spirit and I *like* the way she looks. She looks like me, damn it."

"Darling, you're too silly. You know you're madly attractive."

"You've never seen my baby pictures," he said grinning.

Vaguely, Lily murmured, "I assume she'll improve—with time. She could hardly get worse."

Maxime's colic and heat rash disappeared at the same time. Within six months she had put on enough weight so that her skinny little legs were dimpled and straight, her hair, once it started to grow, was straight and thick and, to Zachary's sweet and triumphant delight, she had a pure white streak exactly the same place as his. As for her spirit, she managed within twenty-two months to break that of the nurse who specialized in difficult cases.

"Madame," Miss Hemmings said, almost in tears, "I've had sick babies, babies so quiet that you knew there had to be something wrong; I've had hyperactive babies who got into everything, including the sewers; I've had babies who could and did climb a tree before they were a year old; I've had babies you couldn't toilet-train for four years, I've had every kind of baby I thought was possible, but Maxi . . . I just have to go away for a rest, Madame, or I'll have a nervous breakdown."

"Oh, no! Don't do that, Miss Hemmings. Please, please don't leave!" Lily begged.

68

"I must, Madame. I love Maxi too much. She's so adorable and she's so *naughty*. I can't bring myself to punish her and that's bad for the child."

"I thought you were supposed to be able to handle that sort of problem," Lily said coldly. The woman was obviously determined to leave. "I'm afraid that Maxi has been spoiled rotten. She wants what she wants when she wants it . . . surely you should have managed to do something about that."

"I've tried, Madame, but . . ."

"But you've failed; it's that simple, really, isn't it?"

"If you want to look at it that way, yes." Miss Hemmings's tone was that of someone who refused to be drawn out and Lily found herself intensely irritated.

"I hold you entirely responsible for Maxi's discipline problem, Miss Hemmings, and I'm afraid I can't give you a good reference."

"That's up to you, Madame. But I doubt that Maxi's problems can be solved just by finding another nurse."

"We'll see about that! I'm sure someone else will do quite well," Lily said furiously.

"I don't like to blame the parents," Miss Hemmings said, her professional pride wounded, "but there's only so much any nurse can achieve. Now if you'll excuse me, Madame . . ."

"Just a minute. Precisely what do you mean about blaming parents, Miss Hemmings?"

"Maxi is spoiled because her father gives her everything she wants and you spend all your available time with Toby. She's trying terribly hard to get her mother's attention and, since you asked me to speak out, she's using her father as a substitute." Before Lily could begin to reply Miss Hemmings left the room and went upstairs to pack. In a long and honorable career she had never spoken her mind so clearly, and as miserable as she felt about leaving Maxi she was rather pleased with herself.

Toby's English nanny, Mrs. Browne, was made of sterner stuff than Miss Hemmings. She took over Maxi, referring to her as "our two-year-old" in a way that explained away everything. Lily, unwillingly stung by Miss Hemmings's remarks, now made a point of reading to the little girl almost every evening before the child's dinner, and of letting Maxi play with her jewels for half an hour on Sunday mornings, perched shoeless in the middle of Lily's antique lace wedding cake of a bed. No one can ever accuse me of being a neglectful mother, she thought, raging with resentful boredom as she read aloud.

It was soon after Tobias's fourth birthday that he began falling out of bed. For two years he had occasionally awakened in the middle of the night and gone to the bathroom when he had to, treading carefully along the familiar route so as not to disturb anybody.

"Could I have a night light, Mother?" he asked Lily one day.

"Oh, my darling, you haven't had one since you were a tiny thing. Did you have a bad dream? Is that it?"

"No, it's just that when I wake up I can't see anything. I can't tell where I am in bed unless I feel around and if I'm near the edge I fall off. And I can't find the bed lamp in the dark. It's happened a few times and it hurts when I fall."

"Perhaps it *is* too dark in your room."

"It . . . it never has been. There used to be enough light on the street to see by . . . but, I don't know, I don't seem to see in the dark anymore."

"Well, I'm sure it's nothing to worry about," Lily said, her heart beating heavily, "but I'll take you for a checkup to Doctor Stevenson. You probably need to eat more carrots, my baby."

The pediatrician gave Toby a thorough going-over. "He's a fine young man, Mrs. Amberville. As for the falling out of bed, I'm sure it's not serious but, just to be on the safe side, I think you should have his eyes checked."

"But you just looked into his eyes," Lily cried.

"By a specialist. Merely to be on the safe side."

"To be on the *safe* side?"

"Please don't worry. Children have all sorts of passing symptoms, particularly when they're growing as quickly as this young man; but it's always a good idea to follow up on them, even if it proves unnecessary."

The famous ophthalmologist, Dr. David Ribin, to whom Dr. Stevenson sent Toby, gave him a complete eye examination. Lily sat in the waiting room trying to read a magazine as the time passed. Suddenly she looked up and saw Zachary standing by her chair.

"No!" she screamed. She knew, the instant she saw her husband, that the doctor had telephoned him to come.

"Lily, Lily." Zachary enfolded her in his arms. "Whatever it is, medicine can cure it. They can do anything with eyes, it's the most advanced field that exists, Lily, I'll take care of it, don't worry. Come on, the doctor is waiting to talk to us. A nurse is keeping Toby busy, I saw them as I came in."

"I'm deeply sorry to have to tell you this," Dr. Ribin said, as they sat before him. "But Toby has retinitis pigmentosa. We don't know the cause of this disease. Night blindness is often the first symptom."

"Disease—what sort of disease?" Zachary asked, taking Lily's hand.

"First of all, Mr. Amberville, I should explain that the retina is a thin membrane that lines the inner eye. It contains rods and cones, which are the structures that are sensitive to light. The rods are the receptors used in dim light, which is why an alteration in their functions, as in Toby's case, causes night blindness before anything else."

"Doctor Ribin, what's the treatment that's used in this sort of thing?" Lily asked, maddened by the length of the doctor's explanation.

"We have no treatment, Mrs. Amberville. The nerve cells of the retina cannot be replaced if they are damaged."

"No treatment? You mean no medicine?"

"I'm afraid not."

"Surgery then? Will he have to have surgery?" Lily cried.

"We have no surgical techniques for retinitis pigmentosa," Dr. Ribin said gravely.

"It's not possible! I won't believe it! Everybody can be treated!

He's only four years old, a little boy, just a little boy," Lily said fiercely, refusal still stronger than grief.

"What's going to happen to Toby?" Zachary asked, holding her hand so tightly that it hurt.

"It's a progressive disease, Mr. Amberville. The sides of the retina are normally affected in the beginning, and although Toby's central vision may stay fairly stable for many years, there will be a progressive narrowing of his field of vision as he grows older. Eventually, we don't know exactly when, he will have only a pinpoint of vision left. But that may not happen for many years. He'll have a long time, I hope, until then, but I can't promise how long."

"Forgive me, Doctor, but couldn't it possibly be something else?" Zachary had to ask, although he knew the answer from the doctor's expression.

"I wish it could be. For your own sense of sureness I'd advise you to get another opinion, but unfortunately the disease, though rare, is unmistakable and quickly diagnosed. There are clumps of pigment scattered throughout the retina, and the vessels of the retina are narrowed. I hate to be so certain. I wish I thought I was wrong, Mr. Amberville."

"But how could he have caught it?" Lily cried in her anguish. "How, oh, tell me, how did it happen?"

"When children have retinitis pigmentosa, unlike its appearance in senile degeneration, it can only be hereditary, Mrs. Amberville."

6

Cutter Amberville was almost tempted to remain in California after graduation. At Stanford, he had made many influential friends and grown to agree with the local superstition that Harvard was second to Stanford in excellence. Sarah Amberville visited her youngest child several times a year but Cutter spent his holidays and summer vacations on the West Coast. He went on to Stanford Business School and, after graduation, worked for a few years at Booker, Smity and Jameston, the San Francisco investment banking firm, whose president was his roommate Jumbo Booker's father, a lean, fit, small man, a passionate tennis player who had delighted in taking a number of games off young Amberville.

However, in the early months of 1958, when he was twenty-four, Cutter decided to move to Manhattan. He had discovered that even in California, there was no one whom he was likely to meet who wouldn't ask him about his brother. Perhaps, Cutter thought, if he moved to China he could escape the inevitable question, but otherwise there was no avoiding the association. Since it existed, he might as well take advantage of it, for the center of all investment banking was in New York City, and to be an Amberville couldn't hurt his career. He intended to make a great deal of money. Zachary must not be the only rich Amberville.

Cutter had been steeped in the Stanford–San Francisco traditions of manners and culture and an aristocratic attitude that extended to the business world. He found it difficult to adjust to the collective frenzy of Manhattan. Who *were* all these people? Why did they run instead of walk? Why couldn't they conduct conversation at a civilized decibel level? Was there really not enough of anything to go around or did they just act as if there weren't?

Within a week he decided simply to ignore most of the city, not to begin to try to understand it in all of its distasteful manifestations. He had discovered that after all, on certain streets his kind of people lived, and his friends from Andover, Stanford and San Francisco had provided him with instant entry to the homes of the only people in Manhattan with whom he could feel at home.

Cutter Amberville was, indeed, more than welcome wherever he went. He was tall, six feet two inches, with a body molded by those sports which build the kind of long, elegant muscles that make a tailor purr. The distinctive looks that had made him outstanding as a boy had matured as he grew older, and now Cutter was an unusually handsome man. He was deeply tanned and his hair was bleached by the sun of California summers. His nose was large and perfectly shaped between eyes as blue as the sea in Sicily, as cold as the water of a fjord, and he had an ascetic, keenly etched mouth that no woman could ignore. He didn't have bulk but he had power, and there was a strong suggestion of what Byron called "the light-limb'd Matadore" when Cutter walked into a room. For all his blondness he had a bull-killer's sternness and dark purpose, he moved with an assurance and a self-esteem so ingrained that no one would ever believe that he had trained them into his stance, with as much will as he had trained warmth and sincerity into his smile.

His undeniable charm of manner was now completed, part of his core, his essence; that pleasing, flattering, *necessary* charm of an envious man whose life was dedicated to gaining the attention and affection he believed had been so unfairly denied him as a child.

The eleven years that separated Cutter from Zachary had come to seem like more than a generation to him. Although nothing could ever happen to make him give up the deep, gnawing hatred he felt toward his brother for overshadowing his youth; although no amount of personal success in his own world could ever compensate for the eternal loss of what he knew had been due to him, his hatred had become so familiar that, from time to time, he could almost put aside his litany of injustices, almost allow the worm in his heart to sleep.

Yet even if Zachary and Zachary's enormous success, success following success as if to torment Cutter, could be temporarily ignored, there was no possible way to simply take them for granted, to come to terms with being Zachary Amberville's younger brother. Cutter could never make himself feel, in his profound self, that Zachary's success did not *subtract* something essential from his own life. He was *diminished* forever, unfairly diminished, and it had to be Zachary's fault. Cutter, for all his singular appeal, a handsomeness that verged on beauty, was a man who wore invisible bitterness as permanently as if it had been tattooed onto his heart. He nourished and cherished his hatred; if it had disappeared he would have had to restructure his world, explain it in some other way. But there was no chance of that, not with the Amberville publications appearing weekly and monthly on the newsstands, their brilliant new covers beckoning, growing thicker with advertising month by month, not with *T.V. Week* an automatic purchase made by millions of Americans each week, visible next to the television set in every library into which Cutter walked.

When Cutter first arrived in New York it had been a year since Tobias's disease was diagnosed, yet except for his night blindness, he seemed to continue to see as well as ever, as far as Lily could tell. She and Zachary had told no one, not even Nanny, about their visit to Dr. Ribin. They had consulted another specialist who confirmed the diagnosis, but since there was nothing anybody could do, they kept their silence. They couldn't endure any discussion of Tobias's future, not even with each other. Particularly not with each other.

"Hereditary." Both doctors had agreed. There was no blindness in the Ambervilles' family history, nor in that of the Andersons, the Dales or the Cutters. But there had been a blind Marquis who had been Lily's maternal grandfather, and a blind uncle, also on her mother's side of the family. No, they couldn't possibly discuss Toby, for the only words either of them could think were words they would never say. Her genes, thought Zachary. My fault, thought Lily. Unfair, utterly and absolutely unfair. They both knew those words were unfair, but they could not, *not* think them.

The enormous silence, the void that was created by this silence penetrated into the heart of their life together and they were as aware of the unspoken words as if they were palpable, a glacier that was inexorably creeping over their always fragile intimacy.

By the time Lily was twenty-four she was recognized as the most impressive woman to emerge in several generations of New York society. Women thirty years older than she, women of wealth, cultivation and immense standing, went to great lengths to meet her, for not only was she the daughter of Viscount and Viscountess Adamsfield, but she was Mrs. Zachary Amberville, wife of the man who had just given a million dollars to the Metropolitan Museum's collection of American paintings, and contributed two million dollars to Columbia University for its general scholarship fund; gifts he gave in Lily's name.

Lily entertained so discreetly and yet so lavishly, with piles of money exquisitely spent, that she stayed out of the newspapers, yet when she departed from New York for a trip to London or to France it was felt as a loss, a diminution of the luster of Manhattan. When she returned every fashionable florist had a dozen orders to send her baskets of welcoming blooms, the homage that was her due, and the pace of the life of the city's society took on a quickness that made her large circle feel that things were in place again, that a gala season had started.

Lily was a generous patroness of every ballet company, and took her hour at the barre every morning without fail. She led in all of the anointed cultural events that brought New Yorkers of a certain class together, yet she was rarely a member of any committee; her mere appearance at a benefit or opening night as delicately dominant as a rising moon, always dressed in Mainbocher, her hair worn back from her face in a heavy chignon, was enough to stamp an evening as significant.

Brisk New Yorkers, quick of speech, rapid in calculating social weights and measures, appreciated the quality of Lily's initial diffidence and understood, with their canny, native perception, that it represented the kind of superiority that they were willing, in fact pleased, to acknowledge. Her superiority only enhanced their own.

76

The mere fact that she had decided never to use her "Honorable" gave them the delight of telling the uninitiated that she was a Viscount's daughter, a nineteenth Baronet's daughter. Soon *not* telling became a matter of pride to those who knew her—who *thought* that they knew her—best.

Long before Toby had shown any signs of disease, Lily had abandoned the notion that there existed some passionate physical pleasure that she would finally experience. She believed that she was made by nature so that she didn't need the kind of sex for which some women seemed to live. There were degrees of everything after all, and some women actually lived for chocolate and others for martinis. Lily wasn't rebellious about her lack of desire since life contained so many delectable and obtainable objects for which she had an endless appetite that never failed, no matter how much she acquired.

Zachary, for his part, had gradually come to think that Lily's coldness was incurable. He never lost his gentle patience, but nothing seemed to bring her to sensual life. She had never turned away from him, but his passion for her grew less as he understood that it couldn't be returned. His love only deepened as it was tinted with a pity for his wondrous girl who never complained.

"This one," said Maxi, pointing to a word on the *Racing Form*. The four men, seated with her in a box at Belmont Park, looked at the little girl questioningly.

"So the kid can read, Zack?" Barney Shore wondered in amusement.

"Can you read, Maxi?" her father asked. Anything was possible with a three-year-old. She might have taught herself.

"This one," she repeated.

"Maxi, why that one?" Nat Landauer wanted to know.

"I like that one, Uncle Nat," Maxi replied.

"*Why* do you like that one, young lady?" Joe Shore asked in a quiet voice. All four men fell silent, waiting.

"I just do, Uncle Joe," Maxi said imperturbably. "That one."

"What's its name, Maxi . . . can you tell Uncle Joe its name?" he persevered.

"No, but I like it."

"The young lady can't read," Joe Shore announced with authority.

"But maybe she can pick a horse . . . maybe she's a . . . you know, an idiot savant, like those guys who can tell you when it's going to be Thursday a thousand years from now," Barney Shore said in excitement.

"Please, a little respect for the young lady," his father commanded. "What kind of expression is that to use in front of a child?"

"Sorry, Dad. Maxi, do you like any of the others?"

"No, Uncle Barney, just that one."

"To win, place or show?" Barney persisted.

"To win," she responded immediately. She hadn't known that there were games where you could just choose to win.

"Come on, Barney, you're not taking this seriously, are you?" Zachary protested halfheartedly.

"It can't hurt to listen to Maxi. The four of us put together can't handicap a mouse. Maybe we just need a fresh point of view. Woman's intuition, Zack. You've always been a believer."

"And how much could it cost?" added Nat Landauer. "Two dollars each, that's not too much to lose . . . last year I figure I dropped ten thousand."

"Two dollars to win for each of us, my treat," Zachary proposed. After all, Maxi was his responsibility.

"I'll go buy the tickets," Barney volunteered.

"Can I have a hot dog, please, Daddy?" Maxi asked. Zachary looked at her perched composedly in her seat, a little like a Japanese doll with her straight black bangs and her thick hair neatly trimmed in a circle just at the nape of her neck. She wore a yellow dress with a white collar, smocked at the yoke and at the cuffs of its short sleeves, white socks and black patent leather Mary Janes. The piquant, droll deliciousness of her face astonished him no matter how often or how long he looked at her.

"Daddy? Please, a hot dog?"

Nanny would kill him if she found out. "No, darling. I'm sorry but the hot dogs here aren't good for little girls."

"They smell awfully good." She gave him a tentative smile.

"They don't taste as good as they smell."

"So many other kids are eating them." Maxi's smile grew more tentative and now it became gently pathetic, the smile of someone who understands why she cannot have a glass of water when she is dying of thirst, the smile of someone who forgives the person who denies it.

"Maxi, it's not safe to eat hot dogs at the track," Zachary pleaded.

Maxi took his hand in hers and nestled against him. "All right, Daddy. I wish . . . I wish . . . ."

"What, darling?"

"I wish I'd had more lunch," she said with patient sadness.

"Are you hungry?"

"Yes, but it doesn't matter, Daddy. I don't mind." She looked up at Zachary, a tiny tear brimming in each eye. "Really, I don't mind at all."

"I can't stand this," Nat Landauer announced. "I can't take it, you inhuman, hard-hearted unpatriotic son of a bitch! Uncle Nat will get you a hot dog, Maxi."

"No thanks, Uncle Nat. Daddy says I shouldn't eat them."

There was a silence. Joe Shore looked pained and gave a deep sigh. Zachary Amberville glared at his brother-in-law. Nat Landauer glared back at him. Maxi looked from one to another, holding her breath. A tear crept down each of her cheeks.

"O.K., O.K.! But no mustard!" Zachary shouted.

"The mustard's the best part, you schmuck." Nat's teeth ground together in anger.

"Young lady, do you like mustard?" Joe Shore asked, a smile restored to his face.

"I like ketchup on hot dogs."

"Ketchup's perfect," Zachary said hastily. Kids lived off ketchup, even Nanny liked it.

He held Maxi up so that she could watch the race. She daintily ate her hot dog while her horse won.

Barney Shore went to cash in the tickets. He returned beaming and extracted an amazing amount of cash from his pocket. "I bet a hundred each to win and another hundred for Maxi. You guys are pikers. Somebody could say 'thank you Barney.'"

"Thank you, Uncle Barney," Maxi said. She really liked this game. She decided to give Uncle Barney a kiss, to reward him for being so nice.

"And of course, I don't have to introduce the two of you," said Pepper Delafield, moving away from Lily and Cutter to greet a new group of guests.

"It would look odd if we shook hands," Cutter said, taking Lily's hand in his and holding it. "I should kiss you on the cheek, but that would be odder still, from one stranger to another."

"The oddest thing of all is that we've never met before. Every time Zachary and I visited San Francisco you were on a trip out of town. And you never came to New York . . ." Lily's voice trailed off and she withdrew her hand. She had no idea that whenever Cutter had seen photographs of her in *Vogue* or *Town & Country* he had turned the page quickly and angrily, dismissing her with scorn as a typically bland little English face whom his brother had probably married for her title, like someone buys a particular cupcake because it has a cherry on top. He'd seen Zachary, of course, for his brother had paid all his bills until he started making a living, but he drew the line at playing the younger brother-in-law to the Honorable Lily.

"I'm here now," he said, "for good." Around them the large party had taken on that sound that reassures every hostess no matter how experienced, the sound of lively, laugh-punctuated, easy conversation, seamless and as constant as the bubbling of a big stew on just the right degree of fire, a sound that covered up the awkward pause that fell between Lily and Cutter. She stupefied him, this woman he could no more dismiss than the law of gravity. Until this minute he had known only American girls, debutantes or postdebutantes of the East and West Coast Establishments, girls, he understood immediately, who had patterned themselves, consciously or not, on an ideal, the ideal that was Lily. How glorious she was! She had a quality of consummate rarity: every detail of her face was heightened, as if he were looking at an enlarged photograph, yet the whole was simplified, as only the purest beauty is simple.

80

Necessary. This incandescent woman was necessary to him, this woman who, of all women in the world, was his brother's wife. She couldn't possibly love Zachary. He knew that fact instantly without a single doubt, because if she loved his brother she wouldn't, she *could not possibly* be looking at him as she was, with wild curiosity, with fear, a fear that made him hear a great tom-tom of triumph, a fear he could clearly see trembling on her lips, quenching her social smile, forcing her to lower her eyes, stiffening her posture so that she wouldn't shake. There could be only one reason for that fear, a reason Cutter understood perfectly, for he felt it himself. It was the fear of someone whose life has, in the space of a minute, changed forever and ever.

"Cutter, by God, Cutter! I've been looking all over for you. Pepper told me you were here. Damn it, Cutter, it's good to see you!" Zachary hugged him with a quick, embarrassed hug he couldn't restrain. He had long been wounded by the cold, distant stiffness his brother displayed toward him, but he couldn't seem to change it, try as he would. There had always been something strained in their relationship which he had never been able to understand. Finally, helplessly, he had decided to attribute it to the decade that separated them, to the cliché of the generation gap. But he was delighted to lay eyes on the boy. No, he corrected himself, the man, for Cutter was unquestionably a man now, twenty-four years old and, in all ways but age, the most commanding presence in the room.

"I'm glad to see you too, Zack," Cutter said smiling automatically. How had he *dared,* how had he had the monstrous effrontery to marry this girl? He had no right to her, didn't he know that? He could deck her out all over with diamonds and sapphires and call her what he would, but she had never belonged to him. He stared down at Zachary, noting the few extra pounds around Zachary's waist, the more obvious since he hadn't had time to have a new dinner jacket made for several years, seeing the strands of gray that had begun to invade his dark hair. There were lines on Zachary's face that were unfamiliar to Cutter, lines that had appeared during the last year, during the long nights that he stood outside of Toby's room where, now, a lamp always burned.

"You look wonderful, Cutter! Doesn't he look wonderful, darling? Listen, have you found an apartment yet? Because if you haven't, you can always stay with us while you look."

"Rented one today, Zack, on East Sixty-seventh, just a few blocks from your house. It's a furnished sublet, just temporary, until I find the place I want to settle in, but perfectly adequate."

"Great, that means that you have to come and see us—Lily, how about tomorrow . . . are we having dinner at home tomorrow night?"

"Yes."

"Is that good for you, Cutter?"

"I'd love it."

"Come early, so you can see the kids. We'll eat at eight but if you can get to our place by six-thirty you can see both of them before Nanny spirits them away."

"Terrific. I'll count on it."

"You're not all supposed to be standing around talking to your own family," Pepper Delafield said, sweeping up to the three of them, and scattering them strategically among her other guests as only she knew how to do.

Lily didn't sleep at all that night, and finally, at five, she got up and wandered around the great house, touching polished wood, picking up heavy silver boxes and putting them down, crushing velvet-covered pillows. When she found herself methodically destroying a bouquet of flowers, plucking petal after petal from the hearts of roses, rolling them in her hands until they grew limp and wet before she discarded them angrily on a table, she decided to go to the ballroom, which had been turned into her dance studio, and work at the barre. It was an infallible remedy for any kind of thought, an ingrained rhythm of body and mind that had never failed her. Yet, as dawn broke, so did her dancer's discipline, and for the first time in her life she did not finish her barre, nor did she care. She was waiting, listening, in the quiet house, for something to happen, something she could not put a name to, and she knew that she was in no condition to face her day's appointments. She would cancel them and stay at home.

She spent the morning flipping unseeingly through a pile of

new magazines in her sitting room. For two years she and Zachary had had separate sets of rooms and the servants were accustomed to her taking an occasional day off from her exhausting schedule and, as now, ordering lunch on a tray. Lily sat looking at the untouched tray, counting the hours until six-thirty. Every few minutes she got up to look at herself in a mirror and each time she saw nothing except eyes that seemed strangely terrified, and burning cheeks. She tried to make a few phone calls but stopped in the act of dialing because she couldn't imagine what she would talk about to any of her friends.

Nothing seemed important, nothing meant anything anymore. It was as if she had had no past and possessed no future. She put her hand to her throat and felt the pulse beating furiously. She walked around and around the room, repeating the few words that she and Cutter had exchanged, such banal words, their only comfort offered by the fact that he had said he was in New York for good. She had seen photographs of him, of course, family photos that her mother-in-law had shown her, but nothing about the pictures of a blond boy with severe, regular features had led her to expect him to be a magnificent man who struck her dumb with mute, primal longing, helpless and quivering and mad with restlessness, bewildered by a feeling of unknown horizons opening before her unto wild and inevitable skies. Again and again she looked at her watch. Five and a half more hours.

There was a tap on the door and the houseman entered.

"Mr. Amberville, Madame," he announced and crossed the room to remove her lunch tray. Cutter stood still, just inside her door. She dared only to glance up once at his face but she couldn't bring herself to meet his gaze or to rise from the couch on which she was sitting. Both of them were motionless until the servant had left, closing the door behind him. Then Cutter came to the couch and picked her up easily until she stood against him, shaking, speechless yet without surprise, astonishingly without surprise. He put one hand on either side of her hot cheeks and, with the utmost deliberation and gravity, kissed her on the mouth, kissed her time after time until they both sank to their knees because they didn't have the strength to stand. They exchanged no words but soon they were both naked, their clothes ripped off in silence, lying on the carpet, panting with haste. He was hard and he had only one goal. She was unsmiling. She had the same goal. Flesh to flesh, sighing, gasping, they made each other whole. They had exchanged no salutations, and no promises, but they had exchanged their separate solitudes, their unrealized selves, their lonely, craving souls. Afterwards, almost immediately, he took her again and this time, now that the world had reformed itself for her, Lily discovered that secret of human passion that she had never known, discovered her own rhythm, a rhythm that had waited, hidden in her body, until this moment in time. What, oh what if he had not been alive? How had she endured so long without him?

"I don't know what to do," she said at last, uncaring, scarcely able to form the words.

"I have to leave you now, beloved. It's getting late and someone is sure to disturb you. Will you make my excuses about tonight? I couldn't stand to see you with him . . . you understand that, don't you? I'll be back tomorrow, at the same time, if you say so. Do you love me, Lily? Do you?"

"Oh, God, yes!"

Cutter put his fingers deeply into her. She was ready for him again; she hadn't closed up and tightened the way women did when they'd had enough. "Tomorrow," he repeated and left.

There were hours of that afternoon, after Cutter left, that Lily could never account for. She supposed that she must have taken a bath, that she must have read to the children and watched them have their supper, that she must have had dinner herself and explained why Cutter wasn't there. But for the rest of her life there were seconds of that first day that she would always remember; the smell of her hands after he had gone; the torn clothing she had hidden in the back of her closet; the way she had to leave the sitting room windows open so that the smell of their lovemaking wouldn't hang in the air; the cream she had slowly, dreamily smoothed on her cheeks where the bristles of his beard had scratched her slightly; the feeling of the carpet under her open legs; the hour she had spent locked in her bathroom, unable to stop sobbing, tears of terrible joy cascading from her eyes; sounds, like those of the newly born, escaping her lips.

After dinner, knowing that she would be unable to function normally without the children or the servants around, she told Zachary that she felt the need of a brisk walk. He nodded, deep in thought, and she left him working in his library on the papers he had brought home from the office with him. Twice, three times she walked around the block, wondering if she could manage to get through the evening without going to Cutter's door. Finally she realized that it was hopeless and she almost ran the three blocks to his apartment. She buzzed. If he weren't there what could she do? She held her breath until the door clicked open and she stumbled up the two flights to his apartment not knowing what she was going to say. He was standing in his doorway, dressed only in a bathrobe.

"I willed you to come here. I've been thinking about nothing else since I left you," he said. She walked into the room without noticing that it was furnished with the most nondescript of rented pieces, worn leather and mustard-colored chairs. He stopped her before she had advanced farther than three steps. "Have you ever done this before? With anyone in the world?" he demanded sternly.

"Of course not," she replied in amazement, her face flushed from the wind, rosy with daring.

"That's what I thought, that's what I knew you'd say," he told her, unbuttoning her coat and leading her into his small bedroom where the open bed waited for her. He pushed her skirt up to her waist and pulled down her brief underpants. She wore a garter belt and stockings and between the top of her pants and the lower edge of her garter belt her blond pubic tangle was framed. He bent down toward it, stuck out his tongue and licked her slowly between those delicately closed lips. She screamed. "Shut up, darling," he whispered, and licked her again, deeper this time, so that the lips parted and his tongue met wetness. Ruthlessly his tongue dragged back and forth, traveling over her clitoris every time it made its trip. Her legs spread as wide as the pants around her knees would permit, her back arched, her mouth opened, she breathed shallowly, concentrated entirely on the voyage of his tongue, knowing, in a delirium of passion, that nothing in the world could make him stop. She lifted her hips off the bed to offer herself more easily to him, she pushed her mound into his face and rubbed it around in a circle, but he wouldn't allow that. He was in charge, he was the boss, and he held her immobile between his elbows, withdrawing his tongue until she whimpered, until she pleaded, until she begged for it, begged out loud. Then he plunged his tongue as deeply into her as it could go, up to the root, in and out, flicking her clitoris every time and when she screamed and screamed he kept going until she was quiet at last.

"Do you *belong* to me?" he demanded.

"I belong to you."

"You have to, don't you, always? Nothing can change that, can it?"

"Never. Nothing. No one."

"Feel me," he commanded.

She put her hand on his penis. It was as hard as it had been when he had first undressed her in her room that afternoon.

"Last night, when I first saw you," he whispered harshly, "I got hard, right away. I was hard all the time we were talking so politely at the party. In my dreams, last night, I came in my sleep and this morning, when I woke up, thinking about you, I had to come again, in my hand, because I was so hard that it hurt. Now I want to come in your mouth."

"Yes," she said. "Yes. Oh, yes."

They took risks only madmen take. They stood up, fully clothed, in the phone booth at L'Aiglon, his hand holding the door closed, while Zachary and Cutter's date had another pre-dinner drink, and he rubbed her against his penis, rocklike under his trousers, until she came, biting back her cries. She went to his office, once he had started working on Wall Street, and while his secretary was out to lunch he knelt on the carpet and she sat on the couch, with her head thrown back and her eyes closed, and slowly, with just his fingers wet with her own juices, he worked her to a shuddering orgasm, watching her face every second.

Often, very often, when they weren't in his apartment, he

would not let her touch him no matter how she begged. He experienced a violent joy in withholding his own pleasure, in creating situations in which she would come but he could not. Lily stopped wearing underpants. She never knew in advance when he would let her have his penis, and he never told her.

He would take her casually by the elbow at a crowded party and lead her with deliberate lack of haste to a bathroom, lock the door and tell her to lie on the bathmat. Fully dressed himself, he would raise her wide skirts to her waist and suck her ruthlessly until she came, and then leave her immediately. The next night, at another party, he would guide her away from the other guests and, once in the bathroom, unzip his fly, take out his naked penis and put it in her with total self-absorption, coming quickly and pulling out, deliberately not waiting until she had an orgasm. He would leave the bathroom first and observe her during the rest of the evening, watching her as she moved across the room, wet with his sperm under her gown, wet with her own wanting, but successfully maintaining her serenity by avoiding his eyes.

During intermissions of Broadway musicals, while Zachary waited in line to buy lemonade, they would stand in a corner, not looking at each other. "I want to suck you," he whispered, licking his thumb and pressing it into her palm. "I want to suck you slowly, for an hour, so slowly, so slowly, and not let you come." He reached under the flap of her evening coat, took out her breast from the low-cut bodice of her dress and held it in his hand, his wet thumb rubbing her nipple. She came, standing up, came in quick, shallow spasms that left her eyes brighter than before, came only halfway as he had known she would, so that she would spend the whole of the second act dying for more, unable to touch him.

Lily stopped wearing lipstick, saying that she had become allergic to it; she carried a tiny hairbrush in her handbag at all times and a small bottle of perfume and carefully folded wads of Kleenex. She kept a small traveling toothbrush and a miniature tube of toothpaste in the same bag, and they both used it when they could, but if they weren't near a bathroom they drank some brandy as soon as they joined any group of people. They were both mad with lust, but not so mad as not to realize that they must smell of sex.

Lily grew addicted to the postponed satisfactions; she gloried in not knowing what he was going to do to her. She refused herself any gratification no matter how he had frustrated her, so that she was melting, fluttering with desire at every hour, particularly as she was dressing to go to one of the many parties to which they were all invited, since Cutter had quickly become a part of the group of people the Ambervilles saw almost every evening of that New York spring season. Whenever she crossed her legs she had a short, quick orgasmic spasm.

Lily dropped out of almost all of her committee work with vague excuses, and refused all lunch dates so that she would always be free to meet Cutter at his apartment if he called. He could take the subway back and forth to Wall Street and still have time enough to spend a long half hour with her in the middle of the day, and that became the only time they would lie totally naked in bed together. But he rationed this pleasure unnecessarily, saying he had to go to business lunches, because he far preferred the chances they took in public places to the shelter of his bed; preferred the dominion over her that he had by merely touching her elbow, taking her away from a cluster of people, particularly when Zachary was part of that cluster. Sometimes Cutter would stand next to Lily, queenly silk-clad, Lily, Lily in her splendid jewels, with her sheaves of hair flowing down her back, for she would wear it no other way now, and talk business to Zachary for three-quarters of an hour, knowing that she was waiting for him to signal her. Then he would walk away with barely an excuse and talk to somebody else. Those were the best moments of all, those evenings when he would deny both of them, when he would merely brush her cheeks with his lips at the end of the party, knowing that at any minute during the past hours he could have had his brother's wife kneeling at his feet, her lips open to receive him.

7

Ever since Maxi was born, the Ambervilles had owned a summer house, a great shingled mansion that overlooked the Atlantic from its perch above the Southampton Dunes. Lily enjoyed those lazy summers. There was something almost English about the quality of utter leisure, the taking of tea, the cutting of roses, the croquet games, the daily visits to the Maidstone Club to play tennis in an atmosphere of protected, soft-voiced, well-mannered distance from the New York crowds. She found more time for her children during the summers and on the weekday evenings, when Zachary was rarely able to drive out for dinner, she often chose not to see anyone, but to eat alone. After dinner she would sometimes walk by herself on the beach, feeling the sand still warm under her bare feet, thinking about nothing at all, and find herself almost happy.

Now as she faced the summer of 1958, a July and August that would separate her from Cutter except for the weekends, Lily tried frantically to find a reason to stay in the city. But there simply wasn't one: she could hardly send Toby and Maxi and the servants out to the beach by themselves while she camped in the city house with a skeleton staff on the pretext of not wanting to leave Zachary alone . . . everyone would find that most unusual and unnecessary, Zachary above all.

It was still mid-June but she thought of little else than the impossible summer ahead. She went through the motions of her life without allowing her preoccupation to become visible, as once she had danced with bleeding feet and a brilliantly fixed smile, until, in the middle of one spring night, she woke up in a state of alarm from a nightmare that she couldn't remember a split second after she opened her eyes. Her heart was beating so heavily that Lily pressed her hands over her breasts bearing down on her fright, unable to sort out her thoughts. Her heart began to slow down as she tried to recollect the dream. What could have so terrified her? She lay still, searching, her hands still cupped comfortingly around her breasts, taking deep breaths, when suddenly a message passed from flesh to flesh and her heart lurched again into a violent rhythm. Only twice before in her life had her breasts felt like this: sensitive, warmer than usual, with a hint of the fullness to come.

There was no question of whose baby it was. She had allowed Zachary to make love to her a minimum of times in the last months, only often enough to prevent any possibility of a confrontation, and each time she had taken every precaution not to become pregnant. With Cutter she had forgotten the meaning of caution just as she had forgotten everything else in her recklessness.

Joy, a joy that accepted none of the problems of reality, invaded her. The fear she had awakened vanished totally as Lily, deeply happy as she had never known she could be, said over and over to herself, "Cutter's baby, *our* baby." She was too excited to stay in bed even though it was not yet dawn. She went to her window and looked out at a city which, for a few minutes, was as close-to-quiet, as close-to-dark, as it ever became in any twenty-four hours, no longer a strange and lonely citadel of hard, bright towers, a city now imbued with the color of her only love, her once and forever love. Here she had first met Cutter, here she had conceived his child, here she had become a woman.

Cutter sat on the edge of the bed and put his arm carefully, protectively, around her bare shoulders. Lily was like an undetonated bomb that might go off at any minute and blow his life sky-high. From the instant she had told him she was pregnant he had been seized by a cramp of such panic that he had barely been able to react. Wordless by necessity he let her bubble on in her lunatic joy as he scrambled in his mind, considering the import of her news.

At her first words he had withdrawn deep inside himself, understanding suddenly but absolutely that she and he were thinking and feeling on two planes that could never meet. Cutter loved Lily as much as he would ever be able to love a woman. She had all the qualities he admired and her inborn sense of superior aristocracy flattered his needy nature. She seemed to be made on purpose for his private pleasure. She was a marvelous sensual adventure, and his lust for her did not lie only in the fact that she was a means of taking hidden, gloating revenge on Zachary. But publicly she was taboo. Lily was his sister-in-law, a married woman with two children, and the fact that she was now pregnant by him was enough to make the past months of fascinated passion vanish from his mind. The only emotion he felt was utter fear and the determination to get out of this situation no matter what he had to do.

"Darling, what do you intend to do?" he asked calmly.

"'Intend' . . . I don't have any intentions. I thought that you . . . that together we . . ."

"Would somehow get married and live happily ever after?" His words were gentle but his hands were balled into fists.

"Yes, I suppose that's more or less what I thought. Oh, Cutter, I can't think . . . I'm much too happy to think. I love you too much to even try."

"Darling, look, one of us has to be sensible. I want a child with you, Lily, I want lots of children with you—but, what about Toby and Maxi? Have you considered them?"

"Toby and Maxime? Well, naturally they'll be with me. We'll all be together—they won't suffer, Zachary would never let them down in any way and eventually things will sort themselves out, the way they seem to in this country." Lily gave a carefree shrug.

Cutter looked at her, his fear growing. This insanely romantic, infantile madwoman could ruin him unless he could control her. Still he controlled his voice.

"The Zachary you know is a doting indulgent husband, more than ten years older than you, who gives you everything you want, my darling. Nevertheless there's no way to predict how he'll act when he finds out what's been going on. If I were in his place I think I'd try to kill you. Certainly I'd try to take away the children. Do you imagine he got where he is because he lets people take things away from him? Do you believe that he lets anybody make a fool out of him? You don't really know your husband, beloved, but

I do. . . . I've known the greedy bastard since I was born. He might, eventually, let you have a divorce, because he'd see that there was no way to keep you, but it would take a very long tough time."

Lily shook her head violently. Nothing Cutter said was right. Nobody could prevent her from having what she wanted. Cutter didn't understand Zachary as well as she did . . . he didn't know that Zachary had never been able to make her love him. It was *all Zachary's fault* . . . all those years and years without love—all those fruitless, arid, passionless nights. She'd been so patient, so innocent. She had given Zachary enough of herself, she thought bitterly, and now it was over.

"Lily, listen to me. There are only two ways we can make things work for us. Either you have to wait to get a divorce until after the baby is born or you have to have an abortion now . . . no, *stop* that, Lily, stop and listen! You can go to a good, perfectly legal clinic in Puerto Rico or Sweden, or to a dozen different Park Avenue doctors, the same ones your friends go to. God knows, sweetheart, I can't stand to think of you having to go through an abortion but there isn't any other alternative."

"I will not have an abortion," Lily declared, her face set in an expression of absolute disdain and defiance.

"I understand why you feel that way but . . ."

"No, you don't. If you did you couldn't possibly suggest it. It's utterly out of the question. Nobody can make me. I'm going to have our baby."

Abruptly Cutter got up and crossed the room and consulted his watch on his dresser. If he listened to her for another minute, laying down the law, so confident in her selfish, shortsighted, childlike stupidity, he'd hit her. There was no telling what she was capable of, what scandal she might unleash, but one thing he was sure of now was that she was fully capable of destroying his career without even realizing what she was doing. He'd be out on the street in five minutes if his firm heard about this, disgraced everywhere in his world, every man he'd ever known snickering at him, stuck with the responsibility for a married woman and her brat at twenty-four, when his life was just beginning, because this God damned bitch hadn't had the ordinary common sense to use a diaphragm.

"Darling," he said, "I'm late for work already. I have to rush. You go home and relax and leave this to me. I'll find a way for us to be together. It's as important to me as it is to you. Now get dressed . . . I've got five minutes to shave and shower."

"When will I see you?"

"Tonight there's that business dinner I told you about and tomorrow is my class reunion at the University Club. Hell . . . it all couldn't come at a worse time but I'm scheduled to make a speech. Look, I'll get away from the dinner as soon as I can and I'll meet you back here. Zachary will still be in Chicago so we can spend the whole night together. Just let yourself in with your key and wait for me."

Smiling, Lily slid out of bed. She didn't mind this enforced separation. It would be lovely to have a little time alone to gloat over her happiness. Men were so preoccupied with details.

A letter was waiting for her on Cutter's bedspread when she arrived the following night.

My *darling*,

If I didn't love you so much I might be able to destroy your life just so that we could be together, but I can't do that to you. You've been protected in a way you don't begin to comprehend. You went straight from your father's house to your husband's house without ever disappointing any-body or being disappointed yourself. You've led a life in which disgrace and scandal and particularly dishonor have had no place, and I can't put you in that position because of your love for me.

I could stand proud under the dishonor of having fallen in love with my own brother's wife because I know the deep truth about the way we feel about each other. But in the eyes of the world, in the eyes of all your friends in New

York, you would be the one who would be blamed. You would have taken all your husband could give you and then turned around and betrayed him. Your parents, in particular, would be heartbroken. Women are always the ones who are considered to be at fault in this sort of thing unless the man is a well-known bastard—it's not fair but you know it's true. The men are considered lucky rascals and the lady is a whore. I can't let you be smeared by gossip and in your case it would be much worse than gossip, it would be headlines in the press, here and in England too.

I've done nothing but think since I left you. Toby will always need the most expensive kind of special education that only Zachary can give him. You know how devoted Toby is to his father. How can I ask you to take a child who's going blind away from his familiar life, his own house, his own father? Maxi could adapt to almost anything but Toby is a special case, and I can't allow myself to hurt him because of our love.

I know that you wouldn't mind living on what I make, I know you don't care about not having the houses and servants and all the other things that Zachary gives you, but I would mind, *desperately*, seeing you reduced to cutting corners, taking care of three children, having to help with the housework, worrying about money. We've never talked about my economic situation but I'm really just beginning my career. Someday, and I know it will be soon, I'll be making enough to support you, but right now it would be impossible with three children unless we were able to depend on Zachary for our income which would mean a kind of sick dependency which would tear us apart.

My beloved, my Lily, you're the only woman I'll ever love, but has it ever occurred to you that I'm only twenty-four years old?

God, I'd give anything to be older, established, able to take you away from him and give you everything and to hell with what people say. *But we must wait.* If you have the courage to wait we can have a life together. You have to

94

make the decision about the baby. Whatever you do will be the right thing to do, the only thing to do.

I'm going back to San Francisco. By the time you read this I'll be on the plane. I'm too much of a coward to say all of this to your face, too ashamed that I can't make it right, couldn't find a way that we could be together. Please, beloved, don't hate me. I hate myself enough for the two of us. I'll always love you and one day we'll be together if you can be patient, strong, brave and forgive me. And wait, *wait.*

Cutter

Lily read the letter once. She folded it and put it in her handbag and proudly walked out of the empty room. How much, she thought, Cutter must love her, to have thought only of how the baby would change *her* life. If only he were here, so she could tell him that there was no reason for him to be ashamed. Hate him? How could she possibly hate him? Every word of his letter told her how much she meant to him. Didn't he realize that their child meant that they would be linked forever? And oh, how well she knew how to wait.

Every Wednesday afternoon there was a meeting of the people on whom Zachary Amberville relied to run his magazines. The group didn't have any formal name, since, as in many privately owned companies without stockholders, there was no board of directors, but Zachary gave a lot of thought to the invitations he tendered. It was understood that anyone who attended one meeting would, from then on, attend all of them. In a magazine business, where top editors are not infrequently wooed by the competition, and issues are planned five months in advance, secrecy about future plans is vital. Zachary waited a long time before asking any employee to come to the Wednesday planning session.

Zelda Powers, Editor-in-chief of *Style,* had some eighty people working for her of whom a handful had their own clearly defined areas of responsibility; among them: fashion, beauty, accessories, shoes—almighty shoes whose manufacturers advertise mightily—and features. Features included all the major articles in *Style* and a front-of-the-book catchall for whatever was new in the worlds of movies, art, television, music, and books, called "Have You Heard?" To have a job in the "Have You Heard?" section of *Style*, a job that paid less than that of any self-respecting saleslady at Macy's, was the equivalent of the honor bestowed on Jean Lannes, Duke of Montebello, the only one of Napoleon's twelve *Maréchals* who was allowed to address the Emperor in the familiar form as "thou."

No poor girl could afford to work for "Have You Heard?" nor would a rich but not terribly bright girl stand a chance. She had to be both well enough off to support herself from outside income, and enormously smart, for the competition for these three assistant editors' jobs started early on the campuses of the Seven Sisters, the Ivy League women's colleges. Young editors were hired by the features editor, John Hemingsway, who enjoyed every second of the power he wielded, for it was he who decided which personalities would have profiles written on them for the main section of the magazine; which American man or woman was ripe to be explored in color photos and three thousand words; it was he who decreed that any given human being merited merely a thousand words and a black-and-white photo, or determined that any particular topic had suddenly become worthy of notice by *Style* and should be assigned as an article.

For his three "Have You Heard?" assistants Hemingsway hired only unmarried women; only those who dressed well; only those who were shorter than he; only those under thirty; because if they were over thirty and still unmarried they were bound to be too neurotic to work as well as he expected them to; and only those who were willing to work nights because if they had too many boyfriends he knew they would be more interested in marriage than in "Have You Heard?" No matter how hard they worked, he hired only girls who were not ambitious enough to want his job, for he didn't trust women at all.

Dozens and dozens of girls managed to qualify for these three jobs at *Style*. Two of them who held the jobs were true to the Hemingsway mold, and the third, who was secretly ambitious and thus the cleverest of all, was able to work late and still keep a half-dozen boyfriends entangled in her web. Fortunately Nina Stern needed very little sleep and worked quickly.

Nina Stern was twenty-five and of all the beautiful, rich, *unmarried* Jewish girls anyone in 1958 had ever heard of, by far the oldest. People had even stopped trying to probe at this problem with her mother. It was taken for granted among the many friends of the Stern family that there was something invisibly but unquestionably wrong with Nina. Even a hint of a hint would be cruel and, what was worse, would have no result. The poor thing didn't even have a broken engagement to her credit. Why meddle if it couldn't help? It was more productive to meddle where there was still some hope.

Marriage, in Nina Stern's opinion, was the end of the line. She had probably flirted with the doctor who delivered her, and certainly with every living creature she had encountered after that minute. The only form of communication Nina knew was one form or another of flirtation; but accused of flirting she truly wouldn't have understood what people were talking about. She flirted with children, teenagers, all adults of both sexes, homosexuals of any persuasion, and any animal she came across. She had never flirted with a rock but she had flirted with many trees and flowers. Her flirtation wasn't specific, neither sexual nor romantic, but merely an instinctive approach to any situation in which she found herself, a general, permanent, immutable inclination toward courtship. Her flirtatiousness was not "correct" in the French sense, meaning proper; it was great, even noble. It was also essentially harmless and it explained why, like businesses that are depression-proof, Nina Stern at any age would always be proof against any shortage of males. Just as she knew her name was Nina she knew that there would always be men for her and she adored variety too much to even consider settling down with just one man.

She liked to meet her college friends for lunch and admire the photographs of their fast-growing families; she felt only sincere admiration when the much younger sisters of these friends displayed their engagement rings, but monogrammed towels reminded her of straitjackets, and new sheets of shrouds. The only shopping in New York she couldn't endure was on the second floor of Tiffany's, where she often was forced to buy yet another baby present. There, certain interior decorators were given a free hand with the vast stock of the store and vied with each other in arranging china, crystal and silver in ways that tables had never been laid before. When Nina confronted the glittering, fantastic tables as she left the gray-velvet-lined elevator, all that filled her mind were images of women standing in line for the butcher's personal attention at Gristede's, cluttered kitchens and dirty dishes. Otherwise she had no time for gruesome fantasies, unless it was to report on the newest horror film for *Style*.

She was, at first sight, the embodiment of the happy medium, although nothing about her was average. Her shoulder-length hair was light brown, but of the irresistible and indescribable shade called *marron glacé*, the color of candied chestnuts. Her height was five feet five and a half inches, mysteriously just the right height for every activity except professional basketball. Her face wasn't distinctively heart-shaped or round or oval, but its shape pleased every eye. It was simply the right shape and her features were the right features and her body was the right body, and her voice was the right voice, in the sense that the slightest alteration in them would have been *wrong*. Seven full pages in the *Oxford English Dictionary* are devoted to definitions of the word "right," but one close look at Nina defined rightness in a flash.

This great flirt, with her definition-defying rightness, sometimes had to work on Saturday if she'd had a particularly full week fending off all the men who wanted to marry her without driving them away for good. One particular Saturday in June of 1958 when the only possible activity for a self-respecting New Yorker was opening up the beach house or painting the shutters in Fairfield County, on a day on which no Manhattanite should have been caught in Manhattan, Nina Stern was forced to go to the office to finish a last column for "Have You Heard?" She took the newly automated elevator to the fifteenth floor. Somewhere between the tenth and eleventh floors the elevator stopped, with a particularly final grinding sound.

98

"Now what?" asked Nina of a male unknown to her, the only other passenger.

"There's a phone . . . I'll call for help," Zachary Amberville said.

Whoever was supposed to be on the other end of the phone was evidently out to lunch. The only sound was Muzak as Zachary tried repeatedly to get an answer.

"I wouldn't mind so much," Nina said surveying him, "if it weren't for that noise. Death by Muzak. They'll find us here on Monday morning, out of our minds, singing 'Rudolph the Red-Nosed Reindeer' for the rest of our lives."

"Do you like rye bread?" Zachary asked.

"Corn rye or regular rye with caraway seeds?"

"Regular. I stopped at Reuben's and picked up a sandwich before I came to the office." He unwrapped the enormous crusty oval-shaped sandwich, sliced on the diagonal in three sections, filled with thick layers of pastrami, Swiss cheese, corned beef, cold slaw, and Reuben's own mustard.

"You even have a pickle," Nina marveled.

"It stimulates the brain," Zachary said with authority. "Better than fish. Why don't we sit down?"

"If only there were some way to turn off the Muzak."

"There is. You have to climb on my shoulders and push that little switch on the top of the door to the left."

Nina surveyed the stranger. He couldn't be a mad rapist or he would have raped her by now. He obviously was kind-hearted since he was willing to share his perfect sandwich when they might have another day and a half before they were released. In spite of child-hood conditioning she wasn't afraid that he was in the white slave trade. Her mother had never let her go to the movies on Saturday afternoon except to the Trans-Lux on Eighty-fifth Street, where a matron patrolled the aisles with a flashlight, because it was well known that any nice New York girl, alone in the movies, would be pricked with a hypodermic by any man who took the seat next to her, pass out and, a week later, wake up as a white slave in Tangiers. Nina thought she would be rather well treated in Tangiers, if it came to that, and anyway this man did not look like the type. He was wearing an expensive tweed jacket, even if it didn't fit him. He had very clean black hair, even if it needed a cut. His flexible, quirky mouth was kind, his dark eyes bright with amusement, and his shoes were handmade.

She nodded agreement to Zachary and he bent down, like a fullback, and she took off her shoes and hopped on his shoulders. "Get up very slowly. I've never done this before," she ordered. Zachary rose inch by inch, while Nina clutched his hair. She eliminated the Muzak with a quick flick of the switch and he carefully lowered her to the floor of the elevator. They both sat down. It was a clean elevator and the only one they had.

"That gave me an appetite," Nina said.

"You can have the middle piece," Zachary offered generously, spreading out the silver foil. The middle section of a Reuben sandwich was always the most succulent.

"Thank you," Nina said. All her life men had given her the best piece, just as she'd always been offered the white meat of every chicken and the crispest piece of bacon and the female lobster with the delicious coral in it, but although she was always grateful she was no more surprised than Morgan Le Fay would have been. She smiled at Zachary. Of all the utterly right things about Nina Stern, her smile was the rightest. Of all the flirtatious things about Nina Stern, her smile was the most flirtatious. What a nice girl, Zachary thought. "Where do you work?" he asked.

"At *Style,* in 'Have You Heard?' What about you?"

"Sales," he said dismissively, with a shrug.

"Unexciting? Horribly boring? Dreary and dull?" she sympathized.

"Necessary," Zachary said stoically. "But nothing you'd want to hear about. I've just spent three days in Chicago at a sales convention and enough is enough."

"Oh, go on, bore me. Tell me about dismal sales, all about pokey, stuffy old sales, everything about tedious, monotonous, unfortunately necessary sales. Stop when I go into a coma."

"I never bore a lady on purpose," he grinned. "Tell me about 'Have You Heard?'"

"If you won't bore me, I refuse to bore you . . . it's all just a lot of chat, basically unimportant. Anyway, wouldn't you rather eat than talk?" Nina's work was too vital to her to discuss with the many men in her life and she had just realized that this stranger was unquestionably going to be a man in her life. It usually did not take her more than a split second to make such a decision but until today she had been terrified of being trapped in elevators and her reflexes were slower than normal.

"We could do both," Zachary said, "at the same time."

"Should we try to make this last as long as possible in case they don't rescue us, or should we just . . . ?" Nina pondered.

"Big bites. You can't enjoy a sandwich and hold back at the same time."

"I'll remember that . . . you're so wise."

Really a bright girl, Zachary thought. Exceptionally bright. I think I'll invite her to the next Wednesday meeting. We can use her kind of brain. And there's something nice about her, can't exactly put my finger on it.

The elevator started just as they were finishing the sandwich. Nina got off at her floor. She held out her hand and smiled at him again.

"Nina Stern," she said.

"Zachary Amberville."

"That's not fair!" she laughed as the door closed. She was still laughing as she opened her office door. Nina, she told herself, you've just blown the chance of a lifetime.

For a smart girl she could sometimes be very dumb.

"'This great big city's a wondrous toy,'" Zachary sang out loud as he walked home much later that day, his work done. "'Just made for a girl and boy.'" As always he hit a false note on the word "boy." He jaywalked expertly across Madison as he reached the last lines of his song. "'We'll turn Manhattan into an isle of joy.'" He hadn't felt like this in a long time, he realized. He hadn't sung his song in months, years. How did he feel exactly? he asked himself, his steps slowing. Was it the brisk, blowing spring evening with the promise of something brightly thrilling in the air that only New Yorkers feel as the days grow longer? Was it the satisfactory afternoon's work shaping a new magazine no one else knew about yet? Was it just New York, intoxicating center of the galaxy, where his ambitions were born and fulfilled? *Good*. He felt good. Why the hell *shouldn't* he feel good? What man wouldn't feel good who was worth so many millions he hadn't counted them lately, what man wouldn't feel good who had the power he had, who had the fun . . . "sales" he remembered, and laughed out loud. Sales, divine sales!

How old would a girl like Nina Stern be? Shit, but he felt *young!* He was thirty-five and he felt like his sixteen-year-old self at Columbia, waiting on tables for enough money for the subway and a hot dog . . . it hadn't been all that long ago, a war ago, a marriage ago, but still, only nineteen years ago. And only six of the nineteen years spent as a married man. He frowned, his mood suddenly almost punctured. If he felt so young, how come he hadn't made love to Lily in the last few weeks? How come they made love so rarely, now that he came to think about it? As Nat, his brother-in-law, would say, who's counting?

He was counting, that's who. Lily had never been passionate and he'd accepted that about her . . . that was just the way she was . . . but she'd always been so willing. Sweet and delicate and docile. He'd had to make that be enough for him, although many and many a night he'd yearned for a wife who would match his hunger. But, in six years, he'd never played around. Funny about playing around: so many men did it, even when they loved their wives, even when their wives were, he imagined, available in a way that Lily, somehow, didn't seem to be anymore, except at increasingly rare intervals. It occurred to him that mentally, if not physically, she had recently turned away from him when he came to her room and indicated in a subtle, graceful, wordless way that she really didn't want him, not that night, not right now. Was there some inward drama, unguessed at, in her life?

Available. So many women were available in this town. But not all of them. A girl like Nina Stern for instance. She wouldn't be available. She was probably married or engaged or had a list of hopefuls an arm long. Girls like Nina, nice and bright, were spoken for, it stood to reason. And she had a healthy appetite too, always an attractive thing in a woman. "'We'll go to Coney,'" he sang, "'and eat baloney on a roll, through Central Park we'll stroll, da dum.'" Someone turned around to look at him and he realized he was singing out loud again. He'd make sure to tell Hemingway to bring her to the next Wednesday meeting. Do the girl good to see how the magazines were run from some other point of view than that of "Have You Heard?" Better yet, he'd send her a personal memo, a special invitation. Motivated, of course, by her deep interest in sales. "That's not fair," she'd said . . . and it wasn't. He should make it up to her. Smiling he opened his front door and entered the gray marble house just as the butler finished crossing the hall. He had a flash of disbelief . . . could this be his own house, did it really belong to him? He felt so young again, so much the way he had felt when he ventured downtown from Columbia and walked all the streets of his city, not even wondering what lay beyond the doors of houses like this one, splendid beyond the limits of his imagination. He passed the butler with a cheerful greeting and mounted the stairs to his private library where he preferred to work, rather than in the big library downstairs.

"Lily?" he said, astonished. She was standing at the window, looking across the garden, and turned impatiently as he entered.

"I've been waiting for you to come home, darling. I do wish you didn't have to work on Saturday, especially after being away most of the week," she said in her silvery, most loving voice.

"It was something that I had to think through, and I think better at the office. Also my desk was piled high with things I won't have time for on Monday. But I love finding you here. What's that? Champagne? Did I forget something? It's not our anniversary, it's not a birthday, what are we celebrating?" He opened the bottle and deftly filled the tulip-shaped glasses standing on the silver tray she had put on his desk.

"A toast, darling," she said, as they touched the rims of the glasses together. "The best possible news . . . another baby."

"Another baby! I *knew* something wonderful was going to happen!" he shouted for joy and grabbed her in his arms, all other thoughts forgotten.

Lily submitted to his hug, her eyes filled with tears. Courage, Cutter had said, and bravery. She would do anything for him. The most difficult part was over. Now the waiting began.

8

Only the blankness of deep shock and the veneer of basic, automatic manners carried Maxi and Toby through the moments in which they had to congratulate Lily and Cutter on their marriage. Words were said, nods were exchanged but neither of them even tried to manage a smile. It was, Maxi thought, as if the four of them were engaged in trying to decently bury the nameless victim of a hit-and-run accident, a victim whose body was that of Zachary Amberville.

The consternation and astonishment that still filled the boardroom was actually welcome because it enabled the brother and sister to retreat quickly, clutching each other's hands and slipping into the express elevator while Lily and Cutter were still engaged with those members of the Amberville editorial group untouched by the death of four magazines, who were able to offer their own good wishes with a naturalness that neither Maxi nor Toby had been able to muster. Elie took them both back to Toby's town house on a quiet street in the East Seventies. Wordlessly Toby stalked to the bar beside his swimming pool which he had constructed out of the entire first floor and garden of the narrow but deep brownstone, and poured each of them a large drink.

"What is it?" Maxi asked.

"Brandy. I never drink it but if ever there was a time . . ."

"I simply don't believe . . . I just can't understand . . ." Maxi started to say but Toby cut her off.

"Shut up, drink it and have a swim. We can't talk about this yet." He stripped and dove into the pool with that fast, flat dive that had helped him become a swimming champion many times over. Maxi joined him, wearing only her black pearl, and they swam laps until she could feel some of the ball of emotions that filled her begin to dissolve into simple weariness. She stopped swimming and sat by the edge of the pool until Toby surfaced at last and easily hoisted himself up to sit beside her. He had splendid muscles and shoulders yet he was almost fragile at the waist, like many other great swimmers.

"Better?" he grunted.

"As much better as I'm going to get. Which is not a hell of a lot. I feel as if I've been hit by a hand grenade—all to pieces."

"I wonder if we haven't both been overlooking a lot about those two, if we aren't naive to be so surprised."

"Do you mean that obviously Mother had been lonely since . . . oh, God, since Dad's death . . . and so she turned to Cutter and obviously they are both about the same age and no matter how much I don't like or trust him, he's objectively an incredibly hand-some man and after all life and sex don't stop in the late forties? And that it's natural that she'd be embarrassed about getting mar-ried to her own brother-in-law and sneak off and do it without telling us in advance? After all, Toby, it was no accident that she told us about it in public. . . . The one thing I can't imagine is that they just decided to elope on the spur of the moment. They're not Romeo and Juliet."

"Yes to all of that," Toby said, "but there's something else that I've noticed and haven't really paid enough attention to . . . there's a *complicity* between them . . . there always has been, to one degree or another, since Cutter came back from England. And when Dad went, so suddenly, last year, it's gotten steadily stronger."

"Complicity? What's that supposed to mean, exactly . . . that they are partners in crime?"

"No, a deep sort of *involvement,* an intense interest in each other's needs and wishes, an agreement that goes beyond agree-ment, so that it creates a bond that is stronger and more durable than the fact that he's good-looking or she needs a man in her life or any of those self-evident things."

"How come you're such an expert?" Maxi asked rebelliously.

"I *hear* it. You know I hear things in people's voices that you don't catch. I hear it in the way they move when they're together. When you're blind, Goldilocks, you learn to hear people moving in hundreds of different ways, and each means something different. They're deeply complicitous. I hear it and, by God, I *smell* it . . . under all the perfume and soap and after-shave in the world I can smell it on both of them."

Maxi squirmed in a primitive resistance to his words.

"Why do you persist in calling me Goldilocks?" she asked, trying to change the subject.

"Because I like the word. If your hair were all white I'd just see tiny bits of it, now and then, so I call you whatever I like. Just don't go bald. Now, back to Mother and Cutter. He's got her exactly where he wants her. It's the first time I've ever known her like this, so dominated, so dependent. While Dad was alive I felt a certain set of things when she was with him, something utterly different. They were kind to each other . . . I supposed they'd come to terms. They were friends, or at least not enemies, but no complicity."

"You're revolting."

He laughed and smacked her on her bare thigh. "Nice and fresh," he said appraisingly. "You should be good for another ten, maybe fifteen years, before you start to lose that special springiness in the muscles."

"Take your hands off me, you degenerate."

"Do you love me, Goldilocks?"

"I love you, Bat." It was their ritual. Tobias's earliest memory was of touching the cheeks of baby Maxi and her first memory was of his hand picking her up when she tripped on an icy street.

"Oh, if only you could have seen those poor bastards at the meeting, Toby. Some of them looked as if they'd just been sentenced by a hanging judge."

"I heard them. That was enough."

"But how can we accept the way he said that he spoke for her? You know that Mother couldn't possibly have made this decision on her own—she's never been involved in running the company. She doesn't think about profits, for heaven's sake! It's all Cutter's doing, God knows why. But he cannot be *allowed* to kill four magazines all at once! We can't let him do it! Our father would *never* have considered such a thing, not for any reason unless he were flat-out bankrupt. Toby, Toby! *Remember Dad!* It's not euthanasia, it's outright murder!" Maxi's voice grew louder with every word.

"But what can we do about it, babe? Mother has the power, clearly, to enforce her 'decision,' whoever influenced her. Whatever she wants to do with the company she has the absolute legal right to do."

"Moral suasion," Maxi said slowly in a voice midway between inquiry and the dawning of an idea.

"Moral suasion? Obviously you've been away from your native shores too long. This is New York City, babe, and moral suasion is found only on the op-ed page of the *Times.*"

"A special kind of moral suasion, Toby. Manhattan style. If you feed me lunch I'll have the strength to pay our uncle a visit in his office."

"Damned if I know what you're up to."

"Damned if I do . . . yet. But dig we must . . ." she chortled.

"For a better New York," he added, joining in the line they both used to explain any and all inconveniences in the city that was, to them, the center of the universe.

"That would be most unwise, Maxi, and it wouldn't get you anywhere," Cutter said, sitting behind his desk in his Wall Street office. "Whatever you and Tobias feel, and believe me, I truly do understand your sentiments and I sympathize . . ."

"Leave out the hearts and flowers," Maxi snapped. "Let's go straight to the bottom line, since that seems to be your favorite place to operate." She hadn't been home to change since her arrival in New York, but the swim with Toby and the superb lunch he had cooked for her had restored her dauntless spirit, and during the ride downtown she had formed a clear idea of what to do, how to attack.

"I don't care if Amberville is a privately owned company or not, Cutter, it's still subject to public opinion. When Toby and I go to the press, as we plan to, with our minority shareholders' report, we are going to tell them that we are convinced that you have obviously exercised undue influence over our mother, your most amazingly recent bride, and put four magazines to death without prior consultation with Toby or Justin or me, all of us shareholders and highly concerned parties." Maxi stretched out her booted legs defiantly and slumped in her chair with every sign of confident relaxation.

"Perhaps your own skin is thick enough to ignore public opinion, but have you thought about your customers?" she went on. "What about your carefully low-profile partners? Have you thought about everyone in the magazine business, the Newhouses, the Hearsts, the Annenbergs and all the others? What attitude will they have, what will they say about you, Cutter? They all know you are not a publisher, never have been, never will be. It's going to be a juicy, big, *nasty* story for the media . . . four magazines folding at once, hundreds and hundreds of people thrown out of work, all based on the judgment of someone who's never spent five minutes in magazines, someone whose only tiny perch in the business was given to him by his wife?"

Cutter turned over a paper knife, rearranged an inkwell, adjusted his desk clock. There was a brief silence before Maxi continued, since he obviously intended to say nothing.

"I wouldn't want to be in your shoes when we hold our press conference, Cutter. I'm certain Pavka will join us. I know he doesn't have a piece of the company but the media adore him, they consider him a genius, which he is, and a grand old man. Remember the lines around the block for his retrospective at the Museum of Graphic Arts? He's an institution and my father gave him his first chance, to say nothing of the fact that *Wavelength* was Pavka's own idea. Zachary Amberville had faith in the future of those magazines, and people had faith in him—that's what you seem to forget. *My father was a legend. He still is.*"

"You're trying to blackmail me, Maxi, and it won't work. Those magazines are out of business as of this morning. The decision was your mother's to make and she made it."

"You," Maxi said slowly, "are a stinking, rotten, filthy liar. Mother didn't decide anything. But you did. I don't know why yet, but it's all your work, Cutter."

"How dare you speak to me like that?"

Maxi had never seen Cutter really angry before. She smiled

right into his eyes, which were frozen and savage with fury. If it had been her mother's decision in any degree, he would never have let such words escape him, not Cutter, always so tightly, beautifully controlled, always urbane.

"And I deny the charge of blackmail," Maxi said, her smile widening, as insolent as a tomcat on its own turf. "Can't you even recognize moral suasion when you hear it?"

"*Moral* suasion—coming from you that's not funny, it's absurd. All right, just what do you want, Maxi?"

"A magazine. I want one of the four magazines and I want a year in which you leave me absolutely alone to do anything I like with it. No strings, no looking over my shoulder, no budget cutting. Particularly no budget cutting."

"Apparently you think you've inherited your father's touch. So you're going to save a whole magazine single-handed? Why, you've barely done a single consecutive week's worth of honest work in your life, and the only time you did work was one summer when you were a teenager. But let's stop fighting," he said, regaining his temper, "it's unproductive. If Lily can be persuaded to give you a magazine, because she's the one who would have to agree, you and your brothers would have to guarantee not to bring the media into a family affair."

"Then we'd be giving you a free hand with the other three," Maxi said, suddenly glum.

"I don't need your free hand, I don't approve of giving in to blackmail, whatever you choose to call it, and I don't think that a press conference held by a well-known playgirl and a man who, because of his unfortunate handicap, can never so much as scan a magazine layout, would be taken very seriously. But, for the sake of family harmony, and because you undeniably have a certain amount of nuisance value, if Lily should approve, which magazine would you single out for your amazing resuscitation attempt?"

"*Buttons and Bows*," Maxi answered promptly. She hadn't the slightest doubt that if her father were still alive his first publication, his talisman, would be the magazine he would care about most of all.

"I'll do my best with your mother, Maxi, but I can't promise anything until I've talked to her."

"Bullshit." Maxi rose quickly and walked to the door. "I consider myself Editor-in-chief of *Buttons and Bows*," she said as she left his office, "as of this minute. No, don't bother to see me to the elevator."

Wearily, but with a sense of triumph percolating in her veins, Maxi arrived home at her apartment on the sixty-third floor of the Trump Tower. She hadn't been at all sure that she could crack Cutter, whose reputation as a sound, if not particularly successful investment banker, might have sustained an attack on his business judgment. Many magazines had died in the last decade, been briefly mourned and forgotten. As Maxi turned the key in her lock, she thought that if Cutter had ever been a member of the editorial board of Amberville Publications, she could never have gotten away with her threats of a press conference. Exactly how, she wondered, do you "call" a press conference?

"Yeow!"

Maxi collapsed to the floor under the weight of a lanky, barefoot, shrieking creature, burdened by a backpack and three tennis rackets, a creature that howled and hugged her until she screamed for mercy.

"Mother, my little mother, my very own tiny little mother," the creature yodeled for joy, "you're home! I just got in and looked in the fridge. There's absolutely nothing to eat in this place, but I know you won't let me starve, oh, little mother of all the Russias."

"Angelica, baby, please get off my bones," Maxi begged. Her eleven-year-old daughter had grown a yard at tennis camp. "What are you doing here? You weren't supposed to come back till next week."

"I split camp when I was eliminated in the eighths finals. It's so tacky to be eliminated in the eighths . . . it's O.K. if you don't get that far and O.K. if you're eliminated in the semis, but the eighths, no way, José."

"Angelica, how did you get back from Ojhi? You didn't . . . oh, my God, you didn't *hitch* did you?" Maxi asked, horrified.

"I called Dad for money. I flew, of course, and he met me at the airport. But he didn't have time to feed me . . . that is he didn't feed me *enough,* just a few hamburgers and a couple of chocolate milkshakes . . . did you see how I've grown? Isn't it great? I'm not going to be a dumb, normal-sized person like you. Maybe I can be a model. Do you think I need a nose job, everyone at camp is having a nose job, where are we going for dinner, did Dad call you in Europe to say I was coming back? I've got a nickname, you have to call me Chip from now on, and I'm going to call you Maxi, it's more mature."

"Call me anything," Maxi groaned as Angelica leaned on her lovingly, "but don't expect me to call you Chip. Somebody has to draw a line somewhere." Maxi put her hands on her daughter's shoulders, pushed her a few inches away and inspected her closely. What particular combination of genes, she wondered, had assembled to create this breathtaking, classic promise of exceptional beauty? The Ambervilles, the Adamsfields, the Andersons, the Dales, the Cutters, had contributed to the amazingly poetic, romantic mixture that was Angelica Amberville Cipriani, and yet the dominant traits in the girl's face were those of her father, Rocco Cipriani; magnificent Rocco, Renaissance Rocco, fascinatingly brooding, darkly luminous Rocco whose ancestors had left Venice—probably the only Venetians who had ever left Venice voluntarily—for the United States less than a hundred years ago.

"Are you also planning a nickname for your father?" she asked, making, as she always did, a point of being polite about her first ex-husband, with whom she shared custody of Angelica.

"Oh, Maxi, you gross me out, you really do. A person doesn't call her *father* by a nickname. Sometimes I wonder about you."

"I see the double standard still prevails," Maxi murmured in resignation. "And don't ask me what that means because you'll find out soon enough."

"Now about dinner . . ." Angelica said, strewing the contents of her backpack around the room. "I thought maybe Thai, or sushi. Tennis camp food was strictly for out-of-towners and you know what that means . . . horrendous squishy white bread, orange-yellow sliced plastic cheese, pale pink baloney . . . I haven't had a decent meal in two months."

"Angelica, we'll get back to your stomach in a second, but how about asking me how I am?"

"How are you, Ma?" Angelica said amiably, trying to find a pair of clean socks.

"I'm the new Editor-in-chief of *Buttons and Bows.*"

"Come on . . . how are you? Did you meet some wonderful human being? I haven't had a stepfather recently."

"You will never, *ever* have another stepfather, Angelica. I've told you that a thousand times. I'm serious about *Buttons and Bows.* I'm taking it over."

"*Trimming Trades Monthly?*" Angelica stopped her fruitless quest in astonishment at Maxi's words. "What do you want with poor, old *Trimming Trades?*"

"What are you talking about?"

"*Buttons and Bows* . . . Grandpa always told me that its proper name was *Trimming Trades Monthly* . . . it says so right on the cover, in tiny little letters. *Buttons and Bows* is just the name some desperate editor slapped on it to try and jazz it up. Not that it helped. He said he only kept publishing it out of pity for the people who'd been there for so long . . . he didn't think they could get other jobs, and a lot of them had been there all of their working lives, but he'd lost interest in it ages and ages ago. Seriously, Ma, when was the last time you saw a copy? I think they're practically collector's items. It must have a circulation of at least two hundred and ten. Boring."

"Angelica, how do you know all of this?"

"Grandpa and I used to talk about the business . . . he said I was the only one of the whole family with a head for publishing. Do you happen to have any socks I can borrow, Maxi? . . . Hey, Ma, do you feel all right? You look a little funny. It can't be jet lag or did you fly a regular airline? Maybe you're just starving, like me. Listen, Ma, when do we leave for Venice?"

"Venice?" Maxi repeated vacantly.

"Ma, we are going to spend two weeks in *Venezia*—you know, the one in Italy—before my school starts," Angelica explained patiently and slowly as if to a very elderly person. "Don't say 'Venice?' as if you didn't have the tickets and the reservations because it was all planned months ago."

"We can't go."

"But you said!"

"No Venice. I'm sorry. I'll make it up to you. I have to go to work. At *Trimming Trades Monthly*."

"Jesus! You're serious. Have we lost all our money?"

"I've made a fool of myself."

"Is that worse or better?"

"Worse, much much worse, infinitely worse. Oh, fuck!"

"Ah, Ma, don't feel bad." Angelica enveloped her in a bone-crushing hug. "We can have dinner at Parioli Romanissimo—so what if I don't get to see the land of my ancestors—a restaurant's almost the same thing as Venice without the canals . . . the pigeons . . . the Piazza San Marco . . . the Gritti . . ." her voice trailed off with pitiful poignancy.

"I can't even have dinner with you tonight, Angelica. I'll call Toby and he'll take you anywhere you want to go," Maxi said, hating herself.

"You have a date?" Angelica brightened.

"A promise. And it's not one I can break. Call it a debt of honor. I have to be at P.J. Clarke's at eight sharp." Maxi sank back into a chair and curled up into a ball of misery.

"Angelica, do you happen to like black pearls? Because if you do, I've brought you one back from Europe."

"Ah, give me a break, Maxi . . . come off the guilt trip. It's strictly not your style," Angelica said kindly.

A customs inspector certainly knows his way around the female human body, Maxi thought cheerfully as she tried to wake up the next morning. Was there a man on earth who could make love like a really straightforward Irishman at the peak of his form? And O'Casey was in the prime of his prime. Her second husband had been Australian but his ancestors had come from Ireland, sweet Bad Dennis Brady, a lovely boy as they would have said in the Old Country, but with an unfortunate habit of combining iced tequila and Buffalo Grass vodka in equal quantities and absorbing several generous glasses of the mixture before trying, without the captain's help, to berth his ship in the harbor of Monte Carlo. Perhaps the marriage might have worked if he hadn't been so otherwise bone-lazy or if the boat hadn't been an oceangoing eighty-meter yacht with its own helicopter pad. Perhaps if the helicopter had been properly fastened down the crash—or was it a shipwreck?— wouldn't have been as embarrassing. Maxi had jumped that particular ship of fools after six months, she remembered sleepily, sadder, but not much wiser.

WISER! The word echoed in her mind and brought her out of bed in panic. Wiser? Who was wiser? What time was it? She had to get to work immediately. The staff at *Buttons and Bows* must have heard all about yesterday's meeting, undoubtedly they were sitting around in doubt and tears waiting for the official ax to fall. She had to get there, wherever it was, and reassure them and take over and do . . . and do . . . whatever was necessary. Yes, *do*, take action, make decisions, take stock, take over, do something, do *anything*. She scampered around trying to draw the curtains open so that she could find a clock or a watch, but she was disoriented, not sure how the heavy draperies worked or where the light switches were.

Maxi had not slept in her new apartment before she had left for Europe two months earlier. At that time, like many of the apartments in Trump Tower, it hadn't yet been finished although Maxi had bought it from floor plans several years earlier from her pal, Donald Trump, when the apartment was no more than his vision of what to do with an all-but-priceless piece of New York airspace. Finally she located the right cords and opened the heavy, interlined, apricot silk draperies.

Maxi stood in front of the windows immobilized by surprise. Was this Manhattan, the familiar, loved and hated city or, while she slept, had her new apartment been dropped gently onto another planet? The sun, which was just rising in the East, behind her, cast its rays across Central Park, which was still in partial darkness, and lit the peaks and spires and towers of the city for as far as her eye could see; north to Harlem; west, across the Hudson River to New Jersey; south, down beyond the Trade Center, to the open Atlantic. Lord have mercy, she thought, it is Manhattan and I've *bought* the whole damn town! She was filled with glee, the kind known as unholy. Manhattan belonged to her! She must be the only person awake this early, the only person with this view, that had been carved out of sky. Perhaps there were taxis and buses and fire engines down there but Maxi couldn't hear them on the sixty-third floor. She was floating, but not adrift, anchored in a nest that had cost her more than four million dollars, a nest that was almost as high as the wispy white Fragonard-like clouds that were turning pink over the park. As she watched the sun rise higher in the sky, flashing on windows which, one by one, sent messages directly to her, messages of a new day, tidings of a new morning, Maxi realized how lucky she was to possess a view that altered the spirit.

"'I'll take Manhattan,'" she sang, "'the Bronx and Staten Island too.'" And she danced and danced by herself to the song her father had taught her.

"Angelica, I have nothing of a publisher-nature to wear," Maxi realized at breakfast.

"I thought you were the new Editor-in-chief, Ma. Have you been promoted already?"

"In the middle of the night I woke up and suddenly realized that *Buttons and Bows* must already have an Editor-in-chief, and it would be an unpopular way to start by waltzing in and taking over somebody's job, so I made myself publisher. Since Grandpa died the publications haven't had a publisher."

"How should a publisher dress?" Angelica asked, eating four fried eggs heavily basted with butter, directly out of the pan, the way she liked them best.

"Like an authority figure, a leader, someone who inspires the troops, someone with unquestionable, impeccable, irrefutable judgment."

"So that lets you out." Angelica sprinkled the eggs with a judiciously thick layer of Tabasco.

"Right. But they don't know that, and if I dress in a dynamic way they'll respond to the image, or so I've been led to believe. However, my wardrobe seems not to start till lunch, a competitively chic Le Cirque lunch, a Côte Basque lunch, not a serious, businesslike publisher's morning. Then I have—too many clothes—for cocktails, dinners, balls, yachts, chalets and beaches. Plus the boots and pants I travel in."

"It sounds like some sort of character test. If you look in my closet you can tell me who I really am," her daughter observed.

"I wish you weren't so honest, Angelica. Couldn't you be a little more tactful?"

"You brought it up. Anyway, what about that double-breasted black Saint Laurent pantsuit you bought last year and never wore because it looked so awful on you?"

"It hasn't changed," Maxi said glumly. "It made me look like a short, dumpy man in drag. You can't tell that I have a waist and it eliminates my legs. I do, you have to admit, have the best legs in New York."

"We all know that, Ma. In the Saint Laurent, with spike heels you'd look like a medium-sized man in drag. And the shoulders are really intimidating."

"Maybe with a sensational blouse?" Maxi said, brightening.

"A severe blouse and a macho scarf flung carelessly over one shoulder. Viva Zapata."

"I loathe that look, and the scarf always falls off."

"You have no choice," Angelica said broodingly. "Listen, Ma, have you ever been seriously in love?"

"I don't answer questions like that this early in the morning."

"If I ever met him, do you think Woody Allen would be too old for me?"

"Not really. But I don't think he'd want to get involved."

"Nobody does," Angelica said sadly.

"It's the malaise of the age. Whatever that means," Maxi explained.

"Whatever," Angelica agreed. She *almost* knew what it meant. "So you really are going to the office this morning? Awesome. Well, good luck, Maxi."

"Thank you, darling. What are you doing today, shopping?"

"Yup, back to school. First I'll check out Armani, Krizia, Rykiel, Versace, Kamali, and end up buying Guess?"

"I wish I were as tall as you," sighed Maxi.

"I think you're cute just the way you are. I like a medium-sized mother. It makes me feel grown up."

"I didn't know you didn't," Maxi grumbled.

9

The offices of *Trimming Trades Monthly* were still located on Forty-sixth Street between Sixth and Seventh avenues, where Zachary Amberville had rented space for his first office. When the magazine had been founded the building was slightly run-down but no more so than the rest of the neighborhood, and within walking distance of the trimming trade industry. Nothing had changed except that run-down had slid into disrepair. Maxi noticed nothing of this as she located the offices and announced herself to the receptionist.

"I'm Miss Amberville. Could you please tell the Editor-in-chief that I'm here?"

"Does he expect you?"

"Just tell him. Maxime Amberville."

Seconds later Robert Frederick Fink arrived in the small reception area. He was round and rosy, some sturdy age between sixty-five and seventy, a natty dresser and absolutely delighted with her visit.

"Maxi!" he cried. "Give your Uncle Bob a kiss! I'll bet you've never forgotten the time you won twelve thousand bucks on the Exacta? Come on into my office and tell me about yourself . . . it's been years and years."

"About twenty," Maxi guessed, smothered by his embrace. She didn't remember Uncle Bob, but she still remembered that race.

"Seems like yesterday. Watch that door, it doesn't open very far."

Maxi squeezed into the editor's office and stopped abruptly. The medium-sized room held eight desks and on top of each desk were towering stacks of paper of all kinds, arranged carefully so that the piles somehow held together with no possible means of support. There was just enough space between the high walls of paper to walk, in single file, to Bob Fink's ninth desk on which the papers had only reached a height of some eight inches. He carefully eased her into the only visitor's chair in the room and then edged himself around his desk and sat down comfortably.

"I don't believe in filing cabinets, Maxi, never did. You put something in a file and you forget it's there and you never see it again. Might just as well burn it. Ask me for a document, any document."

"Huh?" Maxi clutched her serapelike plaid scarf around her with both hands and crossed her arms across her breasts. If she sneezed, she thought, it would take a week to dig her out.

"Ask me to find something for you . . . like a bill or a voucher or an expense account or anything at all."

"A copy of *Buttons and Bows* from, let's see, 1954."

"Nah. Too easy."

"A record of payment for . . . paper . . . from June of 1961."

Bob Fink got up, surveyed his domain severely for two minutes, threaded his way to one of the desks and, with the utmost delicacy, extracted several papers out of one of the minarets. "Here you go. Just look at that! Paper was a hell of a lot cheaper in sixty-one."

"Incredible," Maxi said, beaming at him. "Do you suppose I could see an issue of *Buttons and Bows,* the last one?"

Bob Fink's face fell. "It's right here, but I'm not proud of it. Nothing's been the same since 'Blouson Noir' was let loose."

"Who?"

"John Fairchild. The French designers called him 'Blouson Noir' meaning a motorcycle gang hood in a black leather jacket . . . because he was so tough on them. But what he did for the circulation of *Women's Wear!* A rocket, sweetheart. And when our advertisers saw that, naturally they decided to put all their ad money into *WWD* and if that weren't bad enough, Fairchild publishes *Footwear News* every week, which wiped up our buckle and strap advertisers. So between one thing and another . . . well, we have some subscriptions that still have a few years left to go, some small advertisers who get a kick out of seeing their photographs on the cover; but Maxi, let's face it, *Buttons and Bows* is . . . well, to say it was in trouble would be very kind. If you're in trouble you're still alive, *Buttons and Bows* is in intensive care but the hospital just closed."

"Could I see it anyway?" Maxi asked, not at all discouraged.

He gave her the thin magazine with a brave red cover. There was a photograph of John Robinson of the Robinson Braid Company on the cover and most of the text covered the career of Mr. Robinson. There were a few pages of news of the world of braid and trim and there was an article on the use of buttons on Adolfo suits, illustrated with a line drawing of a cuff with three buttons on it; and there were a few small ads. The two largest of these were from the Robinson Braid Company and the company that sold Adolfo his buttons.

"Uncle Bob, have you heard anything about the meeting yesterday?" Maxi asked, folding the copy of the pathetic scrap of a magazine in half and slipping it possessively into her handbag.

"A rumor, naturally. Well, maybe a dozen phone calls. All right, two dozen. I think it's damn nice of you to come here yourself and tell me the news. Your dad, may he rest in peace, would have done the same thing. I knew it was bound to happen."

"But it is *not* going to happen, Bob! I've been made the new publisher of *Buttons and Bows* and together we're going to make this magazine into a winner again, the way my father would have done!" Maxi almost brought a ton of paper down on her head as she rose in excitement.

"If that's the second prize, sweetheart, I wouldn't like to win the contest. Sit down, for God's sake!"

"I'm not kidding. I'm serious! Damn it, Bob, the sky's the limit, we can do anything that Fairchild can do. We'll turn this place upside down and inside out . . . not your office, of course, but . . ."

"Maxi," Bob Fink interrupted gently, "the garment industry doesn't *need* more than one major publication and what they need is a newspaper, *WWD*, not a monthly. You aren't planning to publish another daily, are you?"

"Well, no, actually not. But what about *W*? We could do something like *W* only better."

"The trouble is that *W* uses stuff that's already been photographed and written for *WWD* . . . sometimes they run the copy a little longer and they use color, but it doesn't cost them anything to lay their hands on it . . . money in the bank for Fairchild and only ten thousand subscribers. Most of *W* is ads, all those great big pretty pictures," he sighed. "I must be getting old . . . I'm not ready for those gorgeous girls wearing boy's underwear. Whatever happened to panties?"

Maxi squirmed in her Calvin Klein jockstrap. They'd added a new dimension to her sex life. Was she a pervert, did she only know perverts, or was Bob Fink old-fashioned?

"How can *W* only have ten thousand subscribers? Everybody I know reads it," she protested.

"That's the point . . . every issue is read by dozens of people and most of them have high incomes, which I guess explains the ads. Maxi, you can't go into competition with Fairchild. They founded that company in 1881 and they've specialized in trade papers before your dad was born, almost before *my* dad was born. And why the hell would you want to? You're an Amberville."

"Bob, I hear what you're saying but I'm convinced that I can turn *Buttons and Bows* around. With your help, of course." How, she wondered, could she get rid of such a dear old man? If only he weren't so pessimistic.

"My help? Maxi, I've been aching to retire for a long time. I just hung around here because I owed it to your dad's memory, but fortunately I invested in real estate at the right time. Most of the ex-presidents of the United States have built their houses on land I sold them in Palm Springs. Only big piece out there that I wanted but I never could get hold of is Annenberg's, golf course and all. Missed that one, but you can't win 'em all."

"Retire? You want to retire?"

"And move west. And watch my palms grow. Maybe learn to ride a horse."

"But . . . all your desks?" Maxi gestured carefully.

"Burn them. It'll cost a fortune to get the stuff out of here, but I'd definitely do that and burn it, if I were you."

"What about the rest of the staff?" Maxi asked wildly. "All those people my father didn't want to fire?"

"Let's see . . . there's Joe who thinks up the ideas and writes the articles, and Linda who buys all the artwork and does the layouts and handles production; and I've been my own ad manager. No circulation department, of course. The receptionist also handles the switchboard and the typing. I put Joe and Linda into real estate with me—and the receptionist could get a job anywhere. Very skillful young lady, hates it here. Have to overpay her to keep her."

"Three people? *Only three?* How can that be possible?" Her head felt light but she must not faint.

"Well, there's also a guy we hire from the building to empty the wastebaskets and dust off once in a while, there's a Xerox place downstairs for anything we want copied and the printer sends someone around once in a while to sell us paper; but otherwise, let's see, yup, three people. And we're still losing money. Rent, salaries, supplies, they all cost money. Of course there's lunch; everybody has to have lunch."

"The company pays for lunch?" Maxi squeaked incredulously.

"Your dad started it, back in the good old days. He insisted. Of course Lindy's was open then. Lunch hasn't been the same since they closed."

"When," asked Maxi faintly, "were you thinking of leaving? I don't want anyone to think I'm in a rush but . . ."

"Today's what? Thursday. We could all be out by Friday. Hate to leave you with this mess though. I'll arrange for the garbage guy to come and get it, don't worry, and Hank, from the building, doesn't mind working overtime so the place will be clean, more or less, by Monday, maybe Tuesday."

"You're sure you don't want to stay?" Politeness was all she had left, Maxi thought.

"Sweetheart, I'm on that plane already. And listen, if you don't mind an old admirer putting his two cents in, that outfit you've got on isn't . . . maybe something more . . . ah . . . *less* threatening? I'd be afraid to meet you in a dark alley, Maxi. Look, if you want, I'll take you wholesale . . . Beene maybe, or Ralph Lauren. There's nothing wrong with you that a change of image couldn't fix."

"You have the nerve to call that lump of mealy mush a Golden Delicious?" Toby roared. "Bite into it, you bastard, and tell me how many months ago it was picked and put in a cold room." With one hand, he grabbed the wholesaler by the back of his shirt and with the other he presented him with the apple. "Go on, bite!"

"I was robbed, mister," the man protested. "I just bought twenty cases from upstate and they swore they were picked this week, fresh off the trees."

Toby let the man go in disgust. "Sure you did. Well, it serves me right for trying a new supplier. Don't you realize I can tell everything about this fruit? All I had to do was touch its skin and I knew it was from last season, it doesn't smell the way a fresh apple smells and if I made myself taste it I'd puke. Go try to sell it to D'Agostino."

He turned away and spoke to Maxi. "Most of the guys here know me and they don't try to pull that sort of stuff; I've never bought from him, thought I'd give him a try."

"That's the last time he tries to rob a blind man," said Maxi. "At least one of us hasn't been robbed this week."

"Will you get your tail out from between your legs and stop complaining?" Tobias commanded, as he turned down the aisle of fruit wholesalers. As he always did in the dangerously cluttered Hunt's Point Market, Toby used his laser cane. Its three beams of invisible infrared light made a pin vibrate that contacted his index finger, telling him if there were objects straight ahead of him, above his head or drop-offs below his feet. He swung it easily, in an arc, using the cane skills he had developed years before. Systematically Toby started choosing samples of apples from various cases, feeling, smelling, turning them over expertly in his long fingers as if each one were being considered for a still life, yet working with an astonishing speed.

"I'm not complaining," Maxi said bitterly. "I'm just so fucking mad at myself. Joan of Arc saving the skin of the man who owns Rancho Mirage . . . to say nothing of thirty years of free lunch. If only I thought Cutter were capable of laughing himself to death."

"Look, you've still got a magazine, an office, and a year to do anything you like. Only your pride is wounded, Goldilocks."

"It's not a magazine, it's pure vanity press. The office . . . well even *you* would have to see it to believe it. Your cane would blow its gasket. How many apples are you buying, for heaven's sake?"

"This is *Tarte Tatin* time, babe, and that means thousands."

"Why the hell didn't I at least have the sense to ask Pavka or Nina Stern before I picked the magazine I wanted? I could have had any one of them! Why did I have to rush into it?"

"Ah, the mystery of human personality. If you'd been slightly cautious you wouldn't be Maxi and if you weren't Maxi the whole world would be a sadder place."

"But wiser."

"Maybe. But wiser isn't all that it's touted as being. Wiser is like celibacy . . . put it off as long as you can." Tobias ordered his apples and led the way out of the huge, ugly complex that supplied at least half the food of Manhattan. He no longer did his daily buying himself, relying on assistants, but from time to time he visited Hunt's Point to check out new developments there for his three local restaurants. He owned two others in Chicago and four on the West Coast, all equally successful.

Tobias had discovered the kitchen sometime before he was eight. It was forbidden territory to him although his day vision was still relatively good. Lily was irrationally terrified at the idea of his being near any kind of fire, which only made him more determined to invade the mysterious room.

One night he waited until the entire household was asleep and then crept downstairs, along all the familiar passageways, and entered the big tempting space. Turning on the light, he began to explore, inch by inch, starting with the lower cabinet and drawers, subjecting every object to his five senses. Already, there had been enough deterioration in his sight so that he used all his senses to investigate strange objects. Each cooking utensil, each empty pot and pan, the chopping blocks and the cooking knives and forks and spoons were all applied to his nose and his fingertips. He smelled the knives, touched them with the tip of his tongue, licked their noncutting edges, ran their cutting edges gently over his hand, pressed them to his cheeks. He shook all the objects, and listened to the noise they made, he hefted their weights and compared them to each other, and, as he learned each one, put it back in its place. On the next night he ventured farther, to the refrigerator, and there, during the long quiet hours of the night, the over-protected little boy fell in love. An egg was a world to Tobias, an artichoke a galaxy, a chicken a universe.

Night after night he spent hours in the kitchen until every corner of it was utterly familiar, until there wasn't a wilted piece of parsley he hadn't tasted, although, obedient to his mother's inter-diction, he had never lit the stove, but only swarmed all over it, inside and out, until it was imprinted on his sense memory.

One night he hadn't been able to forbid himself from cau-tiously cracking an egg into a bowl. If the outside of an egg was fascinating, the inside was utterly irresistible. Another egg followed the first until a dozen eggs swam in the large brown crock, their shells, stacked inside each other, neatly piled on the side of the kitchen table. Obviously they were meant to be mixed with a fork, Toby told himself. He had almost finished, mixing neatly, method-ically and vigorously, when the kitchen door opened and he was discovered by the cook. His first cooking attempt proved only that it wasn't possible to mix eggs in complete silence.

Zachary insisted that Tobias be taught to cook and a chef from the Cordon Bleu School was engaged to work with him every after-noon after school.

Soon Tobias could tell if olive oil was pouring at the proper rate into a mayonnaise he was beating by listening to the noise the drops of oil made as they fell. He could hear that particular second when an omelette was ready to be rolled out of its pan, he could smell the exact moment when an onion had been properly browned, he didn't need a timer for boiling eggs or anything but a sharp knife for cutting the thinnest slices of any fruit or vegetable.

However, as he grew into his early teens Toby was having increasing problems with his vision. In spite of his natural grace he appeared awkward and clumsy, constantly bumping into people and objects he should have been able to see clearly.

Lily, who still refused to accept the fact that Toby would one day be almost, if not entirely, blind, somehow managed to make herself ignore these incidents, but Zachary, who frequently took

124

the children to the movies on Saturday afternoon, realized that in a darkened movie theater Toby was helpless, lost until the house lights went up. Soon it was obvious that he couldn't play team sports, with his poor side vision, couldn't follow the path of a volleyball or a hockey puck, and in spite of Lily's determination not to warn Toby of what the future held—why should he know until it was absolutely necessary, she said—Zachary decided that his son had to be prepared.

Almost nothing was known about retinitis pigmentosa in the 1960s and Dr. Eliot Berson of the Harvard Medical School, to whom Zachary took Toby for an ERG exam to measure the strength of the signals given out by the nerve cells of the retina, couldn't tell him what the prognosis was, except to say that if Toby were lucky he would still have some functional vision after his late twenties.

Even Zachary couldn't bring himself to say these precise words to Toby but he did his best to explain why Toby should concentrate on nonteam sports like swimming and gymnastics, choosing to discuss sports rather than life, referring to the rods and retina rather than to tunnel vision.

"Am I going to go blind, Dad?" Toby asked, after the few minutes of silence that followed Zachary's confused exposition.

"*No!* No, Toby! Not completely, never completely, and not for many years." Zachary's heart broke as he said the words in a manner that he kept as unemotional as possible.

"Still I'd better learn Braille, hadn't I?" Toby asked after more silence. Zachary couldn't answer, couldn't say no. "Braille and touch-typing then," Toby said and rose and went to his room. What he suffered there, no one was ever to know, but he emerged with his whole young soul determined to make the most of his life even if he couldn't conquer his fate.

Braille, which he did not yet need, was best learned as young as possible, and soon he went regularly to Braille classes. He swam with a private instructor in the covered pool that was built for him in the Ambervilles' town garden, with the same energy as he continued his cooking lessons. Toby lived as if he had two lives, one sighted and the other in darkness, and for a dozen years the disease, as was often the case, seemed to grow no worse. By the time Toby had graduated from the Hotel School at Cornell, he had spent eight summers apprenticed to great chefs in France, Italy and Hong Kong and he was ready to open his first restaurant.

For years, like a knight sharpening his weapons and oiling his armor against a far-distant battle, he had investigated the myriad of kitchen aids for the visually impaired, and whenever he found one he liked, like the Magna Wonder Knife, he would adopt it, even though he didn't yet need it. The kitchen of his first restaurant was unique in its impeccable organization. No obsessively neat house-wife would ever achieve the absolute rigidity with which Toby, using his common sense, arranged his tools. His trusty warhorse was a pair of bakers' balance scales from the Acme Scale Company, one of them fitted with an electronic detection device that could measure spices from zero to sixteen ounces, another that could measure up to one thousand pounds of other ingredients, both with weight indicators that had been brailled at half-inch intervals.

His gauntlets were a pair of oven mitts that were seventeen inches long and protected him from heat on the backs of his hands as well as on the palms and fingers; his swords were non-heat-conducting wooden spoons, his double spatulas, his nested measuring cups that could be monitored by his fingers, eliminating the line calibrations of glass. His jousting pole was a battery-operated "Say When" liquid level indicator and his helmets were mixing bowls from Dansk and Copco, all of which had rubber rings at their bases to stabilize them.

In his late twenties, with two restaurants operating success-fully, Toby realized that the blank spaces in his view of the world were growing larger; people and objects swam in and out of them bewilderingly, in a faint, fragmented and increasingly colorless fashion. He had trained himself to make his problems as inconspic-uous as possible but now he realized that he needed highly profes-sional help.

For a period of four months Toby went for training to the St. Paul's Rehabilitation Center in Newtown, Massachusetts. There, all the students, no matter what degree of vision they had, were blindfolded for instruction which ranged from such mundane mat-ters as table manners and counting money to more challenging cane technique. He took fencing lessons that helped in the location of sound, and "videation" or learning orientation and mobility through extravisual means such as judging the speed of wind, the feeling of sun on the face, the textures of whatever was underfoot and all other possible perceptions of the sounds of nature and man and automobiles. By the time he left St. Paul's Toby felt as well skilled as he could possibly be for the future.

He returned to New York and continued to experiment with the enormous variety of systems which had been developed for the blind who work in kitchens. Each time he opened a new restaurant he installed a kitchen that was an exact duplicate of the others. His corps of chefs, all sighted, were trained by him to cook in his way, using his weapons, and soon, if need be, they could all cook in the dark.

Now Toby still cooked from time to time in his first restaurant, inventing new dishes, but the others were run by his chefs, whom he visited, unannounced, on trips to Chicago or Los Angeles. Within twenty minutes of inspection he knew if the most insignificant compote dish had been misplaced. Woe to the *sous-chef* who had been skimping on the wild mushrooms; woe to whoever had misjudged the ripeness of a Brie; woe to the roast cook whose chicken was not moist to the wingtip; woe to the *saucier* who had used an eighth of a pinch too much salt. Woe, woe, to the restaurant manager if the tablecloths lacked a certain crisp finish, if the crystal wasn't like satin to his touch, if the candles were an inch too short or the flowers an hour too old. "Tobias the Terrible" they called him after one of his raids, but afterwards his teams worshipped him even more than before.

Toby nudged Maxi as she brooded. "I'd have had more fun taking Angelica shopping," he said. "Look, you've blown it but it's not the end of the world. Pick yourself up off the floor and pack it up. Don't piss into a violin. Forget the whole thing. Obviously you can't rescue *Trimming Trades* any more than you can bring back high-buttoned shoes and there's no point in your wasting your time for the empty exercise of fighting Cutter. He's won and you might as well accept it. Put it behind you, take that 'kick me' sign off your back, and start being Maxi again."

"For a bat you sound like a wimp," Maxi answered angrily.

"I am a brilliant businessman, which means I face reality every day, I'd like a little respect from you since I'm probably the most eligible bachelor in New York, but hard to get because I don't give a shit about what a girl looks like and I still haven't found anyone whose soul I want to hang out with for the rest of my life."

"A vain, tactless, mean old wimp who isn't even thoughtful enough to offer me a drink when I need it most," Maxi said mournfully.

"It's more like time for Saturday breakfast, babe, or hadn't you noticed?"

"The trouble with you, Tobias, is you're too literal-minded, as your mother would *never* say to you," Maxi said angrily.

"Breakfast calls for a drink, don't you agree?"

"Now that you mention it, why not?"

India West glared at herself malevolently in the mirror on the dressing table of her Beverly Hills bedroom. She made minuscule adjustments in her mind, and her eyes, which were that special brilliant blue of rare Persian turquoises, seemed to deepen or lighten to her order. Supremely delicate muscles moved under her skin and enough happened there to fill the pages of *Les Cahiers du Cinéma*. She fell deeply in love, she endured a quiet depression, was tormented by a secret terror, grew joyful, changed from wanton to nun and was illuminated by a gentle anticipation of rapture. All systems, she noted lugubriously, were still functioning at will, in spite of her catastrophic hangover.

As she gazed, deeply unimpressed by her image, unmoved at that composition of extraordinary features whose perfection bored no one but India herself, she decided that there was something fundamentally and deeply *dumb* about being called the most beautiful movie actress in the world. What kind of a job was that for an adult? Did anybody have any idea what a racket it was? She reminded herself of nothing so much as a Greta Garbo film, with that divine face hardly registering a change of expression and the conditioned response of an audience reading vast emotions into it. Had

Garbo ever felt the same way as she did about herself? India suspected that she had, and had quit before anyone else caught on.

"You're no Meryl Streep, you silly bitch," she said out loud to her glorious reflection, "but you *can* do that thing they call acting." She tied back her shivery waves of amber blond hair and looked in disgust at the Bloody Mary on the table. India West almost never drank but last night had been a horrible exception for which there was only one remedy which would make her liver consider the possibility of going back to work. She swallowed the drink, a goddess resigned to her minute of mortality, shuddered and tottered back to bed.

All her strength had gone into opening the tomato juice and finding the Tabasco, for on Sunday she was alone. There were no maids, no secretaries, no cook in the huge house, all phones were quiet as the great ones of The Industry slept or thought vaguely about brunch as they watched people condemned to live in other places play football on television. Still, India reflected, if it weren't Sunday she'd have to go to her regular workout with her gym teacher, the arbiter of her life, Mike Abrums. If that man even suspected that she had a hangover, and God knows, you could keep nothing from him, he would make her very sorry indeed. He might even *take away her appointments.*

In spite of a well-founded rumor that he possessed—somewhere—a heart of gold, Mike Abrums ruled his pupils with the relentless discipline that he had perfected during his years in the Marines, teaching men how to kill other men with their bare hands. Now he maintained meticulously selected and worshipfully obedient Hollywood bodies in a state of perfection and had a waiting list of hundreds of supplicants. Mike had forbidden her to eat red meat, sugar, salt, fats and liquor, in any amount or form whatever. Last night, in an outburst of rebellion, India had copiously ingested every single item on his list of taboo foods.

"If I weren't so beautiful I could eat a hamburger every day," she said pathetically, addressing the ceiling. "If I weren't a major star I wouldn't have to be perfect. If I weren't rich I couldn't afford to go to that magnificent dictator six times a week, if I weren't famous nobody would give a damn. I have a very bad case of the sort of problems that people always sneer at and say they would like to have, but just because everyone would like my problems doesn't mean *I* have to like them. They are not a transferable asset. A banal thought, I admit, but in my condition I can't rise above it."

India's voice, even though she was only speaking to the ceiling, was winelike, with its infinite shades and range, from darkly potent Burgundy to icy, brilliant champagne; from warm, mellow Bordeaux to the unearthly sweetness of Sauternes. After six years of Hollywood stardom, India no longer found it strange to be talking out loud to herself. One of the less recognized problems of being a star was that there were very few people in the world to whom she could speak frankly. The urge to bask in the glory of being her confidant was all but irresistible and if she confided in any but a trusted few she was likely to read about it in the columns the next day.

"If only my ceiling were more interesting," she observed. A hangover severely limited her options. She couldn't stand the noise of music, she didn't have the strength to focus on print, and worst of all there was nobody she wanted to talk to on the phone. At that thought she began to feel tears forming. She eased herself painfully out of bed, clasped a robe around her, and headed slowly for her pool. Anything was better than lying around feeling sorry for herself.

India threaded her way along the path of her back garden. It had been intended to look tropical and after spending two hundred thousand dollars, her landscape decorator had managed to achieve an unreal Rousseau-like landscape of monumentally exotic plants that seemed, in India's present mood, to be menacing and grotesque. Uneasily she wondered about tigers, sleeping gypsies, and snakes. Suddenly the network of underground sprinklers everywhere sprang to life with an ominous series of thuds. They were only supposed to work during the night. As she stood there, buffeted by a dozen different nozzles, three enormous German shepherds, barking wildly, sprang out of the giant ferns, almost knocking her over.

"Down! Down, you revolting creeps!" she screamed, trying to sound authoritative. They slavered at her ambiguously.

"Bonnie-Lou! Sally-Ann! Debbie-Jane! Down, I say!" They

were all males but it helped a little to pretend they were girls. The huge beasts terrified her but a consultation with the Beverly Hills Police had convinced her business manager and her agent that she had to have them. Apparently the fences and the electrically controlled gates and the television camera at the end of the driveway, plus all the complicated electric eyes and beams that were installed throughout the house, weren't worth even one German shepherd, for real protection.

Muscles aquiver, India continued dripping her way toward the pool, hair drenched, robe soaking, slobbering wet dogs stepping on her feet and licking her hands in what she hoped was affection. Oh God. Had they been fed? She felt increasingly unsure of the future of this particular Sunday.

She finally fought her way out of the rain forest and stopped with a cry of disbelief and outrage. The water of the pool had turned overnight into a vile shade of murky green. Killer dogs, killer sprinklers and now killer algae. It was too much. She fled back to the house and pulled the bedcovers over her head, cursing the pool man who had skipped a visit. "Human beings were not meant to live in Beverly Hills," India groaned into her now damp sheets. "The whole place is a desert, made to bloom only by water stolen from decent, hardworking farmers by the evil founding fathers of Los Angeles. An abomination in the eyes of the Lord. Repent ye sinners."

She poked her head out of the covers and considered the possibility of another Bloody Mary. No. Absolutely not. One was clearly medicinal but two? She would count her blessings instead as her mother had taught her to. First, as ever, health. The only blessing that really mattered. Hangovers didn't count as being sick since they were temporary. Second, her sheets, the smoothest possible pure cotton, from Pratasi, the borders embroidered with tiny scallops, at six hundred dollars the pair. She had a closet full of them, they were her pride and joy—could you be addicted to sheets? Still it was a harmless pleasure surely since you couldn't eat or drink them. Or were the sheets a case of transference?

During the last year she had worked herself out of her transference to her shrink, Doctor Florence Florsheim, psychoanalyst to the stars, and now she seemed to have transferred her affections to her linen closet. Could this be called progress? She'd have to check it out with Doctor Florsheim but she doubted it. What were her next blessings? Beautiful, rich, famous and talented. Even John Simon agreed about her talent, an opinion she allowed to convince her whenever she began to feel self-doubt. But she'd covered all that already and found them less than comforting. Still that made six blessings. Lovers? She didn't have one currently and the last one she'd had was, without the slightest qualification, an error in taste on a scale so great that she blushed at the memory. The *absence* of lovers was perhaps a blessing in disguise. Count it as half a blessing, making a total of six and a half, not too bad for someone with a life-threatening hangover. Youth? She was only just twenty-seven. Yes, youth, if you didn't remember that *thirty* was only three years away. Three years were ages and ages. More than a thousand days. *A thousand days were nothing!* She must not think about it. Christ, but it wasn't easy to be the most beautiful movie actress in the world, it was stress on a major scale, even Doctor Florsheim had to admit that.

India thought of a remark made by Nijinsky when an admirer of the great dancer asked him if it wasn't difficult to hang in the air as he literally seemed to do. He'd answered that it wasn't difficult, "It's just climbing up there and staying up for a little." As good a description of a movie career as she'd heard, India reflected, and poor Nijinsky had died insane. Still, what else was she fit for? She'd wanted her career, worked hard for it, and now she just had to stay up there, defying gravity. Self-pity began to overwhelm India West once more. The phone rang just as she was about to get out of bed and comfort herself with pillowcases.

"Miss West. This is Jane Smith of 'Sixty Minutes.' We've decided to investigate the India West Syndrome and I'll be out next week with a crew to follow you around for a month or so. My particular interest is in the problem of stardom, starting, of course, with the pimple on your ass . . ."

"MAXI! You angel, you blessing . . . how could you go away for so long . . . where are you calling from? . . . Are you really coming here? I'm all by myself and so very lonely."

"No, I'm in New York and I'm not going anywhere, probably

for the rest of my life. I have such a hangover that I don't think I'll live. I called you up to say goodbye forever."

"You too? I'm curing mine with a Bloody Mary. Go make one—I'll hold on."

"What a sickening idea . . . I'd throw up."

"Look, chemically tomato juice is half salt and half potassium. It replaces your electrolytes quicker than a transfusion and you can't smell the vodka if you use enough Tabasco. The best internist in Beverly Hills told me to do it, honest."

"All right . . . but don't go away. I'll hurry."

As she waited by the phone India felt reborn. With Maxi back on the same continent, even a sinister Beverly Hills Sunday seemed filled with promise. Maxi couldn't enter a room without creating a fiesta.

Over the clinking of ice cubes Maxi returned to the phone. "I know why I got drunk but why did you?"

"It was the party last night. I went by myself and there wasn't anybody there I wanted to talk to. Then a definitely fascinating guy walked in and I perked up until he got close enough so that I could read his T-shirt."

"India, I've warned you never to read T-shirts. They're pure aggression. What did it say?" Maxi asked, breathless with curiosity.

"'Life Is Shit and Then You Die.'"

"You've got to get out of that place! When T-shirts start to drive you to drink . . ."

"And eat," India said on a dire note. "Everything in sight."

"Think of it this way," Maxi advised. "One night's eating isn't going to show on your thighs and if you don't get compulsive and *confess* to Mike Abrums, he can't read your mind and you can reveal all the awful things you did when you see Doctor Florsheim because she never makes judgments."

"Oh, Maxi, you're right! When you're not here there's nobody to put me in perspective except myself and I'm not good at it yet."

"It takes two for perspective."

"Maybe *that* could be the title for my novel," India said excitedly.

"Are you writing a novel?"

"I'm going to start as soon as I get the right title. I have a feeling that it's what I should be doing. I've always wanted to write and half the people in town are being published—so why not me?"

"Instead of being the most beautiful movie star in the world?"

"Exactly. What do you think of 'If Hell Is Other People, Then Heaven Is Smoked Fish'?"

"India!" Maxi sputtered. "Not while I'm drinking."

"Then you like it?"

"It's divine, but a little too esoteric. Anything more mass market?"

"How about a science-fiction novel? I rather like 'Chateau Margaux 2001.'"

"No, India, no."

"Well then, 'Married Men Don't Have Wet Dreams.'"

"A hard case to prove."

"How about 'Hamlet Was An Only Child'?"

"What does it mean?"

"I think it speaks for itself," India said with dignity.

"Look, India, I'm worried about you—seriously. Going to parties alone, getting drunk, thinking up novel titles, next thing you know you'll be counting your sheets again. And you know what that means. It's not healthy for you to be alone in that monster house. What ever happened to that heavenly housekeeper who used to do tarot cards with you?"

"Doctor Florsheim told me I had to stop relying on friendships I paid for, so that means no live-in help."

"Are you sure you're neurotic enough to suffer such deprivation?" Maxi asked anxiously.

"If I wasn't when I started, I am now."

"I think you should tell Doctor Florsheim that you need sick leave and come visit me. I need you desperately."

"I would in a second but I'm in the middle of a picture."

"I was afraid of that," Maxi said in tones of utter despair.

"Is it a man?"

"Ten times worse than the worst man I ever met, or even married. Worse than Laddie Kirkgordon."

"Nothing could be that bad . . . you're not sick, are you?" India asked.

134

"No, not unless you count stupidity as a terminal disease. And arrogance and misjudgment, lack of information, acting like an idiot and jumping off the deep end into an empty pool."

"But that sounds exactly like you when you fall in love. I knew it was a man," India insisted, her hangover cured by the sound of Maxi's voice, and the familiar delight of hearing about Maxi's improbable problems.

"If you hold on while I make myself another Bloody Mary," Maxi said in resignation, "I'll tell you the whole hideous story."

"Goody!" India cried and settled down for a lovely long listen.

10

Cutter Amberville's return to San Francisco, after such a relatively short stay in New York, caused little surprise. His friends, all born-and-bred San Franciscans, felt gratified vindication of their own values. They had predicted, before he left, that nowhere in the East would he find the sweetness of life that they enjoyed, and his rejection of Manhattan proved how right they had been. Although some people persisted in calling San Francisco the Wall Street of the West, and others termed it the Paris of the United States, as far as they were concerned it was a city so unique that it need be compared to no other place on earth. Sheer civic pride alone would make San Francisco stand apart, for this quiet Spanish settlement had turned into an international boomtown when gold was discovered at Sutter's Mill in 1848. From that time on successive waves of fortune had deposited millions, indeed billions, in the pockets of the lucky men who led the town, men whose freshly made money grew graciously mellow in less than a century.

None of Cutter's friends—the Bohlings, the Chatfield-Taylors, the Thieriots, the de Guignés and the Blyths—ever knew that he had fled New York because of Lily. He was as welcome as a unicorn, that desirable legendary animal whose horn was reputed to possess magical properties—for was not an eligible yet unattached bachelor almost as rare as a unicorn?

His months in Manhattan had only made Cutter more compelling to look at; deepening the contrast between his blondness and his darkly proud, purposeful manner. He seemed older than twenty-four and more dangerous; a mysterious danger made more seductive by his perfect manners and the unexpectedly warm,

rarely won smile that totally changed his expression, that human-
ized this aloof man. He was well born, he was beginning to be
rather respected by the older men in the world of banking but, as
the women of the Bay City told themselves, he was apparently not
marriage-minded. Cutter Amberville remained resolutely, inexplicably hard to get, fascinatingly, infuriatingly, tantalizingly free
of heart. None of the women who gossiped about him suspected
that his reason for avoiding an involvement with one of the elegant, unmarried girls of San Francisco was a question of clear-eyed
policy: what trouble might Lily cause if she heard about any new
romance?

Cutter was absolutely armored against even the most delicious
girl—if she represented a possible entanglement. But, in spite of a
degree of emotional control that most men of any age could never
achieve, he was utterly unable to dominate his avid, brutal need for
sex. He had to have women and he had to have them often and
now, after Lily, he had to have them in a condition of risk. Not for
him the easy, relatively safe conquest of the women who worked at
his office or women he could pick up in bars. Quite logically he
recognized that there were women within Society, women who
moved in his own world, who were just as restless as he was, who
lived with unslaked desire to the same degree as he did, women he
could possess at will. But to attract him they had to be women who
had too much to lose to become a threat to his public life. He never
pursued a woman who could make a claim on him, never stalked a
woman who could injure him, and if he sensed in a woman any
hint of that crazy, reckless, cap-over-the-windmill view of life that
had been Lily's, he never went after her.

But there were so many others! For a man with eyes to see, a
man who was surrounded by married couples, there were possible
conquests everywhere. Secret swift conquests, made without any
ritual of courtship, conquests that were a kind of mutual recognition of an uncomplicated lust. Cutter was the cleverest of lovers.
He knew how to make danger work for him, how to seize the most
unexpected opportunities, how to sniff out the woman who was as
wild and hot as he was under all the proper trappings of their world.
With a glance he could tell a mere flirt from a woman in heat, and
make his move in a way that drew no attention.

137

Cutter's reputation as the most elusive single man in the city grew with every year that passed. He went out almost every night: at Ernie's, the Gatti brothers both knew that he liked to begin dinner with the local Dungeness crab, served as simply as possible; at Kan's, Johnny Kan himself came to the phone when Cutter called for a reservation; at Trader Vic's his table was always in the Captain's Cabin; but normally he was invited to private homes, not restaurants.

Cutter had realized that the quickest way to total social acceptance in San Francisco was through music. He never failed to attend some twenty of the twenty-six scheduled opera performances and he went to the symphony on both the "fashionable" nights and the "listening" nights. After a few years he was asked to join the Bohemian Club, an institution that was founded in 1872 to promote the arts. By the 1900s it had become a center of all-male power; a club to which the most important men in America were invited for the annual encampments on the Russian River.

Soon Cutter became known to banking leaders like Richard P. Cooley, president of the Wells Fargo Bank; George Christopher, chairman of the board of the Commonwealth National Bank, and Rudolph A. Peterson, president of the Bank of America. He was careful to maintain his New York banking contacts as well. His months in Manhattan had given him that sort of patina that is comparable to a year spent in the best finishing school in Switzerland for a debutante from a middle-sized American city. He hadn't learned anything to which a specific dollar value could be attached, but he had been thoroughly dipped in the currents of the ocean of major American finance.

On his return Cutter had rejoined his old firm, Booker, Smity and Jameston, but soon moved on to another, larger one. By the time he was thirty, he was seasoned enough to become a junior partner in the firm of Standings and Alexander, one of the most influential in the city.

The head of Cutter's new firm, James Standings III, was a fifth-generation San Franciscan. He had been born as royal as any citizen of a republic can be, and he thoroughly approved of Cutter.

138

He invited him to play golf at the Hillsborough Country Club; he invited him to join the Woodside Hunt, to sail from Sausalito Harbor on his forty-eight-meter yacht, and he proposed him for membership in his town club, the Union League on Nob Hill, for James Standings, like Mr. Bennett in *Pride and Prejudice*, was a man with daughters to marry. Not five, as he often thanked the Deity, only two, and although it pained him to admit it, Candice, his firstborn, was far from a beauty.

Along with its view of the bay, its charm, its culture and its restaurants, San Francisco takes justified pride in the beauty of its women. Such girls as Patsy McGinnis, Penny Bunn, Mielle Vietor, Frances Bowes, Mariana Keean and Patricia Walcott, lovely though each was, were not exceptions in the early 1960s, they were the rule. Compared to the average local belle, Candice Standings was, even in the eyes of her adoring father, just . . . average. Not *desperately* plain, mind you, but no, he had to admit, much as he loved her, she was not even pretty. No one had ever even dreamed of calling her Candy. He and his wife, Sally, also a fifth-generation San Franciscan, were just average too, but they both felt that their older child, a sixth-generation San Franciscan, should somehow have been born beautiful, defying all the laws of genetics. After all, their younger daughter, Nanette, showed definite signs of prettiness and she was only fourteen.

Candice had perfect teeth at last, after years of orthodontia, and glossy hair. She had well-developed arm and leg muscles from practicing all the right sports, but an unfortunately boyish body; she'd graduated from Miss Hamlin's and Finch, her pearls were the best Gump's could offer—but she lacked utterly that certain quality possessed even by girls from that lower-class place called Los Angeles, that unfortunately necessary dash of something sexual that appealed to men.

James Standings III was enormously rich and getting steadily richer. Even if Sally Standings didn't send all her dry-cleaning to Paris by air as did Mrs. W. W. Crocker, or possess a Chinese cook of thirty-seven years standing, like Mrs. Cameron, they lived, when they weren't traveling or vacationing, at the Ramble, a thirty-five-room mansion in patrician Hillsborough, eighteen miles south of the city. The Ramble, inherited from Sally Standings's parents, had terraces and formal gardens that were almost as impressive as Mrs. Charles Blyth's Strawberry Hill, but alas, alas, for Candice, Hillsborough was honeycombed with equally vast houses, populated by equally rich fathers of far too many other girls—less plain, so infinitely, incontestably much less plain than Candice, girls who *all* had to be married off in order to produce seventh-generation San Franciscans.

If James Standings III had ever recognized a buyer's market, it was on those many many evenings when he and Sally dined with twenty-five-year-old Candice and waited, just as anxiously as she did, for the telephone to ring. When it did, as it was beginning to more and more frequently, it was always for Nanette.

Cutter was thirty-one. He had never again felt the emotions he had felt for Lily, and he looked back at that time in his life as a form of clear insanity. But he had made a promise to Lily. He had written her the only kind of letter that he felt sure would ensure her silence. Since that time he had written her other letters, carefully uncompromising, not so many that their arrival in New York would cause comment, far, far fewer letters than the ones she wrote him, but cunningly phrased to keep her from any rash action, for Lily was now more determined than ever that soon they must be together. *They had waited seven years!* Zachary had a mistress, she wrote—everyone knew about it, someone who worked on *Style*, a girl named Nina Stern—so there could be no possibility of his succeeding in keeping the children. Lily was wildly impatient. She hated Cutter's ambiguous letters and thought he was being insanely cautious. Cutter could sense her gathering anger in each letter she sent him, asking what he was waiting for in order to claim her.

Cutter had absolutely no intention of marrying Lily and living with her and her children and making his way, step by step, like any ordinary man. He knew his full value and he planned to capitalize on it. He had decided to marry the girl who could do him the most good. He intended, most precisely, to marry Candice Standings, his boss's daughter. He wanted the fat, easy commissions that would fall to him as her husband.

She was fairly plain, true, but not so outstandingly pudding-faced that people could say, without even thinking twice, that he had only married her for her money. She seemed to have a good disposition, she rode and skied, played tennis and bridge, all with equal competence, and would make an excellent wife. Candice would always be utterly *grateful* to him. Their marriage would just be another example of a good-looking man being united to a less attractive woman, an arrangement accepted for centuries. Candice had a nice smile, after all, and he imagined that she wouldn't run to fat, judging from her mother.

His only problem was Lily. What might she not be capable of saying about him if she heard of an engagement to marry Candice Standings, a Society event that couldn't be kept secret? True, his entanglement with Lily was now old news, no matter how unsavory, and gave her no hold over him. *But that boy?* Justin. His son. Even James Standings III would think twice about giving him even a homely daughter if Lily, in rage, were to tell him about Justin. Ever since Cutter had heard of the child's birth he had tried not to think about him. He had never laid eyes on the child that Lily, damn her, had chosen to have out of arrogance and vanity and selfishness. Justin's existence was entirely her responsibility, no matter how she imagined that the boy was a claim on Cutter.

Discreetly, Cutter began to pay court to Candice Standings; so discreetly that he rarely saw her unless her friends or family were around, but he showed her a special warmth that was just enough to be noticed but not taken seriously enough to become gossip. He knew that Candice was in love with him, with a timid, humble love that put her utterly at his mercy. His only chance, he calculated, was to present Lily with a *fait accompli,* to elope with Candice to Vegas some weekend and then let happen whatever would happen. By that time he would be James Standings's son-in-law and heir apparent, and no one could take that away from him. Lily's only solid weapon was that single letter. Even if she were mad enough to use it they were the words of a boy he no longer was. . . . No other real proof existed.

The Standingses skied at Squaw Valley and at Klosters, in Switzerland, but recently they'd bought a lodge in Aspen. They were all expert enough to negotiate the steep, open meadows and thickly wooded trails without difficulty. James and Sally Standings preferred to ski only in the sunny afternoon, but Cutter and Candice were always the first ones up the mountain, ignoring the freezing air and the possibility of frostbite at the high altitudes in order to get the first run down. In her ski clothes and goggles, Candice was as good-looking as anyone else, Cutter thought, and a better skier than most. She could follow wherever he led and he never had to worry about her ability to check her speed on the narrow trails that cut through the thick forests here and there on the mountains.

A love for skiing was perhaps Cutter's deepest emotion—after hatred for his brother. It was the only sport which made him feel utterly free, unbound for a few downhill minutes from whatever people thought about him, from his past, from his future, from himself, particularly from himself, living entirely in the clean, clear present.

One morning, early, as he skied through the icy crust of newly fallen snow, rejoicing in the untouched surface before him, he suddenly realized that he couldn't hear Candice's skis behind him as usual. He stopped and turned. She was nowhere in sight. Cursing, Cutter began to climb back up the trail which was so narrow that he barely had room to sidestep up the mountain. He called her name but there was no answer. No other skiers appeared. After a few minutes he spotted her body off the trail, dangling, motionless, in the branches of two closely growing pine trees, a foot off the ground as if she had been flung from above. She must have caught an edge and pinwheeled, he realized, using all his skill to clamber up through the dense forest. *Caught an edge and pinwheeled.* He shuddered with the knowledge. Anything could be broken in the wild flight of a pinwheel. Finally he reached her. Cutter had seen enough ski accidents in his many years on the slopes to guess, from her unnatural position, that there was a chance that her back was broken. He took off one of her mitts to feel her pulse. She was alive and that was all he could be sure of, for she was unconscious, and he must not try to move her. Cutter left her there, facedown on the bed of icicle-dripping branches, while he dashed on down the trail to alert the ski patrol.

It wasn't his fault, of course. Nobody could blame him. People hurt themselves skiing all the time. Everybody knew Candice was a good skier. A cold morning, a steep narrow trail. No, nobody, not even her parents, could reasonably blame him. However, he could *choose* to take the blame. He could say that he blamed himself, that it was his fault, that he should have known that the snow was too icy, too risky. He could have stopped her, should have stopped her. Yes, he could take the blame. And he could marry her if she lived. He could have everything Candice Standings could bring him and not even Lily could utter a cry of reproach, if he married a crippled girl, crippled by his fault.

It had taken Nina Stern longer than she would have believed possible to seduce Zachary. After the difficult birth of Justin, the Ambervilles' third and last child, Lily had been very ill for months. Maxi, finding herself the least attention-getting member of her family, had proceeded to outdo herself in inventive acts of naughtiness. Not even Mary Poppins could have handled her, Zachary used to groan to himself, as his heart melted at her genuinely contrite tears when she was eventually caught and had to be punished. Thank God television had been invented. Being deprived of her favorite shows was the only punishment that he could inflict on her. He could never have brought himself to spank Maxi or lock her in her room. How had people disciplined their children before television?

Zachary had been too preoccupied to pay much attention to Nina at the Wednesday staff meetings, caught as he was between the problems at home and the problems at the office, for it was a time when all his magazines had to gird themselves to grow or to go out of business. But eventually, as she had always known it would, the classic moment presented itself: the unexpected dinner invitation, made casually when there are only two people left in an office after a hard, long, but satisfying day. Nina had not spent her life practicing for this minute in order to let the occasion pass and the next morning, when Zachary woke up in her bed, he finally knew why other men played around, knew it in pulverizingly precise and staggering new detail and knew that nothing could stop him from being with her.

During the first months of their affair he had been too obsessed with Nina to feel guilty about Lily and the children. But one day he realized that he could never ask Lily for a divorce, he simply couldn't do that to the exquisite, brave, talented girl he had overwhelmed in a single month when she had still been in her teens, the girl who had abandoned her certain and marvelous future as a prima ballerina for him, who knew no other life than the one he had encouraged her to lead, who had given him his children; Lily who was such a marvelous mother to Toby and to little Justin and even kept her patience with Maxi. Lily Amberville had become a queen in New York and he owed her no diminution of that position. One of the results of Lily's illness had been that they almost never made love, not because she was afraid of getting pregnant again, but because Justin's birth seemed to have caused some profound psychic change in her. All the more reason why he could never abandon her.

Painfully, he explained all this to Nina, knowing that she couldn't want to continue with a man who could offer her no future.

"So, I gather that your idea of my idea of a future is that I expect you to get a divorce and marry me?" she had asked, after listening to him struggle to make his position clear.

"Well. Ah. Yes. I see what you mean, I guess. I mean I *don't* see what you mean! Isn't that more or less what a girl like you *would* expect . . . I mean isn't it? Damn it, Nina, don't you want . . . wouldn't you want . . . you're a 'nice' girl . . . your parents . . . any other girl . . . damn it, I guess I took too much for granted. I thought, well I felt, oh *shit.*"

"It's not that I don't love you," she said, trying as hard as she could not to laugh but having little success.

"If you love me," he said, grabbing her, amazed at the enormity of his relief, "why don't you want to marry me?"

"I'm a weird case. I don't like marriage, it's too obvious, everybody does it and then it becomes something you have to do every single day, like brushing your teeth. What I like is what we do: making love and seeing each other at meetings in the office and knowing we're thinking about each other, and sneaking around corners and getting away for weekends and making love some more when everybody thinks we're someplace else, and all that great, corny backstreet stuff. I like to talk to you, but not necessarily every night."

"Are you *sure* you're Jewish?"

"You sound like my mother. You'd better make love to me again, fast, to make me forget that remark," she said threateningly through her tears of laughter at his shock.

Nina Stern liked her freedom as much as she liked her increasing power at *Style*, a power she knew everybody had to admit she had achieved by merit, not by sleeping with the boss. She adored working hard at work she did brilliantly, she enjoyed being able to work nights without worrying about a family, and she was firm about having no one to please but herself. Every day brought her more invitations than three people could accept; she was one of the half-dozen single women in New York who had achieved the same desirability as a guest at a party as a supremely attractive bachelor. Men of all ages had competed for her throughout her twenties, and now in her thirties she was even more mysteriously, definitively desirable than she had been when she was younger, and just as much a flirt. If anything, fidelity to Zachary made her alluring ways more intriguing since they led to nothing and created a challenge few men could resist; surrounding her with the aura of a beloved, successful, deeply happy woman with a distinctly private, private life. When her mother grumbled about Nina's lack of husband and children all Nina bothered to reply was that she had the most interesting life of any woman she knew, a remark that Mrs. Stern regarded as frivolous and totally irrelevant, but which satisfied Nina completely.

Cutter and Candice Standings were married as soon as possible after it was certain that she was out of danger. The degree of her recovery was still in question but within two years of intensive physical therapy she had almost recovered from her accident. Her back would always give her trouble and frequent pain, but it had not been broken. She would never again be able to participate in any active sports but she walked normally.

During these two years Cutter had not only earned the benefit of his in-laws' almost incredulous gratitude, but Candice's love for him had turned into an emotion that was close to worship. It was an emotion so embarrassingly powerful, she was so totally under his dominion, that she had to hide her feelings for fear of being thought ridiculous. As the years passed, her focus on Cutter grew into an obsession that took the tyrannical, feverish form of jealousy, for never, in her hearts of hearts, was she able to convince herself that Cutter really loved her. *Was* it a proof of love that he had married her when she might have been crippled for life? Or was it merely guilt? He had sworn that yes, he did blame himself for her accident, but blame alone, no matter how great, would never have led him to marry her without love, he had sworn it dozens of times, until, one day, she saw that she must appear to have stopped doubting him for his patience was wearing thin.

She mastered herself, with a strength no one knew she had, and to others, even to Cutter, she seemed to be like many another of those rich young married women who were her friends, women who acted as if they took their husbands for granted. But not for one half hour of one single day was Candice free of a lifelong insecurity based on those many years in which men had ignored her. The jealousy that she drove severely underground possessed her spirit all the more ferociously for being unspoken. Cutter became the only meaning in Candice's life and when they participated in the rites of San Francisco social life, into which she was locked by her birth and position, her eyes forever, secretly, sought him out, checking to see if he was talking to a pretty woman. The jealous words she couldn't allow herself to say turned into a wrinkled glass, like a dirty yellow filter spotted with unnamable filth, through which she saw her privileged world as a place where only misery lay.

Candice Amberville started drinking earlier and earlier every day so that, by the time she had to get dressed for a party or the opera, she could feel relaxed enough to face herself in her mirror without comparing herself to every other woman in town, but it didn't help. She spent a fortune on clothes and became one of the best-dressed women in the city, but it didn't help. She went to the hairdresser every other day so that her good hair was always perfect, but it didn't help. She paid her cook twice what anyone else paid and gave the best, most beautifully organized dinner parties of their group, but it didn't help. She was diseased in a way that nothing could cure. When Cutter lay between her legs, even when he was pulsing inside her, she thought of him doing the same thing to another woman, so when she reached her difficult orgasm, even that momentary relief didn't help. Jealousy was killing Candice Amberville and if Cutter had been faithful to her it would not have helped.

She was so befouled with jealousy that she felt as if she had some vile skin affliction that oozed from every pore—to herself Candice was unclean, tainted, crusty with sores and scabs, each one torn over and over until the blood and pus poured out invisible, disgusting.

In a frantic effort to fill her life with something other than her thoughts she bought a pair of golden retrievers. They gave her some surcease, some brief respite, for into their ears she could pour her suspicions, her words of loathing for her peers who had sat next to Cutter at dinner and laughed with him, who asked him to be their partner at mixed doubles or to spend a day crewing for them in one of the many yacht club races. With no sign of her torment she encouraged him to go, to enjoy all the sports in which she couldn't join. She pretended to be anxious to take ski vacations saying that as far as she was concerned, she welcomed the change, enjoyed walking in the snow and having time to read while he was on the slopes.

If she could have had her way Cutter would have played only polo, for there, in the stands, watching him, she could be sure for hours at a time that he belonged to no one else. But whenever he wasn't playing polo her imagination invented scenarios: Cutter, still dripping with the clean sweat of a tennis match, finding an empty room at the club, stripping off his clothes and plunging, already erect, into his only-too-ready partner; Cutter in the cabin of a becalmed yawl, lying back naked on a bunk, his long, thick penis already half swollen, a woman on her knees before him, following his curt, precise directions; Cutter returning early from the mountain and going, unobserved, to the bedroom of any one of the women who skied with him, watching her undress while he explained exactly what she must do to him, exactly what he intended to do to her, while he grew harder with each word.

Candice enlarged her kennels, bought more champion golden retrievers and started to breed them. She now drank more heavily, keeping bottles in the kennels so that she had a place to go, a private place where she could drink unobserved and tell her dogs all the things she could never tell other people because they would think she was crazy. For Candice there could be no acceptance of her situation, no slow slide into resignation, no truce. Her arid, tortured sense of worth lay entirely in *seeming not to know*, in living as if all were well in her marriage, in presenting a perfectly groomed, superbly dressed, confidently smiling persona to the world in which she was convinced that everyone was aware that her husband was faithless.

Actually Candice Amberville was wrong. Cutter's many affairs, though suspected by some, were not common knowledge. He had picked his partners well; they were outlaws like him, all anxious in their own self-interest to leave no signs that could be read by their husbands; women who were part of an underground that exists in every city in the world.

Candice's father, who advanced Cutter's responsibilities every year, would never have believed that the wife of one of the other partners at Standings and Alexander met Cutter twice a week in a hotel room. Candice's mother would have given the lie to anyone who reported to her that her son-in-law had other women, dozens of them. Only one member of the Standings family knew Cutter for what he was: Nanette, who had been fifteen when Cutter and Candice married and who now was twenty-four, pouting, rosy Nanette who had grown up unscrupulous, amoral and game for anything; Nanette who used other women and cocaine with the same sense of defiant curiosity. Why not do it, if it existed? Life was so dull, San Francisco so provincial, and marriage—for she was married—so boring and predictable that it was worth having at least one hard run at anything.

All undergrounds, even the most clandestine, have grapevines, and that of promiscuity is no exception. Eventually Nanette heard enough hints about Cutter's activities to form a new idea of this blond man, so invincibly cool and so darkly intent, this man who had always acted toward her as if she were nothing more than Candice's baby sister.

How had he managed to convince her that he had overlooked her own sexuality, as visible as a brand on her forehead to the kind of man she now knew he was? Did he find her unattractive? she asked herself, deeply piqued. And just how much of what she'd heard about him was true? A man who needed no arousal, a man who always was ready, a man who left every woman satisfied but with a satisfaction that itched for more—a sexual pirate. Could Cutter be all that? Was her horrid sister, so calm and pulled together, so superior and snobbish and disapproving, so busy with those prizewinning dogs and her famous dinner parties—was Candice so smug because she was getting her fill of such a man? Nanette asked herself in petulant irritation.

Cutter resisted Nanette for as long as he could. She was too close to home, he told himself, refusing to admit that that was part of her attraction. He'd wanted her for years, from the time she turned from another little teenager into a voluptuous woman who reeked of carnality, whose animalism was so wanton that whenever he saw her at family gatherings he had become inflamed, against his will and his judgment, wanting nothing more on earth than to take her immediately, to take her without a smile and without a word, take her the way he knew she wanted to be taken, with brutality and violence. How many nights, in the ski lodge at Aspen, had he thrust himself deeply into his wife's untempting, yielding, yearning body while he thought of luscious Nanette, dark, juicy and flamboyant, whose bedroom was only two doors away?

They stalked each other like creatures in a jungle, each the hunter, each the hunted, until the day came when the only question left was *how soon?* Quickly, it had to be quickly. And after they had wallowed in each other, the only question was how soon *again?* Nanette was inexhaustible with a courtesan's skill he had never known in another woman. She was as voracious as a wolverine and twice as vicious. Cunningly she introduced him to the only experience Cutter had never known with a woman before: the thunderous, forbidden rapture of having two women at the same time; wise Nanette who had understood that this was the only way she was sure to keep Cutter for as long as she wanted him; Nanette who didn't mind sharing him with a woman she had already possessed; Nanette who felt a particular, puissant thrill in showing him exactly what it was like when one woman took another while he watched, watched and waited until she allowed him to take her, take the other, take them both. No matter.

But a secret known to three people is only safe if two of them are dead. And this secret was too good to be confined to the grapevine, this secret was too tasty not to be savored and rolled on the tongue by people to whom debauchery was only a word, a fantasy they would never dare to act out. It became a suspicion, it became almost—but not quite—known, and then, as words written in invisible ink become legible with the application of fire, it came, as inevitably it must, to Candice's ear.

Almost from the beginning of her marriage she had endured the scenarios of Cutter with another woman, but the woman was always faceless. For years all her strength and all her emotional energy had gone into nonacknowledgment; her only solace alcohol, her dogs and her pride. Now her pride could sustain her no longer, for now that faceless woman had a face, that of Nanette. Nanette herself had told her, not showing how much she enjoyed the pseudo-confession. Candice's haughty surface had become so perfect that Nanette couldn't resist—didn't try to resist—shocking Candice out of her self-satisfied contentment. Venomously, as if by accident, she left behind a Polaroid shot of herself and Cutter, his face distorted by his orgasm.

She could not endure more, Candice realized. It was not to be lived with. There was no possible hideous future to a life that contained this certain knowledge. She would never stop seeing that picture. It could never become a memory. It would live before her eyes, the purest of agony. Hell had entered the room and eliminated any doubt and without doubt there was no hope.

Candice dressed herself in a beautiful suit, combed her gleaming hair, put on her makeup, went to a hotel on the far side of Union Square, checked into a room on the sixteenth floor, drank half a bottle of Scotch and jumped out of the window into the empty alley behind the hotel.

It would have been considered a case of temporary insanity, of suicidal depression so well hidden that even her mother hadn't suspected its existence. But while she was swallowing the alcohol that she needed to make it easier to open the window, Candice thought of her dogs and scrawled a letter giving instructions for their care, a rambling letter in which her desire to punish her sister won over her desire to maintain to the end that she did not know what sort of husband Cutter had been, a letter in which she accused Nanette.

The detective who found the letter gave it to James Standings III. He had no choice but to believe that Candice was wrong about Nanette, for he had only one child left. All his vengeance turned toward Cutter, now senior vice-president of his firm. In order to avoid a further scandal out of what he could still manage to have treated as a tragedy, all that James Standings III could do was to expel Cutter from the firm and vow that never again would he be hired by any other of the many San Francisco banking houses in which he exerted considerable influence.

James Standings III never realized it but his vengeance was as effective as any other he could have achieved, without a gun, for he took away from Cutter that sure future presidency of Standings and Alexander toward which he had been purposefully moving in so many ways from the day he first met Candice.

Jumbo Booker had never given up the borrowed glory he derived from his position as Cutter's best friend. Enclosed as Jumbo was in the tight pattern of a comfortable marriage, the sinfully exciting life that he could only imagine that Cutter led—for Cutter never boasted—gave him the illusion of participation without the problems that actual participation would have posed. Now, with Cutter so abruptly and inexplicably out of a job, Jumbo exerted himself to find something for his friend, enjoying this welcome sign that his own position, if less glamorous, was still superior.

Jumbo had fund-raising connections with the Nixon administration and he found Cutter an appointment in Belgium within the complicated bureaucracy of the Agency for International Development. Brussels, hospitable if singularly gloomy in its almost perpetual fog, suited Cutter's state of mind and he was soon involved in the complicated diplomatic life of the busy, well-fed capital. Eventually Jumbo got him the opportunity to work for an investment bank in London and there, after a few years, the faithful Jumbo got him an opportunity to return to New York and work in the local office of Booker, Smity and Jameston. It was 1981 and Cutter judged that it was time to go home. Neither the welcome of the NATO wives nor the friendliness of the British quite made up for the advantages he could still hope for as an Amberville on his native soil.

In 1969, twelve years before Cutter came back to Manhattan, Nina Stern had turned thirty-five. Her love affair with Zachary had been conducted so quietly that it had become part of the mosaic of Manhattan life, taken for granted by those in the know and undreamed of by anyone else. Whatever tidal waves of gossip there must certainly have been some ten years earlier had become mere wavelets as Lily and Zachary remained undramatically married. Nina and Zachary were like a minor, little-known institution, some obscure historical society located on a side street which had no fund-raising functions and no inquiring scholars. Only the two of them knew the treasures concealed behind the façade they had built, and as far as Zachary was concerned he asked no greater happiness.

But Nina Stern at thirty-five was not the same free spirit as Nina Stern at twenty-five. She was just as beloved, daily more successful, sure to succeed Zelda Powers as Editor-in-chief of *Style*, but her loathing of everything domestic had not resisted the attack of her hormonal heritage. She had reached the age at which the unmarried career woman faces that classic, unavoidable realization: *now or never*. On the eve of her thirty-fifth birthday Nina had taken stock, asking herself where she would be in ten years, and the answer hadn't pleased her: exactly where she was now, still successful, still with Zachary, but forty-five years old. With fifty fast approaching. Atavistic voices sounded in her mind. *Now or never*. Could she reconcile herself to the *never*? Must she change her mind about what she had believed she wanted just because the sands of time kept running? Nina Stern took a long, honest look at herself. Unclouded by illusion, she realized that, alas, she too was just like other women after all. She wanted the *now*—she couldn't hold on to the *never*. Even if marriage and children would not, in the end, make her happy, she must find out for herself. She was disappointed in this evidence of her ordinary humanity but a little relieved at the same time . . . perhaps, just perhaps, it would turn out to be an interesting experiment.

She broke with Zachary as quickly, as neatly and as sweetly as she knew how, and soon married the most eligible of the many men who had continued to pursue her over the years.

Only her daughter Nina, Mrs. Stern triumphantly told her friends, could have produced twin boys and held on to her job in the first year of marriage. Only Nina, thought Zachary, could have made the break with such decency and such honesty that he was able to go to the wedding and—almost—feel happy for her. Only Nina, thought Nina, could continue to care so deeply for Zachary and yet give her new husband the exclusive—almost exclusive— love he deserved. It was, after all, possible to have the best of both worlds . . . it was all a question of having the right sense of timing.

Lily Amberville saw an opportunity and did not fail to take advantage of it. The wedding invitation would have told her that Zachary was free of his mistress even if she hadn't been able to read the poignant loneliness in his eyes. From the time of Cutter's marriage, six years before, she had lived in a gilded, adorned, extravagantly bedecked emptiness. Now Zachary was as lonely as she and slowly the two of them came together and made their peace with each other, a silent peace—since there had never been any formal rupture to repair—a peace that grew more solid year by year, a peace of dry, resigned, but somehow rewarding contentment. They had each had their great romance. Now they had each other and their children and it was better, so very much better, than being alone.

11

One spring day in 1972 Zachary
Amberville and Nina Stern Heller had lunch together, meeting
unselfconsciously at one of the restaurants they had often gone to
during the years of their love affair, an unfashionable place where it
was unlikely that they would be seen by anyone who knew either of
them. During the years that they had been together they had discovered that there were dozens of such places in Manhattan,
neighborhood places, comfortable and warm, with fairly decent
food. Now, there was no longer a reason to avoid attention, nor
was there a reason to abandon the restaurants they both liked. If an
element of nostalgia, a few moments of remembered pain, of remembered joy, crept into these lunches of the Editor-in-chief of
Style and the head of Amberville Publications it only added a particularly bittersweet flavor to the feast.

"You have to admit," Nina said, choosing her words carefully,
"that Maxi has potential."

"So did Bonnie and Clyde."

"Come on, Zachary, don't be too hard on her. I think she
needs to be motivated, focused on something so she can use everything she has. After all, when she's interested in a subject in school
she can get straight A's . . . ."

"And when she isn't, she just won't bother to study, which
adds up to a D-plus average. What kind of college is going to accept
her with that record?" Zachary wondered miserably.

Nina considered Maxi and sighed. A most perplexing, puz-
zling minx, deeply and fundamentally lovable yet always in some
kind of trouble, managing, even in this permissive society, to get
herself thrown out of a succession of schools and summer camps;
not for drugs or stealing or cheating, but for organizing groups of

her peers into inspired, effective mischief. "She's always elected president of her class," Nina reminded him cheerfully.

"Usually just before she's bounced. All the future I can see for her is to be voted Miss Congeniality but she's not a type they allow in the Miss America contest."

"If only . . ." Nina ventured and then stopped.

"Yup." They both knew that they didn't want to discuss, yet again, the difficulties that existed between Maxi and Lily which made Zachary almost totally responsible for his daughter.

From the time Lily found out about Toby's inexorable eye disease she seemed to have abandoned her unquenchable healthy daughter for the boy who needed her. Maxi was barely three when this happened and, as the months and years passed, she never stopped yearning with all her heart for her mother's inaccessible affection. On Toby, Lily lavished a possessive, watchful, anxious love that was on alert as long as he was awake.

After Justin's birth, her youngest child too became an object of an adoring, excessive passion. Consumed by her two boys, who, like lovers, changed the colors of her world and demanded infidelity, Lily no longer even tried to make the time to read to her intrusive small girl child or let her play dress-up with her jewels.

Maxi had her father all to herself, Lily thought in self-justification when Maxi tried to claim her attention. If she had to cope with Maxi, it would be just too much for her sanity. The child was indestructible, she assured herself as she gave brief, firm, fruitless instruction to one of the procession of nannies she hired for her daughter, and turned quickly back to Toby's learning problems and Justin's health, for he had been premature and frighteningly frail for long after his birth.

But at no point during her childhood did Maxi stop craving and needing Lily's love. She strove for her mother's consideration in every naughty way she could think of, but only managed to get herself punished by her father, whose heart wasn't in it, as well she knew.

She never tried being a "good girl," for she understood that the better she was, the less chance she had to be noticed. Yet from birth Maxi had been bound by the rules of fair play. Some tangible thing called "fairness" was utterly and indelibly precious to her and as she grew older she tried to convince herself that it was "fair" that Toby and Justin should so preoccupy her mother. She had tried very hard indeed to make herself believe this, but she'd never totally succeeded and, at some early time in her life, she began to stop hoping for Lily's love. She never gave up completely but her hope diminished year by year until it was buried so deep that it almost stopped hurting.

Nina stopped eating her osso buco and turned to Zachary.

"There's one thing you've never tried. Every summer you send Maxi away to some new place . . . tennis camp, theater camp, wilderness survival camp, riding camp . . . and every year she's returned to you by air mail. Why not give her a real challenge—I'll bet she'd rise to it."

"What I love about you, among a billion other things, is your optimism." Zachary smiled at her. A beautiful, warmhearted wonderful woman, damn that husband of hers.

"A job, a summer job," Nina continued excitedly. "It would use up all of that crazy energy of hers on something she could sink her teeth into, something that would give her a sense of accomplishment."

"Who would hire her?" Zachary asked. He couldn't imagine anyone deliberately adding Maxi to any business endeavor.

"You, Zachary, you."

"Oh no! Not me! Not Maxi!"

"You know perfectly well that you always have summer jobs available for kids with pull, kids of major advertisers. It's an understood thing. I've got a half-dozen set for this summer on my staff alone, Miss Better Dresses, Miss Panty Hose, and four others, not any one of them as smart as Maxi."

"Pull is one thing, nepotism is another."

"That's a cop-out. I'll talk to Pavka and between us we'll find a place for her. At least try it . . . you've got nothing to lose."

"Nothing to lose?" Zachary asked, amused by her Girl Scout madness.

"What's the worst that can happen?" Nina demanded.

"She'll fuck up," he said.

"But it's worth a try, isn't it?" Nina insisted, looking at him with a special kind of love that her husband had never seen, would never see, in her eyes.

"Are you asking me or telling me?"

"Telling you."

"Then it's worth a try."

Amberville Publications now included three more successful magazines. *Savoir Vivre,* a magazine devoted to the art of living well through cultivation of ever more sophisticated taste buds; *Sports Week,* which had become rapidly indispensable to every man, woman and child in America who had ever worn out a pair of sneakers, and *Indoors,* a magnificent monthly for well-heeled masochists that made its buyers, no matter how rich, feel that they lived like pigs and attracted large numbers of fans who looked at the photographs in each issue with a magnifying glass so as not to miss a single mortifying detail of other people's homes.

Pavka Mayer, who was on the masthead of each of the publications as Artistic Director, sat in his office and contemplated Nina with relish. Even her latest idea hadn't astonished him. He thought Nina capable of anything.

"It boils down to where Maxi can do the least harm," he said thoughtfully.

"*Style* is out because it's fashion and fashion leads to photographers and photographers lead to sex," Nina brooded.

"We can't hide her on *T.V. Week*—those gangsters there won't put up with her. And they might send her to interview Warren Beatty just as a gag," Pavka added.

"On *Seven Days* she'll meet too many other kids. We don't want to encourage our darling's ringleader tendencies and all the editors at *Sports Week* are jocks or ex-jocks or would-be jocks and I don't think it would be a good idea to expose Maxi to so many older men all at once."

"You can't mean you think she's still a virgin?" Pavka asked, shocked.

"I don't know. I've made it a point never to ask. It's none of my business, Pavka. Nothing is impossible no matter how unlikely," Nina replied.

"So that leaves only *Savoir Vivre* and *Indoors*," Pavka realized. "You decide."

"No, you decide. I don't want to be totally responsible."

"Neither do I," Pavka said stubbornly. He pushed a button and spoke to his secretary. "Miss Williams, would you rather work on *Savoir Vivre* or *Indoors*?"

There was a long pause and finally his secretary blurted, "Have I done something wrong, Mr. Mayer?"

"No, just answer my question. Please, if you would be so kind."

"Does this mean I'm fired?" she quavered.

"Oh, my God. No, it's just an election bet."

"Did you win or lose?"

"Miss Williams, I beg of you. Toss a coin if you don't have an opinion."

"I'd rather work on *Savoir Vivre* because I'd rather see pictures of roast pork than of somebody's dining room."

"Thank you, Miss Williams. Well done."

"Oh, you're so welcome, Mr. Mayer. Any time."

Pavka beamed at Nina. "Can I help it if women adore me?"

Maxi was in heaven. Every summer of her life she had been forced into banishment in the country. Beaches, lakes, trees, fresh air and group sports, all were considered to be absolutely necessary for her well-being. Left to herself, a quick trip to Central Park was more than enough contact with nature.

On those rare occasions when she'd been in New York in the summer, for a few hours she'd been conscious of another Manhattan, one that was a hot tropical island where everything moved to a different beat, a city whose rhythm had somehow altered and, in its transformation, had become languid, mysterious, more exciting than ever. Although the office buildings seemed to have the same number of people dashing in and out, there was something different about the people themselves. They dressed differently and they smiled more. A sense of holiday, of a potential party just about to happen reigned in the business district, and in the residential parts of town there was a lazy emptiness, as well-dressed housewives, well-dressed children and well-dressed nannies vanished as completely as if plague stalked the streets.

Now this alluring, throbbing Manhattan in its summer metamorphosis was going to be hers, except for weekends when she and her father would join the family in Southampton. She would go to work with her father in the morning and then—lovely conspiracy—drift away from his side without a goodbye and take another elevator to the offices of *Savoir Vivre* where she would be known as Maxi Adams. Both Pavka and Nina had insisted on the necessity of concealing her identity from everyone but Carl Koch, the Editor-in-chief of the magazine. If her co-workers knew she was Zachary Amberville's daughter, at best they would think she was a spoiled rich bitch who was slumming her way into the magazine business, and at worst they would suspect her of being a spy, planted by the management to see what they were up to, reporting back to her father. Since *Savoir Vivre* was a magazine that had been published for only a little over two years, Maxi was unknown to everyone who worked there and they had decided to plant her in the art department, where she could be put to work on layouts. "She should be able to do wonders with glue and rubber cement and Scotch tape and a ruler," Nina had assured Pavka.

"Maxi and a pot of glue? It won't last two days," Pavka muttered. "But better that than the test kitchens or, God forbid, the wine department. Glue you can always clean up. Glue you can re-glue."

On that first Monday morning of July Maxi woke early and began to prepare herself for her entrance into the world of major corporative responsibility. She was enchanted with the idea of a job, a grown-up job. She had decided to add two necessary years to Maxi Adams's age and tell everybody that she was nineteen.

She walked around in her biggest closet, looking for her oldest pair of jeans, the most paint-splotched, the ones that spoke the most of real work of all the many jeans she owned. She had worn them while painting scenery at her next-to-last school and it seemed to her that they gave off an artistic aura, for was she not going to be working in an art department? With them she put on a clean, pale blue, but equally well-worn denim shirt which seemed to say that she had never spent an unproductive minute in her life, a shirt that she felt was sensible, down-to-earth and adult, above all adult. She wanted so much to make a good first impression. Maxi bound a thick silver-and-turquoise Arizona Indian belt tightly around her eighteenth-century waist. After all, any art department would expect that even its most humble employee would still have a sense of decoration. Shoes? No. She put on one of her many pairs of treasured high-heeled Western boots, four hundred and fifty dollars by mail order from Tony Lama, boots that she was convinced added three inches to her height.

Satisfied with her body she attacked her face and hair. No female, in 1972, ever considered that she had enough hair. Maxi had let hers grow down long beyond her shoulders and liked to fling it around, often adding to it with one of the many hunks of fake hair she had accumulated in the last few years. But today called for seriousness and dignity. She combed all her hair back from her face so that her streak of white was prominent. Makeup? Maxi had as much experience with makeup as any demonstrator on the first floor of Bloomingdale's. Today she wanted to look *old*. The less makeup she used, the younger she looked, so she set about skillfully applying base, powder, blusher, mascara, eye liner, lipstick and eye shadow with a steady hand born of long hours of solitary practice. She added chunky nuggets of turquoise earrings and studied the finished product. She used an eyebrow pencil to darken the beauty mark above the bow of her upper lip.

No, still not *quite* old enough, Maxi decided, and dove into her closet and produced a pair of large horn-rimmed glasses she always wore when she played poker. They had plain glass for lenses but it helped to have some sort of mask, no matter how transparent, when bluffing. Something was *still* missing, she fretted, looking into a triple mirror. It was all that hair, of course. What good did it do to have white hair in front if the rest of it all hung down in the back? She pulled it all into a neat chignon and fastened it securely. Perfection, she thought. The portrait of the artist as an almost-middle-aged woman.

Zachary greeted her appearance at the breakfast table as impassively as possible. Perhaps, he thought prayfully, she didn't look any different from any other girl of her age . . . he didn't go around staring at them so he didn't know for sure. But wasn't there something almost . . . depraved? . . . about the way her jeans and shirt clung to her body? Didn't Maxi realize that she looked sexier in those damn jeans than if she'd pranced around in black lace panties? Shouldn't a girl with such a tiny waist and such . . . a well-developed . . . pair of tits, for want of a less parental phrase, not wear a limp denim shirt that hugged each blossoming inch of her? And those glasses? Since when did she need glasses? They only made the rest of her more—whatever it was that disturbed him. And what had she done to her face? And her hair? Nothing he could figure out for sure, but there was something different about his daughter this morning. Was he going crazy or did she look almost . . . mature? No, not Maxi. Not mature, it couldn't be. *Ripe.* By God, *ripe!*

"Maxi, you look ripe, damn it."

"Thank you, Daddy," she said demurely.

"Don't you think you should wear a dress . . . maybe?"

"Daddy, nobody wears dresses anymore," she said with gentle reproof.

She was right, Zachary realized. Nina wore pants, his secretary wore pants, all his female editors wore pants. The last woman he had seen in a dress was Lily, and hers were all that new mid-calf length. He sighed, hoping dresses would come back soon, and returned to his eggs.

"This is Maxi Adams, your summer trainee," Carl Koch, Editor-in-chief of *Savoir Vivre*, said to his clever, capable art director, Linda Lafferty. "Do with her what you will." He disappeared hastily, and with considerable relief, leaving Linda, who was close to six feet tall and still managed to be dumpy, to cope with the trainee.

Carl Koch had good instincts and he'd been immediately convinced that Maxi was a problem. He just wasn't sure of what magnitude. Those summer kids always were a pain in the ass to deal with. But Pavka had given him firm, not-to-be-questioned orders and *Savoir Vivre* was stuck with her for the summer. But now she was Linda Lafferty's problem.

Linda inspected Maxi with growing wonder. This young person looked to her like a budding intellectual who had somehow become a hooker in Santa Fe, or perhaps an apprentice Simone de Beauvoir who'd strayed into a stag party.

"Howdy pardner," she said finally.

"Howdy, Miz Lafferty."

"Where do you . . . hail from?"

"The East," Maxi answered, skillfully avoiding this leading question.

"East?" Linda persisted. "Far East or Near East?"

"East Seventies," she admitted.

"Oh. Any art training?"

"Only school and camp."

"Camp?"

"Summer camp," Maxi murmured, suddenly unable to find a substitute that would sound more impressive.

Why me, thought Linda Lafferty. *Why me?*

Nothing she had ever done in her life, Maxi decided after a week of work, could compare to the office for sheer fun. The potential for making merry in the art department of *Savoir Vivre* was beyond anything she had imagined. How come she had never guessed that people went to work in order to stand around and tell each other much better dirty jokes than she'd ever heard at school—really good ones—and horse around like crazy and get friendly with each other and goof off and sneak joints in the john and gossip like wild about sex? They all seemed to be making it with each other. To do that all day and get paid for it too—this was the secret grown-ups never told you when they spoke so seriously of something called "business." Business was play on a major scale.

All her new friends worked on layouts, which reminded her of

162

kindergarten, pasting pictures on heavy paper. She loved helping them, leaning over their shoulders and straightening out edges, handing them Magic Markers and sharpening their pencils and making them laugh if they ever got too annoyed with some photograph that wouldn't fit right on a page. She'd shown them things they'd never thought of—the story on foie gras for instance, with photographs of seventeen different slices of foie gras, each one from a different French restaurant—nobody had been able to tell which part of which slice was the top and which was the bottom by the time she'd finished rearranging them.

Maxi's very favorite part of the day was when the bagel-and-doughnut wagon came around, and everybody stopped pretending to be busy and gathered around like nomads stoking up before a trek across the desert. She even came back from lunch early for the afternoon bagel wagon halt at three o'clock. Nobody really needed her till then anyway. Lunch was such a groovy invention! Three free hours to shop. She was on a diet so she didn't bother to eat. Instead, she systematically combed the stores, boutiques as well as department stores.

Maxi had been picking out her own clothes for years but always before she'd had to wait till September to shop. But now the city was full of early fall merchandise and there wasn't anything Maxi didn't try on. When she finally finished her daily bout of pillage and plunder, all charged to Lily's accounts, she brought stacks of packages back to her brightly lit cubicle and pulled all her purchases out of their boxes and modeled them for her co-workers who had such terrific taste about things like colors and shapes and were teaching her a lot about what to wear. She'd stopped using her glasses and doing dumb things to her hair once she'd been firmly established as nineteen, going on twenty, and part of the gang.

The idea of starting her last year of high school in September was too revolting to think about. Maxi had decided to go to art school instead and everyone had advice for her about which school to pick and they were so great about coming back to her office and sitting around telling her about their days in art school and the hell-raising they'd gotten up to there. She hated the end of the day when she had to refuse all the offers of drinks at the bars that surrounded the office and disappear back home, even though she could usually con her father into taking her out to dinner with him.

Linda Lafferty simmered with midsummer rage. Productivity in her art department—*her* department!—had fallen off precipitously since the advent of Maxi. All her workers, who at best had never been as dependable as she would have liked, had turned into randy goats who spent most of their time thinking up excuses to have yet another long conversation with that . . . that . . . she couldn't think of the right word. Maxi was outside of her previous experience, and none of the words she knew managed to satisfactorily categorize that sexy, funny, absolutely lawless, disruptive and yet somehow, in spite of it all—admit it, Linda, you like to talk to her too, she told herself in disgust. The kid was a daily bacchanal. She must be Miss Seagram's or Miss General Foods or Miss Coca-Cola to be allowed such a range of nuisance value, for Carl Koch simply refused to listen to her complaints about the new trainee.

However, Linda Lafferty had a department to run, a department that had always been the single most overworked department at the magazine. Much of the body of the book was given over to photographs and the rest of the thick magazine was stuffed with ads for luxury products. The readers of *Savoir Vivre* were rich people and the magazine, printed on glossy, thick, fifty-pound paper, was expected to drip visual riches that would make its rich readers feel even richer. All the responsibility for the quality and originality of this monthly cornucopia lay squarely on the art department. The text barely mattered although the food and wine articles were all written by top literary figures who were paid enormous sums of money by magazine standards.

She needed a new assistant art director, Linda Lafferty decided in desperation, someone fast and good who would be tough enough to speed things up. A lot of severe ass-kicking could do wonders to kill Maxi-lust, she thought, but something about being so tall made it almost impossible for her to kick ass effectively. She hadn't decided if it was her desire to be liked or fear of killing someone, but at least she was smart enough to know when she needed help.

When she put her request to Carl Koch she was surprised at

how quickly he agreed to let her hire a new top assistant. Although *Savoir Vivre* was clearly a money-machine, Koch, like most editors, didn't like to add any staff if he could help it. In her last job Linda had worked with a young man who was as single-mindedly work-oriented as he was brilliant. She had wanted to hire him for a long time and now Maxi Adams, queen of the rubber cement, Lorelei of paste-up, catnip sorceress of the ruler, was going to give her the opportunity to offer Rocco Cipriani a salary he couldn't resist, for he had always said that only a lot of money could get him away from Condé Nast. Maxi Adams would serve a purpose, would make a contribution in spite of herself.

Linda Lafferty looked at Rocco Cipriani severely. "I'm taking a vacation. I haven't had one minute off since I came to *Savoir Vivre*. I won't be there when you start tomorrow. I don't want people coming to me about you and complaining. You're going to be in absolute charge. They'll all have memos to that effect."

"You want a new broom, mixed with Captain Queeg and a few floggings?"

"Precisely. There isn't one of my bums who's doing a full day's work. I have a major discipline problem on my hands. I'm absolutely counting on you to beat and whack and knock them back into shape while I'm away having that thirty-day nervous breakdown Carl said I was entitled to, and when I get back I want to be ahead of schedule . . . or else." She had decided not to pinpoint Maxi as the source of the trouble. Let him find out for himself. On-the-job training.

"You're cute as hell, Linda, when you get threatening."

"That's why I've hired you, that's why we've spent all weekend going over this disgusting backload of undone work. You're going to save my ass because you're not at all cute."

"And I thought you liked me."

"You're all right for a kid," she said primly, cursing her never-give-up Irish lust that didn't have the good sense to stop raging at the sight of that young and completely untouchable Rocco Cipriani. She looked at him closely, trying to decide how any man so absurdly gorgeous could still command as much respect as he did.

He had an indecent chaos of black curls, heavily hooded dark eyes that were both dreamy and glowing in their intensity, as well as the nose of a Medici prince. In his strong features, for all her acuteness, she could find no single fault. She didn't even dare to look at his mouth. A girl had only so much self-control. Everything about Rocco worked together, relentlessly, powerfully, insistently. It was difficult to turn away from him. He was, she decided, like the model for a great Renaissance painter's masterpiece, a vision of a proud Saint Sebastian. All that was lacking were the arrows piercing his body at those interestingly vulnerable places. Rocco Cipriani explained as much about the high period of Italian art as a trip to the Met.

Yet, at barely twenty-three, he was doing so well at Condé Nast that it was only a question of having a little more seniority, a little more seasoning before he would be the art director of his own magazine. She knew full well that he would never stay at Amberville. This was simply one of those sharp, strategic, sideways moves that some of the best and most ambitious art directors made in order to go ahead faster than they would if they stayed at one company during their entire career . . . she'd done it herself. It made you more appreciated than total loyalty ever did, and it was only risky if you were not very, very, *very* good. Rocco had nothing to worry about.

There are as many kinds of art directors in Manhattan as there are publications and agencies and commercial-makers. Rocco was one of a very special kind, one who never wanted to work on anything but magazines. He harbored no itch to work in advertising in spite of the desirable big bucks those poor bastards who called themselves "creative directors" made. They were bound by the demands of clients and he was bound by nothing but the limits of his own imagination. For Rocco the ultimate joy in life was pages and pages of an empty magazine, pure glorious white space, space without end, space renewed each month by advertising department magic, waiting for him to fill it with layouts that had never been dreamed of before, combinations of type that had never been put together since typography was invented, graphics that would make history, photographs hitherto unimagined, cropped in ways no one had ever cropped before, drawings commissioned from artists who had never been thought of except in terms of gallery and museum walls. Each page of editorial space was to him like a blank canvas to a painter: a new chance to impose his vision of what *could* be, and like a painter, he was never totally satisfied.

Rocco was the not-yet-satiated Alexander the Great of the magazine world, still on the rampage, not with armies but with torrents of talent. He worked at least ten hours a day at his desk and then went home to empty his mailbox into which were stuffed magazines from all over the world, each one of which he devoured page by page, cursing horribly when he saw a new idea he hadn't thought of himself, raping the magazines of the pages he wanted to study, which he taped to the walls of his big Soho loft until they went from floor to eye level, and were gradually covered over by other pages so that being in the room was like living inside a collage of the best international graphic design.

There were only two men in the world whom Rocco Cipriani envied: Alexander Liberman, the genius who was Artistic Director of Condé Nast, and Pavka Mayer. One day he felt sure he was destined to replace one or the other of them, but he also knew he still had a lot to learn, so Linda Lafferty's job offer had an additional allure: he'd be working for Pavka for the first time, indirectly it was true, but still there was always the potential opportunity of picking the man's great brain.

Rocco started at *Savoir Vivre* on a Monday in mid-July. By Friday, Linda couldn't stand it anymore and let herself give in to the temptation to telephone him and find out how things were going.

"We've cleared up all that major lot of undone work and Monday I'm attacking the November issue," he said.

"Already? Are you sure?"

"Well, nobody was thrilled about working till midnight every night all week, but they did it."

"What about the Maxi problem?"

"'Maxi problem'? You mean my trainee?"

"If you want to describe her that way, yes."

"Christ, Linda, she's no problem at all. I can't believe what a help that kid is. Doesn't even take her lunch hour, just bolts a hard-boiled egg out of a paper bag and goes right back to sweeping up and getting rid of eraser crumbs and making sure that everyone has fresh supplies when they come back from lunch. She seems very grown-up for only nineteen. In on time every morning, last one out at night, doesn't fool around in the bagel breaks, brings coffee just before anyone begins to itch for it, keeps my Magic Markers arranged just right, in fact I've never had such an organized desk anywhere. Doesn't smoke, wears those demure little dresses, doesn't indulge in idle chat and doesn't even seem to take time to pee. Maybe she's a Mormon? She's always there when I want her . . . yet she's never a nuisance. A good lady, that one. Not bad-looking too, now that I come to think about it . . . in fact . . . not bad at all . . ."

"Oh SHIT."

"What's that about?"

"Forget it. Just forget it. Carry on, Rocco. I'm going back to the beach and walk into the ocean until I drown."

"If you're planning on working all weekend, Rocco, maybe I can help out?" Maxi suggested casually, holding her breath. She would die for him, she would not just walk on burning coals for him, she would cover herself with them and lie down quietly until it was all over. There wasn't anything in the lexicon of human behavior that she would not do for Rocco Cipriani beginning with leaving home and crossing continents on foot and starving in the wilderness. He had only to ask.

"I don't want to interrupt your weekend plans," he said.

"I don't have any actually. And I could learn a lot while I kept your stuff straight. You know how your layouts disappear under each other when you're working hard. And . . . I could go out for pizza," she added, a suggestion that grew from every bit of wisdom she had absorbed in her life.

"Good thought. I usually forget to eat. And there's that pizza place right next door that takes so long to deliver that the cheese is always cold. O.K., come by on Saturday morning about nine. I'll give you the address."

She took the paper and put it in her handbag to keep forever. She already knew where he lived, she knew his phone number, she knew all about his big family in Hartford, his scholarship to art school, his prizes, his promotions. The advent of Rocco had started a storm of speculation in the art department of *Savoir Vivre* and Maxi had listened carefully, saying nothing but registering every morsel, weeding out the bits that overlapped or didn't seem to go together and ending up with a fair idea of the truth. She knew he had had a lot of girls but no long-lasting one, she knew his enemies and his friends, she knew as much about this stranger she had met for the first time five days before as it is possible to learn and intuit. Maxi's intuition of Rocco was far more than the act of mental contemplation or recognition or consideration. It went deeper than that philosophical definition which claims for intuition a spiritual perception and immediate knowledge that can be ascribed to angelic or spiritual beings. Hers went further and was a good deal shorter. It was Hawthorne's definition: "A miraculous intuition of what ought to be done just at the right time for action."

The first Saturday and Sunday Maxi spent in Rocco's loft were busy ones. Whenever she saw that Rocco was lost in thought before his drawing table she moved about the room, so quietly that he never heard her, finding out where he kept his household supplies. She made his bed with fresh sheets and bundled up all his dirty linen and shirts for a trip to that laundromat which, for the first time in her life, she was sure she would be able to find and figure out. She washed her first sinkful of dirty dishes and put them away; she went through his pantry and made lists of the basics that were missing; but she didn't have time to tackle his drawers or closets. While she bent to these divine tasks she always had one eye on him, and whenever he looked up, needing something, she had it ready for him, with much of the expertise of an operating-room nurse. He gulped down the pizza and sandwiches she brought back for him, sharing them with her of course, but silently, as he thought about the design problems that confronted him. Now that the backlog of old work had been cleared up, Rocco wanted to impose his own style on *Savoir Vivre* before Linda Lafferty came back from her vacation.

He was immediately concerned with the problems created by a magazine devoted to food and wine. He had worked with models and clothes so long that the presentation of objects, whose main relation to the readers was to cause them to salivate, provided him with a challenge which made him oblivious to all else.

"*One* grain, just one grain," he muttered as Maxi sliced another pizza on Sunday night.

"Not hungry?" she asked, worried.

"One single grain of golden caviar, on a full-bleed double spread. The obvious thing to do would be to have Penn photograph it but Penn means Condé Nast and anyway I don't do the obvious. Laser photography? Photomicrography? You can't *draw* caviar—or can you? Maybe, yeah, maybe . . . with gold leaf covering both pages and Andrew Wyeth to draw the caviar . . . maybe . . . is that pepperoni?"

"I asked for everything on it."

"Good." He lapsed back into silence and soon afterwards, seeing that he was about to stop working, Maxi left, so quietly that he didn't notice she was gone.

During the following week anyone coming into the art department of *Savoir Vivre* might have thought himself in the manuscript room of a medieval monastery as the workers bent over their desks with concentrated industry, trying out all the ideas that Rocco flung at them in his search for ever newer, ever more exciting pages.

Zachary was thrilled as Maxi told him about her modest but necessary part in this work and even more delighted when she asked him questions that showed how closely she had been watching the whole process of putting a magazine together. Yet he was slightly concerned by the sheer intensity of her interest . . . if she were so involved, might it not all be over as quickly as it had started? He didn't trust Maxi's enthusiasm. He was relieved that at least she had spent the weekend visiting her school friend India

West, in Connecticut, and was going back there again this coming Saturday.

Sunday night Rocco put down his tools, yawned and stretched.

"That's it! That ought to be it," he said victoriously to Maxi who had just finished putting his recently washed and dried and rolled socks in military order in a drawer where he couldn't miss them. The loft was as immaculate as she could make it without actually disturbing any of the magazines or books or portfolios.

"Pizza time?" she asked.

"Not again. Not another one. I couldn't stand it." He grinned at her. Best assistant he'd ever had, he thought. And he could swear that she'd done something, he couldn't figure out what, which made it easier to get dressed in the morning.

"I could cook a steak, make a salad and put a potato in the oven to bake," Maxi offered.

"Where are you going to find all that stuff on Sunday night?"

"In here," Maxi said, opening the refrigerator which she had stocked the day before. Wilderness survival camp had included basic cooking lessons.

"Great. I'm beat. I think I'll grab a nap while the potato bakes. Wake me in time for dinner, O.K.?"

"Sure."

Rocco sank into a deep sleep almost immediately. It was so late in the day that the setting sun just dusted the air of the loft, but midsummer light still filled the room. Maxi crept close to Rocco's bed and carefully sank to her knees beside it. She had to clench her fists to prevent herself from reaching out and touching his hair. What if he woke up as suddenly as he had fallen asleep? She had never before been able to gaze directly at him for more than a few seconds except when he was talking to someone at the office, and even then she had been aware that if he looked up and caught her staring she would blush humiliatingly. During their two Saturdays and Sundays in the loft she had been particularly circumspect, knowing that if she distracted him in any way he'd throw her out.

Maxi was so much in love and so much in awe of Rocco that her normal reaction had been frozen. She realized that she hadn't been herself since she first laid eyes on him but she didn't know *how* to become herself with this man, who certainly had not been affected by her in the same way as any other man or boy she'd ever met. Love had generated in Maxi a condition in which every ordinary act of Rocco's was invested with absolute charm. If he scratched his head she was charmed. If he bit on his knuckles in thought she was charmed. When he hummed to himself she caught a glimpse of paradise. Maxi's eyes traced the perfect lines of his lips with a mixture of reverence and desperate longing. Her heartstrings pulled her toward him but she stayed immobile, wildly yearning, yearning with a violence that she knew she would never feel for any other man as long as she lived. She was filled with all the unutterable confusion and single-minded passion of first love. If she could just lift one of the soft black curls on his forehead and touch, just touch the skin underneath. If she could just rub the back of her hand against his cheek. But she didn't dare. The risk was too great.

As she knelt there, paralyzed with longing, Rocco's words suddenly hit her.

"Well, that ought to do it," he'd said, and stopped working. She knew him well enough to realize that he had finished with the November issue. Of course the December issue would be attacked next week but without the same need to invent a new graphic style that had been pushing him to work seven-day weeks. She had never thought about this moment before. Somehow she had let herself believe that these weekends in the loft would continue on . . . but her summer job would last only another five weeks. Panic struck Maxi. Tomorrow she would go back to work, just another body in the crowded art department, fetching and carrying and bringing coffee, and that right minute she had never been able to clearly imagine would never present itself—that absolutely necessary minute when Rocco would finally *see* her.

With panic Maxi became Maxi again. The enchantment that had rendered her ineffective, inert, was lifted, a spell broken. Her motto, discovered in French class, was the words of Danton: "Boldness, again boldness and ever boldness." For a minute she paced silently about the loft, and then, whispering "Boldness" to

172

herself, she stripped off her T-shirt and her jeans and her underwear in a few silent but resolute motions. She untied her espadrilles and stood naked, as rosy and voluptuous as a Boucher, with her full, well-separated breasts that were so young that in spite of their weight they tilted upward from her narrow rib cage. Below her tiny, firm waist, where her white flesh was marked by the belt she had just dropped on the floor, her hips swelled out deliciously, in an excellent yet immoderate curve.

Nakedness was as natural to Maxi as to Eve. She was so perfectly proportioned that without clothes she seemed taller than when she was dressed. She ran her fingers through her long hair, shaking her head slightly, unable to move for a second. Boldness, she thought, *boldness!* She tiptoed over to the bed and bent over Rocco, reassured to see that he was in the deepest possible sleep. Carefully, as lightly as a flower, she lay down next to him, her delicate yet lavish body finding a place to nestle. She lifted herself up so that she hung over his face. Boldness, she prayed as she began to kiss him awake, so softly, so sweetly, so gently that it was many minutes before he began to stir and mutter complainingly. She undid the buttons of his shirt and kissed his chest and his throat until he floated up to consciousness, and when she saw him open his eyes she finally kissed him on his mouth, kissed him once and then kept on kissing his lips, moving higher so that her breasts rested on his bare chest, lightly holding his shoulders down on the bed until he woke up completely and tried to sit up.

"Maxi? *Maxi?*" he said in amazement.

She rolled over on her back and looked up at him through the tangle of her hair, looked right into his astonished eyes. She laughed her great, deep, free, joyous laugh that he'd never heard before.

"I hope you weren't expecting somebody else," she answered as he bent toward her and eagerly pulled her to him.

12

A s we used to say in the RAF," India West remarked thoughtfully, "you've bought the farm, Maxi."

"And just exactly what does that mean?" Maxi asked anxiously. India West was never, *never* wrong. She was only fifteen, two years younger than Maxi, but from the moment the two of them had met in school, while trying, as usual, to avoid gym class, they had been best friends, joined by an instantaneous appreciation of each other which included a decided preference for heightened versions of the truth. People sometimes took them for liars, as Maxi once explained to India, but they were only rearranging life to make it more interesting for everybody, a public service, as it were.

"Crashed your plane," India said absently, looking at herself in the mirror. "I think I'm getting rather . . . well, beautiful. What do you think?"

"You know you're beautiful. When haven't you been divinely beautiful? Stop trying to change the subject. We were talking about me."

India had just come back from Saratoga where she had spent the summer with her family. Lily Amberville, the boys and the servants were expected back from Southampton at the end of August. Finally Maxi had somebody she could talk to about Rocco. Rocco was besotted, infatuated, fascinated, her captive. They had been together every minute of the summer, at work and after work, since the first night in July. He was in love with her, truly in love, seriously in love. He had told her so, and Rocco, unlike Maxi, never told anything but the truth. Maxi, in her rapture, couldn't understand why India, usually so insouciant, saw a problem in her flawless love.

"Seventeen is not nineteen. An Amberville is not an Adams," India said.

"My birthday's tomorrow, I'll be eighteen, and I'm exactly the same person he's in love with," Maxi protested.

"Not really."

"You mean you think he won't love me when he finds out? India! That's ridiculous."

"No, I mean something else, and you know perfectly well what I mean. Just because we go to a school which is politely called 'an alternative form of education' doesn't mean that either of us is an idiot," India said severely.

"So, O.K. My father is a rich man . . ."

"Ha!"

"One of the richest men in America, all right? And I don't go to Vassar, after all. I'm still in high school. Do two mere years and a father with tons of money make me a leper?"

"You lied to him."

"I lie to *everybody.*"

"So do I . . . but you said Rocco always tells the truth. That means he won't trust you anymore. How can a self-respecting, hardworking young man from a nice conservative Italian family with a strong sense of his own values carry on a flaming affair with teenaged Miss Amberville, his boss's daughter? What does that make him? You're supposed to be his 'trainee.' What does that do to his career? Apparently the man cares a lot about his work. How can he ever trust you again? You've taken him in completely, poor sucker, and if it had started a year ago you'd be jailbait. And God knows what the consequences will be when Pa and Ma Amberville find out."

India used her voice as effectively as a master bellringer, ringing changes in tones so that no one of any age could ignore her when she spoke. Even Maxi felt effectively subdued, accustomed as she was to the India phenomenon.

"I wish you wouldn't talk to me like that," Maxi said, taking her streak of white hair and twisting it between her thumb and forefinger and pulling it until it hurt. She was, in spite of her bravado, aware that she'd painted herself into corners before, but this corner didn't have any floor left.

"India, I need you," she said nervously. "I have a terrible practical problem. My family's due back here in a week and my freedom will be gone. I've been telling Rocco that they're still in Europe. If I tell him they're back he'll expect to meet them . . . he's old-fashioned about things like meeting parents."

"Ah, so," said India impassively.

"School doesn't start for three more weeks," Maxi continued. "I can tell him they're still away until then if you'll cover for me. I'll tell them I'm with you when I'm with Rocco, and on the nights when I simply have to show my face for dinner at home, I'll tell Rocco I'm with you. Does that make sense?"

"If he's so old-fashioned, wouldn't he expect you to introduce him to your best friend?"

"I'll say that . . . that you have a phobia. You're afraid to leave the house. Agoraphobia, it's well known."

"Why wouldn't he come to see me? You said he's wonderfully compassionate."

"You're afraid to meet strangers. It's another one of your phobias. He can talk to you on the phone. Reassuringly."

"That takes care of him. What about Pa and Ma? How come we're virtually inseparable?"

"I'll tell them that I'm helping you study so you can skip into my class."

"*You're* helping *me* study?"

"Sure. They know I can when I want to. It would be a good deed. And if they call your house to talk to me you answer, and make something up about why I'm not there." India was a much more inventive and believable liar than even Maxi could ever hope to be.

"Which means I have to spend the next three weeks hanging around my telephone," India grumbled. "And what happens when school really starts? And you really have homework? You won't be able to get out of the house so easily."

"Just give me these three weeks with him . . . by then I'll have figured something out."

"There's always the truth."

"India, please," Maxi pleaded, horrified. "You don't seem to understand. This is the most important thing that's ever happened

176

to me. Nothing like this will ever happen to me again . . . I *have* to make it work out. The *truth* . . . please don't even *think* that word. It's too late for the . . . you know what."

"The highest compact we can make with our fellow man is 'Let there be truth between us two forevermore,'" India intoned.

"Why are you torturing me?"

"It's Emerson, Ralph Waldo. I'm reading him. Can I help it if I have a trick memory?"

"Could you please try to remember things on your own time?"

"He also said, 'Keep cool; it will be all one a hundred years hence.'"

"You're a comfort to me, India, you really are. Why did I pick a precocious brat for a best friend?"

"'In skating over thin ice our safety is our speed.'"

"Emerson again?"

"Is he boring you?"

"No, he's making me feel nervous." Maxi's jade-green eyes, widened by anxiety, seemed to absorb all the light in the room into their tantalizing depths.

"Listen, Maxi, is it really all that much fun to fool around?" India asked, with sudden timidity.

"Fooling around," said Maxi, "is the *ultimate fun.*"

"Damn, I was afraid you'd say that."

It wasn't until early October that the truth caught up with Maxi. She had spent so much of her mental energy on hopping and skipping between the lies she and India were telling an increasingly large number of people that she had overlooked one of the normal concerns of most females who are making love as often as is humanly possible. She was at least a month, perhaps two, gone with child, as India delicately put it, when together they counted the weeks since Maxi's last period. They looked at each other in solemn, awed, horrified silence for some time. For the first time since they'd met, neither one of them was trying to interrupt the other. Suddenly the suggestion of a smile that always shaped Maxi's lower lip turned into a huge grin and her delicate, wicked, witty face radiated uncomplicated delight.

"Fun," she breathed, "what heavenly, groovy, fabulous fun. Incredible fun. Oh, WHAT FUN!" She jumped up, lifted India, who was already an inch taller than she, and whirled her around the room in glee.

"Fun?" India squeaked indignantly. "Put me down, you damn fool! Fun?"

"A baby. A darling little baby. A little boy who looks just like Rocco. A bambino all pink and white and chubby with black curls. Oh, I can't wait! I'll learn to knit, I'll take lessons in natural child-birth, I wish he could be born tomorrow . . . didn't I tell you something would happen and everything would be all right? And to have all this fun too, on top of it . . . I can't believe how lucky I am!"

"Lord have mercy." India collapsed in a chair, disbelief in every bone.

"Is that your only reaction? What's wrong with you?" Maxi demanded. "I thought you knew how to have fun."

"Maybe my idea of fun isn't the same as yours," India said faintly. "And, Miz Scarlett, I don't know nothin' 'bout birthin' babies."

"It's my fault," said Nina. "I was the one who thought she should have a job."

"It's my fault," Zachary insisted. "I was the one who agreed."

"It's my fault," Pavka insisted. "I was the one who put her in that art department. And Linda Lafferty says it's entirely her fault."

"Actually, Pavka," said Nina, "it's your secretary's fault, the one who worships you. She picked *Savoir Vivre.*"

"Listen, you two, it isn't anybody's fault except Maxi's. God knows Rocco can't be blamed . . . the poor bastard never had a chance once Maxi made up her mind," Zachary said.

"What does Lily think?" Pavka asked Zachary.

"She's too busy with the wedding arrangements to have time to think. As far as she's concerned, barely eighteen is a good age to get married if you're not doing anything else with your life. She wasn't much older when we got married. But she insists on a big English wedding with all the nonessentials: bridesmaids, flower

178

girls strewing rose petals, pages in velvet pants, the house turned upside down for the reception. The only problem is one of time . . . they should be married as soon as possible. They'd be married by now if it weren't for Lily's plans. But Maxi doesn't care one way or the other . . . she's having too much 'fun' to worry about *how* premature the baby will be . . . I'm beginning to have visions of her doing a two-step down the aisle carrying the baby instead of a bouquet."

"And Rocco?" Pavka said curiously.

"What about him? Linda Lafferty says that the two of you agree that he's doing a fine job," Zachary said, slightly on the defensive.

"I don't mean his work . . . what about his family?"

"They think anything he does is perfect," Zachary replied. "We finally got everybody together for dinner and it went as well as any first-time meeting of future in-laws, better maybe. Joe Cipriani was in the Air Force in Korea, so we told war stories and Anna, Rocco's mother, and Lily talked silver patterns and china patterns and wedding dresses, and Maxi just sat there looking as if she'd accomplished a miracle and won the Nobel Prize for reproduction, and Rocco didn't have anything to say. He looked as if he'd been hit over the head with a club, or run over by a train, or both."

"Then why on earth," Nina wondered, "are the three of us sitting around here and worrying about something that everyone else thinks is perfectly fine?"

"Because we all know Maxi," Zachary answered grimly.

Angelica Amberville Cipriani entered the great world in April of 1973, just a little more than six months after Maxi and Rocco were married, a perfectly respectable degree of prematurity in any society high or low, since the world began counting on its fingers. Rocco had snapped out of his catatonic state once the wedding actually took place and Maxi had delightedly given up her senior year of high school to prepare Rocco's loft for the arrival of the baby.

Lily and Zachary had both tried to insist that the baby should come home from the hospital to a comfortable apartment where

Maxi could have a nanny to help her and someone in the kitchen to cook and someone else to clean. They took it for granted that they would buy and furnish the apartment and subsidize the salaries of the staff, but Rocco had firmly refused to take anything from them other than a traditional wedding present of a silver service. He was making thirty-five thousand dollars a year, and the habit of total financial independence was deeply rooted in him. His own parents had contributed nothing to his upkeep from the day he won his first scholarship to art school, and he had no worries about earning enough to support a wife and child. Maxi was now eighteen, and many other girls in the world in which he had grown up were capable mothers by that age, in competent charge of their modest households.

Maxi approached the future with blissful energy. She went to three different cooking schools so that she could offer Rocco a choice of French, Italian and Chinese food; she took classes in two separate methods of giving birth, just in case she changed her mind in mid-process; she shopped at Saks and Bloomingdale's and even ventured all the way to Macy's, in order to buy a layette complete in every detail. Sensibly, she stored the dozens of barrels of wedding gifts in a warehouse, except for pots and pans, a set of pottery, stainless-steel tableware and inexpensive glass goblets.

Fortunately, Rocco's loft was spacious enough so that with the help of two neighborhood carpenters they were able to divide it into three separate areas: the baby's corner, a kitchen and storage section, and a third space in which they would live, eat, sleep, and in which Rocco would have his work table. Rocco had suggested that the third room be further divided to give him a separate workroom, but, as Maxi pointed out, she intended to continue being helpful to him when he needed her, so that didn't make sense. It would be the perfect harmony of last summer, she thought, with the additional joy of the bambino sleeping snugly away in its own little domain.

Maxi sat on a hard bench in a small neighborhood park with two scrawny trees, rocking the English pram, conspicuous by its size, its brilliant blue finish, its high, elegant wheels and the fringe on the canvas cover that kept the sun out of Angelica's eyes. It was August, and hot and humid as only August in Manhattan can be; the city lay enclosed in a monstrous bowl of airless, evil-smelling gray-yellow stuff that might be air but would kill most Amazonian Indians. Maxi wore shorts and a halter top and flat sandals. Although she'd pinned up her hair on top of her head to keep it off her neck, sweat-wet strands kept escaping. She fanned herself to no avail with a copy of *Rolling Stone*, fighting the urge to foam at the mouth, howl like a dog and demand a recount.

I will think about the fun things, she said to herself rigidly. Rocco is fun when he isn't working on that double-sized Christmas issue. Angelica is fun when she isn't screaming, and keeping us awake. Being married is fun when Angelica is sleeping and Rocco isn't working. Cooking is fun when . . . no, cooking wasn't really what you could call fun. Not when you had to clean up afterwards. That makes about one fun hour in every forty-eight hours. At least one hour that might have been fun if it weren't so hot and humid. NOTHING is fun in New York in August, she thought savagely, unless the fucking air conditioning works.

Their two inadequate window units had both blown from old age when the heat wave started three weeks earlier, and getting new ones in the middle of the hottest summer in years was proving impossible. Day after day Maxi waited for their promised arrival and day after day she was forced to realize that once again they weren't going to be delivered.

Each morning Zachary phoned to beg her to go out to Southampton with the baby, every night Rocco assured her that she was crazy to stay in town, that he'd be perfectly all right on his own during the week, and promised to come out every weekend, but Maxi, stubborn as she had never been before in a lifetime dedicated to having things her own way, refused to budge.

The first summer, she told herself, was the time of testing, the exam that she knew everybody expected her to flunk. But she was going to stick it out in the city; she wasn't going to run off to her parents' like a child and abandon her husband when he was working so hard, leaving him bereft of wife and child and tender care. She didn't intend him to be a weekend husband who missed seeing his baby grow up during these few precious months. To turn tail and run off to the cool breezes and the ocean and servants bringing cold glasses of freshly squeezed fruit juice . . . No! She took out a damp wad of Kleenex and mopped up the rivulets of sweat that crept down her neck.

Why couldn't she stop thinking about white? White linen, white sand, little dabs of white clouds in a blue sky over a blue sea, virgin white Pampers, white tennis shoes, maids in white aprons, big, white wooden houses, white wicker tables set with crisp white lace cloths and white Limoges china. White seemed the last thing Manhattan had to offer this particular August, except for the filthy litter of once-white paper that blew about her feet.

Angelica woke up howling. Maxi picked her up and fanned her frantically. In spite of constant sponging and cool baths the baby had heat rash or prickly heat or some sort of other irritation in half the folds of her plump, four-month-old body. She was a pretty baby, except when her face was screwed up in misery, as it had been for most of the summer. "Poor baby," Maxi crooned, and felt tears come into her own eyes. "Poor, poor little baby. I feel so sorry for you, really I do," she sobbed into Angelica's neck, "oh, poor, unfortunate, brave little baby, what a good little girl you are, and nobody gives you any credit for it, no they don't, they don't, they don't!" Angelica stopped crying and opened her eyes and pulled on a stray piece of Maxi's hair and smiled at her. *"Oh,"* wept Maxi harder than ever, seeing the smile, "you poor little thing!"

She leapt up from the bench and, running, wheeled the pram out of the park. A small cab stopped, seeing her frenzied wave, and Maxi simply abandoned the imported, five-hundred-dollar object on the corner without a second thought, scooped up Angelica and slid into the taxi.

"The Saint Regis Hotel," she told the driver. "Hurry, it's an emergency."

Amberville Publications kept a permanent suite at the St. Regis for visiting customers and everyone at the reception desk knew Maxi on sight. She was escorted to the five-room suite with as much chucking and concern as if she had just been pulled into a lifeboat from engulfing waves. Maxi flopped down on one of the beds, clutching her baby, and for a while nothing mattered except the cool air. As soon as she felt enough energy returning, she filled a tub full of tepid water, took off everything she and Angelica were wearing, unpinned her hair and stepped cautiously into the water with the baby in her arms. She lay back in the big tub and floated Angelica above her breasts, supporting her under her armpits and nuzzling her tiny nose. She made little crooning noises and swished Angelica back and forth; a mermaid and her young.

Soon, restored to full efficiency, Maxi bundled herself and the baby into huge towels and attacked the telephone. First she called Saks for baby shirts and nighties, a crib, another pram, baby bed linen and a rocking chair. Then she called Bonwit's for an assortment of negligees, short silk pajamas and cotton shirts and shorts for herself. Next she telephoned the hotel florist and told him to send up a dozen white vases filled with white flowers. The druggist was instructed to bring up baby oil, baby powder, Pampers and shampoo. Then she phoned F.A.O. Schwarz and ordered a mobile to hang over the crib and duplicates of all her own favorites among Angelica's stuffed animals. She called the hotel desk and dispatched bellboys in every direction to pick up her purchases immediately, and then she called room service and ordered lunch. Yes, they could puree carrots and white meat of chicken, they assured her. Finally, Maxi called Rocco at the office.

"Darling," she said excitedly, "I've just discovered the most marvelous place for us to spend the summer, and it's only a few blocks from your office."

August heat waves are normal in New York but, as any native knows, they can be almost as bad in September. "Autumn in New York" is a song that should clearly specify October, just as "April in Paris" is a song that should mention the necessity to bring umbrellas, warmly lined raincoats and waterproof boots. Maxi, Rocco and Angelica were sheltered by the friendly walls of the St. Regis for another five weeks. Although Rocco couldn't help realizing that the room-service bills alone were more than his weekly salary, he forced himself not to protest. No matter how he felt, he reasoned, he couldn't insist that the baby be subjected to the heat of the loft. Time enough for them to go home when it was cool again.

"I think we should move back tonight," Maxi said to him one morning in late September, as he left for work.

"I thought you were trying to hold out till the first snow," Rocco said, smiling at her flushed, happy face, and nibbling the tip of her impudently pointed nose.

"I'm tired of room service," she murmured, licking his chest as high up as she could reach between two of his shirt buttons, underneath his necktie, a maneuver at which she had become expert while holding the baby.

"I'll try to come home as early as I can and help you pack."

"Don't bother, sweetheart, I have all day and the hotel staff promised to do most of it for me . . . just come back and pick the two of us up."

That evening, when he reached the hotel, he found Maxi and Angelica waiting in the lobby to meet him.

"Everything's done," she said triumphantly. They got into a cab and the doorman gave the driver an address and waved them farewell.

"Why is he going uptown?" Rocco asked.

"I wanted to stop by and see my family first," Maxi said gaily.

"Then why has he passed your parents' house?" Rocco said patiently, realizing that Maxi had planned one of the surprises she loved so much: learning to make tortellini for instance, or framing a group of his sketches with her own inexpert hands, or finding an old dress for Angelica in a thrift shop and producing the baby trailing a cascade of Victorian lace.

"Because they're visiting Toby," she said vaguely.

"And Toby's visiting a friend?"

"Right. You're so smart. Did you know I married you for your acute intelligence and not merely for your impossible brooding beauty?"

"I thought *I* married you because I knocked you up. That's more or less the general opinion," Rocco said, delighted with the mischief in her eyes. He had surrendered to her as he would to a girl in a most improbable, happy dream. Sometimes his young wife was, as tonight, the embodiment of a delightful practical joke.

"Not in front of the baby!" Maxi whispered.

The cab finally came to a stop before a handsome apartment

building on Seventy-sixth Street, between Fifth and Madison. They took the elevator up to the fifth floor and walked along a wide corridor until Maxi rang a doorbell. A uniformed maid opened the door with a smile of greeting.

"Nobody here?" Rocco asked, looking around the big, white-walled, well-shaped room, all brown and terra-cotta and burnt umber, furnished in a way he immediately liked although he didn't know exactly why.

"They must be somewhere," Maxi said, wandering away from him toward a hallway. "Anybody home?" she called.

"Don't you think we should wait in the living room?"

"Come on, sweetheart, they must be here somewhere," Maxi answered from the hall, and Rocco followed her as she flitted through charmingly furnished but unpeopled rooms: a baby's room, a huge bedroom with a four-poster bed covered with an antique quilt, and a shining kitchen, where the maid was cooking busily. In the red-walled little dining room, where the round French provincial table was laid for two, he finally grabbed her and tried to make her stop. "Sit down and wait. You can't just go through someone's house like this, not even you. Or is this some kind of a surprise party?" She eluded him, still carrying Angelica.

"Wait, there's one more room. Maybe they're in there, hiding." She opened another door and Rocco found himself standing in a well-lit room bare of all but his work table, his chair and all his working equipment, everything arranged perfectly, not one familiar item missing.

Maxi faced him, absolutely delighted with herself. "Don't think this happened overnight," she said proudly.

"This . . . ?"

"Is *our* house. 'Surprise party!' You aren't as smart as I thought," she teased.

"You know what I said about not taking anything from your parents . . . how could you do this, Maxi?" Rocco asked quietly.

"I fully respect what you said. This has nothing to do with it," she answered, beaming with satisfaction.

"Then where does it come from?"

"Me. From me to you, from me to me, from me to Angelica."

"What do you mean, 'me'?"

"My very own trust fund. The one Daddy set up when I was born. I came into it on my last birthday. There's another one I'll get when I'm twenty-one and another when I'm twenty-five . . . Justin and Toby have them too, of course. It's a way to give your kids something while you're still alive so that the government doesn't get it all when you die," Maxi explained, not too sure of the precise details.

"Your father, *knowing you,* gave you a large sum of money?" Rocco said, disbelief clear in his voice.

"Oh, once it was set up there wasn't anything he could do to change it. Otherwise I guess he might not have trusted me with so much. But, you see, he would have been wrong, wouldn't he? I haven't done anything wildly extravagant, considering."

"Considering what?"

"That I got five million dollars."

"Five million dollars."

"Honestly, Rocco, including the price of buying the apartment, all I've spent isn't even three-quarters of a million."

"Three-quarters of a million."

"Well, it's not a big apartment . . . just enough for the three of us," Maxi explained patiently. Rocco didn't seem to be too bright tonight. "We'll move when we have another baby."

"Are you expecting another baby?" Rocco asked in a tightly neutral tone of voice. "Is that another surprise for tonight?"

"Not yet, for heaven's sake!"

"Let's go."

"Go where?"

"Back to Soho. If I won't take anything from your parents, how could you possibly imagine I'd take this . . . this place . . . from you?" he asked, pale with outraged fury, insulted to the marrow of his bones.

"But it has nothing to do with my parents. It's totally *different*—I bought and furnished this apartment with *my own money.* Surely I have a right to spend my own money, Rocco? After all, it's for *us,* for us to share."

"I can't do it. I'm sorry, Maxi, but there is no way I can do it. It goes against everything I believe in."

186

"You're just being stubborn and old-fashioned Italian, and typically male," she said, her patient tone wearing thin.

"I'm being me. You should have known me better when we got married. I haven't changed."

"Neither have I," Maxi flashed at him, outraged.

"And that," said Rocco, "is the whole problem. One of us is going to have to change." His hands were balled into fists. He should have known. He'd had warning after warning but ignored them, soft fool that he was, not wanting to believe that she was so deeply spoiled, so thoughtlessly capricious.

"Don't look at me, Rocco Cipriani," Maxi shouted.

"Goodbye, Maxi," he said briefly, afraid that any other words would be irremediably cruel, even more cruel than the end of their marriage. He'd feared this minute from the beginning, but he had tried to overlook his uneasy intuition of Maxi's true character. "I'll send for my stuff."

Openmouthed, Maxi looked at the empty room. She heard the front door close quietly, she waited a few minutes for the doorbell to ring and then she carried Angelica into the lovingly furnished living room and sat down on one of the big, russet velvet sofas. "He'll be back, Angelica," she said to the baby. "He just needs to understand that he can't boss me around like that. Who does he think he is, anyway? *Nobody* talks to me like that, do you hear, nobody!" and she burst into tears of a fearful grief, for she knew already that neither one of them was going to change, neither was capable of change. He couldn't even try, because of his absurd, unnecessary pride, that stubborn bastard, and she would not, would, absolutely, not! She was Maxi Amberville, after all. *So why the hell should she?*

13

Maxi never spent so much as one single night in the apartment she had decorated with such disastrous joy. She arranged for Rocco's work table and supplies to be sent back to him the next day and instructed her real estate agent to sell everything, including the last copper-bottomed saucepan, as quickly as possible, at whatever price was first offered.

The divorce was handled with tactful dispatch and without publicity by the Amberville corps of legal experts. Once Rocco had achieved joint custody of Angelica he agreed that the baby should live with Maxi on a full-time basis. He had returned to work at Condé Nast, and the only alternative arrangement possible for him was to hire a nurse to care for Angelica while he was away at the office, which made no sense since the baby had a perfectly good mother. However, as often as possible, he exercised his right to take Angelica for the weekend, joining the legion of divorced fathers in the park nearby with the doubtful distinction of having the youngest child in his group.

Maxi tried to get through the period of her divorce by concentrating ferociously on each detail of raising her daughter. She became an expert on denial; not thinking, not remembering, not asking herself questions, not wondering "what if" while she conferred with six different but patient Madison Avenue grocers on the quality of their juice oranges and the provenance of their chicken breasts. Nevertheless an appalling, punishing pain located in the very middle of her being vibrated like a tuning fork except when she was actually communing with Angelica, but that healthy baby spent far too much of her first year asleep. Maxi endured the raw torment with silence, for she understood that she had no alternative. Meanwhile she would bathe and feed Angelica and take her downstairs to visit with Lily and Zachary. She had returned home the night Rocco had walked out of the new apartment, seeking the surest refuge she knew.

This period of mourning lasted throughout the fall of 1973 and the winter of 1974. It wasn't until late in the spring of her nineteenth year that finally there came a day on which Maxi realized that she could now dare to take stock. She prepared herself for this process by piling her bed high with pillows and lying back on them after she'd applied the warm, sweet-smelling sleeping body of Angelica on her chest like a mustard plaster. The little girl was over a year old and satisfactorily big enough to provide considerable protection for an adult unfortunate enough to have to examine her own mental condition.

What was her exact position in life? Maxi wondered. How should she define herself? She had a daughter, she was divorced and in a few months she'd be twenty. She was no longer an adolescent, she would never be a debutante, she was not a college girl, nor was she an unwed mother. On the other hand she wasn't a working woman with a career. It seemed that she was left with only one category to fill: that of the interesting, no, make that the *fascinating,* young divorcée. If people still used that word.

What then were the options of this young divorcée who possessed millions from her first installment of her trust fund? In principle the world must be full of endless options for someone with so much money and so much time. Obviously she could stay on living in this great gray house, safe, secure and cared for, yet able to come and go as she chose, since she now had the status of adult rather than that of schoolgirl. Using her parents' home as a base she could venture forth at will to . . . to . . . do what?

In the first place she could—and probably should—go to college in Manhattan, Maxi ruminated, but damn it, first she'd have to finish high school. Years of bouncing around the backwaters and byways of the educational system had taught her that there would always be a high school that could be persuaded to accept her for the senior year she'd missed. Therefore college was a distinct possibility. But did she really feel like taking on the burden of any additional education? Wasn't it now somehow too late and yet too early to return to academia? Scratch college.

Of course there was travel. She could take Angelica and hire a nanny and spend six months or a year in England where her grandparents would introduce her to the world. Maxi's eyes almost closed as she imagined herself conquering London. She'd buy the wildest dresses Zandra Rhodes had ever designed, she'd rent a big flat on Eaton Square, she'd keep a Rolls—no, a Bentley—no, a Daimler, the kind of car the Queen always used that was too wide for American roads, and she'd plunge into all the delights of London society that her mother hadn't bothered about, with the help of the good offices of the nineteenth Baronet and second Viscount Adamsfield. Ah, if only the sixties weren't over. Yet somewhere they must still be lurking, even if the swinging had stopped. Yes . . . London . . . Maxi smiled into the dimness of canopied chintz above her bed until suddenly her eyes popped wide open in surprised pique as reality returned. Rocco, that impossible, doting Italian papa, would never allow her to take Angelica away from him for six months at one time. Never. So travel was not an option except for a week or two at the longest. Scratch travel.

A job? A willingness to do the lowliest task in the art department had landed her where she was now. Perhaps the working world was not for her? Anyway she had a child to take care of. Scratch work.

She seemed to be stuck right here, lying on her bed back at home. And that was out. Out! It *felt* wrong, no matter how much her parents obviously wanted her to stay.

Maxi blew carefully into Angelica's hair and nibbled on one dark curl. Her parents didn't trust her to exist on her own. She could see it in their eyes although they were careful not to say anything to indicate that the present arrangement was anything but temporary. But she could read their anxious minds. They'd like her to stay here until another man, a more appropriate one, appeared to lure her back into a domesticity that Maxi had no intention of attempting again.

The process of elimination had left her with only one option. She must have her *own* place in Manhattan. Out! If she didn't move she'd fall back into the comfortable, familiar, but decidedly outgrown role of the daughter of the house. Maxi felt a licking, brief bite of apprehension. She'd never lived alone. She had gone right from her father's house to her husband's house and then straight back to her father's house.

All the more reason, Maxi thought, her lips tightened defiantly, to get on with it. She'd start house hunting tomorrow. She wanted a town house since she couldn't have London, a dear little brownstone in which she could entertain her friends. What friends? Since that day—oh diabolic day—that she'd walked into the art department of *Savoir Vivre*, two years ago, she'd been so involved in the unfolding drama of her own life that she'd lost touch with everybody she knew of her own age except India who had so selfishly gone to college. Still, she must know *someone*. Hadn't a famous hostess once said that all you had to do to attract guests was to open a can of sardines and spread the word? She would buy a can opener, Maxi resolved, and a case of sardines. If life had taught her anything it was that one thing led to another. If there had been any other lessons along the way, she'd missed them.

Once Maxi had resolved to leave her parents' protection she'd quickly found the perfect small town house and discovered a team of decorators, Ludwig and Bizet, to help her turn it into a setting that had nothing to do with chronology. It was not the home of an impulsive girl but of a serene heiress with a leaning toward eclectic interiors that cunningly defrosted Louis XV with Venetian touches of high fantasy, the combination mellowed with English chintz.

After Maxi's first timid venture into introspection she brooded long and often about her future. She had discarded the category of young divorcée almost as quickly as she had thought of it. There were so many other divorced women in Manhattan, forming a vast, unchartered club she'd rather not join. With far more art and discipline than she had employed in preparing herself for her first day at work, she carefully went about creating a new Maxime Emma Amberville Cipriani, one who would be immediately recognizable as a *widow*. Widowhood—early, cruel, accidental and mysterious widowhood—was a condition so much more desirable than any other open to her. It was a state that combined a certain mournfully elegant status with a distinction and an aura of—poetry?—yes, poetry, if you did it right, she thought, her lips quivering with a suppressed grin.

Maxi worked her way toward widowhood by the elegiac tempering of her smile; by the suddenly tremulous silences into which she fell unexpectedly; by a finely tuned, brave dignity in which she wrapped herself. She dimmed the field of energy in which she usually moved and turned it inward, so that it was obvious—but never immediately or painfully obvious—that she was suffering from an unspoken sorrow with which she would trouble no one. Now she dressed in black at all times: quiet, serious, expensive, indecently becoming black. The only jewelry she wore had been her parents' wedding present, a glorious double strand of Burmese pearls, graduated from twelve to nineteen millimeters, each perfectly round globe radiating a matchless luster, and of course, the widow's necessary ornament, a modest, plain wedding band she longed to throw in the garbage. As soon as Maxi found herself alone at home she changed immediately into old jeans and worn T-shirts but she never left the house unless she was raven-clad from head to toe, even if she were going to the country in black pants and a black silk blouse. Maxi used her makeup skills to achieve a delicious pallor, she threw away her collection of blushers and lipsticks and concentrated on demurely darkening the area around her eyes with smoky grays and taupes. If only India were around to appreciate her efforts, she thought longingly, as she staged her effects.

Just as Maxi forbade herself her belly laugh she made a rule never to talk about herself. Instead she grew adept at drawing people out on their all-time favorite subject: themselves. She learned to subtly sidestep all questions about her private life and automatically refused two out of every three of her many invitations—for the sardines had worked marvelously well—in order to stay home with Angelica. Although she was deeply, constantly tempted, she never went so far as to tell anyone that Rocco Cipriani was dead—stone-cold dead—but she never referred to a former husband, or a previous marriage.

Since the length of time people bother to remember details of each other's private lives in Manhattan is determined by how much fuel is flung on the fire, Maxi achieved established widowhood within a year, by her twenty-first birthday.

It was not a widowhood without distractions. She took with utmost discretion, a baker's dozen of lovers, in not too rapid succession; each one impeccable, eligible, eager to marry her and free of any problems presented by an alliance with a man who might not understand that her money was her own to spend as she liked. Yet not one of them had seemed somehow *necessary* enough to keep longer than a few months. Maxi became convinced that she'd never fall in love again and the thought, although melancholy, was balanced by the freedom it gave her. She had become, she flattered herself, an updated Henry James heroine, a woman with a past that was only dimly known; whose present was tantalizingly private yet illuminated by the blaze of her independence, her family, her fortune, and—why not be blunt—her face; a woman whose future held infinite promise.

One fragrant August in 1978, Maxi drifted toward the entrance to the Casino in Monte Carlo. She idled along alone in the darkness, relaxed in the knowledge that the principality had one policeman for every five visitors and every woman could safely wear all her jewelry in public on the darkest street of the little city. In her bones she felt there was a lucky seat at the chemin de fer table just waiting for her but she wasn't in a hurry to get into the action.

This was Maxi's first evening in Monte Carlo and literally the first time in her life that she was utterly free to come and go as she pleased, alone and on her own, unquestioned, unaccounted for and accountable to no one. Her parents were in Southampton. Rocco had finally been able to arrange matters at the magazine so that he had August off and he had taken Angelica to visit his parents in the country outside of Hartford.

Maxi had refused a number of proposals to be a houseguest or to join traveling friends, and quietly reserved a suite for herself at the Hotel de Paris in Monte Carlo, a corner suite, majestically proportioned, with a great semicircular balcony off the sitting room from which she had watched the sunset. Far below her she could see the crowded port of Monte Carlo; beyond it on a jutting, rocky promontory, rose the palace and beyond the palace was the remarkable sky, meeting the remarkable sea on which dozens of pleasure craft were coming into the harbor. There was no hint from the view from Maxi's suite that every week one more of the charming Edwardian villas that, for so long, were the enchantment of the city, was demolished, each to be replaced by yet another, Miami-modern high-rise apartment building; no hint that every last square inch of Grimaldi territory was being exploited with an unsentimental thoroughness that was far more Swiss than Mediterranean.

August, no matter how hot, is *the* season for Monte Carlo, the month of balls and fireworks, of ballet and of a gathering together of a particular—and often peculiar—assortment of royalty-groupie rich from all over who never miss that once-a-year visit to Monaco. August is the one thirty-one-day bonus period during which those tax exiles from ninety-nine countries whose lawyers and accountants command them to become residents of Monaco, can rent their expensive dwellings and make enough to pay for their upkeep during the other eleven months; the one month during which the harbor yacht moorings are at a premium, the one month in which the myth of Monte Carlo is annually reborn.

Maxi felt intoxicatingly reborn herself. In anticipation of her trip she had assembled a new wardrobe that filled seven suitcases, a wardrobe from which all black was banished; she had armed herself with an enormous letter of credit to a local bank and just that afternoon she had changed so many dollars into francs that her evening bag bulged.

A certain Beekman Place high-stakes poker game, which took place nightly in New York, had occasionally enlivened her sumptuous early widowhood, but Maxi had always had a yen to visit a real casino that would in no way resemble Las Vegas. Gambling, she thought, was a little like shopping . . . you couldn't really do it right as part of a couple. Call it what you will—a question of skill, a matter of luck, or even just picking numbers—all gambling boiled down to choice, and choice was not a collaborative or a cooperative pursuit, arrived at with someone looking over your shoulder and making suggestions. It would be good for her, Maxi thought virtuously, to have a fling. Widowhood was so constricting. She *deserved* a fling, and obviously everyone in the crowd that pressed toward the entrance to the Casino felt equally festive.

The first large rooms of the ornate building were disappointing; filled with casually clad tourists playing slot machines, the high, painted ceilings seeming to look down in grief on such ignoble goings-on. But once past the stern men who guarded the entrance to the private rooms, Maxi discovered that the legend of the Casino of Monte Carlo still existed, as uncompromisingly authentic, as firmly locked into history as if it were a four-masted sailing ship that had somehow sailed out of the past. An Edwardian glamour, voluptuous and unashamed, showered down in gilded splendor; a sweeping waltztime drowned out the mad jazz tempo of the first rooms, a pink glow replaced the popping lights of the slot machines. Low-voiced, purposeful, well-dressed people moved here and there in the air that was charged with an almost unbearable excitement, the thrill that can only be imprinted on a space devoted to gaming, wagering, playing, betting, in short, gambling. No one was immune to its spell, least of all Maxi Amberville.

Curbing her quick New Yorker's pace, Maxi moved into the Casino with felicitous poise, with the self-assurance that can never be feigned, of a beautiful woman who is perfectly at ease *without* an escort. She wore a long, strapless, chiffon dress that was one shade lighter than the green of her eyes and diaphanous to the point of cruelty. Her black hair, which she wore pulled back severely from her face in New York, had been allowed to fall freely over her shoulders. She had transformed her double strand of pearls into one long rope that hung down over her bare white back, she'd thrust a spray of tiny white orchids between her breasts. Nothing about her suggested widowhood . . . nor maidenhood. She looked as fastidiously haughty as she felt; a fine feline female out on the town.

It was too early in the evening for baccarat or chemin de fer she decided. She'd try roulette just to warm up and orient herself. She'd never played it but it looked like a silly, easy kids' game in which no skill was involved.

Maxi went to the cashier and bought chips for ten thousand dollars, receiving a hundred big black chips in exchange, each worth five hundred francs. She couldn't do much damage with that little lot, Maxi thought, as she slid into a chair at the nearest roulette table. She decided to play her age and asked the croupier to put ten chips on twenty-three black. The wheel spun, finally stopped and Maxi was a thousand dollars poorer. Perhaps her next birthday? The twenty-four black yielded nothing. Nevertheless, she thought, if it had come up, she would have made thirty-five thousand dollars since all the numbers paid off at thirty-five to one. Where was the beginner's luck to which she was entitled? On the other hand, roulette was not normally considered an investment, she reminded herself as she pondered her next choice. The man next to her spoke to the croupier.

"Ten on zero," he said in an accent that Maxi couldn't identify. She glanced at him curiously. He was slumped on one elbow as if only that bone was holding him up and he wore the most miserably threadbare dinner jacket that she had ever seen. His dark hair needed cutting, his hollow cheeks needed shaving, and his eyes needed opening, for his lids were so low and his black lashes so long that it seemed impossible that he could see. He looked like a scarecrow, a bored yet oddly elegant scarecrow who had been left out in the fields until the birds had picked him almost to pieces. She drew slightly away. Obviously this was the sort of riffraff to whom a foolhardy fling at roulette was the final episode in a sordid history of debauchery. Surely there was something decadent about his finely cut profile? Yet he had the most beautiful hands she'd ever seen, with immaculate nails. A professional cardsharp? Probably not, for what self-respecting professional could dream of looking so down at the heels, so pathetically scruffy?

Maxi absently lost seventy more chips as she continued to take inventory of the man who had only given her the briefest of glances. Somewhere in his thirties, she decided, and probably Irish, for who but the Irish combined such white skin and such black hair? If his eyes were blue that would be final proof, but they were still hooded. He lost his ten five-hundred-franc chips and lazily put the equivalent of another thousand dollars on the zero again. His expression didn't change and he seemed to take no interest in the rollicking dance of the ball as the wheel turned, first quickly, then gradually slowing to a stop. Maxi lost again as she noted, fascinated, that the man wore ancient tennis shoes and baggy white socks, and that his dinner jacket was worn over a white T-shirt over which he'd looped the necessary tie as casually as if it were a piece of string. It probably *was* a piece of string, and frayed string at that.

Maxi realized that she had only ten chips left. She beckoned to the attendant who hovered by the table and gave him the money to buy another fifty chips. Her neighbor looked up at the sound of her voice.

"Ten for me, please," he said casually, without offering money. Obviously he was hoping for credit from the Casino, Maxi realized.

"Sorry, sir," the attendant said, refusing his request.

"No more?"

"I'm afraid not, sir."

"Not my night." He offered the comment in infinite expressionlessness.

"No, sir," the attendant agreed, going to get Maxi her chips.

So he was Irish, she thought. There was no disguising the classic deep blue of his eyes during the brief exchange. An Irish wharf rat, probably off the crew of one of the yachts in the harbor, who'd come to the Casino in a borrowed dinner jacket and lost his last franc or dime or farthing or whatever he'd had when he came in. Still there wasn't an Irish lilt to his voice but some other accent—English but not British, whatever that meant she thought confusedly.

He reached into his socks and pulled out five black chips from each one with the kind of supremely indifferent look that Maxi knew must mean that he had been saving this stash for just this moment. She felt sorry for the feckless creature, she realized. There was something gallant and touching in the way he refused to show his absolute desperation. He was obviously at the end of the line. Who knew what fate awaited him after he'd lost his last chips? He'd probably borrowed the money he had been playing with. Or even stolen it. Yet he'd put all ten big chips on the zero again, not even holding back a single one to give himself a chance to play one more time. She held her breath as the wheel slowed, as the little ball finally dropped to rest. On the zero. Maxi clapped both hands loudly in delight. Thirty-five thousand dollars—that should keep him from shooting himself. She smiled at him in congratulation and saw, to her disbelief, that his eyelids were not even raised. Should she nudge him? Hadn't he seen?

There was a rustle of interest as the croupier took the next bets but the man next to Maxi never moved. Finally, the croupier said, "Still on zero, sir?"

"Yep."

He was going to let the money ride, Maxi realized in horror. The odds that the zero would come up twice in a row were beyond reckoning. Was he mad, drunk, doped, or didn't he understand the game?

Maxi forgot to bet as she fought not to say something and when the croupier barked *"Rien ne va plus"* she realized that it was too late to give advice. She sighed and waited for the inevitable as the wheel spun, as the ball hopped and skipped, as the wheel slowed and the ball fell. On the zero. A gasp rose from the crowd that stood around the table. The scarecrow had won thirty-five times one hundred and seventy-five thousand francs. Even Maxi's rusty multiplication table told her that it was over a million American dollars. Considerably over. This should make him open his eyes, this should make him look a little less hopeless, she thought, turning toward him and meeting his glance for a second. Was that a smile on his lips? Was that a raising of his lids? Was there a flush of color in his cheeks? No. Absolutely not. He was still slumped on one elbow, he hadn't reached for his chips, he didn't look any less removed or detached than when the attendant had refused him credit. Clearly a mental case.

"Take those chips *off* the board," she commanded him in a low voice.

"Why?" he asked mildly.

"Because otherwise you'll lose the lot, you damn fool. Don't argue. It's the chance of a lifetime," Maxi hissed at him furiously.

"And play it safe?" he asked, almost sounding faintly amused.

Action at the table had been stopped as the croupier waited for a casino official to permit him to accept the bet. The official arrived, looked at the scarecrow with an indefinable expression and reluctantly nodded at the croupier to go ahead. As a big, buzzing crowd immediately gathered around the table, Maxi, in her agitation, again forgot to bet. The man was clearly insane. Criminally insane. The law of averages hadn't been suspended for his sake and there was no possibility that the ball would come back to zero a third time. The Casino knew that as well as she did or they would never have allowed the game to continue. How many men had really been given a chance to break the bank at Monte Carlo? The croupier busied himself with the other players and only when they had all placed their bets did he look again at the scarecrow.

"Will you stay on the zero, sir?"

"Why not?" he asked with a hint of a yawn.

Maxi watched in outrage as the croupier began to set the wheel in motion. There wasn't a sound from the crowd. The croupier's lips opened to say the words *"Rien ne va plus,"* and in that split second Maxi catapulted herself wildly onto the pile of chips on the zero. She scooped them all off the table, scattering them around the man at her side before the bet could be finalized and the chips lost forever.

A roar of scandalized disbelief rose from the crowd. Her breach of casino etiquette was so unthinkable that their attention was switched from the wheel to Maxi. Indignantly she glared at the watchers. Barbarians, she fumed to herself, just waiting to see someone thrown to the lions. Well this isn't going to be your day, you bastards, even if I do look silly. She stared down the jabbering mob in righteous certainty until she realized that the scarecrow was still watching the wheel, not touching a single one of the chips that she had saved for him. Cold sweat covered her in a flash. She had just remembered something else about the law of averages. Each spin of the wheel was a fresh start, as if it had never spun before. Oh no, she prayed, no, *please.* In the sudden utter silence of the Casino only the wheel could be heard. Maxi closed her eyes. A wild incredulous sound came from the bystanders. Zero. Again. Maxi sat frozen, waiting to die. She deserved it. Murder was too good for her. A hand reached out and closed on her upper arm. He was going to break it. Yes, bone by bone, every bone in her body. He had every right. She wouldn't defend herself.

"Nobody will ever call you a cheap date," the scarecrow commented mildly as he rose from his seat, lifting her with him, leaving the chips Maxi had swept off the table to be gathered up by an attendant.

Maxi opened her eyes and burst into tears. She was going to live. He was even more insane than she had realized but not *criminally* insane.

"I don't like to see a woman cry," he remarked kindly.

Maxi stopped immediately. She didn't dare not to. He gave her a surprisingly clean handkerchief and helped her blow her nose and dry her eyes.

"It's only money," he said, smiling for the first time.

"Only money! Over forty million dollars?"

He shrugged. "I'd inevitably have lost it back to the house another day. You don't imagine that they'd have let me bet if they didn't know that for sure, did you? You're not working for the house by any chance? No, I didn't think so. But they do owe you a free drink. Come on, sit down here and I'll order. Champagne?"

"Something much stronger," Maxi begged.

"Good girl. Tequila then, Buffalo Grass tequila." He motioned to a waiter. "My usual, Jean-Jacques, and one for the lady. A double."

"Bad luck, Monsieur Brady," the waiter said sympathetically.

The scarecrow looked closely at Maxi. "Not necessarily, Jean-Jacques, not necessarily." He turned to Maxi. "Drink up and I'll take you home."

"Oh, no, you don't have to do that," she protested.

"Might as well. After all, I *own* you now. Forty million dollars worth anyway."

"Oh."

"You *do* agree?" he asked politely.

"Yes. Of course. It's only . . . fair." And Maxi thought, there could be worse fates. Far far worse. But she'd absolutely have to do something about his clothes.

Dennis Brady was the first remittance man that Australia had sent back to the old country. A century earlier his ancestor, Black Dan Brady, emigrated to Australia from Dublin and struck it rich when he discovered an enormous silver deposit at Wasted Valley in the New South Wales Outback. In the decades that followed, the

Wasted Valley Proprietary Company found vast amounts of iron ore, coal and manganese. By 1972, in addition to the mine operations, its assets included huge steel mills and oil ventures which accounted for three percent of Australia's gross domestic product, and a cash flow of close to a billion dollars a year. Its chief liability was its rebellious chief stockholder and orphaned only heir to the Brady fortune, Bad Dennis Brady, who was bored, bored, *bored* with Melbourne; bored, bored, *bored* with being the richest man in Australia; bored, bored, *bored* with discussions about drilling for oil off the coast of China, finding copper in Chile, or mining gold in South Africa. Dennis Brady had not the slightest interest in extracting another ounce or gram or droplet of anything whatsoever out of this planet. On the other hand he dearly loved a wager. But gambling is not permitted in Australia and the closest casino in Tasmania had lost so much money to him that they had barred him from play forever.

They couldn't call him a black sheep, he told the board of directors meeting of Wasted Valley that he had convened, because a black sheep doesn't pay his debts, nor could they call him a wastrel because he often ended up winning, and, over the long haul, was almost even, although he knew perfectly well that the odds would always be with the house, but no one could call him an asset to the company either. And there was no need to take a vote on that, gentlemen, thank you very much indeed. He'd tried, God knows he'd tried, for twenty-nine miserable years, to be a credit to the Brady dynasty but it just wasn't going to work out. Too bloody *boring* by half. Wouldn't it be better for everyone if he cleared out, went back to wherever it was that Bradys had come from in the first place and left them to get on with the family business? All those in favor say aye—no never mind the formalities—he'd just remembered that he owned more than enough stock to cast the deciding vote. Could he buy anyone a farewell drink?

"What happened next?" Maxi asked, fascinated with his story.

"They said it was too early in the day for a drink but they rather thought I had the right idea and they all shook hands. Good chaps. They're undoubtedly still drilling and smelting and forging away and looking for new companies to buy. They're as industrious as a bunch of giant Santa's helpers . . . motivated, businesslike, patriotic, good to their mothers—useful but all so terribly tedious."

"Did you go back to Ireland?"

"Good Lord, no. Never cared for racing or breeding the beasts—I'm allergic to horses and I can't endure rain. Came straight here and bought this lovely yacht and I've been here ever since. It's not quite the biggest one in the port but it's nothing to be ashamed of and it's the happiest ship in the harbor."

"But what do you *do*, Dennis?"

"Do? Well . . . I just . . . live, you know? A little here, another bit there. Water ski, drink a little, drink a lot, listen to music, sail, fly my helicopter—sometimes we even take the ship out for a day or two. It's a full life. Occasionally I'm so busy I don't even get to the Casino before midnight. I've put myself on a strict credit limit there . . . it might get boring otherwise."

"Are you never bored anymore?"

"Let's say that I'm not bored *now*. I've never owned a forty-million-dollar girl before. I wonder what I should do with you first?"

"Maybe if you thought of me as just a girl . . ." Maxi murmured, trying to make out his face in the darkness of the deck. Most of the other yachts in the port had put out all but their running lights while they talked, and Bad Dennis Brady had almost disappeared in the moonless night. She missed being able to watch his half-tragic, half-fey face, she realized, rather more than she'd expected.

"But if you were 'just' a girl I'd never have told you all this," he protested.

"What do you talk about with girls you don't own?"

"Not much," he said wistfully.

"You're shy," Maxi diagnosed.

"No, basically just Australian. Australian men prefer action to talk when it comes to women. At least that's the general notion."

"But according to you, no one was ever a less typical Australian."

"Well I can't be can I? Poor eye-to-hand coordination, you know. I never was any good at games, particularly soccer. My guardians, when my parents died, sent me to England for quite a while so I don't even sound right. A half-assed Australian and an all-around total misfit, I'm afraid." He sighed pathetically in the darkness and reached out and took Maxi's hand in both of his. The minute she felt his touch she knew that there was at least one sport in which Dennis Brady had won high marks. Feckless, whimsical, admittedly fit only for loafing, but not, oh no decidedly not harmless. Every warning bell in her system went off.

"Ah, poor Bad Dennis, that's a sad story and no mistake," she crooned. "But as much as it pains me to have to remind you—the meter's running."

"The meter? Oh, of course . . . I'd almost forgotten. How much?"

"One million dollars."

"Per week?" he asked hopefully.

"No, Dennis," she said patiently.

"Per day?" He tried to sound incredulous.

"Per hour . . . and you've just spent two of them talking."

"Good Lord! I think that's a bit high. On the other hand, it is slower than roulette. Or should be, if done properly. Well, if you're sure?"

"I am," Maxi answered crisply.

"In that case, perhaps you might . . . care to go below?" he said, springing to his feet.

"I'm yours to command," Maxi answered.

"I like this game," Dennis Brady announced happily. "Even if you can't bet on it."

"Would you consider marrying someone like me, Maxi?" Dennis Brady asked humbly. Startled, Maxi turned toward him as he lay, long, lean and unexpectedly strong, beside her on the bed of the main cabin of the yacht. Without his deplorable garments he was a superlatively well-made man and all the energy he had been too bored to turn toward mineral rights had apparently been saved just for her, to judge by the last day and a half.

"Someone 'like' you? . . . there isn't anyone like you, Dennis, or the world would be a different place—no aggression, no ambi-

203

tion, just sex and casinos . . . maybe paradise is like that." She ached exquisitely in every major and most minor muscles and her mind was so blissfully unhinged that it was almost impossible to speak, much less think.

"Well, actually, to come right down to it, I meant me in particular, yes, just me, Maxi."

"Would I? Marry you?"

"That's the general idea, yes."

"What time is it, Dennis?" Maxi mumbled, remembering.

"It's ten in the morning."

"How long have we been on board?" she asked, yawning hugely.

"Exactly thirty-four hours. Oh, Maxi darling, come on and answer me," he pleaded.

Maxi made an effort to consider. This seemed important. "Let's see. Thirty-four hours plus the two hours you spent talking makes thirty-six so that leaves you four more hours . . . so . . . if you can manage to arrange it before the time's up, what choice do I have?"

"I did hope you'd see it that way," Dennis Brady said joyfully, wrapping a towel around his middle and grabbing the phone at the side of the bed. "Captain, how long will it take you to get out into international waters? What? No, I don't give a damn about the harbor master. *How* many of the crew went ashore? Well, make do, man, make do. By the way, you are a real captain aren't you? I know, I know, of course I've seen your Master's Certificate—have you ever performed a wedding? Just a burial at sea? Well if you can do one you can do the other. Break out your Bible, Captain, and let's get under way."

"I don't have anything to wear," Maxi said automatically, choking with laughter. Mrs. Bad Dennis Brady. What would people think? What did it matter? What a dear he was. What *fun* they would have! She simply wasn't responsible. Everyone understood that a debt of honor had to be paid or you lost your good reputation.

14

"Poor dear sweetie, old Bad Dennis," Maxi said thoughtfully as she and India sat over a frivolous dinner at Spago, their favorite Hollywood restaurant. "He still sends me the saddest postcards and it's over a year since I left him."

India paused in the middle of lifting a forkful of goat cheese pizza to her lips. "Why do you sound even faintly regretful? I clearly remember your telling me that you couldn't take life in Monte Carlo another minute. I even remember your quoting Emerson. 'To live without duties is obscene'—wasn't that it?"

"It was. It still would be. I deeply regret another divorce but I'll never forget waking up and realizing that the darling lad hadn't had a dull moment during the few months we'd been married and I was going out of my mind. Oh, India, it was so boring, boring, *boring* to live with a man who didn't do anything in particular but hang about being an utterly lackadaisical, perfectly joyous good-for-nothing and didn't even feel the smallest twinge of guilt about it. I suppose I kept comparing him to my father, which wasn't fair, of course, because Dennis had warned me what he was like. You know how much my father accomplishes every day and how charged up and enthusiastic he is about his work, and how he communicates that energy, and how much I admire him? I guess he's ruined me for a man who isn't at least trying to *do* something, no matter what. What's more, shuttling poor little Angelica and Nanny Grey back and forth from Monte Carlo to Manhattan every month was just about impossible but that bastard, Rocco, simply wouldn't, under any circumstances, let her spend more than half the time with me. He took a much bigger apartment with plenty of room for Angelica and Nanny and since he has joint custody what could I do? Still, Angelica might have been on the verge of getting too much attention with a crew of twenty all doting on her."

"Did the lovemaking get boring too?"

"No," sighed Maxi. "I wish it had. But you can't base your entire future on sexual attraction."

"*You* can't?" India asked suspiciously.

"Not beyond a certain limit and I didn't want to reach that day so I left before it happened."

"Are you sure you're not still a little bit in love with him?" India said dubiously.

"Actually I don't think I ever was 'in love' with him . . . I just plain loved him . . . he was so needy and lost and . . . lusty. I loved the Australian in him. If only he hadn't been so totally determined to be *shiftless.*" Maxi sighed deeply. "I did care for him, but not enough, India, not nearly enough." She looked severely at her mesquite broiled salmon and wished it were pizza too.

Maxi had flown to Los Angeles to visit India who had a free weekend between pictures. India had slipped into movie stardom with the irritating ease with which she'd gone through school with straight A's and Maxi felt jealous of the demanding film industry that imprisoned her friend so far from New York, or sent her on location to impossible places; jealous of the fun she was certain that India was having in spite of her complaints that making movies was irksome drudgery, comparable at best to being a privileged inmate in a minimum-security prison.

"Well, forget Dennis Brady," India advised, tackling a huge plateful of pasta with wild Japanese mushrooms and duck sausage.

"I did, a long time ago. You were the one who brought him up."

"I simply asked if there were any new men in your life and you said not even one who was worth comparing with Bad Dennis."

"India, how come you've started going to a shrink yet you're still giving me advice?" Maxi asked sharply.

"What does my being neurotic have to do with my ability to help someone else?" India asked, offended. People never understood about psychoanalysis, not even Maxi.

"I don't understand why you've started to think of yourself as neurotic," Maxi replied. "You're no different than you used to be as far as I can tell—precocious, flaky, much too beautiful and kind of weird. But now you're famous."

"I'm a ten-foot-pole neurotic, the kind who won't let a man get emotionally close to her until she meets a guy who's a seven-foot-pole neurotic with a three-foot feather duster attached to his head," India said broodingly. "And fame only makes it worse."

"What's this Doctor Florence Florsheim going to do about you?"

"Do? She's not supposed to *do* anything—I'm the one who has to change. The best thing about her is that she validates."

"You mean that she's supportive, that she believes in you?" Maxi asked excitedly.

"No, Maxi, she validates my parking ticket for the lot next to her office," India explained patiently. *"You're* supportive, *you* believe in me, because you're my friend and you don't know any better. She's my shrink, not my buddy. She listens and doesn't make judgments and every two weeks or so she might ask a question. Also she doesn't give a hoot in hell what I look like, which is the most marvelous relief. There's no point in not telling her the truth because she can't read my mind and if I lie it costs me time and money, since eventually I *have* to tell the truth or I'm not playing fair and won't get helped. I can tell her anything I want to and know she'll never be shocked because there's nothing she hasn't heard already. If I should say anything important she'll certainly remember it."

"Are you absolutely sure about that?"

"No. It's an article of faith. You have to have faith in your shrink, Maxi, and if you start to doubt her you have to tell her all about it which takes another year. The main thing, I guess, is that she's my *ally*. I pay her for it admittedly but still I've got to have a staunch day-to-day ally, especially in this town."

"Did she say she was on your side? How do you know she's your ally?"

"I *feel* it . . . and stop asking for guarantees because she doesn't pass them out. Now, could we stop trying to explain the inexplicable and talk about what you plan to do next with the life you've utterly wasted except for producing Angelica?" India asked kindly.

"I'm going to London next week. I've wanted to spend time

there for years and Angelica's going to be with Rocco all of July this year."

"Where are you staying?"

"With my grandparents, of course. They'd be terribly offended if I didn't. They're in their late sixties now and more alarmingly vigorous than ever. They've planned all sorts of things for me involving jolly entertainment and meeting people including cousins in the second, third and fourth degree, none of whom I know."

"That sounds . . . interesting," India said.

"You mean it sounds perfectly awful."

"That too, that too," India agreed cheerfully.

"There's no point in trying to do anything about it," Viscountess Adamsfield said to her husband in a gloomy tone that was at odds with her feeble attempt at philosophy.

"But of all men to choose, of all possible Scots, and god knows, I like the Scots almost more than any other people on earth, your granddaughter had to pick a *Kirkgordon!* Laddie Kirkgordon no less, and after knowing him less than two months—his family lost almost everything at Flodden Field well over four hundred years ago and they've been going downhill ever since," her husband growled.

"She's your granddaughter too and he is, after all, Oswald Charles Walter Angus, Earl of Kirkgordon, ruined or not."

"Oswald! No wonder he's called Laddie," Evelyn Gilbert Basil Adamsfield fumed. He'd been lucky to extract a miserable "Bertie" out of his name after two dozen fistfights at school.

"Oswald was king of Northumbria from 635 to 642. Apparently the name is a family tradition," Lady Adamsfield said sadly. "Oswald was king for only seven years, unfortunately, but he must have been a very holy man, sending out all those missionaries to convert the heathen, you know."

"No I did not. And I don't care. Why didn't Oswald mind his own business? I suppose Maxi's been educating you? Is that girl bucking for sainthood this time around?"

"She's in love, Bertie. She told you herself. I think you're being perfectly vile about it."

"I'm not going to pretend that I like it, Maxime, and that's that. I had a splendid husband picked out for her, as well you know."

"Maxi said he was a twit."

"No marquis is a twit, and most particularly not one who's practically a duke. His father won't last out the year. He's a bit dim, perhaps, but not a twit. What's more, *his* family has always been loyal to the crown and those wild, daft Kirkgordons are still loyal to the House of Stuart. As far as they're concerned a descendent of Mary Queen of Scots should be on the throne. No wonder they're down and out; idealistic, unrealistic, notoriously eccentric, the whole crazy, stubborn pack of them. And her Laddie the worst of the lot."

"I rather think that's what Maxi sees in him. She said he had a strong sense of destiny, something to live and fight for, a deep meaning to everything he did, a passionate striving, a . . ."

"Spare me, Maxime, my darling. I was at the wedding too and what Maxi sees in him is obvious."

"You have to admit that he is rather gorgeous," Lady Adamsfield said dreamily. "In fact, I haven't seen a better-looking creature in a long, long time . . . that noble head, those *blue, blue* eyes, that wonderfully fresh, ruddy coloring, that sandy hair, almost golden, when you come to think about it, that great height, those *shoulders* . . ."

"That crumbling castle, those barren acres . . ."

"Those historic, twelve-feet-thick walls, that breathtaking view . . ."

"He doesn't have a shilling and she could have been a duchess . . ."

"She's quite rich enough in her own right, pet, she *is* a countess and he absolutely adores her . . ."

"Maxime," said Viscount Adamsfield, "you're a hopeless romantic. I used to think you were a sensible woman."

"Well, I just hope she's settled down for good this time."

"Maxi? Settled with a *Kirkgordon?* I very much doubt it, my dear. Settled down indeed!"

"What's *that*, for heaven's sake?" Milton Bizet demanded, recoiling.

"What does it look like?" his partner, Leon Ludwig, said smugly.

"A telephone-book-sized telegram. It must be from Maxi. Hand it over."

"If you knew, Milton, why did you ask me what it was?"

"To indicate my alarm, curiosity and feverish delight. I've actually been wondering why we hadn't heard from her except for the announcement of her wedding to that utterly glorious-looking Kirkgordon person. Our Maxi and her indecently macho earl must have bought a marvelous house in London by now, I said to myself, and she certainly isn't going to be unfaithful to us and let some English decorators get their beastly little hands on it. Where is it? In Mayfair, of course, but where in Mayfair? Now give me that telegram."

"It's a castle," Ludwig announced, handing over the pages.

"Trust Maxi. We taught her to think big."

"In Scotland," Ludwig said ominously.

"Oh, no."

"Oh, yes. Somewhere between Kelso and Ettrick Forest, so she says, as if we'd know where *that* was, no heating at all except for a few fireplaces that are big enough to roast a whole sheep in, no minstrel galleries, no follies, no marvelous paneling, no family heirlooms, no tapestries, no pictures, almost no bathrooms, tiny little windows so that it could be defended from the invading Royalist troops, whatever that means, Lord knows how long ago. And the whole damn thing has been falling to pieces for at least a thousand years and even when it was in its glory it wasn't vaguely comfortable . . . not a stately home, Milton, oh no, a bloody fortress. She calls it 'Castle Dread.' Maxi wants us to get over there as soon as possible, preferably tomorrow, so we can start to make it *cozy*. Apparently she's found a horrendous problem with dry rot and you know what *that* can lead to. She says the decor consists of a hundred stags' heads and hoards of horrid stuffed fish hanging on the walls and that there isn't even any decent family silver except for some sort of sacred chalice or other. *Poor* Maxi." Ludwig subsided with a tiny sigh.

"Why 'poor Maxi' when money's no object?" Milton Bizet inquired. "I remember when we had to fly to Monaco to redecorate Blissful Dennis's yacht . . . he didn't care what we spent. I did love that job. In fact I rather loved Dennis, didn't you? He looked just like Peter O'Toole in *Lawrence of Arabia.*"

"Only not as well dressed," Leon Ludwig pointed out, with a small, nostalgic smile.

"And will you ever forget the job we did on Maxi's second town house, after we talked her into getting rid of that first little brownstone?" Bizet continued. "She really went the distance on that place. I suppose that she'll keep the new apartment she's bought in Trump Tower for a *pied à terre* when she gets tired of deer stalking or whatever it is she intends to do in Scotland, don't you?"

"All I'm sure of is that money isn't the problem. It never is with Maxi. It's *us* . . . we're going to have to spend months and months in Scotland. What does Scotland mean to you, Milton? Besides deer stalking?"

"Cashmere sweaters, plaids, whiskey, ah . . . shetland sweaters, tartans, Drambuie, ah . . . haggis, bagpipes, trout . . . *kilts!* Leon, is this a quiz show?"

"Rain, cold, fog, wind, discomfort, lonely moors, the hound of the Baskervilles—if Castle Dread doesn't have central heating and decent bathrooms, who in the neighborhood will?"

"Leon, you have no vision. You panic too easily. There's got to be a hotel somewhere and if not we'll just camp out at Claridge's and pop up to Scotland when it's absolutely necessary. But I do wish Claridge's had better lighting in the bathrooms. I can never see well enough to get a decent shave, but where else can we stay?"

"Nowhere," Leon Ludwig sighed. "If we did, people might think we were slumming, and slumming in London isn't chic anymore, alas."

"I'll tell my secretary to make reservations immediately. Maxi sounds desperate. She says she has to have the central heating in by next week and for some reason she can't seem to make the local contractor understand. This is a crisis, Leon. She needs us."

"Milton, when didn't Maxi need us? We're indispensable to her."

"Well, I just hope she's settled down for good this time."

211

"Who, Maxi?! Really, Milton, you've taken leave of your senses. *Settled down*, indeed!"

Angelica ate her hamburger, looking, Rocco thought, more thoughtful than a seven-year-old should look.

"Is there something wrong, sweetheart?" he asked.

"Oh, no, Daddy, I was just wondering if I liked Laddie as much as I liked Dennis, that's all."

"Oh."

"Dennis was so funny but Laddie can play a twelve-string guitar and sing old songs; Dennis taught me to swim but Laddie is going to get me a Shetland pony and teach me how to ride; Dennis had a great big wonderful boat but Laddie has an enormous castle; Dennis showed me how to play Go Fish and he always let me beat him but Laddie gave me a little red fishing rod and when the trout season comes he's going to show me how to . . ."

"It sounds as if they're both simply perfect, two absolutely wonderful guys," Rocco interrupted. "Would you like another hamburger, Angelica?"

"Oh, yes, please, Daddy. That's one thing they can't make right in Monte Carlo or Scotland. I *miss* hamburgers."

"Really."

"Yes, and I miss tuna fish sandwiches and turkey with cranberry sauce," Angelica said sadly.

"Are those the only things that you miss, Angelica?"

"Well, I suppose I still miss Dennis, a little bit. I don't know Laddie quite well enough yet to stop missing Dennis, even though Laddie's so very very tall and so very very handsome."

"I see."

"That's O.K., Daddy," Angelica assured him earnestly. "Maybe people always miss people they like, even when they meet other new people they like."

"Maybe."

"Please pass the ketchup, Daddy. Remember when Mommy was married to Dennis? Remember how every month Nanny and I used to take the helicopter from Monte Carlo to Nice and then the little jet from Nice to Paris and then the Concorde from Paris to

New York to be with you? But I was just a little kid then and I didn't have to learn things. Now I'm in second grade and I can't change schools every month."

"I know, sweetheart."

"So once I start school in Scotland, I won't get to visit you until we have a vacation that's long enough for me to come back to New York," Angelica explained with a look of concern.

"I understand, baby. Your mother and I discussed it for a long time and I had to agree with her that I couldn't interrupt your schooling."

"But I'm worried about you, Daddy."

"Why, Angelica?"

"Because you're going to miss me."

"A lot, God damn it! *One hell of a lot.* But you'll have your mother and Laddie what's-his-name and a pony and a castle and probably dozens of pretty little plaid kilts to wear to school, so you'll be too busy to miss me, darling."

"I miss you all the time I'm not with you, Daddy," she said reproachfully.

"More than Dennis?"

"Don't be silly! It's not at all the same thing. I liked Dennis. I *love* you."

"I was just making a little joke."

"Well, I don't think it was funny. Not at all! Take it back, right away," Angelica said severely.

"I take it back," Rocco mumbled.

"O.K. Could I have a chocolate fudge sundae, please?"

"Of course. You can have anything you want."

"Well, I just hope that Mommy is going to stay settled down with Laddie this time. I don't want to have to miss him too."

"Settled down? Your mother? *Ha!*"

"What does that 'ha' mean, Daddy?"

"I was coughing, Angelica. Just coughing."

"Zachary, just listen to this letter from my mother," Lily said in a tone of alarm, putting down her piece of buttered toast.

"What's bothering her?" Zachary ate his egg patiently.

213

"It's Maxi."

"I know it's Maxi. Obviously your mother's too sensible to get upset about anything minor. What's Maxi done now? I assume people have gotten over being shocked about the indoor swimming pool she installed in the dungeon and the bathroom she insisted on for every bedroom, even though the castle is a historic monument."

"It's nothing that petty. Mother says that Maxi's becoming the talk of London and that's not easy to do when you live in the Border Country. Apparently she's giving house parties that last for weeks."

"Why the hell not?" Zachary stopped eating in quick defense of his daughter. "It took her at least a year to get the old barrack modernized and decorated and it certainly cost her millions. Naturally, she'll want to amortize that, and what better way than surrounding herself with friends?"

"I suppose you're right, Zachary, but it seems that her house parties are simply notorious. They say that Maxi is growing a huge crop of marijuana in the greenhouse and she fills the Kirkgordon Chalice that the Archbishop of Glasgow presented to the family in the fifteenth century with a never-ending supply of home-rolled, Good Lord, Mother writes 'joints'—I didn't think she knew that word—and that Maxi is running a high-stakes poker game every day *including* Sunday in the late earl's trophy room . . . for heaven's sake, dear, put down your butter knife . . . and that she lights great blazing fires on top of the castle tower to celebrate Saint Patrick's Day and Columbus Day and Kosciusko Day and I Am an American Day and every single other American holiday and the local fire department can't get her to stop. She still persists in driving her Ferrari on the wrong side of the road and, Zachary, worst of all, when she was invited to visit her neighbors, the Duke and Duchess of Buccleuch at Bowhill House, she said that she wasn't absolutely convinced that their Leonardo is authentic! That's quite unpardonable, Zachary, and, of course, untrue and she must have known it." Lily flung the letter down in exasperation.

"She's unhappy, Lily. The marriage isn't working out. That's what all this means and I'm not surprised. I always thought that brute of a Kirkgordon was much too beautiful. I don't trust men

214

who look like that, and now he's made her miserable. I admit that Maxi's a little spoiled at times but she's never been self-destructive," Zachary said, taking off his glasses absently and shaking his head in concern. "The only part of that letter that seriously worries me is her driving on the wrong side of the road. I'm going to phone her and find out what's going on. I'd just hoped, I really had, that maybe Maxi had finally settled down this time."

"I know you're a doting father but there should be *some* limits to your wishful thinking. 'Settled down'? Your daughter? Maxi? Really, Zachary!"

"What was it exactly that went wrong this time, Maxi?" India questioned breathlessly. "Tell me everything, take it from the top."

"If you'd ever been able to visit, you wouldn't have to ask. But you were too busy even to pop over for a weekend," Maxi said accusingly. "So, here I am, back on the coast, just to see you."

"That's a bum rap. I didn't have the time for jet lag in both directions and you know it perfectly well. It's not as if you've been living in San Francisco. Come on, stop stalling."

"Basically, it was the dreich."

"Of course it was," India said soothingly. "What's he like this dreich person?"

"It's a Scots word, India, and it means very, very wet, very, very dark, very, very dim and very, very cold. The weather, India, the weather was *fucking* dreich." Maxi reached over and took some pizza off of India's plate. She was thin enough now to risk anything, and the pizza at Spago was irresistible.

"So you got divorced for the third time because of the weather? Interesting. This is the first time I've heard that one. Of course, if you see enough Bergman movies you can begin to understand that gloomy weather does create a definite morbidity and melancholy, but in less than two years? Maxi, leave my plate alone. Wouldn't you like to order your *own* pizza? What about all those tons of central heating you put in?"

"India, what about being generous enough to share your pizza? I gave you half my angel hair pasta, didn't I? What if I told you that

215

my taste in men is probably the worst in the whole world, that I shouldn't be allowed out by myself without a keeper?"

"I'd be forced to disagree. Rocco was, as I well remember, one of the all-time greats, Bad Dennis Brady was, in his own way, supremely delicious, and according to your letters Laddie Kirkgordon was sheer heaven. I quote: 'He has all the best points of King Arthur, Tarzan and Warren Beatty.' Didn't his being an earl even account for something?"

"You try waking up in the middle of the night and telling yourself that you're a countess and see how much difference that makes," Maxi snapped.

"And just why were you waking up in the middle of the night and talking to yourself?"

"All right, India, all right. I give up. I see you've been taking Doctor Florence Florsheim lessons, getting right down to the roots of things, isn't that it?"

"More or less," India answered in a deliberate monotone.

"Laddie is a certifiable lunatic," Maxi said, and fell silent.

"That's it? That's all there is to it? Most men are lunatics, Maxi. Stark, raving lunatics. But you don't divorce them because of it, you learn to live with them. That's probably why I've never married. I know too much up front, in advance. Laddie just wasn't *your kind* of lunatic."

"Damn right, he wasn't. I think he was an overreaction to poor Dennis, but in the beginning I really fell for it: that glorious tradition handed down from generation to generation; the purpose in life; the meaningfulness of being Scots, Scottish, Scotch, you can call it what you will; ancestor worship, the House of Stuart, patriotism, I fell for the lot. But once we got out of bed long enough for me to listen clearly to him, and that took a year, I found out I was much more of an American than I'd ever realized. Laddie began to sound quite obsessed, and finally I realized he was decidedly mad, bonkers, living in another century. He refused to have anything to do with the real world, with one single exception: winning the Selkirk Silver Arrow—I think it's the only thing he cares about."

"Huh?"

"It's an archery trophy, the oldest there is, and every seven years there's a competition of the Queen's Bodyguard of Archers to win the Arrow. Laddie spent at least six hours every day practicing with his bow and don't say it was just a hobby, it was *life* to him, even though the Queen he was doing it for was not Elizabeth the Second. If he'd had better weather he'd have spent more time at it than that, but what with the dreich and all . . ."

"Why didn't you bail out earlier? Between the wet and the target practice I don't understand why you stuck around for so long."

"I was simply just too *embarrassed* to admit I'd made another mistake. I never knew one of my three husbands for more than a month or two before I married him—I only knew poor, sweet, Bad Dennis for thirty-odd—very odd—*hours,* India. What does that tell you about me? Don't bother to answer. Don't say one single word, that wasn't a question."

"What did Angelica think?"

"Oh, she was having too good a time to notice that the laird was a wee bit peculiar. She loved the indoor swimming pool, she loved the local school and she really became quite good with a bow and arrow. Laddie gave her lessons, I'll say that for him. Fortunately I got her out in time, before she started thinking that Bonnie Prince Charlie was going to come riding out of the mists on a white horse and carry her away. I believe Angelica could thrive underwater. I'm the one who isn't adaptable."

"You're just impulsive," India said lovingly.

"Do you think *I* should go to Doctor Florence Florsheim?" Maxi asked with a look of despair. "You can't say that I'm leading life in the fast lane—it feels like oncoming traffic."

"That happens to be the one kind of advice I can't give you. People in analysis are not supposed to go around telling their friends that they should go into analysis too. Anyway, Doctor Florsheim wouldn't take you because you've heard too much about her and she knows too much about you, to say nothing of our being best friends. It would be strictly unkosher."

"Do you talk to her about me?" Maxi asked, with a delighted expression. "I didn't know that! What do you say?"

"When I'm trying to avoid talking about something I don't want to talk about, I do have a tendency to discuss you, yes. But

217

since you're not one of my problems it's just another waste of my time and by now I know that whenever I even *mention* you it's because I'm avoiding something really awful."

"Oh."

"Don't try to understand."

"I won't, India, I truly promise not to."

"What do you intend to do now, Maxi?"

"First of all I'm going to make you a solemn and binding commitment, India. I'm going to vow, with you as my witness, that I will never, ever marry another man. *Never ever another man*, India, do you hear?"

"I hear but I don't believe you. Just because you don't intend to get married again doesn't mean that you won't. You're too young to make such a vow. I warn you not to do it."

"You let me decide that! India, if I get married to another man I'll . . . I'll take out an ad, a full-page ad, saying that I'm not responsible for my actions, that I have no sense when it comes to men, that I'm doing it against my better judgment, that I'm acting in haste and will repent in leisure, that I'm sure in advance that it's going to turn out to be a mistake and that you, India West, are my witness, the only one in the world who knows that I have made a vow to myself, an absolute vow, never, ever to marry *another* man."

"Where will the ad run?" India asked through her fit of giggles.

"In the *New York Times*, in . . . in *Women's Wear Daily*, in the *New York Post*, in the *London Times*, in *Le Figaro*—that should cover just about everybody I know, don't you think?"

"*Weekly Variety* too," India suggested. "You've met a few people in the business."

"Done. I'm absolutely dead serious about this, India."

"I know you are. Oh, Maxi, I did hope that this time you'd settled down for good."

"India, *me?* You should know better than that!"

15

In spite of the discouragement in which she had briefly wallowed over the weekend and on the phone with India, Maxi approached the offices of *Buttons and Bows* on Monday with a tickle of irrepressible excitement. After her long therapeutic talk with her best friend she had convinced herself that the former editor, Bob Fink, was simply too superannuated to understand that something could be made of her magazine, no matter how low it had fallen. He didn't believe in it anymore, if indeed he ever had, he had no competitiveness left, he lacked vision, he had made too much money in real estate to be hungry for improvement, except when it was time for his daily free lunch, Maxi assured herself as she opened the door to the suite of offices, a door that she resolved to have painted as soon as possible.

She stood inside and surveyed the unprepossessing chamber. On the walls of the reception area were framed covers of *Trimming Trades* when it had still been the thriving, prosperous magazine on which Zachary Amberville built his empire. The old-fashioned covers from the forties and fifties just reinforced her conviction that bringing the magazine back to life was a question of using her imagination. The skimpy, recent issue of *Buttons and Bows* that she had put into her handbag and taken home had a cover that was basically similar to those on the walls. Surely something as important as a cover could have been, should have been, totally changed in the course of forty years?

"Miss Amberville, welcome to hard times."

Maxi spun around. It was the receptionist who had announced her arrival last week.

"You're still here? Bob Fink said everyone couldn't wait to leave."

"My salary is paid through the end of the week, and I'm not old enough to retire."

"What's your name?"

"Julie Jacobson."

"Call me Maxi," she said, sitting down in front of the battered desk. "About your clothes, Julie, shall we put our cards on the table?"

"I guess that would be best," Julie answered carefully.

They were wearing identical outfits: miniskirts in a screaming red, with crisp white blouses and exaggeratedly long, black men's ties around their necks. They both had on black tights and high-heeled black pumps. A wool Chesterfield that matched the skirt was hanging behind the receptionist's desk. Maxi was wearing its double. The ensemble was Stephen Sprouse's newest, freshest, and brightest, exactly what a fashion addict with superb legs would choose to wear on this particular day of this particular month of this particular year. Since they were roughly the same height, the two young women looked absolutely alike from the chin down.

"I think we should stop meeting like this," Maxi said, "or else try to make a point of it." Bob Fink had said that his receptionist was overpaid but this suit and blouse had cost over a thousand dollars, not counting the shoes. Just how overpaid was she?

Julie was Maxi's height, but she had little breasts and narrow hips that meant she would always look taller than Maxi in the same clothes. Her short hair was tinted an otherworldly color between Bordeaux and orange that stopped precisely short of punk. It was brushed back uncompromisingly from her forehead to reveal a face that belonged to an impertinent doe: huge challenging eyes, darkly rimmed in charcoal liner and shadow; a slender nose with nostrils so sensitive that they looked as if they could twitch at any minute; delicate lips painted a bright crimson; a chin that was just small enough to give the impression that she shared some forest animal's timidity and yet firm enough to let the world know that Julie Jacobson didn't let anyone order her around.

"But let's discuss wardrobe later," Maxi continued. "I'm going to look around my office. Then maybe you could show me the rest of the establishment?"

Julie sprang up and stood with her back protectively barring the door that led to Uncle Bob Fink's former office.

"I don't think you really want to go in there," she said.

"I don't?"

"It might not be the best way to start the day."

"Don't tell me he didn't get rid of all his stuff," Maxi sputtered. "He promised, damn it."

"No, it's all been carted away."

"Then what's the problem?" Maxi said blithely as she entered. She stopped in her tracks in shock.

The room was completely empty, except for one old black leather chair with a rump-sprung seat. The entire carpet was covered, many inches deep, with layer upon layer of half-disintegrated bits of paper, a mess ten times worse than Broadway after a ticker-tape parade. Cobwebs, she thought in a daze, real honest-to-God cobwebs hung in the corners of the room. Did New York have *spiders?* The walls, now that Uncle Bob's nine towering desks no longer concealed them, were mottled and filthy. There had been leaks over the years and paint had fallen from the walls in long zigzag strips that lay in pieces over the other debris. The windows were so dirty that scarcely any sun lit up the scene, but whatever light came through the grime was desolate.

"At least in *Great Expectations* Miss Havisham had *furniture* to hold up her cobwebs," Maxi said when she could find her voice.

"The last desk, the one he was working at, collapsed when they tried to move it," Julie explained.

"There isn't a broom, there isn't a vacuum cleaner, there isn't any instrument known to man that could clean up this . . . I don't even know what to call it," Maxi said faintly.

"There's always motivation." Julie sounded as if she'd meditated on the problem.

"Motivation?" Maxi was horrified. "You don't mean *me!*"

"In *our* clothes? I was thinking of Hank, from the building. He's been known to become highly motivated by the palm of his hand. Do you have fifty bucks?"

"In cash . . . I don't think so. Will he take a credit card?"

"I'll lend it to you. You can pay me back tomorrow."

"Bless you, Julie! Let's get out of here. It's morbid."

"You're the boss."

"Right? Right! Now where can the boss sit down and discuss the future of *Buttons and Bows* with her staff?"

"Maxi, you don't have a staff."

"What about you?"

"No way. I don't mind lending you money, but that's as far as it goes. I'm purely temporary, not staff, God forbid, in this place."

"Couldn't you just pretend? Till the end of the week. You could put it on your résumé, when you go for your next job."

"I am planning on leaving *Buttons and Bows* off my résumé entirely. But if it makes you feel any better, you can call me a consultant and let me buy you a cup of coffee to cheer us both up. Don't look for a coffee maker, it's broken."

"The nearest coffee shop?"

"You're on."

"Julie," Maxi said earnestly, leaning over the table, "have you ever stopped to think of the possibilities? Every rock group in the world is trimming-crazy, tons of gold braid, uniforms, everything they wear is trimmed to high heaven. Medals are back all over the place. Shoulder pads have never been more important. Claude Montana. Just think of Claude Montana's shoulder pads! The T-shirt craze. What is punk but the inspired use of trimming? And just look at the evening dresses this year . . . if they don't glitter, forget them. Sonia Rykiel's things—all trim. Why, we could do a whole issue on . . . on Joan Collins's puffed sleeves!"

"Hmmm."

"What does that mean?"

"I've only been here two weeks because the assistant editor's job I was supposed to have at *Mademoiselle* fell through at the last minute, but I do know who still subscribes to *Buttons and Bows*. Basically, it's your Mr. Lucas who is worried about selling five thousand yards of passementerie and your Mr. Spielberg whose main business in life is fringe. I don't think they would be intensely fascinated by Joan Collins's sleeves. They would hardly notice if Joan Collins herself appeared stark naked on the cover of the magazine. *Buttons and Bows*, if it's about anything, is about a few of the nuts and bolts of the fashion business. For fashion, Spielberg and Lucas stick to *WWD*. That's not subject to change by you."

"Then we have to widen our base of circulation, appeal to somebody other than Lucas and Spielberg."

"Not *we*, Maxi, *you*," Julie insisted. *"You."*

"Anyway, that's tomorrow's problem," Maxi said, pushing it away into the air. "Tell me about you. All the vital statistics you care to have known."

"I'm twenty-two. I graduated from Smith last year. My mother always insisted that I have secretarial skills to fall back on. For three generations the women of my family have had secretarial skills and I'm the first one who's ever had to fall back on them. I do not enjoy it. In two weeks I'm starting at *Redbook* as assistant to the assistant to the fashion editor."

"Are you a New Yorker?" Maxi asked curiously. Julie was as businesslike a creature as she'd ever met and crisply self-confident.

"Cleveland, Shaker Heights. My father's a neurosurgeon and my mother teaches English literature at the university. Her speciality is Virginia Woolf and the Bloomsbury Group. My sister's working for a double Ph.D. in French and philosophy so that she can teach Pascal, Montaigne and Voltaire, heaven only knows to whom, and my brother's a city planner and chief aide to the mayor of Cleveland. I'm my parents' only failure."

"What is your crime?" Maxi gaped. It must be the color of her hair. Everything else about her was so impressive.

"I'm nuts about fashion. No one in the Jacobson family thinks fashion is a proper way to spend the only life you have. It's frivolous, poorly paid, and doesn't add to universal knowledge."

"It's the fourth or fifth biggest industry in the country."

"They don't think much of industry either."

"They sound a bit . . . Bostonian."

"There's another branch of the family that's lived in Boston forever. They make the Cleveland Jacobsons look like television game show producers."

"I didn't even graduate from high school," Maxi confessed.

"Is that why you've been sent to *Buttons and Bows*—to teach you what happens to people who fail to complete their education?"

"It was my own idea. And I'm not giving it up," Maxi said grimly.

"I don't understand why, with all the other Amberville publications, you should care what happens to pathetic old *Buttons and Bows*. In your place I'd be at *Style* like a shot."

"Let's talk about clothes," Maxi suggested. She liked Julie but she wasn't about to bare her heart and her loss to satisfy her curiosity. The reasons were too emotional, too bound up with her love for her father to explain.

"Clothes Milan? Clothes Bendel's? Clothes American designers?" Julie's eyes lit up with anticipation.

"You're buying the coffee so you get to pick," Maxi said generously.

For several hours that afternoon Maxi sat in what had once been the art department, where two bare L-shaped layout tables and several tottering chairs had been abandoned on a dirty, peeling linoleum floor. In the reception room, from time to time, she could hear Julie answering the phone and coping with the reluctantly motivated maintenance man.

Maxi had supplied herself with a yellow legal pad and a box of ballpoint pens and she decided that the first thing she had to do was to plot the future of a new, revitalized, expanded, explosive *Buttons and Bows*. She had the intention of making lists and sketches and more lists and more sketches. She walked around the room, looked out of the window, sat down, looked at her yellow legal pad, got up and walked around the room some more. Inspiration proved elusive. Maybe it was the fault of the decor, maybe it was the terrible ham-and-cheese sandwiches she and Julie had shared in a coffee shop that had been sold out of her favorite, tuna salad, maybe it was the antics of the full moon or the diabolical influence of Saturn or maybe it just wasn't her day. Maybe it was Lucas and Spielberg. She wished that Julie had never told her about them. None of the ideas that came into her head seemed good when viewed from the Lucas-Spielberg angle, and they were, after all, the faithful core that was left of the readers of *Buttons and Bows*. The magazine, if it were to rise from the ashes, had to appeal to many thousands of Lucases and Spielbergs, wherever they were to be found. Hundreds of thousands. Millions!

"Jesus Christ Almighty!" Maxi said out loud.

"You spoke?" Julie asked, standing in the doorway.

"There *aren't* millions of Lucases and Spielbergs!"

"One of each, I believe. On your subscription list in any case."

"Julie, I'm going for a walk. I think better on my feet."

"It's nice outside," Julie said, eyeing the virgin yellow pad meaningfully. "Oxygen stimulates the brain."

"And it's nice outside. See you tomorrow."

Elie was waiting with the limo downstairs.

"The center of the universe, Elie," she ordered. He made his rapid, illegal way to the corner of Fifty-seventh and Fifth, stopped and opened the door for her. "When will you need me tonight, Miss Amberville?"

"I'm not sure, Elie, but call in around six."

She walked briskly down Fifth Avenue, breathing deeply, relishing the nimble temper of the September city, that perpetual urban high-wire act. She loved the incomparable tension of this island metropolis that felt as if it were perched on the top of an active volcano. "'I'll take Manhattan, the Bronx and Staten Island too,'" Maxi sang, although she had known for years that the song her father had taught her had been skewed to suit his determination since the first three words of the lyric really were "We'll have Manhattan."

Never had Fifth Avenue seemed broader or brighter to her than after the dismal hours she'd spent in her new office, never had the passing throng, pushing and shoving and overtaking each other in the aggressive, *con brio* New York version of a stroll, seemed more fascinating and varied than after the fruitless afternoon she'd spent with her yellow pad. Everyone had a destination, a goal, a reason for being here, in this place, on this street, at this hour.

What, Maxi wondered, what did they all want? *Wanting* was the very essence of the New Yorker. She knew what she wanted.

She wanted to make a smashing success of *Buttons and Bows* and quite suddenly she admitted to herself that she knew it could not be done. Not with *Buttons and Bows*. No way, nohow. There was no *major* demand in this city, where there was a market for everything, for a magazine that was devoted to articles, no matter how well executed, on the mystery of the hand-embroidered glitz on Julio's three-thousand-dollar dresses or the ruffles on Prince's clothes or the definitive word on Linda Evans's paillettes. Probably there was a market for a magazine for contact lens wearers, or a magazine for left-handed people, perhaps even a magazine for people who collected string, but they would always be *small* magazines. Maxi wasn't about to pour her energy into a small magazine.

Scratch trimming, she thought. She needed to find a new idea—a—a *concept*. That was all she needed, a concept, Maxi thought, as she almost danced down Fifth Avenue, in her red miniskirt, a smile on the perfect bow of her mouth. Just a new concept, merely a new, fresh concept that hadn't already been done. That was all. As she sped by, every man who saw her ached to follow.

When Elie called in tonight she'd tell him that tomorrow morning she wanted him to make the rounds of all the newsstands in the city and bring her a copy of every single magazine on sale. She might as well know what was out there already before she invented her new magazine.

"Ma," said Angelica in a voice of supplication, "when are you going to stop torturing yourself? I can't take this much longer."

"Tough shit, kid."

"Ma, that's not a nice way to talk to your little girl."

"I don't have time to be nice. If you want a nice person go find somebody else, I'm working."

"Ma, why are you doing this to me?"

"Because. And stop whining . . . other girls have working mothers and they don't complain."

"Working mothers!" Angelica sputtered. "You're like some kind of loony, a robot, a crazed robot."

"Go play Trivial Pursuit."

"You've been shut up with these magazines for three days

now, you haven't had more than a bite to eat, you read till you drop, you grind your teeth when you're asleep . . ."

"How do you know?"

"Because you fell asleep on top of that pile of magazines last night and I heard you grinding away."

"Just a little stress, just normal stress, Angelica."

"But you've always avoided stress, you hate stress, Ma. Stop it!"

"To be stressed is human, kid, don't you know that? Maybe you're too young, but according to what I read, every female in this country is operating under unendurable stress and it's getting worse even as we sit here and waste time talking. Now go away and let me get back to my work."

"Ma, I'm going to call Toby and get you committed to an institution."

"It takes three doctors to commit somebody and all the doctors in the country are busily writing articles on stress for magazines, so you won't find any who have the time, but you're free to try."

Angelica folded her lanky frame in sections and sat down protectively next to Maxi. Three days before, when Elie had arrived at the apartment with the first shift of magazines, her mother had been like a kid opening Christmas presents. She had installed herself in her new library, with its solar-gray mirrored walls, its book-crowded shelves and its big armchairs covered in off-white glove leather. She had opened each new magazine with anticipation, pounced on it and leafed through it page by page, leaving out nothing from cover to cover. When she had wrung a magazine dry Maxi carefully added it to one or another of the piles of different types of magazines that were beginning to collect around her. Elie kept returning from his expeditions with his arms piled high. From expectation, Maxi's mood grew more subdued. By lunch she began to look slightly dismayed and by the end of that first day she was annoyed. By the evening of the following day she had progressed to outrage, and her outrage had mounted ever since. Still the magazines kept coming, the piles now tumbling down the sides of all but the window wall of the room.

Many of them had been sent away, carried off by the weary

Elie: the only-for-men magazines; the sports magazines; the computer magazines; the car-owner magazines; the audio-freak magazines; the motorcycle-nut magazines; the weekly news magazines; the movie magazines; the soap-opera fan magazines; the magazines for male homosexuals; the aerospace magazines; the business magazines of all kinds and sorts.

Maxi had, by now, cleared a place for herself on the red and white hand-loomed carpet and sat cross-legged, hemmed in by dozens and dozens of publications.

"I haven't found one for lesbians yet," she said in a tired but thoughtful tone of voice.

"Ma! Is that what you're planning?"

"It may be the only major virgin market left."

"Would lesbians go out to a newsstand and buy a special magazine?" Angelica wondered. She heard the front door open. It must be Elie with more dreaded magazines, because the footsteps were those of a man.

"In a country with fifty-nine million single people and a magazine like *Bride's* that claims to reach just over three million, it stands to reason that there's got to be a big lesbian audience out there somewhere," Maxi answered, trying for a tone of sweet reasonableness.

A man entered the carpeted library where they sat so engrossed in print that they didn't hear him. He stood leaning on the doorjamb, casually poised. The mocking cock of his head, the tough jut of his chin, the skeptical glint in his eyes, the clearly bellicose way in which his short, pointy, ash-blond hair stood up from his head, all indicated someone who viewed the world with a certain disdain. He wore battered leather so worn that it seemed a collection of bits and pieces, three Nikons were slung around his neck, and his smile was both knowing and deeply loving. It was evident that he found both Maxi and Angelica very funny, objects of his benevolence, and it was just as evident that only a very few people in the world fell into that category.

"Could I interest you ladies in a subscription to *Boy's Life?*" he said quietly.

"Justin!" Maxi whooped and launched herself across the room into his arms, scattering magazines in every direction. "Justin, you beast, where the fuck have you been for a year, you rotten bastard, you shithead! Justin, darling!"

"Give me a chance at him," Angelica cried, and grabbed him tightly, trying to climb up him like a monkey as she used to when she was a little girl, almost toppling him over in the process. Eventually he extricated himself from the two excited, babbling creatures, separated them and put an arm around each of them. "Let's look at you," Justin said, and they immediately fell silent and subjected themselves to his scrutiny. "Still the ultimate best in the kingdom," he said after a few seconds. He inspected his sister and his niece keenly, his dark gray eyes missing nothing, but whatever his real thoughts were he kept them, as always, to himself.

Soon after Zachary Amberville died so suddenly, so horribly, Justin had taken off without a word to any member of his family. He had a record of disappearing for months at a time since he was fifteen, and the Ambervilles had become accustomed to his comings and goings. He never wrote or telephoned while he was away but, from time to time, photographs would crop up in a variety of publications with the photo credit "Justin": photographs from tiny islands so distant that no travel agent knew them, from mountaintops so unexplored that they had no names, from jungles that were only empty space on most maps; photographs of surfers in Australia, of Brazilian transvestites in the Bois de Boulogne, of the inside of the Royal Enclosure at Ascot; photographs that had nothing to connect them to each other except the unexpected viewpoint of the brain beyond the lens of the camera that captured images that couldn't be skipped over, even in an era when it seemed that the most extraordinary photographs must all have been taken.

His last "trip," as the family called Justin's mysterious wanderings, had been longer than any other he had made, and his photographs had been infrequent, but still no one worried, for by now it was accepted as a fact that Justin was invulnerable.

In his early teens, he had seemed utterly ill at ease in his own skin, jumpy, awkward, and seeking every opportunity to avoid attention. Then, when he was twelve, he had started to study the martial arts and self-defense, embracing a schedule of relentless training that had reminded Lily of the single-mindedness of the ballet. Slowly Justin's bearing, even when he stood still, began to convey an unstated menace. Everything that had earlier seemed vague and alienated in him had been collected into the strength and speed with which he knew he could move. Today he was a presence to reckon with, all dexterity, all sinewy grace; a man of twenty-four, of medium height, whose lean body nevertheless had more density than that of other young men.

Justin looked both lionhearted and unpredictable although he disdained any outward trappings of toughness. His familiar leathers were not studded body armor, just relaxed, well-worn, shabby garments in which he could travel anywhere. When he could be coaxed into a game of croquet in Southampton he exuded the same potential for dauntlessness, wearing white linen trousers and a pastel crew sweater; the quality was built into his hard muscles, into his lack of relaxation, as if he were ready to do battle at any minute.

Maxi had never seen Justin touch another person except with tenderness, yet she often realized that she knew remarkably little about her younger brother although they loved each other unreservedly. He was the most highly defended man she had ever met and whatever went on behind his high rounded forehead, whatever unspoken need made him drift away from home so often was a bafflement to her. Even Toby, with the acuity of his senses, with his way of reading unspoken thoughts, had no clues to the perplexing conundrum of Justin's motivations. It seemed to both of them that he stalked some invisible goal that eluded them, a goal he never had explained, never had described, yet a goal that inexorably lured him on and on.

"What," Justin demanded, grinning, "are the two of you doing? I want an explanation. Toby said I'd find you here but he didn't say in what condition. He said you'd tell me all about it."

"Ma's looking for a new magazine concept," Angelica answered with a shrug of her shoulders, "and I'm trying to make sure she doesn't starve to death in the process. The new cook quit yesterday."

230

"Maxi, why?" Justin said, astonished. "Who needs another magazine?"

"I'm not sure yet, that's the problem. But the rock-bottom reason has to do with Cutter, and a matter of not letting him make an ass out of me."

"In that case, you can count on my full cooperation," Justin said with as much overt ferocity in his voice as he ever displayed.

While Maxi and Toby could have explained in detail what they distrusted and disliked in their uncle, only Justin had always hated Cutter and yet could not have said why. It was an instinctive loathing that went too deep for words, a question of absolute mutual antipathy. Justin had been curious, as they all were, about his father's brother who never seemed to leave San Francisco. When Justin was almost eleven, Cutter and Candice Amberville finally came through New York, stopping for a few days on their way to Europe. The first time Justin met Cutter his curiosity had been transformed into a visceral disgust, a disgust he didn't try to understand. It existed as solidly as a boulder, it was not something to question or ponder, it just *was*, as powerful as his love for Zachary, as obvious as his caring for Toby and Maxi.

"I accept your offer," Maxi said delightedly. For the last three days Angelica had been her only sounding board. Julie was busy at the office winding up the business of putting *Buttons and Bows* into the limbo where all dead magazines still float, items of rare, plaintive nostalgia and trivia quizzes. Maxi had not called on any of the professionals at Amberville Publications who would have been glad to lend her a hand. Pride had prevented her, pride and an irresistible need to do this thing *by herself,* to see it through to the absolute end and then, if she ran dry after giving it her unreserved best, to admit defeat if necessary. But she didn't want to lean on the obviously available expertise of Pavka or Nina or Linda Lafferty, or any of many others who were among the editorial board members. She was twenty-nine and she'd never accomplished much alone in her life except bringing up Angelica. However, Justin's help was different. He was family.

"Where do we start?" Justin asked, shedding several layers of soft leather and making a place for himself on the floor with Maxi and Angelica.

"Don't you want to know why I'm looking for a concept?" Maxi demanded.

"Not necessarily, as long as it has to do with screwing Cutter. How far have you come? Do you have a glimmer of a glimmer?"

"I know what I can't do. I have eliminated all the glossy magazines: the *Vogues* and *Architectural Digests* and *House & Gardens*. Not only are they too expensive to publish, but Amberville already has *Style* and *Indoors* and I don't want to compete with the company. Also they make me so *angry!*"

"Since when? I thought you loved them."

"I used to, I was addicted to my monthly fix of slippery paper, but the more I looked at them, the more I read them, the more furious I got. Justin, do you realize that the glossy books just make you feel like a piece of *junk?* Almost nobody can look like that; wear those damn clothes; use that crazy new makeup; have houses like that or gardens like that . . . you can aspire, you can spend the rest of your life trying to be someone photographed in that one perfect minute, which is the only thing they *ever* show, but you'll never make it for real. They're not selling dreams, they're selling putdowns. They're selling heartache, dissatisfaction with what you have, above all they're selling *envy.*"

"Hey, Maxi, take it easy. They're selling clothes and furniture and cosmetics . . . the editorial pages are just the vehicle for the ads. They make the wheels of American business turn. You know that as well as I do."

"That doesn't make me like them," Maxi said obdurately.

"But you *are* their reader, you of all people. You know perfectly well that you can buy just about anything that you see in those magazines. Look at this apartment . . . four million dollars, or was it five? Look in your overstuffed closets, look in your jewel box, and then take a good look in the mirror. Just what don't *you* have? Except for a fourth husband?"

"I'm thinking about my readers," Maxi said impatiently.

"Oh, so you have readers do you? I knew there was something different about this place but I thought it was the view."

"I intend to have them, Justin, and I'm not going to give them another overdose of how rich people live."

"Bravo! What other kinds of magazines have you decided not to publish?" Justin asked, his curiosity piqued by her vehemence.

"All those damn service books: *Good House, Family Circle, Woman's Day, Redbook, McCall's,* and anything else that digs, digs and digs some more at every woman's guilt. Just look at this *Ladies' Home Journal* ad . . . they surveyed 86,000 women and eighty-seven percent of them said that 'women can do anything.'"

"Well, can't they? You've always acted as if you thought *you* could."

"Look what *else* it says—'We're here as she presses herself for physical excellence. Offering her sensible diet, exercise and beauty plans . . . and we're there as she presses to be better in other ways too. At home. On the job. In her community . . . pressing just as hard for excellence as the seventeen and a half million women who read us every month.' It's a big, lousy, fucking conspiracy, a *tyranny,* Justin, no poor bitch is allowed to be anything but bloody excellent at all times, in all situations. Press on, press on, and if you drop dead from sheer *pressing* for excellence, at least you won't have let your subscription lapse!"

"Angelica, go get your mother a Miltown."

"It's all right, Justin, I just gave her one. It doesn't help. Can it kill you to foam at the mouth?"

"I doubt it, sweetheart, your mother's just suffering from stress."

"Justin," Angelica shrieked in alarm, "please don't use that word."

"Oh, balls," Maxi muttered, throwing down a copy of *Family Circle.* "It's only September, and they've got '101 Christmas Gifts to Make' and 'All-Time Favorite Cookie Recipes' on the cover and Doctor Art Ulene's book on *How to Stop Family Problems Before They Start.* . . . What if you don't bake, what if you *buy* your presents and don't want to know more about your family problems at Christmastime than you do already? How *guilty* will this cover make you feel? And it's the world's largest-selling women's magazine according to the masthead. And look at this magazine, just look. It's called *Lady's Circle* and it's really a joyful book: a piece on stomach-stapling that didn't work, an article about a teenager with a rare, fatal liver disease, another stress article that contains a test on how you rate as a heart-attack victim; and then, for fun, how to crochet a holiday tablecloth. Is crochet a stress antidote? Or a stress add-on?"

"Maxi, why are you even bothering with service books?" Justin asked. "That's not exactly your line of country. I've never seen you making anything more complicated than a vodka gimlet and I remember your being furious that limes had seeds."

"I have to know what people are buying, what *women* are reading, or I won't know what to give them that they don't *already* have," Maxi explained, looking as if she had suddenly turned into a toadstool. "It's obvious."

"But you can't be planning to compete with a *Good House.* . . . Where are your test kitchens, Maxi, where's your money-back guarantee, where's your well-earned readers' confidence? Where's your reputation for excellence and your position as a trusted friend, not a magazine?"

"Justin, how come you know so much?" Maxi inquired suspiciously.

"I had lunch with someone from Hearst once," he said evasively.

"I like to bake cookies," Angelica announced. "Could I have that copy of *Woman's Day*, Ma?"

"With my blessings," Maxi said, smiling for the first time that morning. She turned to Justin and raised astonished eyebrows. Baking cookies?

"What's in that pile?" he asked, pointing to the heap of magazines closest to her.

"I call them the 'so what else is wrong with you?' books. Their premise is simply that things are going so badly that you're desperate for help. Here we have *Woman* and *Complete Woman*, with typical cover lines: 'Why Do You Let Him Walk All Over You?'; 'Beat Those Menstrual Blahs'; 'Conquering Your Shyness'; 'If Sex Leaves You Wondering "What's Wrong with Me?"'; 'So You Are Not Interested in Sex . . .'; 'Banish Boredom, Overcome Hurts,

Fight Insecurity, Beat Loneliness'; 'How to Save Yourself from Yourself.' I could go on . . ."

"Don't! Please don't. Or I'll scream," Justin said, unable to repress a guffaw.

"Ma's overreacting," Angelica whispered to him.

"The hell I am," Maxi snapped. "I'm just seeing what's being sold on the newsstands and having *normal* reactions."

"Like grinding your teeth in your sleep?" Angelica asked.

"Precisely! How about this piece on 'The Number-One Stress Stopper' by Michael Korda. Guess what it is."

"Relaxation?" asked Justin.

"Deep breathing and chocolate cake?" Angelica hazarded.

"No, no, my children . . . 'Do More . . . or How to Be a Confirmed, Happy, Unapologetic Overachiever.' That *SUCKS!*" Maxi flopped on the floor and groaned aloud. "'Do More,' the man says. *More.*"

"Let me rub your back, Maxi, it's probably killing you," Justin said, rolling up his sleeves and flexing his strong fingers.

"How about a brownie, Ma? They say chocolate makes you happy, releases some kind of hormone or something," Angelica suggested anxiously.

"No, don't try to make me feel better." Maxi jumped up from the carpet and picked up the magazines around her and pitched them violently at the magazines that were piled against the walls. "Enough guilt! Enough of your guilt trips about everything from your extra pounds to how you've changed your lover into a tyrant; enough guilt trips about how pathetically little you know about how to handle money, about how you can't accessorize your clothes, keep a neat closet, don't take enough calcium, haven't been promoted at work, can't manage a job and a family too, and need your marriage saved; enough about your nutrition mistakes and how to handle failure; enough about how boring your sex life is and it's probably your fault; enough guilt about your whole life being depressing and why men are unwilling to commit; enough about why you fuck up job interviews. . . . *No more guilt trips!*"

"We agree, don't we, Justin?" Angelica said hurriedly as Maxi whirled around faster and faster but Maxi didn't hear her and kept on talking louder and louder, her bare feet thudding on the thick carpet like enraged hooves.

"All they do is undermine your self-confidence while trying to tell you how to be, seem, and feel *more* self-confident; they make you feel that it's impossible for your body to ever be attractive *enough,* that you can and should be doing better, better, *better,* in the kitchen, the bedroom, the boardroom—what, you mean you haven't been promoted yet? How come you're not an executive and if so what horrible things does your office furniture reveal about your character and when will you learn how to manipulate your boss and make office politics pay? And if you don't work, how come you aren't at home making a new kind of stuffing for the turkey, how come you're such a poor pathetic creature that without this magazine you'd never make it through the night? Oh, thank them—thank the good editors for making you feel better about that heel you married, the dozen men who've left you, the seventeen different things you do wrong in bed, the only man—naturally a shit—whom you can't forget; all of which are your fault, bad girl. *BAD GIRL!* Guilt, guilt, guilt! WOULD ANY MAN BUY A MAGAZINE THAT TOLD HIM EVERY MONTH WHAT A SCHMUCK HE WAS? No, my children, he would not. *If I read one more article about bulimia I'll throw up.* God damn it to hell, isn't there a single magazine a woman can buy that loves her just the way she is? What did I just say?"

"You'd throw up if . . ." Angelica cried hysterically.

"No, after."

"Doesn't any magazine like women?" Justin ventured.

Maxi jumped up and down. "THAT'S IT! That is fucking *it!* The reader-friendly magazine, the magazine that loves you and doesn't try to change you, the magazine that wants to amuse you, that exists for your pleasure and *only* your pleasure. FUN. The magazine that doesn't give a shit if you eat too much or can't find a guy, or should have known better or need help. Fun, I say! There's already more help out on the newsstands than anybody could possibly use. FUN! Did you hear me? FUN!" She opened her arms wide and jumped up and down, flinging the last of the magazines away, kicking as high as any Texas cheerleader, strutting her stuff.

"We heard you, Ma. Everybody in Trump Tower heard you."

"What is this fun book going to be called?" Justin said with a flashing look of pleasure at the sight of his adored sister back to normal form again.

"It's already got a name, Justin. I picked *Buttons and Bows* when I had my chance. But times have changed," Maxi said gleefully, "and so has the name. I'm shortening it to *B and B*."

"*B and B*? What kind of name is that?" Angelica asked.

"Do I know? Does it matter? Bread and Butter, Bosoms and Bottoms, Benedictine and Brandy, Balls and Bums, whatever suits your fancy. It's called *B and B* and that means F-U-N!"

16

Zap-proof. Fucking zap-proof!"
Rocco said, angrily throwing down the issue of *Adweek* he'd been
reading. He looked out of the window of his office on the forty-
third floor of Dag Hammarskjold Plaza and noted with annoyance
the red neon sign of the Pepsi bottling plant on the other side of
the East River. Coca-Cola was his client and Pepsi was the loathed
enemy, until the almost certain day when Pepsi would become the
client and Coke the enemy. "Anyway," he added, "this story is
totally sick. Imagine having to go for zap-proof by shooting eight
and a half hours of film and editing it down to a thirty-second
television spot. No matter how good it might turn out to be, I say
it's a sign of something fundamentally wrong."

"We have nothing to do with that spot, Rocco," Rap Kelly
said soothingly. "It's for somebody's deodorant soap. You should
stop reading the trades."

"Don't turn into a philosopher, Rocco," added Man Ray
Lefkowitz, the third partner of the firm of Cipriani, Lefkowitz and
Kelly, the hottest advertising agency in New York. "When you
give the public remote-control units for their TV sets, it stands to
reason that they're going to zap the commercials."

"If it *had* been us, I'd have killed whoever directed that soap
commercial with my bare hands," Rocco said somberly. "Hitch-
cock he wasn't."

Manny and Rap exchanged glances. Was Rocco going into
another of his occasional phases which they privately called yearn-
ing-for-print-freakouts? When the two of them had lured him away
from Condé Nast three years ago it had been the hardest selling job
either of them had ever gone through, including the battle to get

the Chevrolet account. Rocco hadn't wanted to admit that magazines were dodo birds as far as getting graphics to the attention of the masses was concerned. He had wanted to stay buried in print forever, Rocco had, until together they'd wrestled him out of his fixation.

Manny Lefkowitz, that brilliant copywriter, still remembered his winning argument. "Rocco," he'd said, "it takes more time and energy and decision to turn the page of an ad, particularly when you've *paid* for a magazine, than it does to zap a commercial, since it is your right, as an American, to see a commercial coming at you for *free* every time you turn on the television. Who's the bigger challenge to an art director? The willing consumer, the veritable captive audience of a magazine who's intent on amortizing his investment, or the absolutely fed-up-with-commercials audience watching television who only wants the show to come back on? Don't bother to answer—it's obvious. So if you're the best art director in the world, as Rap and I think you are, then television advertising is the only medium worthy of you. It's your next step, Rocco, you can't help but admit that."

"I admit it . . . but I just don't know . . . where's the *white space*, Man Ray, where's the layout?"

"On that blank screen, Rocco, and you know it. It means you'll be grabbing people quicker and grabbing more of them . . . millions and millions more. And you have to sell them something, not just entertain them. The major difference, Rocco, is that magazine layouts are essentially the print equivalent of jerking off—all you're doing to making pretty pages for the advertisers to plant their ads *around* . . . it's pure self-indulgence. With commercials you live or die in that split second before forty percent of the viewing audience decides to zap you. So you have to be better than in print. Not just good, *great.*"

"Jerking off?" Rocco said, offended.

"With all due apologies to the magazine business, it's a century behind its time. A page doesn't *move* or speak to you and nothing is ever going to make it do so. Get off the pot, Rocco, don't be like that guy who said nobody would ever go to talkies."

"Yeah, Rocco, don't be totally dumb," Rap Kelly chimed in.

He was the cat-burglar, business-getter of the threesome, who specialized in being indecently smarter than he sounded, and won many an account that too-slick talk had lost.

Rocco had looked at the two of them, Manny, the monster-talented chief copywriter and vice-president at BBD&O, and Rap, who was the king of the hill at Young and Rubicam, and realized that the adventure of starting a new advertising agency with these two advertising geniuses was irresistible. The top creative agency job that they were proposing to him had never before been offered to a Madison Avenue art director. Traditionally that job always went to someone who came up through the copy department.

He had been thirty-three then and, except for his brief experience at Amberville Publications, he'd always worked for Condé Nast. But his idol, Alexander Liberman, was going as strong as ever, showing no signs of age, and Rocco suddenly felt that perhaps the time had come to move away from the printed page, at least for a time; perhaps Manny and Rap were right about the challenge. To say nothing about the money. No one in magazines had a chance of making the money that he knew he could make in an ad agency and it was time to think realistically about money.

From the time Rocco and Maxi had been divorced, only a little more than nine years before, he had chosen not to think about money, knowing that it was un-American and unnatural and in some basic way ridiculous not to think about money, as if he'd taken some sort of vow. It was more difficult to work in New York and not think about money than it was not to think about sex or food, but for someone whose life had been as screwed up by money—Maxi's money—as his had been, it was a revolting topic.

And he'd been right about the money he'd make. CL&K, as their new agency was known, was a gold mine from the day it opened its door. They pulled down out of trees clients that supposedly belonged to the venerable giants of Madison Avenue as if they'd been ripe bananas; fickle advertising directors of Fortune 500 companies beat at their doors before they'd finished raiding the other agencies in town for much of their prime talent, for Cipriani, Lefkowitz and Kelly had something extra going for them that no other agency in town had: all three were bachelors without attachments. And much of the prime Madison Avenue talent was female. Man Ray Lefkowitz was a jolly redheaded giant with violently blue eyes which he insisted were a sign that he was of some special tribe directly descended from the Queen of Sheba; and Kelly was a redheaded Irishman with violently blue eyes who had been an all-American quarterback for UCLA and could sing tear-bringing whorehouse tenor when he wanted to, and all three of them had never lost a hair off their scalps or been rude to a lady or failed to observe Valentine's Day. Last year their bill for Valentine's Day flowers from Robert Homma had been over eighty thousand dollars. They had sent his antique Japanese storage jars filled with tall, graceful branches of flowering quince, and it had come back to them as Kelly reverently said, "a million fold."

"Let's go get drunk," Rocco said suddenly, when the Pepsi sign blinked on. "Didn't we just get the Cutty Sark account?"

"Last week . . ." Rap Kelly answered. "It wasn't easy prying them loose from that old boat. I thought you hated Scotch, Rocco."

"Not if they're a client. I'm going to develop a taste. Come, kids, it's that time of day." He put on his tie and jacket and led the way, while behind him, Lefkowitz and Kelly exchanged worried glances. Rocco rarely drank.

"Just a touch of delicious New York vulgarity—just short of actually rough, a hint, merely a hint, of tough chic," said Leon Ludwig, one of Maxi's interior decorators.

"I don't agree. We're talking middle-America; all Mumsy and English country-cottage, tons of glazed floral chintz, and slightly tatty settees," replied Milton Bizet, the other half of Ludwig and Bizet, the decorating team Maxi had used for her last two town houses and the renovation of the Earl of Kirkgordon's castle in the Border Country.

They had not, nevertheless, been able to really impose themselves on the Trump Tower apartment. Their efforts rejected the geometry of the building, since Maxi insisted on keeping favorite pieces bought in her wandering, the spoils of a careless, rich nomad with the instincts of a bazaar keeper. They'd opened up the walls of the adjoining apartment she acquired and done what they could, but the job had left them feeling that their client had not been satisfactorily tamed or subdued.

"Boys," Maxi interrupted, "hold it right there. We're talking office furniture, we're talking state-of-the-art steno chairs. We are not trying to make a design statement."

The three of them were approaching the area in which the office of *Buttons and Bows* was located and when Elie stopped the limousine in front of the building off Seventh Avenue, Ludwig and Bizet stood on the sidewalk in disbelief.

"Here?" asked Leon Ludwig, recoiling.

"Here. The lease has three years to run, all the space on the rest of the floor is available, the rent is much lower than in any of the new buildings, and the neighborhood has associations for me," Maxi said firmly.

"It isn't even Art Deco," Milton Bizet breathed in amazement. He'd never seen this part of New York before, not even on his way to the theater.

"It isn't art anything," Maxi snapped, "unless it's Depression Repugnant. It's a mess and it's utterly inefficient . . . that's what I want you two to fix up. I need it last week. I can't use staff effectively until I have a decent place for them to work."

"Maybe one of those companies that specialize in offices . . . those Itkins or whatever their name is—would suit your purposes better than . . ." Leon Ludwig ventured, unwilling to confide his elegant person to the interior of the building.

"Boys, I have no relationship with the Itkins and I assume you want to continue yours with me?"

"Naturally, Maxi, my delicious, but . . ."

"Then get your bodies upstairs and stop whimpering," she said with her most alarming smile. "It's going to be fun for you, making it all work on a budget," she added thoughtfully.

"And just how much is the budget?" asked Milton arching his eyebrows. It wasn't like Maxi to talk of budget except as something disposable that they would throw guiltlessly to the winds as they went along digging up blissful things without which she couldn't live. He'd known there'd be trouble, ever since Trump Tower had come into her life.

242

"*Half* of the rock bottom minimum you can come up with," she answered.

"Funny girl," Leon purred.

"I have this sinking feeling that she's not joking," Milton said in unfeigned horror, observing the strangely serious expression on the face of their favorite, if marginally difficult, client.

"I'm not. This magazine is going to take a pot of money to produce and I don't want to see it wasted on the walls of the office. On the other hand, cows give more milk in happy surroundings, as do people, so it's essential that the whole office be cheerful, gay, *fun* to work in. I want windows that open, no fluorescent lighting except where it's absolutely necessary, a smashing reception room—do it with mirrors, *cheap* mirrors, Leon, no bevels . . ."

"Maxi, haven't you ever heard that you have to spend money to make money?" Leon said in a last-ditch stand against the all too foreseeable agonies of a strict budget.

"Too often. The money will go into salaries. How else can I get the best people away from their present jobs to work on a new magazine? Well, here we are." Maxi opened the door of the office. The reception room was empty and she vanished immediately in search of Julie. She didn't like to watch grown men cry.

"Welcome back," Julie said in relief. "I've got your keys right here, all the old business is wound up, all debts paid, my desk is cleared out, the phone's still working, and the only thing still hanging around is a blank yellow legal pad and the pencils you left here last week."

"What about my sweater?" inquired Maxi looking at her strangely.

"What sweater? You didn't leave one here."

"I know." Eyes like slits, Maxi studied Julie's new Perry Ellis sweater and skirt costume, the one that would set the standard of adventure for American ready-to-wear that year, two extraordinary ways to use cashmere; one a dazzling tunic, a tapestry of reds, blues, and yellows, inspired by the Cubist work of Sonia Delaunay; the other a longish wrapped black skirt that worked absolutely with Julie's flat black shoes and magenta tights. The sweater, for Maxi too had bought one on Saturday, was eight hundred dollars, and it was too eye-poppingly, too specifically and memorably fall-of-1984 to be worn for more than one season. You couldn't even wear it more than once every two weeks in an office. The skirt, at three hundred bucks, could become a classic, but the sweater was a bravura gesture, the sign either of someone so rich that she could afford it without thinking of price, or someone so clothes-mad that she would buy it, wear it a few glorious times, and then keep it forever for her private pleasure.

Julie Jacobson couldn't be all that rich, Maxi calculated, or she wouldn't have had to take a job as a secretary while she waited for her minor assistant's appointment at *Redbook*. She had undertaken the dreary labor of funeral director of *Buttons and Bows* with tact, dispatch, energy, and remarkable good spirits, setting up her command post in what had been the old art department. As Maxi had fled from witnessing the vapors of Leon and Milton, she had noticed that the offices were now as spotless as they could be, granted their state of decrepitude. Julie was two girls and a half.

"I have a proposal to make to you," Maxi said, sitting down next to Julie.

"No," Julie answered shuddering. "Really, truly, no."

Maxi ignored her. "How much are you going to be paid at *Redbook?*"

"A hundred and seventy-five a week, but that's not the point."

"The point is that you'll be in the fashion department, as assistant to the assistant to the fashion editor."

"Exactly," Julie answered, her eyes gleaming with a vision of herself at some time in a far hazy future, sitting in the front row at the New York fashion collections, pencil poised to make notes of whatever she judged worthy.

"Have you ever played Monopoly?" Maxi asked. Julie nodded, still in her dream. "Remember when you got to pass 'Go' and whiz ahead on the board and collect two hundred dollars from the bank? Didn't it feel good?"

Julie snapped back to reality. "Maxi, what are you trying to con me into? I don't work for you anymore, thank God. As of last

Friday I'm not even on the payroll here. What's more there isn't a payroll anymore."

"But there is a payroll, a new payroll, and I'm going to be meeting it every week."

"How many people are you employing?" Julie asked suspiciously.

"So far, none. Eventually dozens and dozens. Hundreds."

"Doing what?"

"Putting out a new magazine."

"But that's *exactly* what you were planning to do last week! Oh really, Maxi!"

"This has nothing to do with last week. You were absolutely right about my idea for *Buttons and Bows*. It was youthful folly. Since then I've aged a thousand years in wisdom and experience."

"Is that a fact?"

"Trust me."

"I never trust people who say 'trust me.'"

"That was a test," said Maxi smugly. "And you've passed. Therefore I'm officially offering you the job of fashion editor of *B and B* combined with the job of my chief personal assistant in charge of all other details until I find someone who can take them off your hands and leave you totally free to plan the fashion pages."

"'All other details'? Why do I smell snake oil? What is *B and B*? Another remake of *Buttons and Bows*? How many fashion pages would there be? And how much authority would I really have? And what about salary? And what if the magazine doesn't make it and I blow the job at *Redbook?*"

"Three hundred a week, to start with, *you go wholesale for your clothes*, absolute authority within the basic philosophy of *B and B*, which is simply that women are great the way they are—you can't argue about that, can you?—and, oh, there you are! This is Justin, your photographic consultant, Justin, this is Julie Jacobson, the new fashion editor of *B and B*. You two will be working closely together."

Julie spun around and gaped at Justin who had soundlessly materialized in the doorway and stood leaning against the wall with such compact and tightly coiled power that it looked as if he were holding the building up with his shoulder. He advanced toward Julie, who was hypnotized by the battery of Nikons that he wore as familiarly as if they were a scarf tossed around his neck, took her hand and shook it.

"Justin, *the Justin,* is working for this magazine too?" Julie gasped.

"The Justin. I said trust me. That didn't necessarily mean that you couldn't," Maxi laughed. "And here—'hi guys'—as Mary Tyler Moore used to say—here are Milton Bizet and Leon Ludwig who are designing our offices—come in, boys, and greet Julie Jacobson, my fashion editor. She'll be going over your bills, so be nice to her. Julie, you don't have to be nice to them at all. In fact, I would advise the utmost caution. Leon, what color office do you see for Julie, assuming that she doesn't change her hair?"

"A forest atmosphere, lots of batik, tapa on the walls, obviously a kilim on the floor, fishtail palms . . ."

"Leon, I meant the color of the *paint.* We do not have fabric walls at *B and B,* we do not have fabric anywhere. Fabric is too expensive and gets dirty. The fabric-free office is about to make interior design history, isn't it, Justin? Zen and the art of office maintenance. It might get you a story in *Architectural Digest* and then again it might get you the cover of *Plastics Weekly* . . . it all depends on your imagination and talent. If you show enough of it, I may make the two of you my decorating editors, but first you have to prove yourselves."

"An all-white office," Milton offered, deeply offended, "with a large box of Ajax and a gross of sponges."

"Can I just bring one white rose in a white bud vase for my desk?" Julie begged, blushing with excitement. *Wholesale! Justin!*

"I'll supply the rose," Justin announced.

"I'll *lend* you an onyx vase," Leon announced. "White vase indeed."

"Hmm," sniffed Maxi, "I rather thought *I'd* like an all-white office to go with the streak in my hair. We can't have two."

"Julie gets it," Leon decreed, feeling much better. "She's the only one we have to be nice to now."

∼

"Pavka, I'm so glad you asked me to lunch. I haven't seen you in, oh, much too long." Maxi had rushed into his arms in an effervescent swirl of plaid pleats and a sweep of her fine limbs that proved forever that the knee is, under some circumstances, far, far from an unlovely joint.

"I've missed you, but I knew you were busy," Pavka said, careful not to sound reproachful. He was perfectly aware that she had been avoiding him. There were rumors all over Amberville Publications about Maxi's plan, but no one had a single solid detail to contribute.

"We've been painting the office," Maxi said demurely.

"Well . . . that's a beginning."

"I think so." Maxi studied the menu at the Four Seasons Grill Room which had developed into a virtual club of the top executives and agents in publishing, people so important that their perks included the limousines which jammed Fifty-second Street off Park Avenue as if a gangster's funeral were going on inside. As well it may have been, in certain subtle senses of the phrase.

"And when the offices are painted," Pavka continued patiently, after they had ordered, "you will hang curtains, bring in furniture, put down rugs?"

"We'll most likely get around to doing something like that, or at least drifting in that general direction," Maxi admitted gravely, giving the question her most serious consideration.

"And, if I understand correctly, eventually you will publish a magazine?" Pavka pounced, but she didn't flinch.

"Ah, that. I imagine so, eventually. Of course, eventually is never tomorrow, but I suppose that sooner or later we'll putter along and see if we can manage to squeeze out a little . . . a nice little . . . magazine."

"Which doesn't, by any chance, have a name yet?"

"Not a name really. No, I don't think you could say it had a name." Maxi's Imperial Jade eyes had suddenly turned as uncompromisingly and flatly green as a color sample. She was determined not to reveal any details to Pavka. She felt like a mother bird who was being disturbed in her nest while she was hatching her first egg.

"But, my darling, surely you intend it to have a name?"

"In time. In time." She looked sinfully, blissfully lazy. Time was to be ignored, she seemed to say without words . . .

"But Maxi, you do understand the importance of a name?"

"Good Housekeeping, Reader's Digest, National Geographic, Playboy—of course I do."

"I assume you're looking for a name that tells the reader what the magazine is about, hmm?"

"More or less in that general area, yes. Pavka, did you know that Russell Baker says there are only six subjects: sex, God, marriage, children, politics and baseball?"

"So may I conclude that your magazine is about sex?" he pressed.

"I'd never ignore it, not completely. Marriage is good too. So is divorce."

"Maxi! Why won't you tell me anything? You're teasing me, you sound like somebody in a bad off-Broadway play. Don't you know that you have to have an *informative* title so that you can get people to even *glance* through the first issue, which is only one of your problems, and at that, only the *first* of the *dozens* of problems involved in launching a new magazine. You have to get them to open it, Maxi, much less actually buy it."

"Pavka, angel Pavka, I have the most enormous favor to ask of you." Maxi tossed him a look of cosmic prettiness. His heart melted. She really didn't have to bother, she had always had his devotion.

"Anything you want. You know I'll help, whatever it is—do you want to discuss your plans in detail? Or can I help you with the dummy? Nothing is too much trouble for my Maxi."

"All I want you to do is *not* to tell me about my dozens of problems," Maxi answered in her sweetest voice. "I know how much marvelous advice you could give me, but Pavka, you *know too much,* you've seen too many magazines fail. Would you tell a baby who's about to take her first step about the dangers in downhill skiing? About hang-gliding? Ice dancing?"

"Have it your way, my darling, but there is one thing you can't stop me from insisting on saying—you need to hire someone experienced to handle traffic control, someone usually called an executive editor, or managing editor, someone who won't impose

248

his opinion about what goes into the magazine, but who will steer ideas through the many tedious stages from conception to completion, and then get the copy and photos and ads to the printer on time. He should be a pessimist who never believes anything will go right unless he does it himself. A beast of burden, if you will, but a beast you can trust with your life. Otherwise your magazine will be a boat without a rudder."

"I'm the rudder."

"No, Maxi, you're the boat—and the ocean and certainly the wind that fills the sails, but your temperament isn't that of a rudder."

"Hmm." Maxi didn't know whether to be irritated or placated but she rather fancied herself as a boat—a trim forty-eight-meter, three-masted racing yacht. "I suppose you have someone in mind?"

"There's a man I can put my hands on. He was managing editor of *Wavelength* before Cutter's massacre, and he took a vacation when he was fired so he's still available . . . a man named Allenby Montgomery. Allenby *Winston* Montgomery."

"Do I have to call him 'General'?"

"*Évidemment*—by now he doesn't answer to any other name. But there's no need to salute if you don't want to."

"He sounds like an easygoing guy," Maxi gloomed, resignation in her voice. She knew Pavka was right. She needed someone utterly steady around, so she could do all the unsteady parts herself.

"I hope you've thought about an art director," Pavka continued cautiously. If Maxi had been at all clear about what she planned to do, she'd never have been able to keep from unfolding it to him, even if she didn't want his advice. She'd have been too pleased with herself. Did she even have a concept? If she did, and he doubted it, whatever it was, it existed on some half-baked drawing board in the back of her little delicious, maddening head, somewhere under that cockatoo hairdo which went every which way including up and made her look as if she were actively in bed with a few very close, energetic friends.

"An art director?" Maxi murmured vaguely. "Of course I've thought about one . . . but that's as far as I've got. We're still waiting for the paint to dry—I don't need an art director yet."

"I asked a great editor once what was the worst single thing his enemies in the publishing business could do to destroy him and he answered, 'Steal my art director,'" Pavka said, almost to himself.

"What editor?"

"Your father. I was the art director."

"*Évidemment.* And *touché.* But I *am* thinking about people, from other magazines. It's a winnowing-down process, a culling, a matter of finding the pearl in the oyster bed—I'm *considering* it, Pavka, I just haven't made any decisions. Trust me."

"How could I not? So tell me, how are you coming with the dummy?"

"Brilliantly, just . . . brilliantly. I feel just like the cowboy who jumped into the cactus bush. When they asked him why he'd done it, he answered, 'It seemed like a good idea at the time.'"

Laughing, Pavka was able to hide this confirmation of his conviction that Maxi was lying to him. Her summer job at *Savoir Vivre* had indeed led to major events, marriage and motherhood among them; but he doubted that she'd been allowed anywhere near a dummy, much less become capable of making one. He sighed but he was far from surprised.

"Remember, my darling, I'm here if you need any kind of help," he said, keeping up the pretense since she wanted it that way. "And I'll tell the General to call you as soon as he gets back."

"Thank you, Pavka. You're too good to me." The two of them finished lunch laughing at the atmosphere of the Four Seasons, that hotbed of sexual possibilities. They observed editors seducing writers, writers seducing editors, publishers seducing editors and editors seducing publishers, but never saw a writer seducing another writer, for that would be like two professional football linebackers falling in love. In the dignity of the marble room half the people present had been married two and a half times to the other half and were working on the third alliance. Their only permanent relationships were with the headwaiters.

After lunch Maxi found Elie right in front of the revolving door, stolidly resisting the efforts of the doorman to make him move the limousine farther up the street. As she was driven back to her office, she felt relieved that she hadn't been provoked into telling Pavka anything, tempting as it had been. When all was said and done, he was just a little old-fashioned, a bit of a pessimist. He might not have understood that now that she had found her concept the rest of it was *all out there,* all waiting for her. It merely needed a spot of pinning down. Nothing more. Just a little more . . . thought . . . a touch of . . . oh, work . . . yes, face it, work.

That night, refusing three invitations for dinner, Maxi stayed home. She wished that the men she knew hadn't all hooted when she told them that she couldn't join them because she had to work. She frowned as she settled herself in the center of her enormous bed, propping herself firmly on the least floppy of her many pillows, pulling up the white mink throw that lay at the end of the bed so that her knees made a little fur desk.

All the materials she thought would be necessary for the fabrication of a dummy lay neatly beside her. She'd bought ten packages of the thickest paper she could find in a rainbow of vivid colors, five types of Scotch tape, two boxes of special number-three Dutch pencils, a miniature portable pencil sharpener from Sanyo, a vast assortment of ballpoint pens in every color that existed on the market, a complete calligraphy set, and close at hand were the latest issues of all the women's magazines published in the United States. She looked at the magazines scornfully. She had never seen a complete dummy, only scattered pages of layouts, but obviously it must be a magazine-shaped object. She intended to use the other magazines to clip out ads to put into her dummy so the finished product wouldn't just be text and pictures. In fact, she decided, hefting the long, expensive, Swiss-made scissors, why not clip a good assortment of the best-looking ads now, to have easily at hand? Then she could get the magazines out of the way and into the wastepaper basket where they belonged.

Soon she had a thick sheaf of ads, most of them in color. After deliberation, Maxi added a few in black and white; Bill Blass, Blackglama, Lancôme and Germaine Monteil, just for contrast. She shoved the magazines off the bed with a sign of good riddance and, feeling efficient, clipped the ads together in two groups with the paper clips she had not forgotten to buy.

Now.

Now for the dummy.

Perhaps she should just check up first on Angelica, make sure she was doing her homework. No, Angelica's school didn't begin until next week. She'd be in the library waiting impatiently for "Hill Street Blues" to begin. Perhaps she should call India and tell her what she was doing. No, they'd just talk for hours and the evening would disappear. Resolutely she took one of the steel-tipped quill pens from the calligraphy set and experimented drawing an ampersand on a sheet of stiff red paper. The ampersand was tricky to draw but she did a fairly neat job on her fifth attempt. Eventually she inked boldly, *B&B*. At the bottom of the page she made a small circle and carefully inked in the letter C in the middle of the circle. Now she had the copyright on her title; that was all it took. Extraordinary. Perhaps it had something to do with the Library of Congress? Once published it would belong to her. Once published. She never believed the person who had told her you can't copyright titles. She'd like to see the person who could take *B&B* away from her.

Well. So far so good. Now for the text and pictures. Text first, it stood to reason, or how would she know what pictures she needed? Or if they should be photographs or illustrations? Yes, text. No, not text! She wasn't going to write the magazine herself, after all. That was what writers were for. All she needed were headlines. Titles of articles. How lucky she was that she knew what she didn't want, that she'd spent so much time eliminating the sort of thing that made women envious or depressed or guilty. She'd already done most of the work, actually, when you came to think about it. Perhaps she'd join Angelica in the library and see what they were doing up on the Hill this week. Maybe Mick had bought a new suit. Maybe Furillo would fall in love with a blond. Maybe Renko would take up bodybuilding. Maybe Joyce would get a different hairstyle. Maxi sighed deeply. She should have waited till tomorrow to start this dummy. Any day was good for a dummy but only Thursdays brought the Hill. She could just stay to watch the opening shots.

No. She would, *she had to* stay right here. The program was probably a repeat anyway. She reached for the still-empty yellow legal pad that had been malevolently half-hiding under a pillow, picked up a pencil and slowly wrote "Why Short, Fat Men Are

Better in Bed, by Nancy Kissinger." Nancy should be glad to get a chance to tell the world, Maxi thought, and breathed deeply for the first time since she'd arranged herself on the bed. She licked the pencil and reflected deeply. She tugged three times at her white streak and slowly wrote "I Was Wrong About Penis Envy: An Unpublished Manuscript, by Sigmund Freud." A little long, that title, Maxi decided, but it did jump off the page at you. Her stomach rumbled. She had never realized how hungry it made you to think. Resisting the urge to go into the kitchen she scribbled "Why You Must Have Lots of Chocolate in Your Daily Diet." Who was head of the space program? She would get him to do it. Or Jane Fonda. Which one was the greatest authority figure? Jane, of course.

She slipped off the bed and started to walk in circles in front of the window, not even noticing the lights of Manhattan spread below as if she were an alien in a spaceship about to land in Central Park. Suddenly she jumped back on the bed and wrote quickly "The Ultimate Love-Hate Relationship: You and Your Hairdresser, by Boy George." She skipped a few lines, groaned a few times and then grabbed the pencil again. "Real Men Never Fantasize About Thin Women, by . . . by . . . Clint Eastwood . . . no, Mel Gibson . . . no, Mikhail Baryshnikov."

"Monthly column," Maxi said out loud. "Monthly column." She messed about with her hair, scratched her ears, tugged at her toes and finally wrote "Let's Talk Sex, by Tom Selleck." She smiled. The same amount of effort that went into thinking up a one-shot article could make a monthly column. It was an economy of effort, she realized, and decided to give it another try to see if it worked. She closed her eyes for a few minutes, poking around in her brain as if it were Santa's big white bag. After a little while she rubbed her eyes vigorously, opened them and carefully inscribed the words "The First Twenty-five Things I Adore About Women Over Thirty, by Warren Beatty." For another issue it could be women over forty, or fifty or twenty-five, with different writers like Richard Gere or Bill Murray or Sam Shepard or Prince or any particularly attractive man. Even if a reader weren't over the age that was under consideration, she could look forward to it or figure that she was prematurely adorable. "The Best Divorce I've Ever Had, by Liz Taylor." No column in that one, unless you added a Gabor another month and, no, it didn't have staying power. Most people didn't get divorced that often. Some people never got divorced even once, like the Queen of England for instance. Maxi wrote quickly "Queen: The Worst Job in the World, by Anthony Haden-Guest." She paused, wondering if her readers would know who Haden-Guest was, and decided that they probably wouldn't. She crossed out his name and wrote in its place, "by Prince Philip." She sneezed vigorously. This was a dusty business. "Where Do They Put the Kleenex Box? or What Five Famous Women's Bathrooms Really Look Like When They've Finished Dressing, a photo essay by Helmut Newton." With amazement she saw that she'd come to the bottom of the page. "Sex in a Moving Vehicle," she scratched on the next page. By John De Lorean. No. By Paul Newman.

"Ma!" The door to her bedroom opened suddenly.

"What is it, Angelica? Can't you see I'm working?"

"Come quick. Lucy's pregnant. Nobody knows who the father is, or what this will do to her career. Hurry or you'll miss it!"

"I can't stop now. Let me know when you find out. And shut the door after you."

"What happened to your compassion?" Angelica looked stunned. Was this the same mother whose only dream had been to be abandoned on a desert island with all the guys on the Hill?

"They're just actors," Maxi replied and wrote "Twenty Good Reasons Not to Have Children" at the top of another page.

Alone again, Maxi stretched cautiously. All her equipment was still surrounding her. She hadn't made a dent in the dummy yet but she had a strange yet familiar feeling in her stomach. This was . . . making these lists was . . . almost exactly, in fact *exactly* exactly like . . . having . . . *FUN!*

She popped off her bed in excitement at the realization and went to her bathroom mirror to take a good look at herself. She needed something familiar to calm her down from discovering that this thing that she had been avoiding even thinking about, this thing she hadn't told Pavka she was utterly terrified of, this actual writing down of ideas that related to her concept of a magazine that liked its readers, in their natural, imperfect state, was possible after all. She looked pale and messy and all her makeup was gone. The

254

mascara had smeared where she'd rubbed her eyes and if she didn't know how pretty she was she'd have been worried.

"'The Ten Top Models—What They *Really* Look Like,'" she said out loud. Justin could get those photos. Steal them . . . because no model would let him take a picture like that on purpose. But if he snapped them quickly before the makeup people and hair people went to work, the girls would never notice when they automatically signed the usual release forms. That would make a good start for the beauty pages for the first issue and make millions of women happy. Beauty pages, she mused. Yes, there would be all those departments filling out B&B, Beauty and Decorating and Fashion and even Health. Health sounded so institutional . . . why not call it "Living Well: Eating, Drinking and Having Sex" and begin with "The Ten Best Hangover Remedies"? A true public service, that was what it would be. Decorating? She'd make Milton and Leon do a piece on "Think Twice Before You Redecorate," with pages of horrible examples to illustrate the theme, and as for fashion, something soothing. Fashion always tended to make everyone so anxious. "The Ten Indispensable Things Every Woman ALREADY Owns, by Yves Saint-Laurent." With pictures showing how to use them. Maxi tapped her teeth with her pencil as she thought about the pictures.

"Ma, Lucy had a miscarriage," Angelica said sadly, popping her head in through the door. "She must have met a really wrong guy . . . she still won't say who he was."

"'Wonderful Mr. Wrong Guy, the Essential Not-to-Be-Missed Fun Experience in Every Woman's Life,'" said Maxi.

"I don't get it," Angelica said.

"You will, after Don Johnson explains it to you," Maxi assured her.

17

Paper cuts. Nothing helps paper cuts. There is no unguent or pill known to medicine that relieves the tiny but maddeningly painful presence of dozens of paper cuts on every fingertip. Backache. Nothing helps backache except a change of position, exercise and massage, so, if your work requires you to handle many pieces of paper while maintaining a certain back-straining position, you learned to endure backache and paper cuts. Eyestrain. When things got blurry you went to the bathroom and held a cold, wet washcloth over your eyelids, put in a few eye drops and returned to the task because the only thing that would remove eyestrain was to stop work, and that wasn't possible. Not until the dummy was done, because without the dummy *B&B* wouldn't be real.

"I suppose," Maxi said wearily to Angelica who was hovering over her anxiously, "this has built my character." She pushed the dummy aside, got up from her desk and flopped down flat on the carpet of her bedroom.

"You were perfect the way you were," Angelica retorted. She was so accustomed to feeling slightly superior to her screwball of a mother that this new serious incarnation, which of course couldn't possibly last longer than any other of Maxi's fads, was a little frightening. It had all started when she'd canceled that trip to Venice . . . nothing had been the same since. It couldn't possibly last more than another week, she thought. True, Maxi had stuck it out in the Border Country of Scotland for almost two years as Countess of Kirkgordon but this was different; that had been a marriage and this was just a magazine. Angelica shivered, remembering the biting winds of the moors, the drafts at Castle Dread, and then smiled, thinking kindly of her loony second stepfather. Had Ma understood he was nuts? Nicely nuts?

"When will it be finished, Ma?"

"What do you mean 'when'? Can't you tell it's finished now?" Maxi asked indignantly. "Why do you suppose I've stopped working? Could you please rub my back? Please, *please* rub my back. Walk on it in your bare feet, do something about my back, Angelica, if you love me."

"You're lying on your back. Turn over."

"I can't. I don't have the strength."

"Ma, come on, just roll over."

"I will, in a minute. Angelica, isn't it gorgeous? Don't you think my dummy is fabulous?"

Angelica took a look at the object she had grown to loathe. It didn't look any different from the way it had in her mother's first four attempts at making a dummy. It was hugely fat and bulgy and sloppy and exceptionally uninviting to the eye. Just looking at it, she felt that it would fall apart if she touched it. Obscurely it reminded Angelica of school. She was sure she'd made something very much like it in third grade, only smaller and a great deal more attractive.

"It's awesome, Ma, really awesome. I like the red cover. That's a very nice, bright red, definitely eye-catching."

Maxi rolled over, groaning, and looked squarely at her daughter. "What's wrong with it?" she demanded.

"Nothing's wrong with it, honestly. It's hot, I mean I don't know what a dummy is supposed to look like anyway so I don't have any basis for comparison, but the cover is a great red . . . a humpy red."

Maxi stood up and went over to the desk on which the dummy sat.

"It looks like shit," she said quietly. "A bundle of red shit. And it's the best I can fucking do."

"Ma!"

"I'm sorry, Angelica, but I'm not employing any words you don't know . . . and use, from time to time."

"It's not your language, Ma, it's what you said. You've worked so hard. It's *got* to be good. You couldn't be wrong about it—you're just tired. You're not a fair judge."

"You don't have to be a judge of shit. When you see it you know it. I need help. Specifically I need an art director. Who's the best art director in the world, Angelica?"

"Why ask silly questions that you know the answer to as well as I do?"

"Who can always get your father on the phone, at any time of day or night?"

"Me, but you wouldn't want *me* to ask *him* to help *you!* You've always said you wouldn't ask him for a crust of bread if you were dying of hunger or a sip of water if you were dying of thirst."

"I don't want bread or water. I want the best art director in the world."

"Would you settle for second best . . . please?"

"Angelica, that's unworthy of you."

"Well then, call him and ask him yourself. The two of you always talk on the phone. What's the big deal?"

"We only talk about you, Angelica, and who is going to pick you up, and where and when. We never talk about anything else, not even the weather."

"That's too dumb for words."

"But that's the way it is."

"Well. I don't approve. And I'm late for my guitar lesson. Adults!" Angelica said in disgust and disappeared so quickly that when Maxi went running after her, all she saw were the doors of the elevator closing swiftly and soundlessly on the brown and beige carpet of the corridor.

Maxi marched back to her room, not bothering even to glance into any of the many rooms of her new apartment, each one so expensively appointed by Bizet and Ludwig, each one filled with the collection of furniture and paintings and sculpture she had tracked down all over the world, hundreds of quickly purchased objects that had seemed necessary to her until the minute she owned them. She hadn't used any room of the apartment except her bedroom since she'd started work on the dummy a week ago. She'd had her meals standing up in the kitchen, eating whatever the new cook had seen fit to leave for her in the fridge and returning to work immediately with a quick wave to Angelica if her daughter happened to be home.

Her lips tight—talk about the ingratitude of children!—she dialed the number of Cipriani, Lefkowitz and Kelly. Rocco's secretary told her that Mr. Cipriani was in a meeting with some gentlemen from General Foods and couldn't possibly be disturbed. And after that he was due at Avedon's studio. A Calvin Klein commercial.

"But this is an emergency, Miss Haft," Maxi explained. She was put through immediately.

"What's happened to Angelica?" Rocco demanded, in alarm.

"She's fine. Impossible but fine."

"Then . . . why did you call?" he asked coldly.

"Rocco, I need your help."

"Something *has* happened to Angelica! Damn it, Maxi . . ."

"Rocco, your daughter is in perfect mental and physical health. But I have to have your professional assistance on a business matter and I need it fast. When can you come here? I can't bring it to your office. You'll understand when you see it."

"Maxi, whatever it is you 'have to have,' get it from somebody else."

"No."

"I'm in a meeting. Goodbye."

"Rocco—if you don't come to my house and help me I'm going to . . . to . . . put Angelica on the pill."

"She's only eleven, for Christ's sake!"

"Ah, but soon she'll be twelve and she's awfully mature—you know how precocious she is. Girls are ready for motherhood much earlier these days and with your rampaging Latin blood in her, well, anything might happen. Better safe than sorry. Have you read the latest statistics on teenage pregnancies? I remember when I was her age . . ." Maxi's voice trailed off, full of improvised memories.

"Tonight at nine." Rocco hung up without another word.

Humming happily, Maxi called her masseuse and made an appointment. Hilda would be over within a half hour. Then a long bath—she could wash her hair in the shower and take a nice nap. Why, she wondered, did men make life so difficult for themselves? If they would only always be pleasant and agreeable and helpful.

But no, their characters were such that they simply forced you to employ alternative means of persuasion. It went against her better nature not to be direct, but in an emergency you had to use whatever methods were available. Angelica didn't even like boys. It would be another, oh, at least six years before they had to think about the pill. Or perhaps she'd want to remain a virgin until she married. Virginity was coming back in. Maxi picked up her yellow pad and wrote absently, "Try Celibacy and See, by Dan Aykroyd and Chevy Chase."

"It's a *what?*" Rocco said incredulously, staring at the red heap.

"You heard me the first time. I want you to fix it and I want it to be the most beautiful fucking dummy ever made on the face of the earth," Maxi said in a businesslike tone.

"I don't do dummies anymore, Maxi. I believe you're aware of that fact," he said, shaking with rage. This rotten bitch needed a good spanking so badly that it made his teeth ache just thinking about it. To think that he had once married a creature so evil, so low, so utterly vile. So selfish, so self-centered, so . . . to say nothing of using outright blackmail. How Angelica managed to be as lovable, as perfect as she was, coming from a mother like this, was a miracle of the supremacy of his own gene pool. No wonder he'd never even been tempted to marry again. This—this disgrace to her gender would turn any man against marriage for life.

"Why the hell *should* I do it?" he asked. "There are dozens of guys I can recommend who can turn that thing into a dummy. There's no mystery to it."

"Because you'll do a better job," Maxi said inexorably.

"Better by a few degrees, maybe, but what difference does it make? What counts is what's *in* the magazine, not just the dummy. People aren't fooled by a pretty page, they look for content."

"The content is O.K. I didn't ask you for help on the content, only on the presentation."

"Just like that, hm? O.K.? All from your little brain? Would it interest you to know that Time, Inc. has a super high-powered magazine-development group working on new ideas? They've got eighteen top people, including Stolley who founded *People* and Fier from *Rolling Stone* plus seventeen free-lancers and fifteen business types all working like crazy with a budget of over three million a year? Fifty people, headed by Marshall Loeb who made a success of *Money*, the best brains Time could buy. They've already got a finished dummy on something called *Women's Week* and another called *Investor's Weekly*, plus a number of others with covers and boards? What do you say to that?"

"It doesn't bother me. I don't believe in committees. Henry Luce probably didn't believe in committees either, when he was alive. My father didn't believe in committees. Do you have all night to sit around talking shop, Rocco, or do you want to get started on my dummy?" Maxi said evenly. Her ruffled, artfully messed hair remained firmly on her head and Rocco couldn't see her scalp prickling in horror. What if one of Time, Inc.'s brain trust had come up with *her* concept?

"I'm leaving here as soon as I've talked to Angelica about the pill and what taking it too young can do to her."

"Don't bother," Maxi said indignantly. "I'd never let her near it, you ass. You never did know when I was joking, that was your problem. One of the many. Anyway tonight is the night Angelica is allowed to watch MTV and she won't like to be disturbed." She went over to the dummy, picked it up and thrust it into Rocco's arms so quickly that he automatically held on to it.

"Shit!"

"I know, that's why I need you. Sit down, and read it."

"I'll give you three minutes, you lying bitch. And only because Angelica knows I'm here and you'd bad-mouth me if I don't look at this mess. What the hell is *B&B?* That stinks for openers. It's a brand name of an after-dinner drink made by monks, not a magazine name," Rocco puffed, struggling with the floppy mass.

He sat down at Maxi's desk, put the thing on the desktop, and began leafing rapidly through the pages. Maxi held her breath, watching him closely for the sign of any reaction. She had not actually laid eyes on Rocco for over four years. When Angelica was seven she had been quite grown-up enough to be picked up and delivered from Maxi's apartment to Rocco's apartment by one or the other of them, or by Elie, without their having to have the slightest contact. Christ, she thought, the mistakes a girl can make because a man is impossibly beautiful. He looks almost exactly as he did when I first saw him and it just simply couldn't matter less . . . it's as if he were invisible. He has as little appeal as a bottle of gin does to someone who's been in A.A. for twenty years. I wonder when he'll start losing his hair and getting fat? It's inevitable, just a question of time. There must be something fundamentally wrong with him anyway, all those girls he sees, the ones Angelica talks about, and he hasn't managed to settle down. Yet he's thirty-six if he's a day. He'll be a sad, lonely old bachelor soon . . . bad for Angelica because old bachelors die young. Why isn't he reacting? He looked right through the Kissinger article with all those blissfully snooty pictures of Nancy, and didn't even blink, the son of a bitch. He just doesn't want to give me the satisfaction. Well, I don't give a fart about his opinion . . . *B&B* is for women, not sell-out magazine men who've lowered themselves to make commercials. I'm glad he's successful, for Angelica's sake, but obviously the bugger couldn't possibly enjoy his life, not with that pinched, set look he's got on his face.

Rocco flipped through the dummy, came to the end and slapped his hand down on it, closing it firmly, and pushing it away.

"How much is this going to sell for?"

"Rocco! You mean it has a chance? Oh, Rocco! You'd never have asked me that if you didn't think it was good." Maxi jumped up and down, more relieved than she could have believed possible.

"It has a certain . . . quality. I don't mean it has 'quality,' God knows, I mean there's something catchy about it . . . a reflection of your twisted mind. It might sell a few copies."

"I want it to sell for a dollar fifty."

"You're raving. Much too cheap."

"That's what *People* costs, and everyone buys it."

"Maxi, I really don't like to break this news to you but you're talking about one of the biggest-circulation books in the country and it sits at the supermarket checkout counters at point-of-sale where women just automatically put it into their shopping carts."

"That's where *B&B* will be," Maxi said calmly. "It's meant for the same audience, plus the *Cosmo* audience and the *Good House* audience. *Women*, Rocco, women. There are a lot of women in this country who will buy a magazine that likes them *just the way they are,* a magazine that they can have fun with, a magazine that guarantees a good time."

"Where'd you steal that concept?" Rocco demanded.

"Oh, it just came to me. One day. Out of the blue."

"For a buck fifty you have to have enormous circulation—at least four—no, make that five million, to make money. And ads and more ads. You're living in a dream. You haven't even got a distributor, I'll bet."

"I wouldn't take your money," Maxi said with dignity. "I'm quite aware that it's a crapshoot, but then I like to gamble. I'm not interested in special groups; *Bon Appétit* this isn't . . . I'm going for the mass market and if it doesn't work, well, back to the drawing board."

"Big talk, big talk. Whose money are you going to be losing? Lily's?"

"I don't intend to lose. Now let's stop haggling. I want you to make this dollar-fifty magazine look like a million. You can do it with graphics even if the paper isn't up to *Town & Country* standards, even if the binding is perfected instead of saddled. Think of it as a chance to do your tricks with white space again, to do the things you used to do without General Foods and General Motors getting into your act. Freedom, Rocco. I'm offering you complete artistic freedom! You can be honest again. I'm doing you a favor, Rocco, although you don't seem to realize it. In fact, you might show a little gratitude."

"Bitch!"

"But you can't resist this challenge, can you?"

"Easily. I'll send you a first-class free-lancer. I've got forty major clients to service. What kind of megalomania does it take for you to think that I have time to diddle around with the dummy of a new magazine—it's a *huge* job."

"No, I want you."

"You still think you can have everything you want, don't you? It's really extraordinary, it's almost admirable, to be so stuck in the past, like the survival of some prehistoric animal, still breathing even though it's up to its ears in ooze."

"Have it your way," Maxi sighed. "Just send me somebody

really good. Oh, and Rocco, before you go, I have some brochures to show you."

"Brochures? What about?"

"Swiss boarding schools. There are about a half-dozen good ones. It's time Angelica went away to school. It's not just for the French and the skiing. She's subject to all sorts of bad influences in the city. I don't have to tell you that they sell pot and LSD and angel dust in the playgrounds. And the kids she knows are too hip. She really should be in Switzerland. You can see her in the summer—when she is not at camp—even go over for Christmas, if you miss her."

"You . . . you . . ." He was wordless with rage. He'd kill the creature.

"Oh, I *am* pleased that you changed your mind," Maxi said, cooing. "When can I expect the finished product?"

"In three shakes of a lamb's tail," he said, between his clenched teeth.

"What exactly does that mean? A week? Two weeks?"

"I'll show you," Rocco screamed and grabbed her, turned her upside down on her bed and smacked her as hard as he could on her bottom. *"One,"* he shouted, "and *two."* He hit her again. "And *three!"*

"Coward," Maxi panted, and tried to punch him in the balls. He grunted and hit her again, falling on the bed from her strong blow which had landed on one knee. Maxi grabbed his hair and pulled it as viciously as she could while he tried to gain a purchase on the mattress to give her a shaking that would break her spine. She slithered away just before his hands could close on her shoulders, did a sort of semi-jackknife and grabbed his penis firmly in both hands. He went totally immobile. God knew what she might do, starting with emasculation. Neither of them moved a muscle, waiting in a silence broken only by their breathing, for the next move. The silence grew longer and, to his utter disgust, Rocco felt his penis hardening in Maxi's unrelenting grip. Harder and harder. There was nothing on earth he could do to stop the damn thing from reacting. He tried mightily to pull away but she had him too tightly. After half a minute it became slightly less important to get out of her hands, and as soon as she felt the change in him she used

264

one of her hands to unzip his fly while, with the other, her grip changed from that of a prison warden to that of a woman, opening and closing her fingers around him in a rhythm he'd never been able to resist.

"Bitch," he grunted.

"Shut up," she replied, and began to caress his penis with delicate feathery strokes, while she cuddled his balls with the hand that had unzipped his fly. He attacked his belt buckle and pushed his trousers and tight jockey shorts down below his knees to give her more room to move in, but Maxi concentrated her attention on his penis, never straying away to touch the rest of his body. She didn't intend to give him an instant to think. A penis, as every woman knows, has no brain. It was jerking strongly as it grew bigger, almost twitching away from her while she lapped it with her tongue until she heard his unwilling groan of pleasure. She dragged her tongue slowly up from the base of his penis, pausing every now and then as if wondering whether to go further, putting her entire open mouth around his shaft as far as it would go, sucking hard for just an instant, and then resumed her leisurely progress toward the full, pronounced and tender line at the base of the tip. There she paused and made her tongue into a hot little arrow that circled the swelling head, but she didn't take it into her mouth. He'd have to ask for it, she thought, as she slid out of her underwear without his noticing her rapid movement beneath her skirt.

"Please," she heard him breathe, *"please."* At his words, she raised herself slightly and lowered her mouth down on the enormous head of his penis, first just holding it and exploring the hot pulsing shape with the whole of the inside of her lips and her now-flattened tongue. He pushed his hips up from the mattress in strong demanding movements and at that well-remembered signal Maxi began to suck with all the power she had, maddened now by the need to possess this flesh, to own it, to draw it into herself. From a distance she heard his breath coming faster and faster. At that she pulled her mouth away but still held his penis. With a quick move she slid upward on the bed, and put one knee on each side of his body. Quickly she lowered herself down onto him, so that he was totally enfolded in her wet, waiting nest. Savagely intent, she rode him, raising and lowering her pelvis, eluding his grasping hands

265

that tried to slow her down, moving faster and faster, giving it to him, giving it to him good, caught up in a relentless rhythm as she felt her own orgasm growing with each thrust she made, with each time she plunged down onto his body and her clitoris came into contact with the base of his penis, rubbing quickly and deeply before she rose up again. Madly they moved in unison, until their backs tensed, arched, held still for a tiny instant and then, bodies remembering, came together in a wildness, a long, drawn-out, shaking, heaving burst of magnificent release.

Maxi collapsed on top of Rocco. His eyes were closed and he had gone completely limp. She mustered up the force to roll off his body. Both of them still had their shoes on, she noticed in part of her mind, as well as all their clothes except for her panties. His lips moved but she couldn't hear what he had said. She pulled herself up closer and his lips moved again.

"Grudge fuck," he croaked.

"Mercy hump," she hissed, and pushed him with the little energy she had left, so that he almost fell off the edge of the bed. Weaving, he managed to get to his feet. With difficulty he pushed his shirt into his trousers and zipped them and stumbled around, disoriented.

"You forgot the dummy," Maxi murmured. He picked it up wordlessly and stumbled toward the door.

"How many ad pages can I count on from CL&K?" she called as he fumbled for the doorknob.

"God help me," he muttered and tried to slam the door after him, with no success.

Maxi lay on the bed and rolled her eyes at the ceiling. Every man has a weak point, she thought, and it was the same one with all of them. If you understood that simple fact, you could beat the odds every time. What's more, she had discovered the cure for paper cuts.

266

18

Cut. And . . . print!" The director's valedictory tone marked the final second, the final take of India West's latest picture.

She almost ran to her dressing room, radiant with liberty and the unprecedented fact that her shrink, Dr. Florence Florsheim, was on vacation at the same time as the picture wrapped. This conjunction of events hadn't happened in the years since she'd become a star. She was at liberty to rush to the aid of Maxi whose last phone call had been so disturbing. There must be something seriously wrong. Maxi hadn't called in two weeks and since that Sunday, whenever India tried to telephone her the only person she could reach was Angelica who had developed an interesting talent of lying convincingly. "Ma's working and absolutely can't be disturbed," she'd said each time, and if India didn't have a profound knowledge of her friend's character she would have believed the child. Well, it was probably hereditary, that talent for lying. Angelica was as believable as Maxi herself.

But whatever sinister mystery was going on "back East" as she found herself saying, in the same way the English stuck for life in some Indian garrison town used to say "home" when they meant Britain, India intended to find out about it at first hand. Tomorrow she was flying to New York, her bags were packed, the beastly dogs were in a kennel that charged only a little less than the Beverly Hills Hotel, and by evening she'd know what was up with her oldest and her only best friend.

Maxi couldn't have been serious about that absurd plan she had to publish a magazine about . . . zippers? Her story had been hard to follow, interrupted as it had been by bouts of self-recrimination and violent outbursts against her wretched uncle. Except for

Lily, who was so often photographed, it was hard to visualize Maxi's family, India thought. She'd caught glimpses of Toby and Justin a few brief times all those years ago when she and Maxi were both teenagers doing their homework together. After Maxi's first marriage, her contact with the Amberville family had been maintained purely through what her friend told her. If Maxi hadn't visited from time to time during these last six years in California they would scarcely have laid eyes on each other since Maxi's first divorce, when India was in the process of leaving Manhattan for her freshman year at college. She had managed to catch up with Maxi and to spend a few days on board the yacht when her friend had decided to take on heavenly Bad Dennis Brady, in Monte Carlo, but she'd missed the miserable Scottish years entirely. A shame about that; the Countess of Kirkgordon must have been a priceless, not-to-be-forgotten piece of miscasting.

Now Maxi *was* her family, India reflected. Her own parents were dead, but Maxi had remained the one fixed point in her life. Even though ninety-nine percent of their contact was by phone, they could read each other's minds through the receivers. What's more, she was Angelica's godmother, and made up for her lack of physical attendance by sending her marvelous presents. You wouldn't think a nice little girl would lie like that to her own darling, lovable, gift-sending godmother, would you? She'd have to have a long talk with the youngster about Emerson and the importance of the truth. With Maxi for a mother there was no way of knowing what bad habits she might have fallen into, India told herself with a dubious shake of her head. She'd straighten the kid out. Give her the benefit of some of Doctor Florsheim's insights, buy her some decent sheets.

Maxi was having a Rolodex housewarming. Everyone listed in her Rolodex had been invited, and had accepted. Working through one morning with Julie, neither of them off the phone for a minute, out of sheer *joie de vivre* at the thought of her precious dummy being transformed by Rocco, she had put the party together in the way she liked best. "Parties should just pop up out of nowhere, for the same night," she said to Julie. "If you give people time to plan what they're going to wear and get their hair done and wonder who else will be there, you take the bloom off the rose. And if they've made other plans, they can always bring their friends with them. It's like a marvelous surprise package."

It was a zoo, a very choice zoo for only the best species. Gazelles, peacocks, antlered stags, superb panthers, sleek seals, self-satisfied lions and, here and there, a delicate monkey. Manhattan animals all, the decibel level of their voices reaching a pitch that no group in any major city of the world could, or would desire, to produce.

The front door was left wide open because the doorbell could not be heard inside. India, followed by the elevator man carrying her luggage, paused on the threshold, bewildered. She started to turn around and leave. Obviously this was no time for a surprise visit. She'd go to the suite the studio kept at the Palace and call tomorrow. Parties made her more horribly shy than usual.

"Godmother!" Angelica, as reverently as possible, lifted her six inches off the floor and looked at her, stunned. "It's you! You yourself, in person. Totally awesome! Ma tried to call but you weren't home. How did you know about the party?"

"You . . . are . . . Angelica?"

"I know, I've grown. I'll put you down. I didn't hurt you, did I?"

"Of course not. You just—surprised—me. Now, listen here, Angelica, you told me your mother couldn't be disturbed because she was working and I walk in on a madhouse. What's going on?"

"She *was* working, Godmother, until last night. Macabre! Now she's relaxing."

"And why do you have three holes punched in each of your ears, Angelica? And why are you wearing feather-tufted studs in them? Have you joined a religious cult?" India asked as severely as possible in the face of the consternation Angelica's unexpected beauty caused. Had she any idea of what she would become?

"I went for it, Godmother," Angelica explained. "Do you think it was a mistake? I feel like a freakazoid, to tell you the truth. But do you like my to-die-for denims? Hot, huh? I think they were made in a leper colony somewhere. Macabre!"

"I can relate to them," India said carefully, reaching as far

269

back as she could into the seventies for a suitable response. "The holes in your ears will grow back together if you take the studs out and could you please stop calling me Godmother?"

"If you insist," Angelica agreed, a little crestfallen. "I'll take your bags to the guest bedroom . . . India." Angelica lifted them easily and began to lead the way into the apartment.

"No. Stop. I couldn't possibly stay here. It's jammed," India said, ready to flee.

"The bottom line, India, is that I will clear the guest room out for you in five seconds. You're the guest of honor. Could you be totally into that?"

"Do you always talk this way, Angelica?"

"I try. I try," Angelica said, picking up India's luggage and clearing a pathway for her.

That child needs help, India thought, as she quickly changed her clothes in the locked guest room. It was lucky she had come. It might not be too late. Obviously Maxi had neglected her education. India wafted out of the room, wearing a dress of white lace and white chiffon from Judyth van Amringe that floated so lightly that it seemed to be held together only by her brooch, an antique Greek coin set in cabochon sapphires and emeralds, which she'd pinned just above one hipbone. Her beauty was a creature of seasons, lacking only a winter; a changeable, endlessly mesmerizing parade as she flowed from the embodiment of bewitching spring to full summer to ripe autumn, depending on the demands of the director or the script. Today, left to her own decision, she was springtime in all its promise, all its freshness.

Shy as she was, India was realistic. There was no way to find clothes that would make her disappear at parties so she might just as well look like a star. People expected it and essentially it aroused less attention than did the tatty, ratty, why-should-I-bother-to-dress-for-*you*, Diane Keaton look that just made people curious and hostile. Nor, in a year in which clothes glittered, would she give in to it, because anything that sparkled made her feel like an Oscar presenter and she was, after all, an Oscar winner.

India went in search of Maxi, moving with a deliberate drift, a technique she'd perfected for parties, designed to keep her in motion at all times. If stopped, she still suggested constant movement by the way she leaned away from the person who talked to her. She never carried a glass so that if she found herself stuck in conversation she could say, "Oh, I must find a drink, I'll be right back," and disengage herself. Or she could ask the man she was talking to— women never seemed to want to say anything to her—to be an angel and get her a drink and then escape in another direction. If India actually wanted a drink she went to the bar, got it from the bartender, drank it straight down and gave the glass back immediately.

India always looked into the air above people so that they couldn't catch her eye, zigzagged slightly as she drifted, so that she presented a moving target, and wore an expression that instantly conveyed that she was intent on joining someone she knew terribly well on the other side of the room. This combination enabled her to attend the necessary Hollywood parties without actually having to speak to anyone except the agents from Creative Artists who were everywhere and who ignored her act and tended to hug her a lot. As a client, she didn't intimidate them, for how could they be intimidated by any woman, no matter how fabled a beauty, when that beauty was theirs to sell and her income was automatically reduced by their commission?

Actually, India thought, as she drifted, hoping that she was insulated by her mannerisms, she never felt shy with her agents or the men who were physically involved in the making of movies. They knew she was just another girl, once they'd graduated from apprenticeship and reached the stage of second assistant to a second assistant to someone or other. Doctor Florence Florsheim said that there was no difference between being an elusive motion-picture star and a plain, everyday wallflower, India thought, fighting the beginning of panic.

"What was the worst thing that could happen if you did get involved in a conversation?" Dr. Florsheim always wanted to know. India couldn't explain to her own satisfaction. Her mind blanked out at the conversation itself. It *was* the worst thing. Something about the way she looked stopped conversation dead, leaving the burden of human exchange on her incurably reluctant shoulders. The best thing about Dr. Florsheim was that she never looked at India, except when she came in and when she left the office, and she never permitted small talk.

Maintaining her seemingly purposeful course, but picking up speed, India went from room to room, panic mounting as Maxi didn't appear. Soon she'd have to start looking at people instead of above them, and that meant the risk of catching someone's eye.

"I'm *sorry!*" She had bumped directly into a man, causing him to spill the two glasses he was holding all over his suit. "My God, I'm clumsy, I wasn't looking, let me help mop up, oh dear," she babbled, blushing with confusion.

"It's just vodka, don't worry. No harm done," he reassured her, and there was something in the resonance of his voice, something that she caught at his first words that utterly dissolved her panic. He would probably be in control of the situation if *he'd* spilled the drinks on *her*, she thought, amazed at his ability to calm her down. Only a few film directors had ever been able to do that with so few words, and they had been the great ones.

"You seem to be looking for somebody," he remarked. "Can I help?"

"No," India heard herself answering. "I was just wandering around." Maxi could wait, she decided, daring to actually look at the man she'd just drenched. He was almost a head taller than she was, probably in his early thirties, and as he stood there calmly, ignoring his wet jacket, she found herself wondering what he'd look like if he were in love. A passing waiter took away the two glasses he was still holding. She grabbed a handful of cocktail napkins. "Couldn't I just . . . you're dripping on the carpet," she laughed, making a tentative swabbing motion. He took the napkins out of her hand and held them.

"Vodka evaporates and doesn't leave a stain. There's enough body heat in this room to make it disappear in a minute." The words were simple enough but there was a meditative expression on his face, as if, somehow, he were dreaming and as if the dream were one of gallantry. So fascinated that she forgot her habitual fear of anyone unknown, India found herself looking at him as particularly inquisitive and tactless people sometimes looked at her, as if they could learn something just from the way her features connected

272

with each other. There's a courtliness to him, she thought, something to do with being kind and firm and confident, something about his mouth, formed for . . . no, *by* bravery. And an impatience at the same time. There was a kind of impact of . . . was it concentration? He was, somehow, electrokinetic. She hoped he wouldn't go away to whomever he had been bringing the drinks, but he seemed disinclined to move. They stood together in the middle of the restlessly busy room, an island of two tall, isolated people. She peered into his eyes and it seemed to her that he was looking at her urgently, with intensity, yet with no sign of recognition, of the deference or bedazzlement she was resigned to seeing.

"I like your voice," he said.

"Thank you." For the first time in her life she didn't feel that she had to apologize for a compliment. His confidence seemed to be contagious.

"It makes love to the air," he added.

"Well, you know that there's always the chance that perhaps it's just a trick," she answered, using, in a sudden, unexpected rush of her old sense of mischief, the accent she had learned to play Blanche DuBois, slurring her pronouns with a kind of breathless, giddy emphasis on the verbs, ending the sentence with her voice vaguely going up at the end of the phrase.

He smiled as if she were deliciously, childishly silly, and India felt ridiculously proud of herself.

"A plantation voice," he said, "I've always liked a girl with a plantation voice, but it's not precisely suitable to you. You're too timid to be Southern . . . that's their charm . . . they never let their shyness show so they don't arouse it in others."

"And mine shows?" she asked, downcast. She'd always believed that she hadn't been really good as Blanche, even if everybody said she had been.

"Instantly. To me, anyway. But I like that too. To be timid at times is universal to the human race, but in this city people become aggressive just so that their natural, normal, inevitable shyness won't be revealed. The result"—he gestured—"is what you hear. It's tiring to listen to, and hard to combat. Half the time I whisper . . . you can be heard more easily under the noise than above it."

"I had a coach once who told me that."

"A coach?" He bent toward her and peered at her even more closely.

"A . . . vocal coach," she said, bewildered.

"Are you a singer?"

"I've been known to sing," India answered, utterly astonished. It had been so many years since she had met someone who didn't know who she was that she hardly knew how to treat this fact. Her eyes sharpened with sudden suspicion. Oh Lord, let him not be one of those people who pretended not to recognize her. They were worse than gawkers. No, whatever he was he simply wasn't a moviegoer or a magazine reader. In his household she obviously wasn't a household word.

"What else do you do?" he asked, giving her no time to ask about him. He had a habit of command, she realized as she replied.

"I . . . work . . . and, well, you know, live, like everybody else. I feed my dogs and go to exercise class and read a lot and swim and, well, go to a few parties, and that's about it. I guess that doesn't sound like a very full life . . . oh, and I go to my shrink, of course, Doctor Florence Florsheim . . . stop laughing! I don't see what's so funny about that, it's a name like any other, she can't help it though . . . with Florence for a first name perhaps she shouldn't have . . . married Mr. Florsheim." India was reduced to a puddle of giggles. "She must have been madly in love, or maybe it's her maiden name."

"Did you ever ask her?" he wanted to know.

"She rarely answers questions. She's very orthodox about that anyway."

"My shrink answers questions."

"Then he's not a Freudian," she pronounced with a superior air.

"He told me that, like every other shrink, he stood on Freud's shoulders, but he'd thrown away the stuff he didn't believe in . . . if you say you hate your mother he assumes that your old lady was a tough number, until proven otherwise, not that you wanted to make love to her when you were three."

"I like the sound of that. But I'm stuck with Doctor Florsheim . . . she knows too much," India said darkly.

"Other people's shrinks always sound better than your own.

It's the first rule of analysis. However, I agree about your life, it doesn't seem exactly full. What about a husband and children?"

"Nonexistent. And you?"

"Never married, no kids."

"Aren't you interested or haven't you had the time?" India inquired cautiously. There had to be something wrong. There always was.

"It's just never happened yet, but it will. Meanwhile I'm available, shamelessly available, and I'd like to get out of this hellhole and take you to dinner. Shall we go?"

"Oh, *yes*," India replied.

"*India! What* are you doing here?" Maxi asked, so surprised that she squeaked.

"Hello, darling. I'll tell you later. I have to go out to dinner now," India said ruthlessly, trying in one glance to convey love, support, and the absolute necessity of Maxi's letting her escape the party with this man, this heavenly, heavenly man, before another second passed and someone—perhaps the person he'd been getting the drinks for—appeared and tried to get him away from her, because she would not, could not run that risk.

"But Toby, you just can't disappear with India like that," Maxi wailed, outraged. "She is *my* friend, damn it, not yours, and nobody ever even told me she was here."

"Toby?" India whispered in a voice of wonder that held both shock and the beginning of choice.

"India? *That* friend? The one who's the most beautiful girl in the world?" Toby stopped dead, a complex set of emotions appearing on his face, hesitation first among them.

"Oh, shut up!" India said, timid no longer. "You said you *liked* me four times. So don't act like a . . . dumbbell. Anyway, it's too late now, isn't it?"

"My, my," Maxi cooed, "I think the two of you are going to have your first fight. Oh, good! Can I listen?"

19

Cutter Amberville seemed intent on retracing his exact path, as if he were putting his feet into footprints he'd made on a wet and sandy beach, as he walked back and forth on the carpet that lay in front of the window behind his desk. His hands were clasped tightly together behind his back, his knuckles cutting off the circulation to his fingertips so that they were much redder than his fingers. Maxi watched him as he walked, perched on the arm of the chair she had chosen, refusing the low chair he had offered. Instead, taking her time, she had picked out a chair with a reasonably wide arm, and pulled it to precisely the spot she intended to be in, at a distance too far away from his desk for his comfort.

She swung her legs, clad in high shining riding boots and brown velvet jodhpurs laced from boot-top to knee. She caressed the frilled neck of the Victorian lace blouse she wore under a brown velvet, shawl-collared jacket, nipped in at the waist, a Chantal Thomass fantasy that was never meant to come near the saddle of a horse.

"Cutter," she said, breaking his fuming silence, "my driver is double-parked downstairs. Would you disgorge whatever you seemed so anxious to see me about, so that he doesn't get a ticket?"

Cutter turned and finally stopped his pacing, leaning with both hands on the top of his enormous desk.

"I can see that I underestimated you, Maxi," he said.

"Couldn't you have told me that on the phone? I'm a busy woman, and this trip downtown has fouled up my morning. Time is money, Cutter, time is money!"

Weeks had passed since Rocco had finished the miraculous dummy, dozens of expensive people were on Maxi's payroll, the work of completing the first issue and laying out those to follow was going on at top speed, all propelled by Maxi's flood of energy, working seven days out of seven.

Not only was the door to her office always open, the room did not, by her instructions, even have a door, nor did Maxi have a desk. There was a big table in the middle of her office covered with cases of cold soft drinks and urns of coffee, tea and Sanka which were always kept full by the cateress Maxi had hired for that task; a woman who kept platters piled with cookies and brownies and made stacks of thick, delicious sandwiches that were constantly replenished. A number of high, round tables surrounded the feast, with bar stools invitingly placed about them. The tables could easily be pushed together when the group around them grew larger. Her office was as close to the kind of eighteenth-century coffeehouse in which Samuel Johnson would have felt at home as Maxi could devise, and the result was the one she had planned for: everyone on her brilliant, young, constantly growing, highly paid staff wandered in at least once or twice a day, knowing that they were permanently welcome and would be royally fed. They tended to hang around and talk about *B&B*, people from all departments getting to know each other; and from this constant rubbing together of the best talent in the magazine business, from these excited "why the hell not?" conversations, came a steady stream of new ideas for the magazine, not one of which was ever lost, for Maxi noted them all down, unobtrusively perched on one or another of the stools. When she was busy elsewhere, or on the phone, one of her rotating staff of three secretaries replaced her. The only reason that Maxi had agreed to come down to Cutter's office was that she wouldn't let him see her own. He'd contaminate it.

"I never would have believed you had it in you," Cutter continued. "No, not even you."

"But you haven't even seen the first layouts," Maxi answered, annoyed. Could someone have leaked him pages? Did he have a spy planted on her staff?

"I'm not talking about your magazine, Maxi, whatever it may be." Cutter looked her full in the face and she realized that he was flushed, almost crimson, with suppressed rage. He pushed a pile of paper across the desk to her.

"These are what I'm talking about, *these!* Bills for millions of dollars, bills that those damn fool accountants have been paying automatically, because they were signed for by an Amberville, paying without asking me, without questioning them, bills for paper, for rent, for furnishings, for salaries, for photos, for articles, for expenses, for . . ."

"Food," Maxi interrupted. "Start-up money is always more than you expect," Maxi added with composure. "It won't be as expensive once *B&B* is actually out and, naturally, as soon as we start making money the whole picture will change."

"No, don't play that game with me, Maxi. I know, and you know that I know, what we agreed on. *Buttons and Bows!* That was the magazine you wanted and that was the one you got. A trimming magazine with almost no budget at all. This thing, this *B&B,* whatever it is, has absolutely nothing to do with the deal we made."

"Not so," Maxi said coolly. "It's as much *Buttons and Bows* as *Buttons and Bows* was *Trimming Trades Monthly.* It even says so on the masthead. You never said I couldn't update the magazine, Cutter. You didn't utter a word about not changing it into something more viable. You gave me a year and I'm taking my year, and that year has barely begun."

"I never gave you the right to spend millions," Cutter said violently, hitting the desk with his fists.

"I hope that desk isn't valuable," Maxi commented with a tiny yawn. "It looks authentic, but then they make such good copies these days."

"Millions of dollars . . . I never said . . ."

"Ah, but you didn't say I couldn't, did you, Cutter?" Maxi smiled lazily at him, and readjusted the lace at her neck, preening, and then flicked a spot of dust off one of her boots. Her eyebrows rose in amusement until they were hidden by her bangs. "It's too late now, you see. I've already—and in person—sold six months of advertising, at very special introductory rates, to dozens of major advertisers. They also all advertise in the other Amberville publications, and, naturally, they have every reason to believe that when an Amberville comes to them with a splendid concept for a new magazine and an absolutely smashing dummy, they're spending their money safely. Amberville Publications is *committed* to *B&B*, Cutter, totally committed as far as the advertising and business community is concerned. As long as the magazine is being published we *have* to run those ads, or else give them their money back and look, at the very least, frivolous, unbusinesslike. Especially since you just took it upon yourself to fold three other books. They all know that *B&B* has your special blessing, Cutter. I've made sure they realized that. You can't *touch* my magazine without making everyone suspect that the entire company is about to go under."

"Do you have any idea what the money you spent is going to do to our balance sheet?" he demanded.

"Punch a giant hole in it, I imagine. And, Cutter," Maxi said, rising and moving toward the door, "about those bills, it's only fair to tell you, because your blood pressure looks dangerously high to me, the bills on your desk are only the beginning. I've gone way out on a big, long, lovely limb for the first six months—you have to spend money to make it, and I can't risk disappointing my readers. 'First catch them, then keep them,' as my father used to say." Maxi reached the door and held it open while Cutter sat immobilized by sheer rage behind his desk. "Another thing, I've taken a series of ads in all the major magazines and newspapers that are read by media people, telling them about *B&B* and our plans for the future, an introduction to the newest Amberville Publication as it were. You should be getting those bills very soon. Don't bother to get up—I'll see myself out . . . as usual." She went through the door and half-closed it behind her. Then she turned, cast a glance at him, looked closer, shook her head and made a little tut-tut sound of concern. "Goodness gracious, Cutter, you *do* look upset." She shut the door softly but not until she'd asked, "Was it something I said?"

"Lily, love, come and sit closer to me," Cutter said, patting the space at his side on the couch. Obediently, Lily left her chair and took the offered place, her pliant, slender body curving into his side.

She sighed in a satisfaction almost deeper than love. These moments together, when he came home from his office, these long-awaited moments were, she often reflected, the reward for her years of patience. Even more of a reward than physical passion, although the endurance of that unquenchable, living connection of their two bodies was her great pride. The years that had separated them had left the embers of a fire that needed only a breath of wind, another match, a twist of paper and a bit of wood, to make it flame into hot life. But to be able to sit together at the end of a day and talk quietly, as she had never totally enjoyed doing with Zachary . . . ah, that was the even more delicious joy. It was at moments like this, when the easy comfort of their long-sought, so-long-delayed intimacy, was combined with the new happiness of being married to Cutter, that she knew that she finally had what she had always wanted, had always *deserved.*

"Darling, something happened today at the office that suddenly made me think about you, about the future of our life together," Cutter said.

Alarmed at the gravity of his tone, Lily lifted her head from his shoulder abruptly.

"No, no," he laughed, "nothing to worry about. Something to dream about, something that I would never have initiated on my own, but still, a piece of business I can't not tell you about."

"Business?" Lily asked. "You promised that we wouldn't waste our time together talking business. I've never understood it and when Zachary used to drone on and on, I'd get a headache just from having to sit and listen."

"It is business, and yet, in a way, it isn't. Not boring business. You have to listen, darling."

"All business is boring," Lily said willfully, "but I'm the patient sort, as you should know."

"I had an extraordinary phone call today from a man at the United Broadcasting Company, a perfect stranger to me. He wanted to know if there was any possibility of your meeting with him to discuss . . . to talk about an eventual sale of Amberville Publications."

"What! But he's mad! Who on earth does he think he is? *What utter nerve.* What makes him think the company's for sale? I just can't imagine anyone rude enough to make a call like that out of the blue," Lily said, stung into indignation, as if her jewelry had been stolen while she looked on helplessly.

Cutter laughed indulgently. "That man from UBC's not trying to take advantage of you, my darling. He's just doing his job. It's not some sort of attack. In fact, it's an enormous compliment. All I have to do is to call him tomorrow and say you're not interested, that Amberville Publications isn't for sale. And he'll go away, or maybe he won't. But one way or another you can expect to get more and more calls like that."

"Because Zachary's dead?"

"Even if Zachary were alive, it wouldn't make any difference. He'd be getting the same queries. It's the trend of the times. Lots of companies, particularly major conglomerates, are all out looking for magazines to buy."

"Well, I'm not interested. Why should I be? Anyway, I only own seventy percent of the stock. You know the children have ten percent each."

"They can't sell their stock except to you and you're the majority stockholder. You can do absolutely anything you want, Lily. They can't stop you. When I explained why we had to stop publication of those magazines that were losing money, I thought you understood."

"I did. You convinced me that it was necessary. But selling . . . I never thought of selling. Zachary spent his whole life building the magazines . . . he never sold one. I don't know if he ever would have, under any circumstances, for any amount of money."

"Oh, Lily, you can't stop being loyal, can you? Have you ever thought of the many ways you were sacrificed to those magazines? *You*, Lily? All that business talk that bored you so, all those business trips when you were left alone, all the times you had to cope with the children and their problems by yourself because Zachary was working, the endless weekends he spent shut up in his office, all that business entertaining and being charming to people who didn't interest you? Those magazines were built on *your life*, Lily. Years and years of the only life you'll ever have. And now you're still thinking about what Zachary would do with them if he were still alive. *He is not.* There's no one who's in charge whom you can trust but me. Would you put your shares in the hands of Pavka? He's an old man; brilliant, yes, but old. He'll retire soon, I imagine. And the rest of the editorial board? Could you rely on them to keep the magazines afloat? They're just employees, creative employees, I grant you, but not managers. Zachary was a manager, but he never built a second rank of managers to replace himself."

"I hadn't really thought . . ."

"I know you hadn't, darling. I've been keeping things going so that you wouldn't have anything to worry about. I left Booker, Smity and Jameston and opened my own office just to keep your affairs in order. Still in my heart of hearts I'm not at all convinced that the magazine business is necessarily the one you should be in."

"Is there something going on, something I don't know? Some reason why I should sell?" Lily sat up very straight at the faintly ominous tone of his voice.

"Lily, the magazines are all doing well . . . at the moment . . . but the reality of 1985 publishing economics will include great increases in paper costs and much higher distribution expenses. That doesn't have to mean that we'll make less money next year than we did this year, but it makes it a damn sight more difficult. Right now our profit-and-loss statement, our balance sheet, is still perfectly healthy. I can't begin to imagine how much money you could get tomorrow for Amberville Publications—a great deal. However, in a few years . . . who knows? I don't have a crystal ball, and I hate like hell to see you chained to something that doesn't even interest you, even if Maxi is infatuated by it to the point of . . ."

"Maxi?" Lily questioned. "What's she up to now?"

"Nothing for you to worry about—a little of her usual over-enthusiasm. I'll manage Maxi, darling, so that she doesn't get burnt. Of course, if you sold, the children would all be able to realize their inheritances."

"But what about you, Cutter? Are you trying to say that you don't want to be in the magazine business? That you wished you hadn't left Booker?"

"If it's what you need, my love, then I'm more than willing to stick it out. I never wanted to join Zachary, you know that. He suggested it a dozen times but I always refused. However, since that phone call from UBC today, coming out of the blue, I've been asking myself if it weren't some kind of sign, some kind of . . . turning point . . . something to which we should pay attention."

"Sign? Sign of what?"

"A new life. A life for us together, without being tied down to worrying every month about page rate increases and the rising cost of pension plans and the million and one other details involved in Amberville Publications. You *could* sell, darling, if you wanted to. And then we'd both be free. There wouldn't be anything in the entire world you couldn't do. You could have your own ballet company . . . no? . . . we could spend the best months of the year in England, we could buy the most wonderful house in the South of France, we could start to become *serious* collectors of everything you love. Oh, Lily, there's got to be more to life than my sitting in an office in New York, able to be with you only after a long day's work is done. But it's not my stock, it's not my company, it's for you to decide if you're even interested in the possibility. That's why I had to talk to you about that phone call. Business, 'boring' business, if you will, but I could hardly keep it a secret."

"No, no, you couldn't," Lily said slowly.

"Think about it, darling, or don't think about it. It's entirely up to you. You've given as much of your blood and your heart to Amberville Publications as anyone possibly could, and perhaps you should keep on that way. I only want to see you happy."

"I will think about it. I promise. It's not something . . . I could decide about right away . . . is it? No, of course not."

"It's important to take all the time you need, Lily. It's a very serious step," Cutter answered, and rose to make himself another gin and tonic.

Amberville Publications, he thought, Amberville Publications, that enormous creation of his hated brother, would soon be just another item on the balance sheet of a giant conglomerate; its identity lost, its key employees scattered, its real estate sold, and, most important, Zachary Amberville himself quickly forgotten, with the disappearance of his name. Within a matter of years it would only evoke a nod of recognition from a few people with long memories. *Thank God he was still young enough to wipe out Amberville Publications*, to fling it to the winds, to rid himself of its hold, to be free of his brother at last, to destroy what was left of him. As for

UBC, he'd call its president tomorrow and make a lunch date, find out if they really were in the market. There were dozens of potential suitors out there. That much was absolutely true. He had foreseen this day when he'd shut down publication of all the magazines that were losing money. All except one.

"You know, Justin, it isn't easy being fashion editor of a magazine that exists to tell women that they're just fine the way they are. Fashion is what hasn't been seen *before*, damnation. Fashion pages should make you itch to buy."

Julie spoke rebelliously but her voice was like a slightly electrified love song. Her infatuation with Justin had reached the point where she could list each separate and virtually identical piece of clothes he wore, she could even tell each of his three Nikons apart. She knew when he'd cut his nails. Every detail of the man was under her constant but imperceptible scrutiny and the very fact that her emotions seemed to be unreciprocated made them more profound. If Justin had shown a lively interest there would have had to be a progression, for better or worse, in their relationship. She would have been miserable, or in some stage of happiness. But in the weeks they'd worked together he treated her with a pleasant and maddeningly *un-fraught* mixture of friendliness and working cooperation that Julie Jacobson of Shaker Heights, who had never, since first grade, failed to get her man, no longer regarded as a challenge. It had become a painful longing for some sign that they might have a future.

"Do you wish you were on a conventional magazine?" Justin asked idly. "Do you regret not taking that job at *Redbook?*"

"Never. But this idea . . . I mean after all, imagine a whole fashion feature that tells about why you should never, ever throw away your favorite bathing suit? How am I going to explain that to Cole and Gottex and O.M.O. Kamali and all the other bathing suit manufacturers who've given us ads?"

"Explain Maxi's theory—that when a woman feels good about herself, after she's read an issue of *B&B*, she's got to react to their advertising in a positive way, even if the editorial material doesn't make the reader believe that she has to rush out and spend money just to survive the weekend."

"Do you believe that? Or is it just Maxi?"

"As a matter of fact, I do too. Basic, acquisitive human nature will take care of the shopping instinct and *B&B* will put women in the right mood to pay attention to the advertising."

Justin surveyed his studio, the first he'd ever had, with well-hidden consternation. He'd always shot on location before, traveling light with just a couple of duffel bags and camera cases, but in order to turn out the work Maxi asked of him for *B&B* he'd rented a studio with all the infinite variety of equipment it contained, and hired the necessary assistants to answer the phone, work in the darkroom, and help him with lights and props. Of course it was all paid for by *B&B* but it was the first time in his life that he'd had the impression of being attached to a particular place of work. It made him uneasy and restless, but since he'd taken a proprietary interest in the success of *B&B*, he couldn't just disappear again until he was sure that Maxi had managed to get the magazine off the ground and running smoothly. Or until it turned out to be a failure. And either possibility, he thought, was still very alive. He was used to Maxi's new projects, he'd observed the frenetic pace of her life, the ceaseless search for something that was more fun than the last thing, and he was far from convinced that she had the staying power to do more than launch a magazine. She'd probably be sick of the thing in six months.

No one, he often thought, understood her better than he did, for he was like her. He too had never found whatever it was that could tempt him to settle down and stick around. He too was an impermanent person with few long-lasting attachments. He had loved his father deeply and his death had been a tragedy to Justin. He would always miss Zachary Amberville, yet they had rarely had intimate conversations. Justin had avoided them and Zachary, understanding, hadn't sought them out, hadn't forced them on him. There had been a mutual but unspoken understanding between the two of them that Justin's desire for privacy must be respected.

On the other hand, he thought grimly, his mother seemed to have been after his soul from the day he was born. "Justin, come here and talk to me." Every day when he'd come home from school he'd heard her irresistibly lovely voice, so grave, so poignant, calling to him from her sitting room. There hadn't been any choice but to go in and give her the kiss she reached up for and let her smooth his hair and try, without squirming, to give satisfactory answers to all the questions she persisted in asking him. "How was the math test, Justin? Weren't you cold in just that sweater? Why didn't you take your coat? Who's your best friend this year? And who's your second best? What about that new boy who moved from Chicago? Do you like him? When do you have to turn in your English paper? If you need any help you can always show it to me, you know that, don't you?" Her constantly probing, gentle, devoted, poetic voice, wanting to know everything he did, everything he thought.

He had never told her that he didn't have a best friend, or a second-best friend, or really any friends he cared about at all because that would only have led to more questions, to concern, to trying to do something about it, when he wanted only to be left in peace to try to deal with his fears of growing up, to learn to live with the idea that there was no one he could count on to solve his problems except himself. Yet he had never refused to lend his presence, never had the heart to turn his back on his mother because he sensed keenly how deeply needy she was, how somehow bereaved, like a young widow, in spite of her beauty and her jewels and her never-ending social life. In her devotion to him Lily was, he knew without words, really begging that he take care of her. And he had done his best.

Only when he'd discovered the martial arts and started taking lessons, had he managed to spend the late afternoons free of the burden of the maternal emotion that his mother hadn't shown his sister; a kind of emotion that seemed tinged, even tainted, by a feeling he couldn't quite define but had learned to hate in spite of his love for her. Almost a kind of . . . worship. It was because he was the youngest child, he had decided. Maxi had been in constant trouble with their mother and Toby had been so independent, so special, in spite of his slowly approaching blindness, that perhaps he had been the only one left for her to lavish her feelings on . . . but still he, Justin, had had to bear the particular burden of that special child, the *favorite*.

286

As soon as he knew clearly that *B&B* was either a failure or a success, he'd be off again, to someplace he'd never been before, resuming the only role in which he'd learned to feel comfortable: that of the inconspicuous observer, a part of every scene, the quiet outsider who nevertheless, because of his camera, was at home everywhere. And nowhere.

"Justin," Julie cried, holding up a flowered bikini that could only have been made in the late 1950s, "do you *believe* this? And it's still in such perfect shape that it probably never even hit the water."

"Maybe most favorite bathing suits don't," he said, shrugging.

"That's what Maxi says. 'If a woman ever finds a suit that really flatters her, that hides what she wants to hide and shows off what she wants to show off, she won't get it wet unless she's forced to, and even if she gets too fat to wear it, she'll keep it somewhere, with the idea that eventually she'll fit into it again,'" Julie quoted. "Maxi is just encouraging magical thinking, if you ask me," Julie added in disapproval.

"Whatever you think, love, we've still got those dozen old suits to shoot. How many models did you book?"

"Three girls and two dozen boys."

"You're mad. Why so many boys?"

"That was Maxi's idea too. Each girl is going to have a big bunch of assorted guys around her, darting flattering looks," Julie said tartly. She hadn't had time to go wholesale for an entire week, thanks to the hunt for ancient bathing suits.

"What are you putting the boys into?"

"I have four dozen identical—objects—from Ralph Lauren Bodywear in a million different colors. Identical but not exactly old-fashioned. I don't know if they're bathing suits or underwear but they don't waste fabric, do they?" Julie held up just enough of a garment to cover a man's pelvis and give him something to put his legs through. "Bellybutton City. It's a disgrace. We're encouraging women not to buy new suits and men are allowed to parade around all but naked."

"Where are we going to put that mob?"

"The girls get the dressing room to themselves—what with the hairdressers and makeup people they need all that space—the boys will just have to use your office, Justin. This studio isn't big enough."

"How often do you book twenty-seven models at the same time?" he asked reasonably.

"This is a first, but I still think you should find someplace with a second dressing room."

"I probably will," said Justin, knowing he wouldn't. He had chosen the studio precisely because it demanded improvisation. This interior space set aside exclusively for his work made him nervous. The smaller it was the better, the less likely to seem to be a commitment or an announcement that he had come to stay. This place was only rented on a month-to-month basis, although Maxi had given him a free hand. His own office contained little more than a desk, a chair, a phone and a couch where he could flop and relax after a session was over.

The girls all arrived at once and Justin looked them over critically. Julie had booked them for the neutrality of their good looks. They were beautiful but not too beautiful. Their hair was new—no Farrah Fawcett flowing manes—but not so short as to be alarming, and the two makeup men had been instructed not to try anything outrageously different with their faces. "No pink eyelids and no blue lipsticks," Julie had ordered. "We're not trying to sell any one of those awful new looks in cosmetics. We're trying for your average American woman if she knew how to put on basic makeup."

The three girls passed his inspection and as the two dozen anonymously handsome male models started to arrive, while the girls were being made ready, he busied himself with his cameras. Like many photographers, he never let his assistant touch the cameras before a shoot, and only permitted him to reload film while he was working. Soon the first girl was ready, and for the next half hour Justin, Julie and the models all worked steadily, yet without managing to achieve the certain rhythm that would make each girl, surrounded by a dozen almost unclad men, look perfectly at ease.

"Wet them down, Julie," Justin finally said.

"Why?"

"They're still too stiff. Bathing suits indoors look posed and that's no good. There are some buckets in the darkroom. Boys, some of you go and fill the buckets with water and we'll try it that way."

"Are we going to get *wet?*" one of the girls asked in disbelief. "Nobody at the agency said anything about water. I'm going to call my booker."

"Relax, I'm just wetting down the boys," Justin said curtly. He wished he were back on some unknown street in some unknown city, free to take a picture or not, instead of here with twenty-seven of the most expensive-per-hour bodies in the United States, each refusing to flow naturally, the way real people did in real surroundings. The Ganges, that's where he could shoot them. In fact it would be a pleasure to push them all in and hold them under for a while. Meanwhile he'd have to make do.

The water did the trick. It loosened them up as nothing else could have, turned them all into kids again, dumping buckets of water on each other and on themselves in a competition to get wetter than anyone else, creating the illusion of a swimming pool or beach that no amount of props could have achieved.

Jon, a male model with shaggy dark red hair and a grin full of animal vitality, was the ringleader. It was he who threw the first bucket of water on one of the female models. "Don't you dare!" she shrieked, and received another bucket of water over her head. After that it became a free-for-all, the two dozen boys and three girls awash, forgetting the camera totally, the hairdressers standing by shaking their heads but not discontented, since they could still be paid their usual seven hundred and fifty dollars an hour. Julie, at a nod from Justin, pulled out each dripping girl when he'd finished a shot and took her to change her suit, not an easy job on a wet body. She should have booked a dozen girls or at least brought towels, she thought, but who had anticipated a water fight?

Finally the sitting was over, all the wet suits were collected, the girls had been blotted with paper towels and dried down by the blow dryers and everyone including the assistants had been sent home. Julie looked wearily around the studio, pleased with what she knew would be an exciting set of pictures.

"Don't worry. I'll get it cleaned up tomorrow. Go on home, Julie," Justin said gently.

"I should stay, but . . ."

"Don't be silly, you're beat. Out, love, out."

Finally alone, pushing aside sheets of wet and dirty paper, Justin put his cameras away carefully. He opened the closed door of his office, wondering what kind of shambles the boys had left it in.

"You took your sweet time, Justin. I thought you were lost." Jon, his red hair still slightly damp, sat behind the desk, his bad-boy grin appearing as he saw Justin enter. He looked as much at ease behind the desk as if it belonged to him.

"Couldn't you find your clothes?" Justin asked quietly, his composed tone belying his stance, the posture of a man trained and ready to defend himself.

"They're exactly where I left them when I came in."

"Do you enjoy sitting around in a wet bathing suit?" he said sharply.

"I'm not. I took it off." Jon smiled again and stretched, as lazily as a big jungle cat.

"You can't be comfortable," Justin said, his expression tightly vigilant. "And that happens to be my chair."

"I'd be more comfortable on the couch, as a matter of fact," Jon answered, but made no move to stand up.

"I'm sure you would be," Justin said, as if decoding the statement with his deepest concentration. "But what makes you think that I want you there?"

"Justin," Jon mocked him, half reproachfully, "do you think I don't know what you want? Do you think I don't know how much you want me? On the couch or on the floor or anywhere you can have me? Do you think I don't know what you wish you could do to me, what I need—and intend—to do to you? Do you think I'm stupid?"

"Just what gave you that idea about me?" Justin asked, the menace with which he always moved more in evidence than ever, without his having to take a step in any direction.

"Nothing you said, nothing about the way you look, or walk or talk. Nothing 'gave' me that idea . . . I know it. I have very good instincts."

"Do you? Are you really sure? Or aren't you just trying it on for size? Something you pull with any photographer on the off-chance that you'll be right? And that there'll be something in it for you?"

"I don't want anything, Justin, except the same thing you're aching for. I love it, just as much as you do, only, unlike you, I'm not afraid to ask. I've been hurting for you since I walked in here . . . it wasn't easy not letting it show in that bathing suit. I'm so hard now, Justin, I'm as hard as I've ever been before, and *so are you.* I can see just how much you want me all the way from behind this desk. So come here and stop playing games. Come, give it to me, Justin. Any way that makes you happy. Any way, anything—I can take it all."

Wordlessly, Justin moved toward Jon, wordlessly and willingly.

20

The trouble with you, Maxime, is that you're too impulsive," Lily said, her opal eyes narrowing as she inspected her daughter with her familiar air of withheld criticism.

"Mother, I know I have a history of recklessness and I'm not proud of it, I promise you, but B&B is something absolutely different. It's not fair of you to assume that this is just another toy until you've seen how I mean to make it work. Look, I've brought you the dummy of the first issue so that you can see for yourself." Eagerly, Maxi held the dummy out to Lily.

"No, Maxime, I can't judge anything from looking at that. I've never been a clever judge of magazines, particularly new ones. Even your father had to admit that, try as he would. Put it back in your attaché case, dear, so you don't forget it here when you leave."

"Please, Mother, just take a quick look. It might make you laugh," Maxi pleaded. Somehow she had to *reach* Lily. Since her return from Europe they had barely seen each other. Maxi had been too busy to meet her mother for the occasional lunch and ballet matinee that had, over the years, developed as the easiest and least abrasive way of maintaining their relationship. Today, however, she'd had to make time to accept her mother's unmistakable summons to come for tea, the one resolutely British ritual that Lily had maintained since she'd arrived in Manhattan more than thirty years ago.

"I'd prefer not to, dear. Of course I'll read it when it's properly printed, but until then I'd rather wait. I'm hoping for a pleasant surprise. The reason I asked you to interrupt your work today, Maxime, is that I've been giving some thought to Amberville Publications recently and I was curious to find out just how much money is being spent on this sudden whim of yours . . . this notion that you have turned into a publisher, or an editor, or whatever it is you think you are."

"Do you mean Cutter hasn't told you?" Maxi asked, astonished. It had been several days since her interview with Cutter in his office and she had assumed that he would have told her mother the whole story.

"No. As a matter of fact he was very vague about it. It seemed to me that he was avoiding the subject. That's precisely what made me wonder what was going on, wonder if there weren't something in the air—something between you—that I should know about."

"'In the air'? You mean am I having a problem with Cutter? Is that what you mean?"

"Precisely," Lily answered, pouring Maxi another cup of tea.

"We're having a bit of a hassle, Mother. He thinks that I'm spending too much money and I *know* that I can't spend a penny less and hope to have a success. If I stop now all the start-up money will be a total loss. It's either do it right or not at all and I haven't been able to make him understand that. Father would have known exactly what I'm doing. It's only fair to say that I haven't been exactly tactful with Cutter—in fact, not tactful at all—but Mother, he's just *not* a magazine person, he's got a Wall Street balance-sheet mentality. That's natural considering that he's always been an investment banker but it makes a reasonable conversation impossible with him. If Father . . ."

"Maxime, your father is dead. Your problem with Cutter stems from your personal resentment of him, an illogical grudging resistance that's made me very unhappy, a problem that doesn't come from any lack of knowledge or interest on his part."

"Mother, it's not that at all . . ."

"Just one minute, Maxime. Let me finish. I've tried to understand your deep . . . antagonism . . . toward Cutter. I know that anyone at all who presumed to come into my life after your father died would have aroused those primitive feelings in you. You always were a daddy's girl and you'll never get over it." An old, familiar bitterness had crept into Lily's voice, into that voice she kept under such delicate control; the voice that told Maxi that her

293

mother was entitled to everything she wanted without having to even ask for it.

"You don't appreciate what Cutter means to me," Lily continued, "or, if by some miracle you do, you don't care. I'm fifty years old, Maxime, and in January I'll be fifty-one. I'm sure you think that I'm too old to be concerned with my emotions. What must fifty seem to you, at twenty-nine, with most of your life ahead of you and a past that wasn't exactly uneventful? At twenty-nine what can you even guess of my feelings?"

"For God's sake, Mother, fifty isn't old! And I'm not stupid enough to think that you don't have a heart and a body. Give me some credit at least. Maybe fifty sounded old to you when you were my age, but times have changed." Maxi put her cup of tea down in such agitation that Lily flinched when the porcelain hit the table.

"Times have changed, but only in principle. Human nature remains the same," Lily continued relentlessly. "And it's human nature to classify your own mother as a bloodless antique. It's inescapable, although, heaven knows, you've tried to avoid it with Angelica and so far you've succeeded. You're so breathtakingly unpredictable that she just participates in your life and you take that for granted—she's the tail to your comet. But one day she'll classify you too, Maxime, mark my words."

"How did Angelica get into this conversation?" Maxi said, deeply annoyed. "I thought you wanted to talk about the money I'm spending on *B&B.*"

"One day, Maxime, you'll know what it feels like to be young forever in the trap of a body that grows older no matter what you do to preserve it," Lily continued as if Maxi hadn't answered her. "I look at the models in the fashion magazines and I think, ah, yes, *now*—but in twenty years those photographs will be *unendurable.* To *have been* beautiful is a life sentence, not a blessing. To have been *anything* wonderful that you've lost . . ."

"Mother, you're getting morbid. You are beautiful, you were beautiful, you will always be beautiful. What does it have to do with this tea party?"

"I should have known it was hopeless." Lily sighed and ran her hands over her smooth, heavy chignon. "I've been trying to explain something about Cutter and me, but your insensitivity, as usual, makes it difficult. Well, Maxime, how much is this whole magazine business costing?"

"I can't give you a final figure, not yet. Because it will cost one amount if it works and a very different amount if it doesn't."

"Then just tell me how much you've spent so far."

"Somewhere close to five million dollars has been committed, over the next six months."

"Is that a normal amount of money to spend before you know the results of your venture?"

"Absolutely. In fact it's on the low side. Take Mort Zuckerman for example. He's poured eight million into *The Atlantic* and doesn't expect to see a profit for more than a year, and then there's Gannett's enormous investment in *USA Today*, even with that terrific Cathy Black publishing it, and the fortune it took to make *Self* work . . ."

"Spare me, Maxime. I can't endure it when you talk numbers like that. You sound like a parrot of your father but at least he knew what he was doing. So you've spent five million dollars since you came back from Europe, five million dollars of Amberville Publications' money."

"Yes, Mother, I have. Five million and I wouldn't try to pretend that I've finished yet. You won't regret it, I promise." If Lily had been studying Maxi's face she would have recognized Zachary's expression of eager resolution.

"You promise." Lily shrugged her shoulders with a movement almost too faint for irony. "Well then, I won't worry about it anymore. Can I give you another cup of tea?"

"No thanks, Mother. I really have to get back to the office."

"I understand, dear. Give Angelica my love. If she's free next week I have ballet tickets on Saturday afternoon."

"I'm sure she'd love it." Maxi kissed Lily goodbye. It was no good. It had never been any good. The trouble with you, Maxime, is that you're insensitive, that you don't appreciate Cutter, that you are a daddy's girl, that you want me to care about your work. The trouble with you, Maxime, is you expect too much from your mother.

As Lily rang for the maid to take away the tea tray she thought how wise she had been to have had this interview with Maxime.

Her daughter was running true to form. Five million spent and nothing but a dummy to show for it. Lily might not like to talk business but she knew that if Maxi admitted that she'd not finished spending money yet there was no telling how much could be lost. A dangerous toy in the hands of a thoughtless extravagant child, who'd never had to make a penny in her life. Five million dollars thrown out of the window in a matter of a few months. There was no point in getting upset about it, not when Cutter assured her that the balance sheet was still healthy. It was merely a confirmation, if she had actually needed one, that with Zachary dead, the Amberville family should get out of the magazine business.

It wasn't merely the loss of money, Lily thought, as she walked upstairs to her dressing room, it was the wear and tear on Cutter. It had been typically unselfish of him not to have told her the dismaying details of Maxime's spending spree. He must have been wild with anger, and yet he hadn't wanted to disturb her with the maddening account of her daughter's pretensions. He was consideration itself, almost to a fault. He should have told her. Maxi running berserk as publisher of a magazine, indeed! She scanned her closets critically. How she missed darling Mainbocher. And just who, she asked herself, could tell what Toby and Justin, much as she loved them, would decide to do in the future? Together they owned thirty percent of the Amberville stock. No, thank you, she didn't want her children for partners. She might not know much about business, Lily thought with the shrewd, self-centered practicality she had always managed to hide from everyone including herself, but she knew that much.

"Get away from here," the man behind the pushcart snarled at Angelica.

"How come you're selling leather whips?" she asked him curiously.

"Never mind, kid, just beat it." Sadomasochistic paraphernalia would never move if brats hung around. This tall one with all that long hair would drive away trade. "Here," he said, and gave her a dollar. "Go buy yourself a hot dog."

"Thanks." Angelica walked away to the Sabrett man directly

in front of the entrance to the residential section of Trump Tower. She'd have to bring her gang, the Trump Tower Troops, to visit the pushcart tomorrow. A free hot dog each? Why not? As she ate her hot dog she inspected the various pushcarts on Fifth Avenue. Wallets, belts, scarves, jewelry, all made halfway across the world and laid out on the once-immaculate sidewalk in front of the finest retail stores in the world. The Troops had never seen Fifth Avenue in the days of its glory. That roving gang, who varied from eleven to fifteen members, were the only children who lived in the building, and to them the street vendors were a constant source of amusement and interest, part of their world, a natural counterpoint to their multimillion-dollar apartments.

The Troops knew everything about Trump Tower. They knew how to get through the concealed security booth, manned twenty-four hours a day, which led from the dignified, small, luxurious, basically beige lobby of their building into the vast, six-story-high, pink marble atrium of the building's retail arcade where a truly marvelous waterfall ran by magic and there was always someone in a tailcoat playing the grand piano in the entrance. Tired New Yorkers gratefully entered to sit down for a while, listen to the familiar songs and perhaps eat a sandwich while in one of the many wildly expensive boutiques only a few floors above them, four-thousand-dollar nightgowns were being sold to women from many lands. The Troops knew every store, they knew about the floor where the live-in maids' rooms were located, they knew the beautiful blond Mrs. Trump and had persuaded her to let them visit the garden of her triplex which covered the entire top of the Tower and was planted with full-grown trees.

Angelica was the leader of the gang because she was American and had the biggest apartment, an "L" combined with an "H." Most of the others were foreign and their apartments were only considered *pieds-à-terre* by their parents who were forever on the move from one capital city to another. However today Angelica wasn't in the mood to seek out any of her cronies. She was worried about her mother, and she wasn't exactly sure why.

For one thing, she mused, as she bought another hot dog with her own money, Maxi was getting so bizarrely organized. She'd found a cook who actually showed every sign of staying on the job since Maxi now left her detailed lists of everything that was to be done in the course of each day and had provided her with a cleaning woman to do the heavy work. Maxi—who had never planned anything—had started to plan meals a week ahead so that the shopping could be done efficiently. As a result Angelica was certain that they had the only cook in Trump Tower who didn't just telephone Gristede's but actually picked out the produce herself on Lexington Avenue. Where were the last-minute phone calls to the places that delivered? Angelica wondered. She remembered years of odd and ethnic improvised feasts, or former careless, carefree meals, often eaten right out of the cartons in which the food had been delivered. Her kind of eating.

And it wasn't just the fact that she and her mother sat down to dinner together at night. Maxi had actually begun to supervise Angelica's homework. Not to understand it necessarily, for today's math naturally was beyond Ma, like yesterday's math, but to make sure that it got done on time. What's more, she had started to take an interest in Angelica's wardrobe instead of letting her wear whatever she wanted to, charging it at any of the stores in town as she had been in the habit of doing since she was ten. "Appropriate clothes," she'd said just the other day, "aren't necessarily all bad." Now what kind of macabre statement was that for Ma to make?

And then there was the matter of her love life. Ma didn't seem to have any and she didn't seem to care. Could she be in menopause? Angelica considered Maxi's age and decided that twenty-nine was probably too young. But as long as she could remember there had been a man in Ma's life, one right after another, and sometimes, Angelica suspected, two at the same time. Humpy guys as older men went. But *B&B* left her no time for anyone, humpy or not. When she wasn't at the office or with Angelica she spent every evening working with Justin or Julie or one or another of the people from the office, or, astonishingly, often alone, actually alone, in her own bedroom bent over a yellow legal pad, occasionally letting out great hoots of laughter, at her own wit, Angelica supposed, since the television wasn't on. Was this what people meant by obsession? And wasn't obsession supposed to be bad for you?

Yet she couldn't see any signs that Maxi was beginning to fall apart, Angelica ruminated. It was just the opposite, she was getting it all together, going for it, totally going for it, and that was the worst part of all, because a Ma who was going for it wasn't as much fun as a cute, crazy Ma who had to be *supervised*. A grown-up Ma with a whole bunch of grown-up ideas about how to do things wasn't what Angelica had bargained for. Ma was changing, that was for sure, and Angelica didn't like it. No. Not one little bit. Because, if Ma was the grown-up in this family, what did that make her?

No Cipriani in memory had ever bitten through his own bottom lip, Rocco suddenly realized and made himself ease up on the painful grip of his upper jaw.

"Obviously I've avoided the classic mistake," Maxi said, attacking her codfish gumbo in its incendiary sauce as if it were as bland as mashed potatoes.

"Which classic mistake?" Rocco asked, wondering why he had let her talk him into having dinner. He supposed it was curiosity. After all the work he'd put into the dummy, after he'd found her Brick Greenfield, a stunningly good young art director, to carry on where he'd blazed the trail, he felt a reluctant interest in the future of *B&B*, but Maxi's insouciance was turning his temper as hot as the Creole cuisine of Chez Leonie whose smiling Haitian proprietor had taken them under her wing and ordered for them.

Rocco had already heard, from entirely too many people, how Maxi had visited most of the major advertisers in person, using his—*his*—dummy as her calling card, and talked them into taking space in her magazine, using every bit of guile she possessed, every ounce of wile and winsomeness, all of her Amberville credentials. Even he had to admit that the basic concept of *B&B* could sound logical when presented by Maxi at her most devious, *if* you had no previous experience with her. If she were a stranger, for example, and you could be conned into thinking that a reader-friendly magazine was what you needed to round out the kind of totally balanced media buy that a top agency like Cipriani, Lefkowitz and Kelly would provide with the help of a highly trained team of people whose whole life was media buying. If you happened to be some damn foolish horse's ass of a national advertiser and some ditsy girl who called herself a publisher and acted as her own ad manager as well came along, bypassed your rightful ad agency, and sweet-talked you into making commitments you'd never have made in your right mind.

"Rocco, why are you doing that with your teeth? You're drawing blood, or is it only this red sauce?" Maxi offered him her napkin in concern.

"Put that away, I've got my own napkin, damn it! I think I bit right through a giant hot pepper. Hell!"

"I warned you to be careful." Maxi looked around Chez Leonie, a First Avenue restaurant only big enough to hold six tables but full of an atmosphere she loved: old records of old Caribbean melodies being played on an old phonograph somewhere in the back; candelabras everywhere, dripping wax as if it were a Cocteau movie; the softest, almost yellow walls on which Leonie's family photographs were hung here and there. It made Maxi feel as if she'd gone on an Island holiday. Obviously Rocco had become so Madison Avenue that he didn't understand the poetry of this place. And that from a man who used to live on hot peppers. Sad.

"Which classic mistake?" Rocco asked again, his dignity restored.

"Of not understanding that I have two customers for each copy: the reader and the advertiser. You can't get the ads without the readers and you can't get readers without ads, because they're suspicious of a thin magazine. That's why I practically *gave* away the advertising space for the first six months. Well, I didn't give it entirely, but it is much, *much* cheaper than it should be. Absurdly cheap. The first issue is going to be nice and heavy and reassuring, like a great plump chicken. My reader will be able to just heft it and know that at a dollar fifty she's getting a bargain. Rocco, leave some room for the main course."

"Isn't this it?"

"Wait," said Maxi with a particularly provoking smile, her beauty spot riding above the perfect bow of her upper lip in a way that made Rocco feel the impulse to give her a good slap and see what would happen.

"There's only one problem you don't seem to think you have

all figured out," he said, "and that's how to get your magazine distributed. You can have the world's most beautiful book, with every other page a four-color ad, and you still have to scare up those millions of readers you've been assuming you'll get. And if people can't find *B&B* how can they buy it?"

"Rocco, did you ever hear of a man named Joe Shore?"

"Nope."

Maxi sighed. "He was a wonderful old man but he's been dead for, oh, fifteen years I guess. I used to go to the track with him right up to the end. He let me have as many hot dogs as I could eat. He died the way he would have wanted to, in his box at Belmont Park, with a winner. Of course he'd only bet two dollars, but still he'd won."

"Maxi, what are you talking about?"

"Uncle Joe, Uncle Barney's father. Well, naturally I've never lost touch with Uncle Barney. He was awfully upset when I divorced Laddie Kirkgordon . . . he loved my being a countess. He and his wife came to visit us at Castle Dread and they had a wonderful time."

"Uncle Barney? J. Bernard Shore? The head of Crescent?" Rocco waved away the enormous platter of braised pork ribs, chicken, yellow rice and roast duck. "*Crescent?*" His voice cracked.

"Well of course, Crescent. You have to have a national distributor, Rocco," Maxi explained with sweet patience.

"I'm fully aware of that, Maxi," Rocco said carefully. She *was* trying to kill him. Creole food and aggravation, red hot peppers and deliberate malice. He wondered if he had an ulcer yet or was he just getting one now? Crescent was the most important national distributor in the United States. Naturally Amberville Publications was an important account for them, but as for *B&B,* they'd just laugh. Or should, if they had any sense.

"Anyway, I went to see Uncle Barney and told him my problem. He knows that I've always been able to pick a winner, ever since I was three, and so I signed a contract with him. Of course they get their usual ten percent of the cover price, he couldn't do anything to lower that, but he did put me onto the Front Line Rack. *Rocco!* Leonie! Come quick, I think he's choking. My God,

Leonie, were there fishbones in that gumbo? Rocco, put your arms above your head, no, Leonie, don't hit him on the back, Rocco, do you want the Hug of Life? The Heimlich maneuver? Oh, make up your mind! Run your fingers across your throat if you can't breathe . . . oh, you're O.K. . . . Christ . . . you frightened me. I'll never bring you here again, so help me. Leonie, could I have some of your Haitian cognac, please? I feel faint."

"The Front Line Rack?" Rocco whispered, gasping between each word. "Are you sure that's what he said?"

"Absolutely. He said he'd make the space if he had to build bigger racks himself."

"How much?"

"Well, that's another problem. I have to pay the retailer directly for that. About five dollars every three weeks. Per store, I mean. Surely you don't think that the supermarkets put magazines at the checkout counter out of charity, Rocco? Is that how *People* and the *National Inquirer* and *Cosmo* get up front where you can't miss them? After all, business is business," Maxi said briskly, recovering from the shock of Rocco's choking fit by eating his portion of chili-flavored ribs as well as her own.

"You're going to lose a fucking fortune!" he roared.

"Rocco, will you keep your voice down—or at least moderate your language? Maybe I will lose a fortune but my eyes are open and I'm betting on me. And so is Uncle Barney . . . he's acting as my banker for the Front Line Racks for a year. I picked an Exacta for him once. The only time it ever happened in his whole life . . . and I was only three, couldn't even read. Oh, Rocco, for heaven's sake, have some of my cognac . . . I'm worried about you. Have you thought of having a checkup? I know a good internist who specializes in nervous advertising men, as if there were any other kind."

It was a solemn group that descended from the plane at the airport in Lynchburg, Virginia, on the day that the first issue of *B&B* was to go to press, printed at the gigantic Meredith/Burda plant located outside of Lynchburg. On arrival, they separated into two groups because one rental car wasn't big enough to hold all seven of them. Justin, who had come along to lend Maxi moral support, drove the first car, with Maxi beside him and Julie and Brick Greenfield in the back. The second car was driven by Allenby Winston Montgomery, the managing editor suggested by Pavka. His long, gloomy face was set in its normal expression of someone who, with resignation, dignity and patience, is mounting the steps of the guillotine, but his personality had changed a little on the day that Maxi decided that "Monty" suited him better as a nickname than "General." He had actually smiled at her once, and although he hadn't smiled since, he seemed, to those who observed him, quite likely to smile again before the year was out. He was accompanied by Angelica, who had refused to let Maxi get on the plane without her, school or no school, and by Harper O'Malley from Editorial Control, whose job it would be, every month, to stay at the printing plant during the entire printing process, inspecting copies as they came off the presses and making sure that they were being printed correctly, and, if not, making immediate changes.

Maxi clutched the precious bundle of First Color Proofs on which she, Brick Greenfield and Monty had made their final corrections, after the two preliminary sets of "Blues" and Second Color Proofs had already undergone the process of correction and been returned to Meredith/Burda. Maxi's eyes didn't register the Virginia countryside as she tried to remember when she had last felt the same set of emotions that she was now enduring, and which she would have scorned to call fear if she honestly could.

Yes, she had it now. It had happened before, about three days before Angelica's birth. She and Rocco had gone to a movie and suddenly, during the film, she had been overcome by the knowledge that the baby inside her, the baby she had blithely carried for almost nine months, had no exit from her body except one. This unspeakably absolute fact, which somehow she had managed to ignore until that moment, had struck her with such force that she had only one thought: how to get out of it. There must be, there simply had to be some way to *avoid* having the baby. But as she looked at her enormous lap, even Maxi had had to bow to a certain incontrovertible logic. There was no way around the fear. She had to go through with it. The pile of proofs that lay on her lap now had to go to press just as Angelica had had to come into the world.

She relaxed slightly and patted the proofs lovingly. Whatever their future, she had given them the best she could give.

Except to Harper O'Malley and Brick Greenfield, who had been to the plant when they had worked for other magazines, the sheer size of Meredith/Burda was enough to inspire awe if not downright terror. Inside the plant the gigantic automated presses snaked around the vast room, five stories high, where a few of the top printers waited to greet them. The noise, drowning, deafening, almost unimaginable, made conversation impossible, but they all shook hands and mimed greetings as Maxi handed over the proofs. It was like being trapped inside of Chaplin's *Modern Times*, she thought, with *Star Wars* improvements. Computers blinked here and there, constantly checking the yellows, reds and blues of the inks, and the little group from *B&B* waited, huddled together, tense and unsmiling, for the first copy to come off the press. In spite of automation and computers, there was still the need, there would always be the need, of a human eye to scan each page and make sure that the page looked as it had been intended to look. When the first copy appeared they all crowded around and flipped through it.

Except for Angelica and Justin, they each thought that they knew exactly what to expect, for they had gone over every word and picture many hundreds of times, but it was a totally different experience to see the magazine bound and trimmed, between covers, than it had been to see it in segments and double spreads; almost as different, Maxi thought, as the mound she'd seen in her lap at the movies and the baby she'd seen in the delivery room. Almost but not quite.

After she, Monty, O'Malley and Greenfield had each given their final approval, the first run of *B&B* started to come off the press, bound by huge machines into big bales tied in plastic strips and conveyed on belts to an outside loading dock where a great fleet of trucks was standing ready. Within four days of distribution there would be copies of the new magazine on every major newsstand and in every major supermarket and drugstore chain in the United States.

Maxi, followed by the others, walked out to the loading dock to watch the first trucks leave. Monty shattered the sudden silence as, with a note in his voice that almost broke, he said, "Well, there they go." Suddenly he smiled as if watching a flock of baby birds taking their first flight. Maxi sighed deeply and Angelica, who was standing next to her, turned and lifted her a few inches off the dock, gave her a crushing hug and a kiss on each cheek.

"Hey, Ma," she said, "what's going on? You're crying!"

21

Maxi prowled around the Eastern newsstand in the Pan Am Building. It is one of the largest and best stocked in Manhattan since many hundreds of thousands of people pass it every morning and evening, looking for something to read. It is located at one of the key intersections of New York, a building that must be crossed or entered to get to a hundred different places, including the subway and Grand Central Station. Every publisher, from Newhouse to Annenberg, from Forbes to Hearst, has its representatives checking out the sales situation at the Eastern newsstand a dozen times a day whenever the new issue of its magazine goes on sale. Experts with searching eyes circle the newsstand, people who can calculate the number of copies left in a stack and, returning in an hour, recount and know immediately whether the cover photo or blurbs have pulled a big audience or bombed out, or performed as usual.

It had been four full days since *B&B* hit the loading dock in Virginia and Maxi had forced herself to wait till this evening before going to the Eastern newsstand. She had refused to let anybody from the office go with her. This was not a communal effort as putting together the first issue had been. This was a solitary affair. Playing roulette was something you did in a group but when you went to cash in your winning chips or else rose nonchalantly from your chair after you'd lost everything, it was better to do it without company or fanfare.

Slowly circling, she moved in closer and closer, at first confused by the sheer abundance of magazines and the hurly-burly of customers around the newsstand, but little by little the scene came into close focus. Uncle Barney had told Meredith/Burda how many copies to send to each of the local wholesalers in different parts of

306

the United States. Normally the wholesalers decided how many to send to each retailer, on the basis of past experience. In the case of *B&B*, since the magazine was brand-new, Uncle Barney himself had indicated the numbers he thought should be distributed. A newsstand doesn't have the same few choice checkout positions as a supermarket, but it will inevitably group the fastest-selling magazines together so that customers don't have to hunt for them. To give *B&B* a fighting chance it was supposed to be stacked—for this month only, since even Uncle Barney, with all his power, could do no more—next to *Cosmo. Cosmo* sold ninety-two percent of its copies as individual newsstand or supermarket purchases and just being next to it would give *B&B* a special opportunity to be noticed by women.

Maxi located the stacks of *Cosmo*, which had come out a few days earlier, and realized that they were half-depleted compared to the still-high stacks of most of the other women's magazines. She inched closer, peering anxiously right and left, but nowhere could she spot the screaming red cover of *B&B* that Rocco had chosen because it was precisely the color of a stop sign, the one color everyone had to pause and notice except the color-blind. And she damn well wasn't color-blind, Maxi thought. Could the magazine not have been delivered yet? That seemed impossible. Four days was the period in which every single city and bus stop in the country was supposed to have its copies. The Eastern newsstand had unquestionably had them as soon as, or sooner than, anyone else.

Was it possible, she asked herself, that the newsstand boss had left the bundles of *B&B* unopened, so busy with his sure-to-sell merchandise that he hadn't bothered to unstrip the new bales? Monty, in his infinite wisdom, had told her a dozen horror stories like that: when it happened, for whatever reason, you were dead. Dead. Stone-cold dead in the water. No matter how carefully you had planned every detail in the entire publishing business it all depended, in the end, on that special unknown person who opened the bale of magazines or box of books or bundle of newspapers and put them out for sale. If that person had the flu and had been replaced by someone less experienced, you were dead. Or if he were tired or had had a fight with his wife and didn't hustle as he usually did . . . dead. *Damn the human factor,* Maxi thought as she grew more agitated. These things should be done by computer and robots.

Unable to control herself, she stood directly in front of the pile of *Cosmo*. She gaped, gasped and blinked. A tall stack of *The New York Review of Books* was nestled right next to *Cosmo*, where *B&B* should have been. She should have known! Double-cross! The beastly New York newsdealer, some kind of weirdo intellectual, with utterly phony, pseudo-liberal pretensions, who probably had a son who wrote poetry or even intended to be a harpsichord critic—the bastard had usurped her place! Gaining brownie-points with *NYRB* for his rotten kid. She'd see about that! Maxi pushed her way into the sacrosanct center of the newsstand, swarming with busy newsboys falling over each other as they tried to make change for impatient customers.

"Where's the boss?" she demanded at large. "Show me the boss, and fast!"

"You're not allowed in here, miss. And I'm the boss. Would you move outside?" A large man made a shooing gesture, and almost turned away. New York must be full of beautiful, loony girls, with messed-up hair and furious green eyes.

"The hell I will." Maxi pulled him around. "Where'd you put *B&B*, God damn it? Why aren't they out there next to *Cosmo*? And don't try and tell me you didn't get them because I'm sure you . . ."

"Did. Yeah, we did, and whatever they are they're all sold. I called the rep for the retailer and he's bringing me another couple hundred. So don't blame me, lady, I'm saving its place with that fink sissy newspaper and that really hurts."

"They're gone?" Maxi whispered. *"People bought them?"*

"Don't look at me like that, lady. I don't know any more about them than you. They just melted away. Never saw anything like it in my life. Hey, lady, stop it! I don't even know you . . . stop kissing me, lady . . . well, all right, just stop crying all over my shirt . . . mascara, lipstick . . . sure, I agree, it's wonderful that I'm not a robot." Too bad she was crazy, with legs like that: they were gams, real old-fashioned gams like you used to see on Marilyn and Rita and Cyd Charisse. Too bad he was too old for her . . . anyway she was holding up traffic.

Pavka Mayer and Barney Shore barely knew each other. Although Crescent had been the national distributor for Amberville Publications for almost thirty-seven years the sophisticated, profoundly elegant Artistic Director had had little contact with the rough-and-tumble tycoon whose chief reading material remained the *Racing Form*. Yet, three days after Maxi went to the newsstand in the Pan Am Building, Pavka Mayer found himself being taken to lunch by Barney Shore at *Le Veau d'Or*, the kind of small French restaurant in which they both felt at home, a restaurant that had surely been in business longer than either of them, a restaurant as urbane as Pavka, as down-to-earth as Barney, an un-fancy and excellent restaurant not known to non–New Yorkers.

"I had to celebrate with somebody who'd feel the same way I do," Barney said.

"I'm glad you called me," Pavka agreed gravely.

"It's been a week now and it's sold out in every major city in the country. Nobody's seen anything like it since that first issue of *Life*. My computers are going crazy. It didn't do anything to make peace in the war between Fort Worth and Dallas when the Dallas ladies drove all the way to Fort Worth and the Fort Worth ladies drove to Dallas, all assuming that the other place would have copies. Couldn't even bribe the clerks at the checkout counters . . . they couldn't sell what they'd sold out. Same story in Chicago, L.A., San Diego, Boston, Milwaukee . . . same story everywhere. I miscalculated, should have printed five times as many . . . or ten. We persuaded Meredith/Burda to go back to press—they kicked and screamed and we paid double time—so you'd better keep your copy as a first edition, a collector's item." Barney Shore's grin grew broader.

"You don't happen to have any extras at your place, do you?" asked Pavka.

"Sorry, but my wife graciously passed them out to her friends, without asking me, every last one . . . my daughters are ready to strangle her," Barney replied, chuckling in delight. God, he loved to follow a hunch, and Maxi had always brought him luck.

"I was afraid you'd say that. My wife's friends never do their own shopping and when they finally resigned themselves to enter a supermarket it was too late. The gals at the office who were too blasé to be interested, who spend their lives knee-deep in magazines, are taking turns going to the newsstand in the building to be there in time when the next batch is coming in. Wouldn't you think that Meredith/Burda might have been thoughtful enough to save a special bale for us?" Pavka's delighted eyes and triumphant expression belied his grumble.

"My secretary had the idea of stealing one out of the folder at her hairdresser's but the owner of the shop had already taken it home for himself and won't bring it back. Says his clients are all confirmed kleptomaniacs and they won't enjoy it as much as he does anyway. Well, Pavka, here are our drinks."

The two men raised their glasses and touched the rims briefly. Their eyes met and their smiles faded.

"To Zachary Amberville," Pavka said.

"To Zachary Amberville," echoed Barney Shore.

Rocco buzzed his secretary. "Where are Lefkowitz and Kelly?" he asked.

"In Mr. Lefkowitz's office. Shall I ring them?"

"Never mind, Miss Haft, I'll go in."

He found his redheaded, blue-eyed partners just returned from lunch and not even out of their coats. Kelly, who slept with a copy of *Gentleman's Quarterly* on his night table, was wearing a tailored dark gray Chesterfield overcoat with velvet lapels and a homburg, its brim curled to the side and dipped at the front and back. Lefkowitz, who had been deeply marked in his early twenties by the Belmondo movie *Stavisky*, wore a Borsalino, which, as he frequently reminded Kelly, was made by Borsalino Giuseppe e Fratello of Alessandria, Italy, and not one of your average wide-brimmed felt makers. He turned down its brim on one side only so that one would confuse him with F. Scott Fitzgerald, and he too still wore his reversible tweed raincoat from Cesarani.

"You guys cold?" Rocco asked, "or auditioning for a remake of *The Sting?*"

"Rocco, look at this thing!" Lefkowitz said excitedly.

"We almost trampled a couple of broads but we got one," Kelly said triumphantly. "Rocco, take a look. What do you think . . . wasn't it worth being half clawed to death?"

They made room for Rocco to look as they turned the pages of *B&B*, with the fine-tuned perception only possible to men whose whole lives were defined by the necessity to sell people things they had not yet realized they needed.

"Nice," Rocco commented.

"Nice?" Rap Kelly snorted. "Thank God we made those page buys at the right price. 'Nice' is all Rocco finds to say. Do I detect a little jealousy, pal?"

"Come off it, Rap. Why the hell should you think a dumb thing like that?" Lefkowitz asked.

"Man Ray, let's face it, the look of this book is very, very special. I haven't seen anything that comes within light-years of it. Christ, just look at that use of white space, at that typography, those graphics, the layout . . . maybe you guys think that all I know how to do is get new business, but I'm not blind."

"I said it was nice," Rocco repeated heatedly, looking at the pages he'd laid out for Maxi, pages he could never now claim as his own, at the risk of looking an absolute fool.

"He said it was nice, Rap, what more do you want?" Lefkowitz said hurriedly. "Listen, Rap, back when Rocco was doing magazines, he was at least as good as the guy who laid out this book, easily as good, anybody will tell you."

"Yeah," said Kelly, "if there's anybody who still remembers."

Justin, dressing rapidly, hours late for Maxi's office party, to celebrate the success of the first issue, didn't hear the first knock on the door of his modest, walk-up apartment. The second knock was louder, more impatient.

"Open up, police."

What the hell, Justin thought, and hurried to open the door. Two men, casually dressed, stood there.

"You Justin Amberville?"

"Yes. Why?"

They showed him their badges. "New York City Police. We have a warrant to search your apartment."

"Search? What for? What's going on?" Justin said in surprise, moving swiftly to block them from coming into his apartment. Expertly they shouldered him aside and when he fought back violently with all his sinewy strength it took both detectives to pin him to the wall. "Harry," one of them said to the other, "you look the place over. Justin here thinks he's pretty tough and he has objections, so let's make sure we really give the place a going-over he won't forget. Here's the warrant, Justin baby. Cool it." The scorn in his voice when he said Justin's name was blatant, provocative, but at the sight of the paper Justin realized that there was no point in struggling with the man and, in any case, he had nothing to hide.

He watched, momentarily silenced by sheer disbelief, in the muteness of a dreamer, as the first policeman rapidly searched his living room, slitting open all the couch and chair pillows, sweeping all the books off the shelves, taking apart the speakers of his stereo. Still immobile against the wall he listened to the noisy, exhaustive wrecking of his bedroom. Harry came out. "Not there, Danny, unless it's under the floor. I'll try the other room."

"That's my darkroom. There's thousands of dollars of valuable stuff . . . for Christ's sake, be careful."

"Sure thing, Justin. That's what we're here for, to be careful," Harry sneered. He flung open the darkroom door, turned on the light and started his search, violently flinging down everything that didn't interest him. One by one Justin watched his Nikons hit the floor, their lenses shattered. As the third camera was tossed out he broke Danny's strong hold in a single swift, fluid movement and went after Harry, easily tossing the heavy man on his back. Harry grunted in pain, unable to move for a moment. "Bastard!" Justin spat and turned quickly to face Danny. His kick shattered Danny's elbow. The fight that followed was short, ugly and brutish. Without their illegal saps the detectives would both have found themselves doubled up, on the floor, unable to breathe, but instead it was Justin who was finally beaten into semiconsciousness, and handcuffed.

"Harry, you missed that little closet," Danny gasped, nursing his elbow. "This slick fucker has to have the stuff somewhere." The second detective, panting from the damage Justin had inflicted, jerked down a pile of boxes from the closet shelf and riffled through the photographs that had been carefully filed in them. He unbuckled Justin's empty camera cases and threw them away in disgust. Finally he unzipped the duffel bag that Justin had put away after his last trip.

"Pay dirt," he grunted, lifted the bag and put it down on the floor so that the other detective could see its contents. "How much does it look like to you, Danny? Whataya say, Justin, huh, whataya say, creep?" He kicked Justin hard in the ribs. "Looks like about three kilos of blow to me, the whole fucking side pocket's jammed full of the stuff. Millions of bucks worth, on the street. He must have thought he found the perfect hiding place. Too obvious to bother about, huh, Justin? Come on, Danny, I'll take him in, read him the Miranda. You just get downstairs. I'll come back for the bag. You gotta be hurting bad." Viciously he pulled Justin upright by his handcuffed wrists.

"Come on, Mr. Amberville, we've got a date downtown."

After Justin had been booked for possession of cocaine, with suspicion of intent to sell, fingerprinted and photographed, he was allowed one phone call. Bewildered, dazed, hurting badly, instinctively reaching out to the one person he dared to call, he dialed Maxi's number.

When the phone rang she had just finished putting a woozy Angelica to bed. Maxi sat at her desk, weary in every bone, yet so euphoric, so utterly content that she didn't want to go to bed herself and end the celebration that had lasted until long after dinner.

"Justin! Why didn't you come to the party? We all waited . . . What? *What!* No, it's impossible . . . I don't understand . . . of course, I'll be right down. Jesus, Justin, shall I bring a doctor too? A lawyer then? No? you're sure? All right. I promise I won't say anything to anybody. I'll be there as fast as possible . . . yes, my checkbook. Just hang on, I'm on my way."

It was after eleven when Maxi reached the Midtown North precinct house, yet only a quarter of an hour after she left her apartment; a quarter of an hour of nightmare, nightmare conjecture, nightmare streets glimpsed from the taxi window, a quarter of an hour in which the precise conditions of a nightmare were duplicated; something hideous, not quite known, yet long dreaded had happened. It was more than the fact of Justin's arrest; it was the feeling that somehow she had expected it for reasons she had avoided looking at. There was a revolting whiff of the familiar, something of the half-understood, the half-suspected, the unseen that had been hidden, just out of sight, deliberately, even scrupulously unacknowledged, something more frightening than anything she had ever thought about in the light of day. Her thoughts weren't clear and she shivered uncontrollably in spite of her fur coat. Her checkbook. It was in her handbag, the one solid reference point in the universe.

In the crowded, confusing station Maxi finally located the sergeant who was in charge.

"No, ma'am, no way you can get him out on bail. Bail hasn't been set yet. He's not here, ma'am. After booking he was taken down to One Police Plaza to await arraignment before a judge. The man should have called his lawyer, not his sister. What's the charge? Possession, it says here, and suspected dealing. How much drugs? Enough, a lot more than enough. That's all I can tell you. No, of course you can't see him. Not till arraignment. And bring a lawyer with you. What's that? He doesn't want one? Well, you listen to me, lady, he needs one. Bad."

After another half hour of fruitless quest in the police station for someone who might be able to tell her more, Maxi was stopped by a young stranger.

"Miss Amberville? I understand that your brother was arrested tonight . . ." the man said sympathetically.

"Who are you?" Maxi demanded.

"Perhaps I can help. I saw him brought in. He definitely needed medical attention and I thought you should know."

"Who are you?"

"Apparently a large amount of cocaine was found in his apartment. He claimed that it wasn't his, that it must belong to somebody else. Do you have any idea who could have put it there? Could it have been someone he trusted, some acquaintance, some friend, somebody—"

314

"Go away," Maxi screamed. She raced down the stationhouse stairs, waving frantically for a taxi. A friend? An acquaintance? Someone who hid cocaine in that apartment where even she had never been invited, where Justin guarded his privacy as though it were a fragile, infinitely precious object. *Oh, Justin, what kind of people do you call friends?* Who knows you better than I do? Poor, sweet, lost Justin . . . I've tried so hard not to guess. Wasn't that what you wanted, more than anything else in the world, that none of us should guess?

There was no help for it, Maxi thought, as she picked up the phone by her bed to telephone Lily. The only lawyers Maxi herself could contact immediately specialized in divorce. Justin obviously needed the highest-powered law firm that Amberville Publications could summon and, in any case, Lily would have to be told as gently as possible before she read about Justin's arrest in the newspaper tomorrow.

"Hello, Mother."

"Do you have any idea of the time, Maxime?" Lily's voice said drowsily.

"Yes, it's after midnight. I'm terribly sorry to wake you but . . . something's happened, something . . . no, *nobody's* been hurt, Mother, it's something else, Justin's been arrested."

"Let me take this on another phone," Lily whispered. In a few seconds she had picked up another extension. "I didn't want to wake Cutter. Where is Justin now?"

"He's in jail. They've taken him down to One Police Plaza."

"What did they arrest him for, Maxime? Was it . . . was it soliciting?" Lily asked in a low, terrified tone.

"My God, Mother!"

"I've been afraid of that for so long. Was it that, Maxime? Tell me," Lily implored.

"No, Mother, not that. It's some kind of terrible mistake. They say that they found cocaine in his apartment. They suspect him of dealing. It's all utterly impossible. The only thing that I was able to find out was that he said someone hid the drugs in his place."

"If that's what he said, that's what happened." Lily's voice was relieved, calmer. "Justin is not a liar. And of course he's not a drug

315

dealer. I'll call Charlie Salomon right now. He'll know exactly what to do, how to fight this. We'll get him out of jail in the morning, first thing."

"Mother, more than anything Justin didn't want anybody to hear—to guess. But there was a reporter there and he got a photo of me . . . he knew the essentials, about the drugs."

"We have to be prepared for that." Lily's grave, silver voice had never sounded this note of lament, not even for herself.

"Oh, Mother, I feel so horribly sorry for him, poor, loving, harmless Justin. Why did this have to happen to him?" Maxi asked, and as she asked she knew how childish the question was.

"Maxime, something—like this—has been waiting to happen to Justin for a long time. It's not his fault, dear, but it was bound to come. Try not to worry. Charlie Salomon's the best lawyer in town and thank God, Cutter is here for all of us. Goodnight, Maxime, and . . . thank you, darling. Thank you for going to help."

Before she went to wake Cutter, Lily telephoned Charlie Salomon, chief counsel to Amberville Publications, at home, finding him still watching television. Precisely, displaying almost no emotion she told him what had happened, as far as she was aware of the facts, and made an appointment to meet him at One Police Plaza in the morning.

Then, wrapping her robe around her she walked slowly from her sitting room to the bedroom she shared with her husband. He had had a particularly tiring day and she knew that he had to get up early for a breakfast appointment, but she couldn't put off waking him any longer. The reassurance she had given Maxi, the short conversation she had had with the lawyer had left her with an intense need to be held in Cutter's arms and told that everything was going to be all right, that he would carry on for her now, that she was no longer alone.

She looked at his sleeping face, as distinguished in unconsciousness as it was in wakefulness, for the relaxation of his lean facial muscles left the clean, fine, aristocratic line of his bones and his skull unchanged. Only the dark, brooding sternness, that perpetual bull-killer's watchfulness had disappeared from his expression. She sighed with unconscious pleasure. Even in this moment of long-dreaded trouble there was joy for her in looking at him.

Gently she ran her fingertips over his forehead. He turned to one side to avoid her touch but she continued and eventually he woke, dazed, from the depth of sleep. "What? Lily? What's happening?" he muttered, not fully awake.

"Wake up, my darling, I need you."

"Lily, are you sick?" He sat up in bed, alarmed.

"I'm fine. It's one of the children, one of them is in trouble . . ."

"Maxi. What's she done now?"

"No, it's Justin, our child, Cutter. Oh, Cutter, hold me tight, hug me hard, I've been so afraid, so afraid for so long, and now it's happened." Lily flung herself into Cutter's arms and tried to burrow into a safe place. He held her and kissed the top of her head and comforted her for a minute, but then he pushed her away far enough so that he could see her face.

"Tell me, Lily. What about Justin? What's happened, for God's sake?"

"He's been arrested. The police searched his apartment and found drugs—cocaine. They've taken him to jail. He called Maxi but it was too late to do anything tonight. I've already talked to Charlie Salomon and he'll get him out first thing tomorrow."

"Wait a minute. How much cocaine did they find?"

"Maxi didn't know, they wouldn't tell her, just that it was 'enough'—enough to book him as a suspected dealer."

"Christ!" Cutter jumped out of bed and tied his bathrobe around his waist. "Christ almighty, as if that kid didn't have enough money! How the hell could he have been so stupid? I could strangle him with my bare hands . . . suspected of dealing cocaine? An Amberville dealing cocaine! Do you have any idea of the disgrace that is? It's as low as—"

"Wait! *He's not guilty*, Cutter! Justin couldn't possibly be guilty of that. He's not evil, he's not a criminal, how can you even think it?" Lily was panting with outrage. "Somebody left it, concealed it, in his apartment. He didn't know it was there. Maxi learned that much."

"Oh, Lily. Couldn't that dumb kid have thought up a lie that sounded a little more convincing?"

"You assume it's a *lie?*" Lily's voice rose.

"Justin is somebody with something to hide. I knew it from the minute I first saw him. He's never been honest with me or with you or anybody else in the family. He vanishes for months without saying where he's going, he has an apartment we've never even seen; it all adds up, Lily. I know you don't want to admit it, but it adds up. And now we get the whole rotten mess dumped in our laps. Justin's a lousy rich dilettante drifter whose dividends and trust funds aren't enough, so he sells coke on the side and gets caught, the little prick."

Lily looked at Cutter, striding up and down the bedroom, ruthlessly throwing his words like stones at her feet.

"Cutter, listen to me." She forced herself to speak as calmly as possible. "You don't know Justin, but even so, surely you must understand that he would never ever do anything to hurt anyone but himself. Unfortunately, he does know the kind of people who would hide drugs in his place. When I realized that the two of you didn't get along with each other, when you and Justin never grew close, when you made no effort to get to know him better—*your own son*, Cutter—I thought the reason was because you knew, because you sensed, well—because somehow you instinctively realized that he was homosexual. And I thought that perhaps you blamed yourself in some crazy way, thought that—"

"Homosexual?" There was a moment of dead silence. The word seemed to bounce back and forth from one wall to another of the bedroom that was filled with Cutter's stunned disbelief and Lily's incredulous realization that he had *not* known, not seen, never even bothered perhaps, to be sensitive to his son, to wonder at Justin's evasive mode of life and ask himself why.

"He can't be a homosexual, Lily. It's not possible," Cutter finally said in harsh denial.

"You believed he was a cocaine dealer. Immediately, with no questions asked. Why can't you believe he's a homosexual?"

"My son a faggot! No, never. If it had been Toby . . . but not *mine*. God damn it, Lily, I never wanted you to have him, but you, no, you wanted what you wanted. *He should never have been born.*"

318

"Never been born?" Lily looked straight at Cutter as she echoed his words and he saw a face he had not dreamed could exist, contorted, ready to strike out at him, the face of a woman stripped down to the bones of an emotion he'd never seen before.

Swiftly he walked toward her and forced her, struggling, into his grip. "Lily, Lily, beloved, I'm sorry, Jesus I didn't mean it, not a word, not a single word. I just went crazy for a minute—I have a thing about . . . homosexuals . . . a phobia, I guess. It's some kind of primitive reaction, I just couldn't take it when you said that Justin . . . Lily, it sounds nuts but it's my problem and I'm ashamed of it. I don't blame you for being upset. You know how people can say things when they've had a shock, things they don't mean. Lily, I'm glad we have a son—truly, deeply glad. So glad, my Lily." He felt her relax in his hold and begin to weep. "O.K. now, darling? I love you so much. Please say you forgive me. Look, I'm going to get us both a drink and we'll talk about it, about what we can do to help the poor guy, about what I can do for my son."

As he made his way down the stairs to the bar Cutter swore at himself for being the worst kind of a fool, a man who let his tongue slip when dealing with a woman. No amount of anger was an excuse. Since the minute he'd first made love to Lily he'd schooled her to be controlled, to be dominated, so that now he could turn her in any direction that suited his purpose. To carry out his intention to break up Amberville Publications meant that he must continue to have Lily's complete confidence, her entire trust. He'd managed to make her stop publication of three magazines but there were seven more still left whose identities must be wiped out as fully as possible. He'd almost blown it. That wouldn't happen again, he vowed, as he carried the glasses back to the bedroom. Not even if it meant saving Justin's ass, that sick, sullen little faggot. He'd always hated him and now he knew why.

22

At breakfast time there is always a traffic jam at Park and Sixty-first Street, for in front of the Regency Hotel the police allow limousines to triple-park while less privileged taxis are forced into a single file to pass this expensive but basically unremarkable hotel. Its dining room has, for reasons unclear, become the most popular place for powerful men to do business with each other over coffee and dry toast. The Plaza is too far downtown, the Carlyle too far uptown, the Waldorf too far east, the new Plaza Athenée too new, so it has fallen to the Regency to garner the Tisches, the Rohatyns, the Newhouses and the Sulzbergers of the city, who often accomplish more real trading in the course of a one-hour breakfast than they may do in the rest of their day. No two men ever meet for breakfast at the Regency just to eat, unless they are a pair of rare, unaware tourists who can't bother to wait for room service.

Cutter Amberville had, by virtue of consistent and precisely right overtipping—never so much that he seemed insecure, yet never so little that it failed to impress—nailed down the second banquette on the right facing the Sixty-first Street windows. He had picked this table three years ago when he first came back from England, because it allowed him to sit with his back to the wall. He could not understand the men who allowed themselves to be seated at the center tables, exposed to all eyes. Obviously they knew that they would be observed, since the Regency breakfast was a declaration of courtship, potential or protracted, but why, he wondered, go out of your way to attract attention? Cutter made sure to arrive several minutes before his guest, Leonard Wilder of the United Broadcasting Company, thereby establishing subliminal proprietary rights from the beginning of the conversation. He concentrated on the man he was going to meet, sparing no thought for Lily, who had already left to get Justin out of jail.

Leonard Wilder was a man famous for his impatience. He wore two watches and constantly checked them; he normally made two breakfast dates in a morning, one at eight and one at nine, and he never bothered to eat. He had been important for too long to bother with the courtesy rituals, the minuetlike to-ing and fro-ing of corporate affairs, and his favorite phrase was known to be "Cut the baloney, what's the bottom line?"

Cutter rose as Wilder was brought over to the table by the headwaiter.

"I'm delighted to meet you, Mr. Wilder," Cutter said as they shook hands, "and I'm particularly pleased that you could find time for breakfast on such short notice. My wife and I watched your 'Ragtime Special' last night, and we both agreed that it was excellent entertainment."

"Wasn't bad, did well." Wilder replied in his rapid-fire, impatient way.

"Well then, shall we order?" Cutter studied the menu critically, giving it his complete attention. "Henry, I'll start with the fresh strawberries and Mr. Wilder will have—no, nothing to begin with? After that, the English porridge with fresh cream. Let's see— ah, yes, I'll have the buckwheat cakes with Canadian bacon. Be sure the bacon is lean and cooked to a crisp, and remind the chef that my buckwheat cakes must be freshly made." He turned to Wilder. "I'd have the same if I were you. No? They make a batch all at once every morning and then put them on a steam table to keep them warm . . . they're no good that way so the chef always makes a fresh batch for me." Wilder grunted. "And hot coffee, really hot. You can bring that right now. What will you have, Mr. Wilder? Only coffee? I guess it's the transplanted ex-Westerner in me, but I find that with a decent breakfast I can do twice as much work before lunch than if I only gulp a cup of coffee. You're sure? All right, Henry, just coffee for Mr. Wilder."

Leonard Wilder glanced at Cutter's trim waistline. Cutter intercepted his look.

"Breakfast like a rich man, dine like a pauper. I've always followed that advice. Still, diet isn't enough, you have to keep in shape too. My wife and I are both ardent weekend athletes and we have a gym in the house so that we can work out every day. What do you do for exercise?"

"Walk to work."

"Ah, there's nothing like walking," Cutter agreed, "but I don't find it exercises the whole body unless you run and in this city you can't do that, unless you're willing to be killed by a taxi driver."

He sat back and sipped his coffee. "Waiter, this isn't really hot. Could you bring another pot, please, and fresh cups? And take away Mr. Wilder's coffee too. It's only lukewarm."

Leonard Wilder ground his teeth and checked his watches. Cutter relaxed and waited for the fresh coffee.

"I knew your brother," Leonard Wilder said abruptly. "Wonderful man."

Cutter sighed. "We all miss him. It's been a great loss."

"One-man show. Best in town. Things a mess now?"

Cutter chuckled. "Well, Mr. Wilder, that can happen in a privately owned corporation. We both know too many cases where the founder of a business died and the business fell apart at the seams. But fortunately Amberville Publications is in a different situation. Henry, these strawberries aren't ripe. Take them back, please, and bring me a compote of mixed fruit." He turned back to Wilder. "That's the trouble with out-of-season strawberries, you can never be sure. Usually there are good ones from Algeria or Israel this time of year, but those really weren't worth eating."

"Amberville's all right, then?"

"As a matter of fact, our profits will be up considerably this year. My brother loved to tinker with the magazines. He had lost interest in the bottom line years ago. His passion was starting new magazines and giving them all the time they needed to prove themselves. You know how costly that can be. And risky. When my wife—as majority shareholder—asked me to mind the store, I decided to cut losses to a minimum. I'm afraid I had to make an unpopular decision—nobody likes to lose his job—but it turned out for the best. Henry, you can clear the fruit away. Sure you won't join me for porridge, Mr. Wilder? It's particularly good here. No? Henry, bring another pitcher of cream. This one is only half full." Cutter attacked his porridge with relish, adding a judicious amount of butter and sugar to the steaming bowl.

"Profits up, you say?"

"Definitely. Every one of our magazines is showing increases in ad revenue and, as you know, that's where the money is."

"'Up' can mean anything with a privately owned company," Wilder said, repressing the desire to peek at his watches.

"I don't feel it's indiscreet to tell you, Mr. Wilder. I'm talking about fourteen or fifteen percent, possibly more."

"Hmm. Nice going."

"Yes, it's been a most satisfactory experience. On the other hand, Lily, my wife, is British and she misses England. She's been really stuck in New York, except for whirlwind trips to Europe when Zachary went on business, for more than thirty years. She's still a young woman and she'd like to spend more time abroad. Hunting, theater, all of that . . . Lily says there has to be more to life than the magazine business. You're married, aren't you, Mr. Wilder?"

"Call me Leonard. Yes, married twenty-five years. You said up fourteen or fifteen percent, Cutter?"

"Right. Ah, thank you, Henry. Those look good."

Leonard Wilder wriggled on the banquette. He was already late for his nine-o'clock breakfast and Cutter Amberville had just started on his buckwheat pancakes.

"Could we talk round figures?" Wilder asked.

"Round figures?" Cutter poured some maple syrup on the pancakes. "I don't see why not. You're known never to repeat things. Something near one hundred and seventy million in pretax profits."

"Near? Which way? Up or down?"

"I don't like to overstate, Leonard, but I expect a higher figure. There's still some deadwood to be trimmed here and there."

"Business for sale, Cutter? That's why you called me?"

"Yes, as a matter of fact, there is that possibility. As I said, my wife is longing for a change and she deserves whatever she wants. I've urged her not to rush into any decision, told her to take her time, but spring's in the air and she's always been impulsive."

"So the business is for sale."

"It wouldn't be fair to make any promises . . . but it might be. It might very well be. At the right price."

"Naturally."

"Now take Bill Ziff for instance, and his company," Cutter said, between bites. "Interesting deal he just made. If you'll forgive me for mentioning the competition, Leonard, CBS just bought twelve magazines from him for three hundred and sixty-two million dollars, books like *Popular Photography* and *Yachting*. Then he sold Murdoch twelve trade publications, *Aerospace Daily* for one, and *Hotel and Resort Guide* for another, for an additional three hundred and fifty million. Twenty-four magazines in all. Now, admittedly we've only got six books to sell, but each is the leader in its field, each a classic. Major magazines, Leonard. We can leave *B&B* out of the discussion—it's an experiment, at the moment, unproven. But the others have revenues well above Ziff's, far, far above. So you have to understand that we're discussing a very large sum of money, certainly near a billion. Henry, more hot coffee, please."

"UBC is cash-rich, Cutter. That's not a problem. You talked to anyone else?" Wilder demanded, his other breakfast date utterly forgotten.

"No. Not yet. Lily only brought up the matter a few weeks ago and I didn't see any reason to hurry. I like to give new ideas time to mature, to ripen. All in good time and no regrets."

"Cutter, I don't believe in kidding around. I'm interested. Been looking for a major magazine group for years. Always liked Amberville. Got a three-man executive committee. They can commit whole board. Only ask one thing; don't speak to anyone else before we have a chance to get together on this."

"That sounds fair enough, particularly since I'm in no hurry. In fact, our next statement isn't due for almost three months and I'm so sure that it's going to show an interesting jump that I'd prefer to wait until then. If Lily is still of the same mind, then your accountants can go to work, and judge the values for themselves."

"Three months . . . you're sure you want to wait? We could get started a lot sooner."

"I'm sure, Leonard. But during that time, why don't we get together for dinner with our wives? I feel I owe you something decent to eat. You missed a wonderful breakfast."

"Does anybody else know about this?" Toby asked India suspiciously, running his fingers down her belly.

"Could you be more specific?" she asked lazily, drifting up from the glowing globe of great joy in which she floated, feeling the complicated, compelling sense of bliss she experienced at the sound of his voice.

"This tiny scar, right here, below your bellybutton and to the right."

"Appendix, when I was eight. Even Barbara Walters doesn't know about it. On the other hand, she never asked."

"That's the one hundred and seventeenth thing I know about you that nobody else knows. Your ears are distinctly different sizes; your nose is out of line to the right, only by a hair but still nobody could call it straight; you have thinner eyelashes on your left eye than on the right, and correspondingly, less hair under your left arm than under your right, shave your armpits though you will; there's a tiny mole under your pussy hair on the left outer labia—"

"Toby!"

"I suppose it's not your fault if you're not perfect. You were billed as being perfect but, good Lord, the things I've found would fill a book, and I've barely begun to look. And as for taste, let me tell you, young lady, you don't taste the same way two days in a row. A man likes a little consistency in his woman."

"Am I your woman?" India wondered, knowing she shouldn't ask, but unable to resist.

"My woman of the moment. The only woman of the only moment. But you know how I feel . . . I've never—"

"Spare me . . . never committed yourself. Coward! Revolting, timid coward. I wish I had a penny for every fink man in the country who goes around counting pussy hair and not committing himself. Have you no shame?"

"I didn't count your pussy hair, I counted your underarm hairs."

"It comes to the same thing and you know it. How did women get into this? Why are you allowed to make me love you and then refuse to love me back?"

"I do love you back," Toby said in a low voice. "You know I do. I loved you as soon as you threw those drinks over me to attract my attention five months ago. But commitment is something else."

"Where I come from, when you love somebody and she loves you and there's no reason why you can't agree to hope to keep on loving each other for good, logically that will lead to a commitment for some kind of permanent arrangement . . . called marriage," India said with the same dogged persistence which had kept her flying back and forth from Los Angeles to New York almost every weekend since she'd met Toby. She had moved half her wardrobe, little by little, to his closets and now even his bed, on which they were lying, was covered with her very own hand-ironed Porthault sheets.

"'Is not marriage an open question, when it is alleged, from the beginning of the world, that such as are in the institution wish to get out, and such as are out wish to get in?'"

India sat up fuming. "You dare to quote Emerson to *me*—I invented quoting Emerson, you skunk."

"'By necessity, by proclivity, and by delight, we all quote,'" Toby declaimed in perfect Emersonian dignity.

"It's Maxi, I know it's got to be Maxi. She told you how I used to torment her with Emerson, didn't she?"

"She may have mentioned it, in passing, as an example of girlish affection."

"Then the two of you have been talking about me?"

"Naturally. It wouldn't be in Maxi's character to maintain a discreet silence, when her brother is in love with her best friend."

"What does she think?"

"She thinks that I'll have to make up my own mind."

"Some best friend," India said bitterly. The phone rang and startled her.

"Don't answer it," she said.

"It might be from one of my managers," Toby sighed. "The restaurant business never sleeps." He picked up the bedside phone, listened for a moment and then hung up angrily and abruptly.

"Not him?" India asked anxiously.

"I'm afraid so, darling. It was your 'biggest fan' again. And my unlisted number was changed only last month."

326

"Oh, Toby, I'm sorry. That crazy guy. He writes me three times a week, and tries to call long distance. My secretary just tells him I'm not available. Forget him, it's the price of fame."

Toby unplugged the phone and turned back to India.

"Now listen, my love, you really have the most extraordinary and admirable facility to avoid facing facts," he said, resuming the interrupted conversation. "Let's cut to the chase. I'm blind, we can't pretend that I'm not."

"You're not really blind," India said stubbornly. "You can see something, you told me that your field of vision was less than five degrees, but that's still *something.*"

"Less than five degrees out of a normal field of one hundred and forty in each eye, and that's only when I put together a tiny bit here and a tiny bit there, where there are still a few cones functioning in my retina. It's all fragmented, a nothing, not even black, just a kind of flickering, a now-and-then reality that has no color, no borders or stability. And it will probably get worse, certainly no better. And there's no cure, no hope at all."

"But your blindness skills, everything you learned at Saint Paul's! You can do so much, Toby, you learned so much while you could still see . . . all those *years* of seeing, more than twenty-five good years. You told me yourself that you have an enormous number of visual clues, thousands of memories that help to piece things together, to make a pattern recognizable, it isn't as if you'd been born blind. Anyway, what difference does the exact percentage matter, when you can function? When you can work? What does it have to do with the two of us? So what if you've never seen me? When I get old and wrinkled and lose my looks you won't care about it. You don't love me just because I'm beautiful. Don't you realize how much that means? Besides Maxi you're the only person I know who doesn't base some of his feelings about me on my particular face, you're the only person I can trust to *like* me for no other reason than that I'm me. Doesn't that make a difference to you? Don't I make sense?"

"Perfect sense, up to a certain point. I don't think it's fair to you to involve you in my problems."

"Fair? What's fair is to take the happiness you know exists for you, now, this very minute, without doing any harm to anyone else, the happiness that exists if you just stretch out your hand," India said, her voice trembling.

"You have an incredible ability to oversimplify, India, sweet, imperfect India. I can't allow you to choose a man with my particular handicap, for it is a handicap, say what you will, even if you're convinced, at this particular time, that it's what you want. You have no idea of what the future holds, you can't know how long I'll be able to make you happy."

"I *know* you're the man I want," India said, her voice golden with the intensity of her sureness, "and I know I'm not going to change my mind."

"What, may I ask, does Doctor Florence Florsheim have to say about us?" Toby asked.

"Don't change the subject."

"She must have said something, analyst or not."

"She said that it wasn't recommended to make major life changes during the analytic process. Not that I couldn't, just that it wasn't recommended."

"That's all?"

"Word for word."

"Well, I think she's right."

"Oh *rats!*" India howled, pounding her fists against his bare chest. "I knew you'd say that. You make fun of her all the time and suddenly when it suits you, you decide to agree with her."

"Just because she's your shrink doesn't mean she's necessarily wrong. Hey, what's this I've found? Oh, oh, India, poor baby, I think you've got a crow's foot in its earliest stages. It probably won't be noticeable on the screen for a few years, maybe even five if you never smile from now on. Let me kiss it and make it well."

"You're a first-class sadist, Toby. You know something? For the first time I'm absolutely convinced that you and Maxi are brother and sister."

The morning of Cutter's breakfast meeting with Leonard Wilder, Charlie Salomon had called and told Lily to meet him at the courthouse. He had used his considerable influence to arrange for Justin's hearing to take place immediately following the judge's arrival.

"I'll go with you, darling," Cutter said, "just let me cancel my breakfast date."

"No, I don't really think it's a good idea," Lily answered. "Not that I don't want you there, but I believe it would be easier on Justin if we treated this as . . . routinely . . . as possible. Anyway, I promised Maxi to let her know as soon as he could get out of that awful place. I'll call her and tell her to come with me."

"Maxi, for moral support?"

"Well, you know how close she is to him."

"All right, Lily, if you're sure, but—"

"I'm positive. I'll call you as soon as I'm back home."

Lily picked up Maxi on the way downtown to the courthouse. There they met Charlie Salomon and two young lawyers from his office whom he had brought along. When Justin was brought in, handcuffed, Lily grasped Maxi's hand tightly, and lowered her eyes so that if Justin happened to glance at her he wouldn't see her watching him until the handcuffs were removed. How stubbornly defiant he looked, Maxi thought. His stance was as dangerous as it had always been, his head tilted at his characteristically aggressive angle but he limped slightly and no amount of toughness could disguise the dark bruises around his eyes, forehead and chin where the detectives had hit him with their saps. His spiky blond hair was matted in several places. Maxi flicked a glance at her brother and caught his eye. On impulse she winked broadly and smiled as if she were remembering a private joke between them, but Justin looked away, without acknowledging her.

"The defendant is a very rich man, Your Honor," they all heard the assistant district attorney say. "Two detectives found almost three kilos of cocaine in his possession and he forcibly resisted arrest. If found guilty of conspiracy to distribute cocaine he will certainly face years in prison. Under these circumstances there is every reason to expect him to leave the country rather than stand trial. The state asks for one million dollars bail."

Bring your checkbook, Maxi thought. Oh, Justin, how naive

we both were last night. The reporter who had accosted her the day before was scribbling away in the row behind them.

"That's an unreasonable amount, Your Honor," Charlie Salomon said. "My client has no record of any previous offense."

After a few more minutes of argument the judge made his decision.

"Bail is set at two hundred and fifty thousand dollars."

Justin was handcuffed again and taken to a holding cell in the courthouse until the money could be produced. Lily telephoned her bank manager and made arrangements for a cashier's check, to be delivered by a messenger on a motorcycle. After an hour and a quarter of waiting the check finally arrived and was handed over. The necessary paperwork for release took another half hour.

"Charlie, thank you so much for your help," Lily said. "I think you and your colleagues should go now. Maxime and I will go back uptown with Justin."

"I think I should stay here with you till he comes out. I have to talk to him anyway, Lily."

"Tomorrow, Charlie," Lily commanded and the lawyers left.

"That reporter from last night is here again today, Mother, and he's got a photographer with him today," Maxi warned.

"Justin is not guilty, Maxime. If they want to take pictures, there's nothing we can do about it."

"Shall we both smile for the camera, Mother?"

"Why not, Maxime? There's nothing to be ashamed of."

"All I need is a good hot shower and something to eat," Justin insisted when Lily suggested that she call her doctor and ask him to examine Justin in case there was serious damage to his skull from the saps the detectives had used. Nothing could sway him so the three Ambervilles went back to the great gray stone house and eventually found themselves sitting, at Lily's insistence, over the lunch table making conversation as if nothing more serious than an unremarkable head cold were at issue. Even Maxi felt gripped by the compelling force of Lily's superbly maintained composure, yet without looking at her mother or her brother she felt the hurt that suffused their souls. As a rack of lamb followed the cream of asparagus soup the tension in the room grew greater with every evasive word they each uttered, with the mounting total of essential words that hadn't been spoken. The servants came and went.

"Mother, could we skip the dessert and have coffee, just the three of us, in your sitting room?" Maxi asked.

"Certainly, dear," Lily answered as if this were the most normal request in the world.

They went upstairs, Justin moving with the tightly controlled restraint of a man who is keeping all his capacities for action in reserve. He looked as psychically remote from his sister and his mother as if he were a bullfighter being dressed in his suit of lights just before the *corrida*. It was almost, Maxi thought, as if he weren't there at all.

"Sugar?" Lily asked.

"Please," he answered and took two lumps with the close attention a heart surgeon might give to opening a chest.

"Tomorrow," Lily said, with no change of tone, "I'll have Charlie Salomon look into the question of defense lawyers, the best ones available. The fact that you're innocent is hardly a sufficient defense."

"Thank you, Mother," Justin said with a lopsided shadow of his go-to-the-devil smile.

"Of course, you realize," Lily said nervously, fiddling with the handle of the coffeepot, her words tumbling out in a way that wasn't natural to her, "that whatever life-style you choose will never make any difference to us, that we love you anyway—very much—no matter what."

"Life-style? You mean even if I were a vegetarian or took up computer fraud? How about murder-for-hire?" Justin challenged her.

"What the hell are the two of you talking about?" Maxi burst out. "This isn't a time for twenty questions, Justin. We know that there's only one reason that cocaine was found in your place."

"Maxime," Lily said warningly.

"Mother, we can't keep waltzing around." Maxi got up and

took away Justin's demitasse and put it down on a side table. She knelt on the floor by his side and wrapped her arms around him and gave him a deliberately loud smacking kiss on the cheek. "Look, kiddo, there's got to be a guy who has a key to your place or who's been staying with you, somebody who put that stuff there without telling you, some guy you're *involved* with. Can't we just get this out in the open, Justin, so Mother and I can stop trying to act as if we didn't know that you're gay?"

Justin leapt up savagely and stalked to the window without a word, turning his back on them. Maxi ran after him and grabbed him around the waist. "*Gay*, Justin, or whatever word you prefer. *We know*, we've known for a long time, Mother and I, and we don't give a fuck! Come back and sit down. It's not the end of the world. Gay is one thing, stupid is another, and in either case going to jail is not recommended. So turn around so we can discuss this sensibly."

"You don't know anything. You can't possibly know anything," Justin said, his voice corrosive, his back still turned, gripping the windowsill. He stood as if he felt contempt for them rather than any stronger, more personal emotion.

"But I do, darling," Lily said, more evenly now. "I've known for years. I saw no reason to talk about it with anyone, ever. It was your private life, until now."

"I had no idea that Mother realized anything until last night when I had to call her," Maxi said, without slackening her grasp. "Nobody but people who love you very much and know you as well as we do, and God knows, you've made sure there are damn few of us, would even begin to wonder. But this is a tough conversation to have with your shoulder blades. Please?" She planted a row of delicate kisses on the back of his neck, holding on to him as hard as she could, all the while.

"Justin, who do you think put the drugs in your closet? That's really the point, isn't it?" Lily spoke as if she were asking him if she should dismiss a light-fingered butler.

He turned, finally. Only two patches of red on his sharp cheekbones and the long, thin muscle that worked in his throat displayed any emotion. "I haven't the slightest idea." His tone was almost ironic, formal.

"But there is somebody, *some man,* who can get into your place when you're not there?" Maxi persisted.

His face twisted in a spasm of shame so mixed with pain that it brought tears to Lily's eyes.

"Yes." The one word so quietly spoken hung in the air like a long sigh. Briskly, Maxi broke the silence that threatened to overtake them all.

"Do you think he did it?"

"No. No, he couldn't have. Absolutely not. He's simply not like that. He's just a guy I met on a shoot. But we've done a lot of . . . entertaining . . . people always dropping in—it could have been anyone. That duffel bag's been sitting there empty since the last time I came back to town." His voice was so empty that they felt fear.

"Do you know where he is now?" Maxi asked. "What's his name?"

"He's out of town," Justin said. "It must have been somebody else. And his name is none of anybody's business. I refuse to start blaming someone I trust just to prove I'm innocent. *Christ, I hate this city!"*

Maxi and Lily sat silently after Justin had rushed out of the room.

"Thank you, Maxime. Without your kind of directness I don't think I could have persuaded him to say anything. But it must have seemed unfair, the two of us cornering him like that," Lily said. "I feel somehow ashamed, not for him, for us."

"Unfair? Yes, but only if we'd wanted to know for any other reason than to keep him out of jail. But in these circumstances, no, absolutely not. And, Mother, he must have some sense of relief now that it's out and he knows we love him just as much as we ever did, that it doesn't make any difference. He's been guarding that secret all alone for much too long a time."

"Oh, but Maxime, you saw his face . . . he looked . . . oh, as if he wanted to vanish, as if he didn't believe in anyone or anything in the world and never would again. He's always been so alone, so apart, he's always kept so much to himself. I've worried about him all of his life but I could never break through to him."

"It's not your fault, Mother. Not mine. Not Justin's. It just *is* and it has to be dealt with. It's reality and nothing could have changed it."

"I wish I could believe that," Lily said wistfully.

"Mother, do you really imagine that on one particular day when Justin was just a little boy you could have said, 'Now darling, when you grow up, the only people you'll want to touch will be girls,' the way you taught him good table manners?"

Lily smiled slowly, reluctantly and ruefully. "That would have been too good to be true, but what a wonderful idea. You do have a way of getting straight to the point, Maxime."

"Thank you, Mother," Maxi said almost shyly. "I have to rush to the office now, but what's the next step? How can we help Justin?"

"I'm going to call Charlie Salomon at once and tell him what Justin just told us. But, on one hand he didn't tell us much that would help, as far as I can see, and on the other hand wouldn't it be better not to use it? I so desperately hope that we can keep that part of his life out of the newspapers . . . the man with the key to his apartment, the parties. If only we could do that much, at least."

"Every paper in the country is going to have the drug story, Mother. Plus the *Star* and the *Inquirer* and the news magazines. I don't see how we can keep it from being a media circus. It's only a question of time before they sniff out the rest of what Justin told us. There's nothing we can do to protect him. All it will take will be one lead, one person talking to one reporter. I don't think there's much hope."

"I thought . . . if only he could keep that bit of dignity. He cares so terribly much," Lily said soberly.

"I don't think you should be optimistic about protecting Justin's private life. The most important thing is to prove him innocent of drug dealing. He's an Amberville after all, and the media is going to be out in full force, dancing on his head."

Lily sighed as Maxi got up to leave. The two women embraced, a little awkwardly, with more warmth than either of them could remember showing each other in years. Lily, in her familiar gesture, pushed Maxi's hair back from her forehead.

"It's still wrong, isn't it, Mother?" Maxi asked wryly.

"The trouble with you, Maxime, is that you always jump to conclusions. I was just thinking how charmingly you wear your hair. It wouldn't really look like *you* any other way, would it?"

23

As Maxi and Lily were saying goodbye to each other, Cutter was meeting in his Wall Street office with Lewis Oxford, Vice-President for Financial Affairs of Amberville Publications. Cutter could more easily have established himself in a suite of offices in the Amberville Building uptown but he found it useful to force everyone who worked on the magazines to make a time-consuming trek to see him, and it kept him at a useful remove from anyone who wanted to talk about minor matters.

"Oxford, I wish you would stop doing that," Cutter rapped out.

"Sorry, Mr. Amberville. It helps me to reflect," Lewis Oxford answered, regretfully putting away the pencil with which he had been tapping his teeth.

"There's nothing to reflect about. My wife's orders are clear enough."

"Clear, perfectly clear. The only thing I was wondering was if it wouldn't be better to follow her instructions over a period of six months, or even a year. Three months isn't much time and I'm going to have to make a lot of waves."

"I've given you three months, Oxford, and if you can't manage I'll find someone who can. I'm sure you know that it's more merciful to cut off a dog's tail in one clean sweep than bit by bit. Every single one of the Amberville magazines has a thick strip of fat running through it and I want that fat cut out, starting immediately. Our next profit statement must reflect this change. By my estimates at least fourteen percent of our operating costs can be eliminated. Maybe more. Preferably more."

Lewis Oxford shook his head. "I still think it may be a mistake to move so rapidly."

"I'm not interested in anything but results, Oxford. Mrs. Amberville wants the paper quality on each and every magazine to go down one level. No more fifty-pound free sheet for *Style*—it doesn't have to look like *Town & Country* to sell. Everything that's being printed on forty-pound stock will be printed on thirty-four-pound stock from now on, as soon as you've used up the paper already in inventory. *T.V. Week* goes to thirty-four-pound ground-wood stock. Is that understood?"

"Yes, Mr. Amberville."

"As for the bulge on each magazine; the staff salaries, writers' fees and photo fees, I expect to see impressive results. Cut all staff by fifteen percent immediately. Mrs. Amberville wants every article and photo story you have in inventory to be used. *Eat up that inventory*, Oxford. You have hundreds of thousands of dollars worth that's just getting out of date. What's more, no more expensive writers' fees are to be approved. This article by Norman Mailer on 'Miami Vice'—can you give me one good reason why we should be paying for Mailer instead of some unknown free-lance we can get at a cut-rate price?"

"It's classy, Mr. Amberville, and it might attract readers we wouldn't ordinarily have."

"We don't need class in a television magazine with seven million readers. It's sheer editorial ego to use class writers."

"Excuse me, sir, but that's not quite fair. The editor of *T.V. Week* feels strongly that Mailer and other name writers will impress Madison Avenue. He's ordered a series of ads in *Adweek* and *Advertising Age*—"

"Cancel them. For the next three months Amberville Publications is not blowing its own horn. We've been around for almost forty years and the advertising community is hardly unaware of us. I want promotion and publicity eliminated."

"Yes, sir."

"These photographers' bills are insane, Oxford. Insane."

"That's what all the top photographers are getting now, Mr. Amberville."

"Send out a notice to the Editor-in-chief of each magazine that they are to stop using the same photographers they've been relying on for years. One of our editors' problems is that they've been letting the photographers do the imaginative work they should be doing themselves. I want them to use new photographers, the least expensive they can find, particularly women, people who will work for a great deal less and work harder. What's more, I want thirty percent fewer color spreads, replaced by black and white. That can be just as effective as color, used properly. As for models' fees, they're killing us. Whenever possible I want celebrities to be used for models—they don't cost us anything at all."

"Mr. Amberville, I must object. There's a limit to how many celebrities you can use before the magazines will all begin to look like *People*. Mr. Zachary Amberville never—"

"I'm not interested in repeating the past, Oxford. Readers want to see celebrities and we're going to give them what they want. I'm very disappointed in our profit for the last quarter. It has to come *up*, Oxford."

"It will, sir."

"Won't advertisers supply free articles and pictures if their products are plugged?" Cutter asked.

"It's been known to happen, but not at Amberville."

"Well, make it happen, Oxford. As often as you can. And another thing, just look at these travel expense accounts for our ad and sales representatives," Cutter went on. "They're an absolute scandal. Let each rep know that we're watching him and tell them that we expect a reduction of thirty-five percent in the next set of figures."

"Hell, Mr. Amberville, the reps live off their T-and-E's— everybody knows that."

"They're living too high, Oxford. Every rep who doesn't change his ways will be replaced. Be sure and put that in the memo."

"But the reps have to maintain relationships . . ." Lewis Oxford's voice trailed off at the mounting rage he saw in Cutter's face.

"Amberville Publications is not a God damned gravy train, Oxford! I can see that these cuts are long overdue. I blame you for letting things go on in this way. And do *not*, if you value your job,

338

tell me that Mr. Zachary Amberville wanted it that way. My brother was a great editor, Oxford, but I can see he wasn't keeping a tight ship, as Mrs. Amberville and I have suspected. Do you have any more suggestions, Oxford? or have I covered everything?"

"There are small things, tables we take at magazine industry dinners, the lunches we give for major advertisers, things like that."

"Leave those alone. They don't amount to enough to make a difference and I want our presence maintained on that particular level. Don't worry, Oxford, when the profit is up, we'll take out media ads and let everyone know about it. Three months from now."

Cutter waited a few seconds and Lewis Oxford, hoping that the conversation was over, began to pull his papers together in preparation for departure.

"One more thing, Oxford. *B&B*. How much are we losing on it every month?"

"I'd need time to get the exact figures, Mr. Amberville. But I'll send Miss Amberville all your cost-cutting directives."

"No, don't bother. How long will it take for *B&B* to break even, assuming that every issue does as well as the first one?"

"Many months, I'm afraid. As you know, every start-up is a major hemorrhage of money, sir. But that's only normal. Once they're back in the black profits should be tremendous."

"Stop publication of *B&B*, Oxford."

"What?"

"Don't you understand English? Cancel it, eliminate it, finish it! No more *B&B*, Oxford. Give the printers instructions not to print any more copies. Let all the creditors know that they'll be paid in full for whatever is currently owed, but beyond that Amberville Publications will not honor a single bill that Miss Amberville runs up. Warn them, Oxford. Not a dime. And fire the whole staff except for Miss Amberville. She's not on salary."

"But the magazine is a success, Mr. Amberville! The biggest success story since *Cosmo* or *Life* or *Seven Days*."

"It was a successful experiment, Oxford. But we can't afford the loss over the next year, or even over the next six months, not if we plan to raise our profit to where it should be. Even you would have to admit that whatever you save everywhere else will be more than offset by B&B's losses."

"Well, yes, in fact I assumed that those losses were why you were taking such drastic measures."

"Never assume, Oxford," Cutter said with a pleasant smile, and rose to show the man to the door. "Never assume anything in a privately owned company."

Angelica stood on Fifth Avenue, between Fifty-sixth and Fifty-seventh streets, leaning disconsolately against a tall, metal city sign. "Don't Even THINK of Parking Here," it said, and added, for emphasis, "Red Zone, Tow Fine, $100 Minimum. No Standing at Any Time." Behind the sign, sitting around the fountain of the Steuben Glass Building, were the usual collection of waifs, drunks and tourists, some of them eating falafel, schnitzel or chicken nuggets from the pushcarts that stood conveniently at hand, others dipping their aching feet in the fountain, and still others studying the contents of the shopping bags they had just filled up and down the avenue. It was an affluent North American version of Calcutta.

The stern no-parking sign was Elie's favorite place to sit in the limo when he waited for Maxi. He had reached a tacit agreement with the cops on the street to start the motor and pull up a symbolic inch or so whenever they came along. But this afternoon he was late in bringing Maxi home and Angelica scanned the passing traffic with impatience.

Finally the long blue limo pulled up and Maxi hopped out.

"Oh, no," she groaned, seeing Angelica and the copy of the *New York Post* that she was holding, open to the story of Justin's arrest. How could she not have realized that there was the chance that Angelica would see the story in the paper before she'd been told about it? The lunch with Justin and Lily, followed by a few hectic hours at the office, making up for the work she hadn't done that morning, had driven the thought of warning her daughter out of her head.

"Ma?" Angelica's voice was blurred with tears.

"Baby, it's all crap. A giant setup. Uncle Justin has absolutely nothing to do with selling cocaine. Don't worry about it for a second. He's totally innocent," Maxi said in a rush.

"I know he's innocent, Ma, for goodness' sake, you don't have to tell me that. But how come you and Granny are smiling in that picture? That's what I want to know. How could you be so heartless? You look like two freaked-out beauty queens—Miss North Carolina and her lovely mother. *Honestly.*"

"How do you think we should have looked? Frightened, miserable, horrified?"

"A little cool wouldn't have hurt. I mean, after all, you're not supposed to be thrilled about a bum rap. At least Uncle Justin handled himself properly . . . he looks terrific, tough, grim, indifferent, just like Sting, yeah, exactly like Sting."

"Angelica, I think you should seriously consider a career in public relations. Come on, let's go home."

"Can I have a falafel first?"

"You'll ruin your dinner. But go ahead, if you can pronounce it you can eat it, as far as I'm concerned," Maxi said, too exhausted to argue.

"You're losing your grip," Angelica said in relief, "but I'm not surprised. Today I found out that Cyndi Lauper's thirty years old. She's older than you are, Maxi."

"Please, a little respect," Maxi said, stung into firmness.

"I'll try," Angelica said hastily, feeling better. Cyndi Lauper might be older but Ma was . . . her mother.

Rocco opened the *Post,* his head snapped upright and Angelo, the barber downstairs at the St. Regis, who dispensed his forty-dollar haircuts to a chosen circle, narrowly missed nicking him with his scissors, although his reflexes were finely conditioned to the aberrant reactions of executives under stress.

"Hey, Rocco, trying to lose an ear?"

"I have to get to a phone. Don't bother to finish." Rocco stood up and started to undrape himself.

"Sit! I'm half through. You can't leave here like that."

"The hell I can't." Brushing off hairs, Rocco ran up the staircase. The phone booths in the lobby were all occupied. He rushed out of the hotel and saw that even if he could get a cab it couldn't move in the late-afternoon traffic. Where could he get a phone? All of the booths on the street were permanently out of order, vandalized as soon as they were repaired. The office was too far to run to. Angelo! He ran back to the hotel, descended the stairs three at a time and took unasked possession of Angelo's private phone. The barber, who could get a president of a Fortune 500 company a previously unobtainable reservation at the Hotel du Cap at Antibes during the busiest week of the year, merely raised an eyebrow. Rocco was crazy but his hair was a pleasure to cut. Old Country hair, thick, curly, healthy, the real thing, should last him till he didn't need it anymore.

"Maxi, I just read about Justin. What can I do to help?"

"I don't know. Mother's busy mobilizing legal talent but Justin hasn't the first idea of how the cocaine got there. Apparently he's been doing a lot of entertaining . . . he insists that it could be any one of dozens of people. However, he did say there had been some guy who had a key to his place but all he would tell us was it was someone he met on a shoot and that it couldn't possibly be him."

"Why not?"

"Apparently he's just too perfect a person," Maxi said dryly. "And Justin absolutely refused to tell us this saint's name. What's more the wonderful human being is out of town."

"Can you follow it up?"

"That's exactly what I've been asking myself. The first bathing-suit shoot Justin did for me used twenty-four male models. The next fashion feature was the one called 'Celebrity Closets, or The Positive Effects of Creative Disorder,' and the following month we had Bill Blass showing you thirty different ways to wear your oldest sweaters. Besides the fashion shots, Justin's done a lot of other stuff for us . . . I'm looking over the pictures now."

"Twenty-four male models? All from the same agency?"

"No, Julie booked them from four different agencies, or maybe even five."

"Look, get hold of the bills. They must be there at your office. Then give them to me and let me make a few phone calls. I'll let you know if anything checks out."

"I'll go get the bills now."

"Tomorrow morning is soon enough. I have to talk to people in their offices, people I can't call at home."

"I'll have them delivered first thing. Rocco, look, this is really extraordinarily sweet of you, and I'm deeply, deeply grateful," Maxi said. "I won't ever forget it."

"What the hell," Rocco said, ignoring her emotion. "You know I've always liked Justin. That poor bastard. How's Angelica taking it?" he asked, his voice suddenly anxious.

"In her own way."

"What's that supposed to mean?"

"If anyone survives this, it will be my daughter," Maxi sniffed.

"You don't understand her," Rocco said, "my daughter's an exceptionally sensitive little girl."

"Angelica has finer feelings I couldn't possibly comprehend, I suppose."

"Exactly. She's probably suffering a trauma you wouldn't even recognize, much less cope with."

"Rocco, I have an idea. Why don't I have Elie bring her over to your place? You can take her out to dinner tonight and help her deal with the shock."

"Uh. Well. As a matter of fact I have a date. Of course Angelica could join us, I guess, or maybe that wouldn't be such a great idea. No, probably not, on second thought. Angelica's going to be spending the weekend with me. We'll talk it all out then."

"You do that. Thanks anyway, Rocco. Talk to you." Maxi hung up softly, and looked around for something to throw at the wall, something guaranteed to break into a billion pieces and make one hell of a lot of noise. But nothing too valuable. That miserable pissant wasn't worth it.

"Sue, this is Rocco Cipriani."

"Oh, hi there, Mr. Cipriani. What can I do for you?" she chirped.

"There's a little question I'd like to ask about four of your guys," Rocco said lightly. Sue was the best booker of models at her agency.

"Sure thing. Which of our glorious boys interests you?"

"I'll tell you in a minute. It's a little delicate, Sue, but I'm sure you understand that sometimes I have to ask a, well, a somewhat hard question."

"That's what I'm here for," Sue proclaimed perkily.

Rocco gave her the names of the models from her agency who had been in the bathing-suit shoot and added, as if he were asking their chest measurements, "I'd like to know if one or more of them uses cocaine."

"Is this a complaint, Mr. Cipriani?" Sue asked after a tiny pause.

"No, Sue, nothing like that. Nothing to be alarmed about. But I figured that if anyone else had been having trouble with one or more of the guys, if there had just possibly been some complaints, you'd know about it before anyone else."

"Mr. Cipriani, you know as well as I do that if a model is on dope he won't last long. If we get enough complaints we drop him." Her upbeat voice had disappeared completely, replaced by the firmness that had made her a power in the industry.

"Of course you do. On the other hand, Sue, it's not impossible to get away with a few complaints here and there if you're really hot. A model in real demand can get away with murder, much less a few toots."

"Not here," she insisted. "This isn't Hollywood."

"Your people are special, Sue, we've always known that." Rocco's voice curled sweetly around the compliment. "I also want to find out if any of the guys I'm curious about are living high, spending more money than they could be earning."

"I still don't understand what you're driving at," she said, managing not to sound defensive.

"Why don't we put it this way?" Rocco said soothingly. "My instinct tells me that among the male models in this city, there are a few who are either heavy users or dealers in cocaine or both. One way or another, I really need the information."

"Not a model with this agency, Mr. Cipriani, no way, absolutely not."

"Maybe not. I'm pretty sure you're right. But something *is* going on. I'd also like to just suggest that the best interests of the entire modeling agency industry would be served if it polices itself.

Call it a pre-police action, because, Sue, if, for some reason or another, I don't get those special names, I'm awfully afraid that the police are going to be out in force, crawling under and over every agency in the city," Rocco said. "In fact you can count on it," he added gently.

"I'll do everything I can to help," Sue said, determinedly businesslike. "I'll definitely ask around."

"Right, you do that little thing. By the way, I've been checking out the bookings CL&K did with your agency last year. Four hundred thousand dollars, wasn't it? No, actually quite a bit more than that. What do you know? You people really can pick 'em. Goodbye, Sue, and oh, if by some remote chance, you should happen to learn anything helpful, let me know fast, won't you?"

"Of course, Mr. Cipriani."

"By three-thirty or four this afternoon, let's say, in fact no later than the close of business today. And Sue, I'm really looking for a dealer, not just your dime-a-dozen user. I know that you're far too bright not to have realized that, aren't you? I'm not all that interested in your ordinary users—but I want their names anyway, just in case."

"In case?"

"Just in case. *A dealer and the people he sells to.* That's what I'm after, Sue. And that's what I'd better get. We're all equally concerned, aren't we? I'll be hearing from you, one way or the other, won't I?" The smile in Rocco's voice grew deeper.

"Sure thing. Absolutely. You can count on it. One way or the other. Oh, and thanks for calling, Mr. Cipriani."

"It's always nice to talk to you," Rocco said pleasantly. "A dealer, Sue, and the people he sells to."

Rocco spent the morning making four similar phone calls to the four other agencies who had supplied the models for the bathing-suit story. All of them did a great deal of business with CL&K. He got the same set of resolutely negative answers but by five in the afternoon he had a longer list of names than he had anticipated and behind the scenes at five agencies a lot of very worried executives were consulting each other. This sort of thing wasn't supposed to be going on except at other agencies, they told each other. They could afford to lose CL&K's business if it came to that, but none of them could afford a scandal in the modeling industry. They had given Rocco every name they could pry or threaten out of their male models and their bookers, as well as the names of every model they had had vague suspicions about themselves. But exactly what had Cipriani meant by a "pre-police action"? they wondered. And why had he been so uncharacteristically pleasant? So terrifyingly *mild*?

Two days later Rocco telephoned Maxi at her office.

"Justin's in the clear, Maxi. I thought you'd like to know. All charges have been dropped."

"Rocco! Are you sure? Are you absolutely sure?"

"I just had a call from Charlie Salomon. He confirmed it."

"What did you do? How did you do it?" She was so excited that she almost dropped the phone.

"Oh, I just asked around."

"Rocco, don't drive me crazy. Oh shit, you're so wonderful—"

"Cut it out, Maxi. It was no big deal. I asked around for names and I got names and figured out who the guy was from your list and I gave the name to Salomon, plus the names of some people who'd been buying from Justin's friend and who were . . . urged . . . strongly urged, by their agencies, to agree to testify against him . . . nothing your average amateur detective couldn't do if he knew where to look."

"You're so incredible, you're the most marvelous—who was he?"

"Some beauty named Jon, a relatively minor-league dealer who was caught doing a little business with some much bigger fish down in Florida. He tried to cop a plea, putting the blame on Justin. He'd left his merchandise at Justin's place, unfortunately for Justin. Jon's not a very nice guy, basically. As Angelica would say, he has a massive attitude problem. Anyway, the cops managed to pick him up. A relatively simple matter once they knew who he was, or so I gather."

346

"Why do I have the feeling that there's something you're not telling me?"

"You always had a suspicious nature. Too bad Justin didn't. Anyway, that's that. I'm glad it's over. Goodbye, Maxi."

"Rocco, wait! Don't just hang up. Please let me thank you," Maxi pleaded. "You don't have the faintest idea of what this means to me. I'm just . . . I don't know what to say . . ." Her words fell over each other in a cry of thanksgiving. She sounded almost childish in her immense joy and gratitude.

"Oh, come on, cool it. I did it for Angelica and Justin. And your mother, of course. Salomon's calling her right now. Justin will be in the office sometime Monday, business as usual. He said to tell you."

"When did you talk to him?" Maxi asked incredulously.

"A few minutes ago. I figured he should be the first to hear the good news."

"What did he say?"

"Not much. He was relieved, naturally, but more than anything else he didn't want to believe that Jon had been the one to set him up. He had some very serious illusions about that creep. Your brother is one of the last of the great romantics. So, if I were you, I wouldn't act all bubbly and Mary Tyler Moore and thrilled when he shows up for work. Just try to act natural, like it's not the end of the world or something. Make it easy for the poor son of a bitch."

"I'll do my best," Maxi said softly.

"Try not to be too sloppy, O.K.?"

"Right, Rocco. Will do." Maxi looked for something satisfactorily resistant to grind under the four-inch heels of her new Mario Valentine pumps. "Good show. Well done. The family appreciates your efforts on our behalf and there will be a turkey for you in your Christmas basket, my good man."

All right, thought Maxi, all right, probably she had sounded as if he were Superman and she were Lois Lane tied to the railroad tracks, maybe she had let her happiness get out of control, but wasn't it normal to be grateful? How could anybody, even someone as thoroughly crusty and grumpy as Rocco Cipriani, not want to be thanked? How did a man get so contemptible? she asked herself furiously, sitting in a lump in the middle of her bed, her chin resting on her folded hands, her elbows on her knees, unmoving, brooding, a solid mass of resentment. He never lost a chance to try to make her feel feeble-minded, even when he was doing a good deed. He had actually accused her of insensitivity, warning her how to treat Justin, as if he expected her to be gauche and goofy. He'd always had that arrogant streak, that unbending vein of sheer shitheaded vanity that made him think that his way was the only right way. His trouble was that he thought he was the center of the universe. Nothing had ever really happened to him to make him realize that he was just a pinheaded pretty face who was clever with a pencil. Humility. Rocco needed to learn humility. She said the word out loud, savoring it, tasting the sweetness of it. But, unlike him, she was not a small-minded, petty, grudging, miserly person. She was happy to see that the father of her child was good in a crisis. He had done the Amberville family a gigantic service, and he was going to be rewarded for it whether he wanted to be or not. Rewarded royally, rewarded until it made him sick!

Suddenly gleeful, Maxi reached out for her now ever-present yellow pad and started to make notes. First, an Alfa-Romeo Spider convertible. What did it matter that he wouldn't be able to find a parking place for it and that a car like that was an invitation to vandals? She'd take whatever color was immediately available although she'd prefer black because it showed dirt faster. Next; that set of delicately etched antique crystal wineglasses she'd seen at James Robinson. Three thousand dollars and they had to be washed by hand, preferably in a rubber-lined basin, and dried with exquisite care. He'd probably break the lot in six months. What else? Why not a full set of antelope suede luggage from Loewe? The Spanish leather-goods makers had a shop downstairs and she'd been eyeing covetously their soft-sided pale gray bags, trimmed in burgundy, but of course they were too fragile for airplane travel; they'd be ruined in one trip. The smallest carry-on bag alone was almost six hundred dollars—maybe he could manage to keep that one looking decent for a while. Ah-ha, she had it, that glorious Art-

Deco sterling silver coffee set from Puiforcat. So what if it was forty thousand dollars—it had to be kept polished if it were to look like anything, just like any ordinary piece of silver. But you couldn't say it wasn't thoughtful.

A string of polo ponies? No, Maxi decided regretfully. They were only ten thousand each but even Rocco, unsophisticated as he was, would realize that they were inappropriate. Ponies needed a groom and boxes and regular feeding—either she'd have to throw in all the upkeep or not give them to him at all. Anyway he knew that she knew he couldn't ride. It would be delicious to give him a small Learjet 23 but three hundred thousand dollars seemed just a bit too much to spend to indicate her everlasting gratitude. Still, the list lacked something. It was skimpy. Why not a pair of tickets for a long Caribbean cruise? It would be good therapy for a devoted workaholic like Rocco. Perhaps two, no, make it three dozen of those lace-edged bath towels she'd seen at Barney's the last time she'd shopped retail. In beige, of course, or, better yet, plain white. Not an obviously feminine color. He should be able to find a fine hand laundry somewhere, if he looked hard enough. And just to show that she harbored nothing in her heart but sincere generosity, a case of Glenfiddich, his favorite pure malt whiskey. That should confuse him nicely, Maxi thought. What she'd really like to give him would be a folio of drawings by Leonardo da Vinci. That would show him the extent of his tiny talent as nothing else could. But the Queen of England had cornered the best of them and the Morgan Library had most of the rest.

There was a tap on her door and Angelica came in.

"Why aren't you with your father?" Maxi asked in surprise. It was Angelica's weekend to be with Rocco. "Don't tell me he canceled on you?"

"No, Ma, you know he'd never do that. He's got the most awful cold in the head. He just called and said he was sure he was contagious, swarming with germs and that I should ask if he could trade weekends with you."

"Sure you can," Maxi answered. Angelica looked even more doleful than before. "Don't you want to?"

"Well, actually, the Troop had planned something special for today because a lot of kids are home for spring vacations and I kind

349

of hate to miss it. I mean, it's happenin' *this* weekend, not next weekend and anyway I'd like to have some time to myself, you know, to jam a little. Nothing bogus, Ma, just a little time raging with my people."

"You make it sound like rape and pillage," Maxi said, hairs lifting on her nape. "Raging?"

"I am referring," Angelica said with dignity, "to an afternoon at the circus followed by a dim sum rage, or, as you would put it, a nice time with nice young ladies and gentlemen, including refreshments."

"Be my guest," Maxi assured her. She had the greatest faith in the Troop and their activities. Angelica vanished skipping in a resounding whoop of joy, free from her guilt-ridden parents who took up far too much of her private life making up to her for their divorce. Didn't they know that everybody got divorced sooner or later?

Maxi started to get dressed for her shopping trip to buy Rocco's thank-you presents. Maybe he'd still be home sick when they were delivered. A terrible head cold could last a week. Spring vacations? Hadn't Angelica just said something about spring vacations? She looked out of the bathroom window and verified that spring had come to Central Park without notice, as surprisingly overnight as it had in *Mary Poppins*. A head cold and spring vacations. Why hadn't she realized it sooner? The malignant Cipriani hay fever had struck and Rocco, clinging stubbornly to his traditions, had refused to admit it, insisting, as he did every year, that it was unthinkable that he should suffer from such a sissy ailment since no Cipriani in history had ever had it. How could you get hay fever in Venice? Maxi had asked once, many years ago. She felt that the question was still valid.

Standing, rocking with laughter, in her pale lavender satin chemise, one foot about to be thrust into the right leg of a pair of sheer black stockings embroidered here and there with butterflies, Maxi was struck by a most kindly, most charitable, most open-hearted impulse. She would just dart over and make Rocco more comfortable in his misery, like a higher form of visiting nurse. Indeed an angel of mercy.

She knew where Angelica kept the key to his place and she

knew just the treatment for the Cipriani hay fever. There are some things you never forget. On her way to Rocco's, Maxi speculated about his apartment. He lived barely three blocks away, in a duplex on Central Park South, but she had never deigned to ask Angelica to describe it. She remembered Rocco's old longing for someplace monastic, austere and calm, as if he were a Japanese monk. Perhaps by now he had mastered the minimalist school of decorating, subtracting everything that made a house livable and spending all his money on fanatical detailing that nobody else would ever notice. Or else he'd gone in for hideously uncomfortable Mackintosh chairs and black-and-white tiles from the 1930s that had been ugly to begin with and hadn't improved with age in spite of their highly touted, inexplicable Andrée Putman chic. Maybe he was heavily invested in industrial objects, steel pipe sections and neon tubing, and slept on a mat on the floor. On the other hand that was all démodé. Perhaps by now he'd gone in for the Santa Fe Calvin Klein look—a nightmare out of Georgia O'Keeffe, with three meaningful stones on the mantel whose magic arrangement must never be changed, adobe walls on which the plaster was encouraged to flake and one perfect cactus, dying slowly. Or possibly he just lived like half the design snobs she knew, with all white walls and horribly boring and expensive Mies and Breuer furniture, punctuated by the obligatory Frank Stellas and Roy Lichtensteins. It was too much to hope that he was into the truly atrocious 1950s and laminated plywood. Probably, like most old bachelors, his place was bound to be basically a mess.

Quietly, Maxi used Angelica's key to open the front door. The entrance hall was a good-sized room she observed disapprovingly. How odd of him to have used fine old parquet, rubbed to a golden glow. What a strange place to put a life-sized Maillol torso of Venus, a powerful, darkly gleaming presence that held its own, magnificent against the melting magic, the receding rainbow tides of the two large Helen Frankenthalers on facing walls. No furniture, she noted, with the exception of a superb Regency table against the third wall, all curves and carving and unquestionably authentic to her experienced eye. Well, it's not all that difficult to buy good art if you have the money, she thought, closing the door softly behind her, and she disapproved of the art-gallery school of decorating on theory. Maxi listened for the sound of life in the apartment but heard nothing. Cautiously she made her way into the living room. Well, Rocco had certainly developed a taste for luxury that was quite out of keeping with his mingy high-mindedness, a luxury that seemed to be set with a divine incongruity in an old barn in the country instead of on Central Park South. Sunlight poured into the two-story room and turned the walls, covered with wooden siding, into a source of subtle information on the beauty that weather can work on wood. Deep, downy, gray velvet sofas, separated by a Parsons table lacquered in Chinese red, turned their backs on each other in the center of the long room and faced the great twin fireplaces that were on each of the side walls. Old Indian cashmere paisley in tones of biscuit, red and coral covered the supremely elegant Regency armchairs; here and there on the old brick floor were scattered Chinese silk rugs in muted, rare colors that echoed the sunlight.

Maxi sniffed as scornfully as possible. The most valuable piece in the room was clearly the Egyptian sculpture she'd given Rocco for their first Christmas together, an early Ptolemaic piece, a statue of Isis almost two feet tall, made from red quartzite. You could see every detail of her body, for the Egyptian goddesses wore robes more sheer than any Bob Mackie creation and the Isis had the most delicious breasts and bellybutton, almost as nice as her own, but no head. And the Maillol Venus had no arms. Apparently Rocco didn't like women enough to have one around who didn't lack a part of her anatomy.

She jumped at the sound of a violent sneeze, and a smile of anticipatory relish curved her tightly appraising mouth into a dangerous weapon, the particular smile that even Maxi was not vain enough to know drove men mad.

She crept softly upstairs toward the sound of sneezing and swearing and the blowing of a nose. All ugly and swollen she knew it would be, like a caricature of W.C. Fields at his worst.

The door to Rocco's bedroom was three-quarters closed. Inside she could see that it was dim, almost dark. He must have drawn the draperies and gone to ground under as many covers and quilts as he owned. No man had ever been brought so low by a head cold as Rocco Cipriani. Bad Dennis Brady treated them by switching from tequila to hot grogs and Laddie, Earl of Kirkgordon, simply ignored anything less than pneumonia. It was the weather, he explained. His ancestors had *always* had colds and what was good enough for Bonnie Prince Charlie was good enough for him.

Maxi coughed lightly to warn Rocco. There was no point in sending him into cardiac arrest when she'd come to make him feel better.

"Angelica, I told you not to come near me."

"It's just me," Maxi assured him. "Angelica was so worried about you that she insisted that I come over and make sure that you didn't need a doctor."

"Bugger off," he snarled, sneezing deliberately in her direction. All she could see of him was a gloomy hump of Dickensian churlishness.

"Now Rocco," Maxi said soothingly, "you're just making yourself miserable. There's no need to act as if you're at death's door just because you have a little head cold."

"Go ahead, gloat, but get the fuck out of my house."

"Isn't that a little paranoid? Why would I gloat over the suffering of any human being? Particularly the father of my child? I only came to reassure Angelica. However," Maxi said cheerfully, throwing open draperies, "since I am here, I'll do what I can to make you more comfortable."

"I don't want to be comfortable. I want to be alone! In the dark!"

"Typical, typical, everyone knows how men love to suffer. I bet you haven't even taken any vitamin C," Maxi said, eyeing the giant sprays of budding forsythia that stood in a superb Florentine jar on a table near his bed. Renaissance majolica unless she was badly mistaken. There was the source of his cold, although he'd never believe it.

"Vitamin C's a crock. It's never been proven," Rocco wheezed, sliding farther down under the covers and trying to pull a pillow over his head.

"But we don't know for sure, do we? Anyway even you know you need liquids. I'm going to make you a pitcher of fresh orange juice and leave it for you."

"Just leave. I don't have any oranges. Out. Out!"

Maxi disappeared, closing his door, before he could actually rouse himself to throw her out bodily. She had brought a bag of oranges from home, anticipating this deplorable state of gender-specific need. Men, in her experience, never had oranges at hand. Lemons, yes, apples sometimes, but not oranges. She tiptoed down the stairs and found the kitchen. It was, she saw at once, four times as big as her own, and much more cheerful. Of course, it didn't have a view of the World Trade Center, she told herself while she squeezed the oranges, but it did have a highly polished eight-burner cast-iron range, a floor of golden travertine marble, a huge wooden worktable that looked Pennsylvania Dutch and a burnished bronze refrigerator full of champagne. She peeked into the freezer. As she had thought, many bottles of vodka, all frozen to that thick, glacial condition that makes it go down the throat like a kiss blown by a friendly iceberg. Thoughtfully she added three-quarters of one entire bottle to the pitcher of juice and tasted it. You couldn't even tell it was there because of the sweetness of the fruit. She put the pitcher in the refrigerator to get colder and went in search of the linen closet. Nothing made a sick person feel better than clean crisp sheets. Well! So India wasn't the only person she knew who was depraved on the subject of linen. Rocco had everything you could buy at Pratesi, all in solid white with severe geometric borders in dark brown, navy blue and deep purple. Did himself well, didn't he? Pratesi could be even more expensive than Porthault although if you flew to Milan for it the trip paid for itself. She gathered up thousands of dollars worth of pure Egyptian cotton and returned to the kitchen for the juice and a big glass and made her way back upstairs.

Noiselessly she opened his door. As she had thought, he was fast asleep. Maxi burrowed under the covers and found Rocco's big toe. It was the gentlest way to be awakened. She tugged on his toe with a light touch until he stirred, and kept tugging until he emerged from under his pillow.

"Juice time," she trilled as prettily as Julie Andrews.

"I don't fucking believe it," he moaned and sneezed ferociously. She gave him a fresh Kleenex and a full glass of orange juice, holding it with impersonal dignity. He drank deeply and

354

grunted something that could be taken for thanks. She poured another full glass and put it into his hand.

"You're dehydrated. That can be dangerous," Maxi warned him.

"Later. Just put it down. And go."

"I will, but only when you've finished," she promised. He drank it quickly, to show her how anxious he was for her to leave, and then fell back on his pillow and closed his eyes. Maxi waited a few minutes for the vodka to have its calming effects on his nervous system.

"Rocco?"

"Yeah."

"Feel any better?"

"Maybe. A little."

"In that case I suggest that you take a nice long shower, and while you're doing that I'll make your bed."

"Shower? You're crazy. Change of temperature at a time like this could kill me. Kill me."

"Don't take a hot shower, take a room-temperature shower. I guarantee it'll make you feel so much better, honestly."

"Sure?"

"Positive. And fresh, cool, lovely sheets . . . wouldn't they feel good?"

"Couldn't hurt. Since you're here. Then you'll go? You promise?"

"Of course. More orange juice?"

"Maybe—try another glass. Seems to help." He tottered happily toward the bathroom, carrying the glass with him. Maxi bustled about. One thing she could do was make a damn good bed. She heard him in the shower, not singing but not sneezing either. She moved the forsythia to the hallway with the pile of discarded bed linen and pulled the draperies almost shut.

Ten minutes later Rocco emerged to find an empty bedroom, with just enough light in it for him to make out his newly made bed with the quilt pulled high, just the way he liked it. With a sigh of relief he flung himself into the heavenly sheets and stretched out, groaning with pleasure.

"*Aiiiii!*" He bounded off the mattress. His foot had just touched something alive.

"For goodness' sake, it's only me," Maxi whispered. "I thought you could see. Sorry."

"Whatcha doing in my bed?"

"I must have fallen asleep. It's such a big bed to make, so hard to get around."

"You're naked," he pointed out.

"I am?" she said sleepily.

"Uh-huh."

"Hmm . . . that's odd, so I am." She yawned. "I must have thought I was at home. Do forgive me."

"Don't scare me again. Hate being scared."

"Of course you do," Maxi murmured maternally, pulling his head to her marvelous breasts like sun-warmed fruit of the gods. "Of course you do, poor thing, poor, *poor* Rocco, it's so terrible to have a cold."

"I'm catching," he sighed, starting to suck on one of her nipples.

"No, no, don't worry, I never caught your colds." She was kissing his shoulder and a particularly tender spot at the back of his neck where he was especially fond of being kissed if memory served.

Memory served. Blissfully, sweetly, and soon irresistibly, memory served, lulled by Russia's gift to the world and assisted by Maxi's dexterous lips and limbs, memory was gloriously celebrated.

Hours later, toward twilight, Rocco woke up with a floatingly light head and a profound sense of uneasiness. Something had happened. He wasn't sure what. He wasn't sure when or how but *something* had happened. Instinctively, with inching caution he explored his bed. It was empty. Something was still wrong. He turned on his bedside light and looked around the room. Nobody was there. He got out of bed and listened to the sounds of his apartment. He could tell at once that he was entirely alone. Why did he feel so worried? He returned to his bed and gazed at the ceiling. Memory returned. Oh God. Oh no. *That bitch.* Memory unveiled itself further, disclosing details. Not once, not twice, but

356

three times. He knew it. She was trying to kill him. Three times in a row. What was he supposed to be, fourteen fucking years old? She'd raped him, that's what she'd done, or was it sexual harassment? Could you claim rape three times in one afternoon? Angrily he realized that he was grinning like an imbecile. Rocco whacked his pillow until the feathers flew out of it. How like her, to take advantage of a sick man. A vampire, that's what she was. She knew, that vicious, unpardonable, victimizing, manipulative, unspeakably evil creature, she knew perfectly well that when he had a head cold he always got horny.

"So, schmuck," he said out loud to himself, "how come you're not sneezing?"

24

"axi, could you come into my office for a minute?" Monty asked, grabbing her by the arm. "Your office is a madhouse and we have to talk."

It was early in the morning of Monday, April 15, and Maxi had just started working on the final corrections of the proofs of the September issue of *B&B* which was to go to press in a week. The article by Madonna called "The Easy-to-Come-by Joys of Narcissim" needed more pictures and Dan Rather's piece, "Nobody Knows How Shy I Am," had developed into a regular column, with celebrities vying with each other to expose the adolescent terrors they still endured. "Those Necessary Lies: Why You Must Never Feel Guilty" by Billy Graham had brought so many readers' letters that more of them had to be reprinted on the letter page than anyone had expected and the "I Wish I Were" monthly article for September, in which Johnny Carson wished he were Woody Allen and Elizabeth Taylor wished she were Brooke Shields, had somehow gotten screwed up, so that the way it read now Woody Allen wished he were Brooke Shields. What was more disturbing, something in the "pace" of the issue that was laid out, pinned page by page on the walls of her office, was slightly off to Maxi's eye.

"Couldn't it be after lunch, Monty?" she pleaded. "This stuff is urgent."

"Now, please." When Monty said something in that emphatically unalarmed tone of voice, Maxi had learned to question him no further. She led the way to his office, tucked away in a far corner of the additional space she'd rented after the first issue had sold out. On the way she passed Julie's all-white office where her fashion editor was huddled over the telephone. Ever since the story linking Jon and Justin had appeared in the newspapers Julie had tried to avoid her, but Maxi had seen her proudly concealed anguish and immediately guessed at its cause. She felt intense sympathy for Julie but to express it would be to show her that she knew why her friend was so deeply wounded, and Maxi judged it was best to let her be for a little while. Eventually time would heal, Maxi thought, as she walked along the busy corridor and responded to greetings. It was an old cliché, cold comfort indeed, but it happened to be true. If she had found out that Rocco was gay when she worked on *Savoir Vivre,* how much time would it have taken her to get over him? Six months? No. More. A year? Probably more. Her reverie was interrupted by Monty who ushered her into his office, closed the door firmly behind him, and stood with his back to it so that nobody could come in.

"Lewis Oxford just called. He must have gone crazy but he sounded sane. He told me that he was putting us on notice that Amberville Publications is shutting down *B&B.* Everybody here is fired as of the end of this business day. He has already called Meredith/Burda to notify them that Amberville will not authorize payment for printing the September issue. They're calling all our suppliers to tell them not to extend us a penny's credit. He's acting on direct orders from Cutter Amberville, who is acting for your mother."

"She would not do that. He's simply wrong." Maxi spoke with the anesthetized coldness of shock.

"When was the last time you talked to her?"

"Just last week, when Justin was freed. We're on the best terms we've been on in years. Look, Monty, this is some trick of Cutter's. He's trying some new tactic that I can't understand until I talk to her. You just sit on this absurdity until I go uptown and see her—she's always home in the mornings. And keep your lip buttoned, or whatever."

"Obviously. But I'm worried about the printer. If we lose our time on the presses, if they've already replaced us for next week, we won't get the issue out in time even when you straighten things out. They sell their time months in advance."

"Call Mike Muller, the Burda business guy at the plant, and tell him that I personally guarantee payment. Me, Maxime Amberville."

"Will do," Monty said, looking as if he would like to ask more questions. Maxi hurried out of his office and rushed downstairs to where Elie was waiting for her.

She burst in on Lily who was conferring with her chef about a dinner party.

"Mother, we have to talk right away."

"Maxime, I've been trying to reach you all weekend. Jean-Philippe, I'll finish this menu later. Where were you, Maxime? I've been so anxious to speak to you."

"Out," Maxi answered mechanically. "Mother, Lewis Oxford just called to say we didn't have any more credit, that *B&B* was out of business."

"Oh dear, oh dear, this is exactly what I didn't want to have happen! That fool Oxford! I warned Cutter that I wanted to have a meeting with you and Toby and Justin all together, first, but obviously Oxford didn't check with me to make sure it had taken place."

"What does that mean, 'first'? Why do you want to talk to the three of us? What does it have to do with *B&B?*"

"Maxime, do stop shouting. Oh, dear, I *so* wanted this to be an orderly event, and now it's spoiled." Lily actually wailed in distress.

"Mother, you are going to drive me out of my mind. What in holy hell are you talking about?"

"I can understand that you're upset, dear, hearing it like that. I wanted to tell you all at the same time." She paused for a few seconds and then continued, resolutely, "I have decided to sell Amberville Publications to the United Broadcasting Corporation, but now it's been announced in the worst possible way." Lily twisted the head off a rose in a silver bowl.

"Mother! I don't give a damn what *form* this decision comes in! *How can you sell?* I . . . I don't understand anything you're saying. Sell *our* business? Sell Father's business? Sell Amberville? It's . . . it's—you just can't do it—it's—*unthinkable.*" Maxi sat down opposite her mother, her legs drained of strength, her heart sinking as she read the stubborn expression on Lily's face, only agitated by the way in which she had to present a decision on which Maxi could see she was determined.

"Now, Maxime, do listen to me and stop saying the first thing that comes into your mind. It's not at all unthinkable. It makes great sense. Since your father died the company has been without its founder. It's kept on going by momentum but that momentum can't last forever. UBC is interested in buying the company and Cutter believes that in three months, when the sale will take place, the price will be close to—well, more or less a billion dollars. This is an opportunity that may never come again and it's obvious that I have to act on it. Maxime, you and Toby and Justin will receive a hundred million dollars each. There's no way in which any of you can realize your ten percent unless I sell, but that's not the only reason I'm doing it."

"Mother . . ."

"No, *wait*, Maxime, don't interrupt until you hear me out. I can't run a magazine publishing company, Cutter doesn't want the responsibility and I don't blame him, Toby obviously has his own life, Justin has his, and although you're having fun with your fling at turning out a magazine, you obviously aren't cut out to run a vast enterprise. If the company is ever to be sold, the time is now, not later. I know that *B&B* is having a dear little boom but you have to admit that it's costing the company a fortune. Cutter reluctantly had to tell me how much money *B&B* loses each month and I was horrified. It's too expensive a toy even for you, Maxime, and UBC will be buying Amberville on the basis of what Cutter called a very sick-looking balance sheet if it continues to be published."

"So it *was* on your orders that Oxford called?"

"Yes, of course, but I had intended to explain it all to you before any of you heard from him. Nobody is supposed to know about the sale until it's gone through, except the family. I'm deeply distressed that you had this shock. If only I'd been able to reach you over the weekend . . ."

"I was out," Maxi repeated. "Mother, don't you understand that a new magazine automatically loses money no matter how big a success it is, until it starts getting enough income from the advertisers? I literally almost *gave* away the advertising to get the magazine off the ground, and it costs more to print an issue than I can sell it for on the racks."

"That was clever of you, I suppose, although I'm no judge . . .

it sounds to me as if you willfully took a big risk. But that's neither here nor there, Maxime, since the decision to sell is mine to make, and I've made it. I'm being guided by Cutter in how to handle Amberville affairs until the sale is official and he is quite adamant about stopping publication of *B&B* right now. I'm sorry for your disappointment, dear—"

"Disappointment." Maxi's echo was flat. The gap between the way she and her mother felt about *B&B* was so vast that no words could bridge it, no emphasis of tone could make any difference. Her mother would never be convinced by anything she could say that *B&B* was not just a plaything but the only tribute that was in her power to make to Zachary Amberville and the great love she had for him.

"Well, I know you've been having a terribly amusing time and I'm really proud of how well it's selling, but obviously you couldn't have done it without using the company's money, could you?" Lily continued.

"No, as a matter of fact, I couldn't. No way," Maxi admitted.

"Well then, you do see, don't you? It's not like a real magazine, is it, dear? It's subsidized, it's not paying its own way."

"No, that's wrong, Mother. It is a *real* magazine. *Millions* of women pay a dollar fifty for it every month. I have a fantastic staff working their hearts out. *B&B* exists, it's growing like mad, the September issue has two hundred and fifty pages, it's crammed with ads and photographs and articles and we get thousands of letters from our readers, it's as real as any other magazine, it's just *young,*" Maxi said passionately.

Lily laughed indulgently. "Maxime, Maxime, I'm pleased to see you sticking to something for such a long time, and if your father were alive he would have been delighted, but you just have to accept the reality of the sale of Amberville. It's in all of our best interests."

"Mother, look. If, *before* the sale goes through, I can show you that Amberville Publications isn't losing money because of *B&B*, if the company is worth just as much as it would be without *B&B*, would you reconsider your decision to sell?" Maxi asked quietly.

"First of all, you don't know how Justin and Toby will feel.

I've told you how Cutter and I feel. No, Maxime, I can't promise to reconsider."

"If I don't ask you to 'promise' to reconsider; if, just before the three months are up, I come to you and just ask you *to think about it again* . . ." Maxi asked imploringly.

"I'm afraid that the answer will still be no, dear, but, of course, you can always come and ask," Lily said gently. She found it hard to refuse Maxime absolutely when she obviously cared so much and was being so reasonable. There was no harm in letting her "ask" again since it was obvious that she couldn't accomplish the impossible and publish without money. And if she didn't insist that her daughter accept her decision right now, it would end this upsetting interview so much more quickly and pleasantly. She'd have time to finish planning the menu for her dinner party before lunch.

"Where to now, Miss A.?" Elie asked.

"The Amberville Building," Maxi answered. She must talk to Pavka. He was the only person to whom she could go for advice. At the offices of *B&B* everyone would be looking to her for leadership but she needed help herself as she had never needed it before. She prayed that he was in his office and not out enjoying one of the long lunches for which publishing was more guilty than Hollywood. She had to talk to Pavka before she went to speak to her accountants to get the money to keep *B&B* operating.

"Is he in?" she asked Pavka's secretary anxiously, skidding to a halt before her desk.

"He's in your father's office," the secretary answered and Maxi could see that she was puzzled. "He's been in there for a half hour and he asked me not to put through any calls. But of course he'd see you—perhaps if I just knock—" Maxi was gone before she could even get up, headed at a half-run down the corridor to the door of the office which nobody had used or changed since Zachary Amberville's death.

"Pavka?" she questioned softly. His back was turned to her and he was standing at one of the windows, his head bowed, leaning on the sill with both hands in a position she had never seen him in before, a posture of helplessness. He turned and the amused and knowing look she was so used to seeing on his alert, dandy's face was gone. In its place there was a gravity that matched hers and something she recognized as deep grief. And yet he could not possibly know about the proposed sale yet. Lily had said that only the family would be told now.

"You must have received one of these too," Pavka said, holding out a sheet of paper, without even greeting her.

"No, nobody's sent me anything—not on paper anyway. Aren't you going to give me a kiss?"

"A kiss?" he asked absently. "Did I not kiss you?" He gave her a brief peck, very unlike his traditionally close and appreciative embrace and for the first time since she'd gone to see Lily, Maxi felt real terror.

"Read this," he said, handing her the memo from the office of the Vice-President for Financial Affairs. It listed all the changes and cuts that Cutter had outlined to Oxford. Copies had been sent to the editors and managing editors and art directors of all six Amberville publications. Maxi read it in silence. Nothing was said about the sale of the company.

"I intend to resign," he told her abruptly. "I don't have the power to prevent these measures but I refuse to have my name associated with them; using the cheapest writers and photographers we can find; cutting the number of color pages; throwing everything to celebrity models; getting editorial pages from advertisers for plugs; using inferior paper and eating up everything in inventory, including those many projects that didn't turn out well enough to come up to our standards. This memo is vile, Maxi, vile!" He quivered with rage and frustration.

"Pavka, please sit down and talk to me," Maxi implored, B&B forgotten in the shamefulness of what she had just read. They both sank into the weathered leather armchairs that faced Zachary Amberville's desk and fell silent. In spite of their anger and concern, as soon as they stopped speaking they became aware that in the office something was still happening. They felt it immediately. Some activity was continued within the room that didn't need a human presence, something alive and powerful and joyous, imprinted in the very walls; a sense memory of Zachary Amberville hung in the air, as robust and enthusiastic as he had been when they'd last seen him. Pavka and Maxi both drew deep breaths and, for the first time, smiled at each other. Still they didn't begin to speak as they looked around the big, always disordered, wood-paneled room, its walls covered with the originals of some of the famous covers and illustrations that he had published over the years and, here and there, signed photographs of Presidents of the United States, of writers, photographers and illustrators. Nowhere was there a photograph of Zachary Amberville himself, but the memory of his excited, amused, vibrant, living voice seemed to echo in the room, his appetite for excellence, his belly laugh, his roar of approval when an associate made a good suggestion, the outpouring of his energy, ardor and fervor that had been concentrated on every issue of each magazine he had ever published—all this lived on without him.

"Pavka," Maxi said, "am I right in thinking that the price paid for a company is based on how much profit it's making at the time of sale?"

"Normally yes. Why do you ask?"

"If," Maxi continued, not answering his question, "you resigned, but the magazines continued to be published, incorporating all the changes that Oxford has ordered, how soon would the economies show up as profit?"

"On the next balance sheet, in three months. But, Maxi, that's beside the point. The magazines would be cheaper to produce but they could never be the *same*. We'd know it right away as we worked on the new issues, and in time our readers would see the difference, no matter how cleverly it was done. They might not be able to tell you exactly what was wrong with *Seven Days* or *Indoors* or the others but they wouldn't look forward to a new issue with the same excitement, they wouldn't read them with the same satisfaction, and eventually, after a year or so, they would either accept them in their diminished, cheapened state—as so much *is* accepted by consumers—or stop buying them altogether. We've never settled for less than our highest possible degree of excellence, but this memo takes the idea of excellence and spits on it."

"My mother intends to sell Amberville Publications based on

the earnings shown in the next balance sheet," Maxi said tone-
lessly.

"Ah." There was a world of sadness and disillusionment in his
sigh. "So that explains it. I should have guessed. What a fool I am,
not to have thought of that. It is the only possible explanation for
destroying what your father stood for. Still, I'm amazed that she's
doing it this way. The magazines could be sold untouched, intact
and proud. There would be no dishonor then in selling them if
that's what she has decided to do."

"But less money?"

"Oh, yes, less, unquestionably somewhat less, but still enough
for any family until the end of time," he said bitterly. "She'll have
my resignation within an hour. I predict that many other people
will resign too. I came in here to escape their outraged phone calls.
They don't realize that even I can't fight this. Soon the editors who
knew your father best and longest, the key people, will decide that
they don't want to have any part of it, if they haven't made that
decision already. Also, they've been around long enough to know
that inevitably they'd be on their way out after the sale. The new
owners, whoever they are, will change the magazines to suit themselves, put in their own people. In a few years you won't know that
this group of magazines was once Amberville Publications although
the magazines will probably have the same names. That's all that's
being sold now: brand names."

"How can you be so sure that the new owners won't want to
keep on the people who made the magazines great?"

"Oh, Maxi, perhaps they will try, after all. Perhaps they will
be wise. But good editors must spend money and this memo makes
that impossible. When a company that has been created by one
man is sold, the heart goes out of it, the soul if you will, the spirit of
the founder, the vision of that one man can't possibly be retained.
Look, right here, on this memo, it's started already. I'm appalled by
your mother, Maxi, appalled. As long as Amberville Publications
lived, so did your father." He shook his head with something far
deeper than sadness as he thought of the high hearts and great
plans with which he and Zachary Amberville had embarked on
their publishing adventure almost forty years ago.

Slowly Maxi rose and walked the few paces to her father's desk and sat down in the chair that nobody but he had ever used. In her mind she turned over everything her mother had said. *B&B's* future was only a small part of the puzzle. What was happening was the willful dismembering of Zachary Amberville's achievement, an achievement that had continued on past his death, that had lived and prospered for a year and could endure indefinitely with the group of loyal people he had drawn together around him, far into the future. Six enormously prosperous, powerful magazines were to be cheapened, degraded and then sold to no necessary purpose. A lifetime's achievement was being destroyed, her father's lifetime. The dividends that came from Amberville Publications had supported his family in luxury until now, and would do so as long as people could still read.

Cutter. There was only one person whose interests could be served by tearing down the monument that Amberville Publications was to her father's memory. Cutter. Everything Maxi knew or had observed about Cutter, everything she sensed, everything her instincts told her, everything she and Toby and Justin had felt about this younger brother who had married their mother, gathered into a cloud and the cloud began to take a form, to solidify into a shape, the shape of a great hate. *A great envy.* Envy even more potent than hatred. First he had taken his brother's wife. Then Cutter had strangled the last of Zachary Amberville's new creations, those three magazines that hadn't yet hit their stride. And now he was sucking the guts out of the sturdy giants and selling them as quickly as he could. Only envy could answer for his actions, only her father's death had given him the chance to first mutilate and then betray a life's work he could never have matched.

She wasn't going to let him do it.

"Pavka, don't resign," Maxi said. "Please, for me, don't resign. I'm going to fight this sale. I think I can influence my mother not to do it. If you can keep everybody calmed down and working for the next few months, making these infernal changes as slowly and as imaginatively as humanly possible, trimming here and there but not enough to seriously compromise the October and November issues, dragging your heels on absolutely everything, making Oxford pin you to the wall on the tiniest detail, commissioning articles and photographs by the best people you know, *as of yesterday*, if you can do all that, Pavka, I'm going to fight Cutter."

"Cutter?"

"None of this started as my mother's idea, Pavka. Cutter has led her into it, I promise you. It could never have happened without his influence."

Pavka came close to the desk and inspected Maxi gravely, without the familiar overtone of flirtation and mutual charm that had always colored their relationship. She sat there, where he had never seen anyone but Zachary Amberville sit, with an unthinking ease, a sureness, a right of possession. He would not have dared to use that chair, yet she had taken it unconsciously. And she spoke with a firmness, a cleverness, a cold purpose, a gathering together of forces, that he had never dreamed she could call upon. This was not the girl he had watched so long as she flitted after fun, living as if her life were a gigantic sack of brightly colored lollipops, to each of which she'd give one experimental lick before discarding it for another. He had rarely caught sight of Maxi since her return, he realized, and in the months since that shocking board meeting she had changed profoundly. She had not, he thought, aged, no, that wasn't the word. She had grown up. Maxi Amberville had become a woman.

"Why are you going to fight Cutter? If you leave things alone the only thing that can happen to you is that you will become richer," Pavka said, and there was a warning in his tone. Maxi, grown up, was still not a match for Cutter, with Lily under his domination. "I know you detest him, but that is no reason to engage yourself in a corporate battle."

"It's not a personal vendetta, Pavka. I'm doing it for my father," Maxi said simply. "I'm doing it because I loved him more than anyone in the world and this is the one way I can show how much he meant—how much he *means*—to me."

"In that case, I too will do my best. For my dear friend, your father."

Maxi had telephoned her accountants from Pavka's office and made an appointment to see Lester Maypole, of Maypole and Maypole, who had acted as her personal accountant from the days she had first had the spending of her own trust fund. On the drive downtown Maxi thought about money. It was not a topic on which she usually spent much time. It was as familiar as one of her senses, taken for granted as much as touch or smell. Her mother had talked about a hundred million dollars but Maxi did not see why, when she had always had everything she wanted, she should be interested in such a sum, impossible to comprehend. It would only create problems. Right now she was rich in the same way that she had ten fingers and ten toes. A hundred million dollars would be like having two heads.

She had been born rich, she reflected, as the limousine slipped through traffic like a long, blue snake, and she'd grown up rich, and when she'd been poor, or living as if she were poor, during the time she and Rocco were married, she hadn't liked it at all so she had simply arranged to stop being poor. It had been the same as taking off an uncomfortable pair of new shoes endured during a necessary hike; she had just stepped out of poorness and resumed the comfort of the richness that had been there waiting for her all along. Of course the detour into an early marriage and early motherhood had kept her from getting trapped in the rich girl's world; the silliness of debutantes and fortune hunters; or else the obvious solution of a solid match with somebody appropriate, followed by the accumulation of country houses and dogs and horses. Instead, she supposed, she had fallen into the category that the late-night movies would label "madcap heiress."

B&B had taught her what it cost to budget a magazine but it hadn't influenced her habits of private spending. Nameless people in Lester Maypole's office paid all her bills and since she'd had no complaints from them she could only assume that there was more than enough to sustain her style of living: to pay for the upkeep on the apartment; the travel; the servants who cooked and laundered and cleaned and drove; the garage; the caterers who did the parties; the florists who sent in flowers twice a week for every room in the apartment; the clothes she wore for the season in which they were fashionable and then replaced; the buckets of jewelry she hadn't had time to add to since *B&B* started. And then there was Angelica. Rocco paid for half of Angelica's clothes and school because

369

he insisted on it, so Angelica really was one of the least expensive items in her life, somewhere between food and flowers, so much more necessary than one, so much more beautiful than the other. Of course, there were her collections, Maxi reminded herself. The antiques, the precious boxes, the old silver; so many collections that had had to be put into storage when she moved to the Trump Tower from her old town house in the East Sixties.

What, Maxi asked herself, did her accountants do with all of the money she received that she didn't spend? Did they reinvest it in stocks and bonds? Did they risk it in the market or buy the safest possible securities? She had no head for the subject and no need to force herself to take an interest in it. That was what she paid Maypole for. But it stood to reason that she must have pots of money. And anyone with money could always get more, everybody knew that.

Lester Maypole looked at Maxi as if she were a cross between a mermaid and a hippogriff, a mythological creature who had materialized in his office with a list of what would have been perfectly reasonable questions if it weren't for one fact: Maxime Amberville had always lived up to her huge income, from her trusts and her Amberville dividends. Not beyond it, just within it. And she didn't seem to realize this fact which had been writ large on the bottom of every month's statement they had ever sent her.

"But you never *warned me*, Mr. Maypole," Maxi protested, disbelieving, just beginning to be angry.

"Miss Amberville, we're accountants, not keepers. We just receive your monies and pay your bills. There's never been any reason for us to think that you didn't know that you were spending up to the limit so long as you didn't exceed it. You never expressed any interest in investments or we would have told you that you had none. Your art objects and your apartment and your jewelry are all assets, of course, but as for the rest—" He waved his hand expressively.

"I've just pissed it away."

"Oh, don't be too hard on yourself. After all it did cost you almost three million dollars to refurnish Castle Kirkgordon . . ."

"Laddie Kirkgordon had sold practically everything but his bed to pay death duties . . . it seemed the least I could do . . . and there wasn't any central heating, none at all," Maxi explained, remembering those frozen, titled years.

"And then, in Monte Carlo, your pearls were stolen . . . twice. The double strands were worth almost nine hundred thousand dollars and you didn't have insurance. Each time you *replaced* the pearls."

"It wasn't really *in* Monte Carlo. The police there are very effective. It was pirates on the high seas . . . or at least that's what they looked like to me. I couldn't get insurance, Mr. Maypole. Any wife of Bad Dennis Brady's, even a short-term one, was considered to be a bad insurance risk, with good reason, but a girl *has* to have her wedding pearls," Maxi said indignantly. It wasn't as if they had been diamonds after all.

"On top of that, you're in the highest possible tax bracket, you give very large amounts to charity and you've lost several major fortunes in casinos." He coughed, just short of disapprovingly.

"It's such fun to gamble, but nobody sensible expects to *win*," Maxi explained.

"That's more or less my point," Lester Maypole said quietly.

"It's *all* gone?"

"I would hardly put it that way. You are a very rich young woman. You own ten percent of a great company. Why shouldn't you spend your money freely?"

"Pissed it away," Maxi repeated furiously.

"You could have employed someone who specialized in estate management . . ."

"But it's too late now, isn't it?"

"For the past, I'm afraid so, but there's enough in your account to carry you until the next yearly dividends are declared in June, unless you've just bought something I don't know about."

"How much will the dividends amount to?" she pounced, hope suddenly restored.

"That will depend on your mother. The owner of the controlling interest in any company declares dividends as he or she sees fit."

"Would you care to bet on the size of this year's dividends,

Mr. Maypole? Never mind. What about my ten percent of Amberville? I'd like to borrow on that up to the maximum."

"That stock can't be sold to anyone but your mother," Lester Maypole said. Surely she must know that much.

"It's still stock," Maxi objected wildly. She felt as if Maypole were torturing her for his own pleasure.

"You can't borrow on it, Miss Amberville. Not a penny."

"You mean it is as if it didn't exist? It doesn't *count?*"

"Miss Amberville, please, don't get so upset. It exists, it counts, it belongs to you. You just can't *borrow* on it, because you can't *sell* it to an outsider."

"You're saying that I don't have any money."

"You could put it that way, for the moment, yes, I suppose you don't actually have any, well, any *cash.*"

"Thank you, Mr. Maypole." Maxi was gone like lightning striking too close, leaving Lester Maypole sweating in alarm. She didn't seem to understand the difference between money and cash and he, for once, had lost track of it himself. He looked in his wallet. Twenty-four dollars. He buzzed his secretary. "Linda," he said, his heart beating ridiculously, "get me my investment portfolio, right away. And then take a check to the bank. No, I just want some cash in fives. And make it snappy."

Maxi pushed her way through the crowds listening to a pianist and violinist playing "Alice Blue Gown" in the lobby of the Trump Tower. She didn't notice the eighty-foot-tall waterfall which was running at the highest of its three speeds, or the walls and floor of shrimp-pink and mango-colored Breccia Perniche marble, nor did she spare a glance for thriving ponytail palms and the lovers kissing on the escalators. She took the first elevator to the right and went straight up to the large suite of offices from which the building was run.

"Louise," she asked the warm, blond woman who was vice-president of Trump, "can I hock my apartment?"

Louise Sunshine didn't look surprised. Years of working with restless, unpredictable Donald Trump had made her immune to shock of any kind. "The Residential Board doesn't like liens on apartments, Maxi. What's the matter, gal, want to buy the Pentagon?"

"More or less. Is Donald available?"

"To you, always. Just let me check and make sure he's not on the phone."

Maxi waited impatiently but her heart contracted as she looked out of the window. There, but at a much lower height than her sixty-third floor, was the view that she loved so intensely; the view invented to drive people to extremes of adoration or hate, a view of a city that everyone took personally, as an affront or as a challenge or as something to which it was virtuous to be indifferent. New York was never *just* a city, it was a place that had to belong to you or be chased from your consciousness. And from no other location could the city look so heartbreakingly beautiful, so truly the dream and not the reality.

"Go right on in," Louise Sunshine said, startling her.

Donald Trump, the brilliant, ambitious young real-estate man whom even his enemies had to admit was disarmingly unaffected, rose to greet Maxi.

"Hey you, pretty girl, what's the problem?"

"I need cash, and I need it fast."

"That happens in the best of families," he grinned.

"Can you sell my apartment, Donald? This week?"

"Hold on a minute, Maxi, are you sure you want to do that?" Suddenly he looked totally serious. "I've always got a waiting list for your apartment—next to mine it's the best and biggest in the whole tower, but once it's gone, it's gone forever. And there will never be another great one like it. It's an 'L' and an 'H' thrown together—it's a world-class apartment." His concern was genuine. There was a certain normal amount of turnover in apartments in the building but generally they were those which had been bought specifically for investment. Maxi, who loved her apartment the way he loved his, as a part of herself, as an extension of her capacity for life, would never sell unless she was in serious trouble and had nothing else left to sacrifice.

"Can you promise I'll get my money this week?"

"Maxi, how much money do you need exactly? Maybe there's another way . . ."

"I don't know the exact amount, a minimum of six million dollars—probably more."

"That much? And right away?" He considered a moment and then he said, "No, there's no other way. Look, it will take me a little time to make the best possible deal for you but if you want to turn the apartment over to me I'll write you a check for six million. Then, if I can sell it for more, and I hope that I can, I'll give you the rest when the deal closes."

"Where do I sign?" Maxi asked.

"I just hope it's worth it, whatever it is," he said, shaking his head, and picking out a checkbook from his desk drawer.

"It's worth trying, Donald, even if I don't win. Give me your pen, damn it. And a fucking Kleenex."

25

Once Maxi had found herself, after two hours of intense looking, at the far end of the great second floor of the Louvre, the longest gallery of paintings in the world. She had been overcome by a staggering case of total visual overload. She knew that if she saw another masterpiece she would never want to go into a museum again, yet three hundred and fifty yards separated her from the exit. She had solved the problem by walking back the length of the gallery as quickly as her tired feet would allow, with her head bent so far down that all she could see was the floor. Not even the edge of a frame entered her peripheral vision and she made it to the Winged Victory and down the marble steps to the exit without mishap.

It was in this fashion that she walked through her apartment, her ex-apartment, and headed straight to the telephone next to her bed, which was still her bed, and made arrangements for an expert from Sotheby's to come as soon as possible to take inventory of every valuable she owned, including the objects in storage, and put them up for auction as quickly as possible. Now, she thought as she put the telephone back, she was sitting on her ex-bed, for the carved and gilded eighteenth-century *lit à la Polonaise* hung with its original crownlike pouf of embroidered silk would bring a good price. Was she sitting on her ex-mattress? Probably, she thought, not quite sure if she had ever seen a mattress up at auction with the bed it belonged to. Better not to know.

"Maxi? Where are you?" she heard a voice calling.

"I'm in here, in the bedroom," she answered, suddenly unable to say "*my* bedroom."

Angelica, flushed from her day's adventures, appeared at the door.

"Have you hugged a mother today?" Maxi asked, in a small voice.

"You don't look as if you need a hug," Angelica observed, approaching her cautiously, "you look as if you need intensive care. Maybe a transfusion. You've been working too hard."

"Try a hug," Maxi advised. Angelica enveloped her in her strong, athletic grip, lifted her up, twirled her around a few times and then flopped back on the bed with her mother still pinioned in her arms.

"Did that help?" she asked Maxi anxiously, peering at her closely with her truthful, undefended eyes.

"Very much. Thank you, darling. I have something not nice to tell you."

"You *are* sick!" Angelica said, stricken, sitting up abruptly.

"No, damn it. I'm not sick at all. I'm perfectly fine. But I had to sell the apartment. We can't live here anymore."

"You promise you're not sick?"

"I swear on—what do I have to swear on for you to believe me?"

"My head."

"I swear on your head that I'm a totally healthy mother. Satisfied?"

"Yup. So why did you sell the apartment?" Angelica asked, vastly relieved.

"It's a long, very complicated story, but basically I need the money."

Angelica's face wrinkled up in an attempt to understand words she'd never heard her mother utter in her entire life.

"To buy something with?" she asked finally.

"Yes . . . and no."

"Ma," Angelica said patiently, "I really think it would be helpful if you'd tell me the whole story, long though it may be. I'm old enough to understand."

When Maxi was finished there was a silence while Angelica considered the situation.

"The way I see it," she said finally, "is that you did what you had to do. This is just like real life. In fact—it *is* real life. That's— interesting. It's not exactly fun but it's chewy. Now, the next problem is where do we live? I'd pick Columbus Avenue because that's where it's happenin', but I know you'd never go for it. And anyway we should really live on nothing, right? So why not invite ourselves to Uncle Toby's? It's free, he's got some extra room and the food will be great. He'd probably be glad of the company. And another thing, after school every day I can come down to *B&B* and work at anything that needs doing, delivering packages or mailing letters or helping out in the art department."

"Don't you go *near* the art department!"

"What's in there, snakes? O.K., I won't, but there's no reason I can't pitch in, lend a hand, is there?"

"None." Maxi looked for Donald Trump's damp pocket hand-kerchief, for he carried nothing as common as a Kleenex, and applied it as inconspicuously as possible to her streaming eyes.

"And the third and final thing, and I don't care if you do disapprove of my choice of language," Angelica pronounced. "In my honest opinion, Ma, Cutter eats shit."

Maxi looked around and wondered what it was that was familiar about her surroundings. She and Angelica had been immediately welcomed at Toby's but they'd had to cram themselves into the two small rooms on the fourth and top floor of his long but narrow brownstone. The first floor was devoted to the swimming pool and kitchen; the second floor was all one big living room. The third floor was Toby's domain. Somehow Maxi had imagined that they would be given the big extra bedroom next to Toby's but that was before she discovered that India and Toby were living together on alternate weekends. The extra bedroom's closets were full of India's clothes and, Lord have mercy, even some of India's sheets. Not for anything in the world would Maxi want to be on the same floor as a couple delicately involved in tentative nest-building. In fact, if she had actually realized that India was spending so much time in New York she wouldn't have called Toby at all, but once she had, he had insisted on her moving in with Angelica.

Did she feel as if she were their chaperone, she wondered? No, nothing that adult. Summer camp! That was it. She felt as if she and Angelica were at summer camp together, uprooted from their

377

familiar surroundings and bunking in a strange place, with only a few stuffed animals of Angelica's, her school books, and some of Maxi's framed photographs to make them feel a sense of familiarity. Her own clothes hung on the cumbersome metal racks she'd had to buy because the closets weren't big enough. Yes, a cross between summer camp and a tiny, overcrowded designer's showroom, she decided.

Thank God she'd bought all her spring and summer clothes before the ax had fallen, Maxi thought, looking at the laden racks. They took up almost all the space in the room. She needed to look expensive and authoritative and totally carefree at the daily lunches she spent wooing potential advertisers, but fortunately for the female editors of many magazines, the public-relations people at most ready-to-wear houses will "do a personal" and bring up the designer's clothes to the editor's office for her to choose from, at wholesale, of course. But tonight she could relax, she thought, putting on Zoran's baggy pull-on ivory cashmere pants and his ivory cashmere and silk boat-necked pullover, cut short and ribbed all over, the two pieces three times too expensive and worn, as they should be, about three sizes too big. Cashmere was as comforting as mother's milk and a good deal easier to come by, Maxi reflected as she laced up her sneakers. She wasn't anxious for the rainy April weather to turn into a warm spring. If she could, she'd wear six layers of cashmere at once until she won her battle with Cutter. Maxi sighed as she realized that the most costly wool couldn't warm away the worry she lived with now. A wave of infinitely sad longing for Uncle Nat and Aunt Minnie swept over her. She could have confided in them as in no one else, but after Uncle Nat had died of a heart attack in his early fifties, Aunt Minnie had gone to live in the Landauer family compound in Palm Beach. Now it wouldn't be fair to disturb her with the convoluted problems of *B&B* but, oh, how she missed the two of them.

Maxi padded downstairs and stopped outside the entrance to the kitchen–dining room in which Toby was busy cooking. She heard him say, "It's a meat loaf, and you can consider yourself lucky to get anything that complex at a chef's own table." Was Toby talking to himself at such a young age? They were supposed to be having dinner alone together since Angelica was with Rocco and India was in Hollywood. Curious, Maxi peeked into the big double-purpose room. A trail of tattered leather oddments, shed here and there in the kitchen, informed her immediately of Justin's presence.

Maxi swooped on him with joy, for she'd been so busy with Monty working on the budgets for future issues of B&B that she hadn't seen him for days.

"I wanted to surprise you," Toby said, pleased with the success of his invitation.

"Have you got anyone else up your sleeve?" Maxi asked.

"No, just the three of us. I don't think that we've had dinner together alone like this since we were kids," Toby answered. "After I went away to college and you got married there were always other people, mainly one or another of your husbands. This is a post-nursery evening for cultivated adults who like meat loaf, and have a certain special common interest."

"Such as?" Maxi questioned.

"The future of Amberville Publications," Justin answered. "You don't think you're the only one who's concerned about it, do you?"

"Of course not."

"You never came to us for help, Goldilocks," Toby said seriously. "Don't you think that you should have, before you went and sold your apartment and planned to strip yourself of everything you own?"

"No, I don't," Maxi countered. "It's a fight I volunteered for. What's more, I'm not at all sure that if I win it, you won't be disappointed. Maybe each of you would rather have the cash you'd get if the sale goes through. That's what I really *should* have asked you about."

"Whatever it was you should have asked us about, you didn't. And we're both peeved, to put it mildly. This dinner is a setup, in case you haven't realized it yet," Toby said pleasantly, basting the meat loaf with a fresh-tomato-and-basil sauce.

"I was beginning to have my suspicions. So you wouldn't mind if Mother sold the company? You want me to cave in and fold B&B and stop making a fuss and, in general, act like it's all right with me?"

"Toby, have you noticed that Maxi has a tendency to over-react?" Justin asked.

"Actually, since you've brought it up, I'd say that the trouble with Maxi is that she jumps to conclusions," Toby answered.

"Or," Justin added, "you could say that the trouble with Maxi is that she jumps overboard and never looks around to see if there's a life preserver on board."

"No, that's not quite it. The trouble with Maxi is that she confuses herself with General de Gaulle. *L'Etat c'est moi*, you know. Amberville, *c'est elle*, or something like that."

"De Gaulle didn't say that, Louis the Fourteenth said it," Justin corrected. "He too had a tendency toward grandiosity, but that was so long before the Revolution that he could be forgiven, but Maxi, no."

"I don't think you're as funny as you both seem to think you are," she said, annoyed.

"The trouble with Maxi is that she doesn't know when people are trying to lend her money," said Toby.

"Oh, so that's what this is all about. *No way* am I going to come to the two of you for money! You've got your own lives, you've got your separate interests, why should I expect you to lend me money for something that is totally a decision that I made myself? Keeping my magazine afloat until it can swim by itself is a personal problem, and the money *has* to come from me."

"I work for *B&B*—doesn't that give me a say?" Justin asked.

"Look, Justin, I know you hate doing magazine photography and that you're only sticking with it for my sake. That's as much of a contribution as I'd ever expect you to make and I'm very aware of what it costs you to be tied down like this," Maxi said severely. "So don't expect me to hit you up for a loan on top of that."

"What about me? I'm your older brother, Goldilocks. You might have tried me," Toby insisted.

"Come on Bat, you've never had the slightest interest in the magazines," Maxi replied. "You can't convince me that you do. No, Toby, this one is my baby. It just wouldn't be fair to rely on either of you. Surely you two are sensitive enough to understand that, for once in my life, I want to win something *on my own, by myself.* I've had a free ride in life and I haven't made much out of it. This time it's different!"

"Hear, hear," Justin said with a slanting, loving, ironic and surprised glance.

"The real trouble with Maxi," she continued, "is that she's always starving, always hungry, always needing to eat. Such a bore, that girl. She gets mad when she gets hungry, so butt out of my business, you guys! Back off, you bums. When is the overrated, probably overcooked meat loaf going to be ready?"

"Maybe you should have taken their money," Monty said doggedly, for the third time, as he watched Maxi sign checks. "Or, at the very least, you could have asked them how much they had in mind."

Maxi shook her head. She couldn't explain to Monty that Lily was planning to sell the entire company. This meant that she couldn't tell him about the hope she had pinned on the survival of *B&B*, about the possibility that Lily would change her mind. It was a thin possibility, she knew, but the only one she had. If she allowed herself to indulge in self-doubt now, all would be lost without question. Maxi changed the subject to lure Monty away from his lust for her brothers' money.

"Monty, our last month's circulation figures were hovering at four million copies. If we can maintain that number, when those six-month advertising contracts are up, we'll be able to renew them at a huge hike in page rates, isn't that so?"

"Yeah, if all your advertisers are willing to stand still for the size of the increases you plan to ask for, which is by no means certain and you'd better not count on it. After all, you still don't really know precisely who those four million dames are, and what their income level and age level are. *Demographics,* Maxi, demographics. Madison Avenue buys specific audience with specific needs. But assuming that the advertisers do renew, you'll start to begin to see daylight with the seventh issue. Right now every copy we're selling at a dollar fifty is costing us two dollars and five cents to produce, not including the money Barney Shore is putting up for rack space. You're such a raving success that you're losing fifty-five cents a copy four million times a month or, to make it easier to understand, two million, two hundred thousand dollars monthly."

Maxi raised her eyebrows so high that they disappeared under her rumpled bangs. "With three more issues to go, that's over seven million dollars . . . still, it's not as bad as the Defense Department. My auction had better break some records."

"Don't try to increase your circulation," Monty warned her. "Success kills."

"Don't worry. I do understand that much. Is this the only business in the world where the product costs the manufacturer more to make than it costs the person who buys it?"

"Ever heard of movies?" Monty asked sadly. "Or theater? Or ballet or opera or concerts? Or television shows that don't work?"

"So, essentially, we're in show business?" Maxi summed up.

"Damn right we are," Monty brooded.

"If you had money, would you put it into show business?"

"No," Monty mourned. "Show business is two dirty words."

"If you don't cheer up, I'll goose you," Maxi threatened. He gave her a bleak grimace that tried to pass for a smile.

"We'd better pray that the price of paper or printing or distribution doesn't go up," Maxi said thoughtfully.

"And that Barney Shore doesn't drop dead," Monty added helpfully.

"I hope you can run faster than I can, you bastard," Maxi exclaimed, charging at him, her middle finger already in position. "Here I come!"

"Frankly, Maxi, I think you're bonkers, obsessed, over the hill," India said as she unpacked the nine suitcases she had brought for a week's stay. "If someone wanted to buy my family business, and the payoff meant that I'd have more money than I've ever heard of, I'd jump at the chance. You can't even be sure that your father wouldn't have sold if UBC had made him an offer."

"He was only sixty-one when he died. I'm positive that he would never have sold and retired. What would he have done with the rest of his life? He lived for his magazines. They were his anchor, and he was my anchor. Don't you understand?"

"And you identify with him? A sort of transference?"

"I guess someone like you would feel the need to put it into that particular, simple-minded jargon. I see you've discussed it with Doctor Florence Florsheim."

"Naturally," India said with dignity. "I try not to talk about you, but it's getting more and more difficult since I met Toby."

"And what did the good woman say?"

"She said maybe you didn't want a hundred million dollars."

"Oh, so she's started to have opinions, has she?"

"About other people, sure. She's human, after all. She just doesn't have opinions about *me,* or at least she doesn't tell me about them bluntly. She lets me arrive at my own conclusions about her opinions."

"India, would it surprise you to know that she's right? I don't want a hundred million dollars."

"Why ever not?"

"Ever since you became a movie star you've been complaining about how being publicly beautiful is a drag. How many women do you know who would understand that problem? And sympathize? You keep moaning about how this special and particular arrangement of your chromosomes has turned you into some kind of freak; how strangers get all sorts of delusional notions about you because of the particular way your cheekbones slant, because of the size of your eyes and their color; how millions of people project impossible dreams on your frail little shoulders based on the shape of your chin, the length of your nose, the color of your hair, and God knows what else. You say that no one can see 'the real you' but an old friend like me, or Toby, who's blind, or your analyst, who doesn't care. You complain that you intimidate people just because of an accident of birth; that they make you shy because you know what they're thinking; that you can't make friends with other women because of envy; that your looks invite the unwelcome attention of all kinds of sick creeps like that guy who keeps phoning and writing you those awful letters. Are you still getting them, by the way?"

"Unfortunately, yes. *Please* don't mention it in front of Toby—my 'fan' called here today, he's getting crazier by the minute. But let's not talk about him. And anyway, what do weird types like that have to do with money?"

"Money invites the same kind of fantasies, only worse. You used to be smarter, India. People would read about the sale in the papers—whenever a private company is sold the details get spread all over the financial pages and leak over into the regular press, and I'd never seem even remotely human again. I'd be one of those immensely rich women whose fortunes get listed in magazines and any chance I still have of leading a normal life would disappear. As it is, it's bad enough. When people meet me for the first time I can actually see the pupils of their eyes change, as if I glowed in the dark, had a halo or an aura. They can never see me without it; it taints every word they say, and makes them shut up and listen when I make the most banal remark. Money is great and it's also a serious barrier to being allowed to join the rest of the human race." Maxi sighed, and twisted her white streak into a corkscrew curl.

"There are times, particularly at the office, when I'm genuinely just one of the gang, and it's heaven. Being an Amberville obviously means being rich, but nobody knows exactly *how* rich, and it's that particular detail, that number, that dollar value, that Americans get off on. And not just Americans. Everybody. It makes them crazy. And as bad as it would be for me, it would be much worse for Angelica, because at least I'm my own person, I more or less know who I am, and who my friends are, but Angelica would be so exposed, so much in the spotlight as she grew up. Now she's still a regular little girl."

"She may be regular but she's not a little girl anymore. Not the last time I looked, which was this morning," India said.

"She's only twelve and a bit," Maxi said defensively.

"Going on thirteen and watch out! Raging hormones. She'll be rich *and* insanely beautiful. She's got Rocco's looks, that kid. You're still terribly pretty, Maxi, even if you are almost thirty," India said, giving her a slow, professional, critical assessment, "but nothing to compare with Angelica. No offense meant."

384

"No offense taken, creep. After all I only married Rocco because he was so handsome."

"If I remember correctly, there was just a bit more to it than that."

"The worst thing about old friends is that they don't have the grace to disremember. Rocco always was a miserable grouch but as he gets older he gets worse. He's so flawed that it's hard to pick out his worst aspect but I think that probably it's his ingratitude. I cured his head cold and he's never called to thank me."

"Do you know how to cure head colds? That could be valuable; science has been looking for a way for years," India commented dubiously.

"Only certain head colds. What's more I almost gave him a bunch of presents for something he did for Justin. I didn't because that's when my money ran out, but it's just as well. He has a basically odious nature."

"I always liked Rocco," India announced with determination. "He must still be divine to look at, at least."

"Some people might think so, I suppose, but it won't last much longer, no beauty does, you know," Maxi said. "Not even yours," she added in a compassionate voice.

"Tell me, Maxi, how's your sex life?" India inquired, her turquoise eyes unswervingly observant. "Something seems to be biting your ass. I detect a little oversensitivity, a degree of irritability. Knowing you, it's got to be a new man."

"Ha! Who has time for sex? I've forgotten about it. When you're as busy as I am, sexual appetites just go away somewhere and you don't miss them."

"So that's what it is, lack of libido. On the other hand it's the only thing I can think of to keep you out of trouble. Remember, you've taken a vow never to marry another man."

"Who would I marry? And more to the point, *why* would I marry? Who was it who said, 'I've been a man and I've been a woman and there's got to be something better'? That's the way I feel about marriage."

"I think you're scrambled. Didn't Tallulah Bankhead say, 'I've *had* a man and I've *had* a woman and there's got to be something better'?"

385

"Never mind," Maxi said. "You know what I mean."

"Actually not. I can't think of anything I want more than marriage," India said wistfully.

"Not having tried it, naturally you're tempted. Anyway, Toby is a hundred times superior to any of my husbands. If you can only manage to talk him into it."

"That would make us sisters-in-law and I don't know if I could live with your currently pessimistic view of the world. Cheer up. If everything falls apart at *B&B* and you end up wildly, ridiculously rich you can give it all away to charity. Or you could start your own cult. You could buy the Getty—no, you wouldn't have enough for that. Well, you could buy a movie studio and get rid of the money that way, faster than you think."

"Why don't you write a novel called *Unsolicited Advice?* Or maybe one called *I Also Do Windows?*" Maxi suggested, tweaking India's famous nose. "I appreciate your thoughts and comments, but, you see, I am in show business already."

Man Ray Lefkowitz and Rap Kelly, Rocco's partners, having lunch together, sat in the Perigord Park eating shad roe and covertly eavesdropping on Maxi who was at the next table working over the most important space buyer on the Seagram account. Her voice, as it drifted over to them, was as potent as a dose of nitroglycerine wafting up a man's spine, yielding, addictive and yet businesslike, maintaining a firm borderline that never crossed over into the overtly seductive.

"We've finally got the demographics, George," Maxi said. "You're one of the first to know." She sounded almost clandestine yet somehow ingenuous. "Naturally it took time to collect them, but our four million readers are, on the average, working women as well as wives and mothers. She's between nineteen and forty-four years old and last year she personally earned over twenty-six thousand dollars, which is roughly twenty-two percent of all the income earned by all the women in America put together. And George, teetotaler she most definitely is not. She buys *B&B* because it makes her feel good—that you know already. But did you know that seventy percent of our readers read *B&B* while they're enjoying a drink? Maybe relaxing from their work, maybe just sitting around waiting for their guys to arrive, maybe making dinner—we don't have the breakdown on that yet, but the figures should be in soon. *B&B* is simply not the sort of magazine you read when you're on a diet and have decided to cut out wine and liquor—our reader is too busy being nice to herself, day in, day out. She's the sort who celebrates . . . and if there's nothing to celebrate, she decides to celebrate anyway."

"Are you sure she's not an alcoholic, Maxi?" George asked. Maxi turned slightly toward him, with the faintest necessary movement, the minimal successful movement of someone who knows that she has the best legs, the best posture that shows off the best breasts, the best shoulder pads and the best haircut of any woman in the room.

"You have a delightful sense of humor for such an attractive man," Maxi said, with enough of a twist of diabolical mockery mixed into her winsome flattery to make him wonder exactly what she had meant . . . all that night long. "So many otherwise sensational men lack humor. They take themselves so seriously."

"I know what you mean," George assured her, pedaling like mad. Where exactly was she coming from? "Interesting demographics. Very interesting. Four million women, all sipping a drink and reading *B&B*."

"Now, George, I never said that. Only seventy percent of my four million readers drink *while* they read *B&B*. The others do other things. *Then* they drink. That's why I have so many liquor clients who want to buy next year's run of the back cover."

At the next table the two men eyed each other with faces that were a study in willful blankness.

"Kelly, she can't get away with that," whispered Lefkowitz. "George won't buy it. Nobody would buy such a blatant lie."

"Wanna bet?" Kelly hissed at him.

"Actually, no. I mean, look at her, for goodness' sakes. Yum."

"After all, what does it cost him? He's not spending his own money," said Kelly, finally laughing.

"Where do you suppose she gets the demographics?"

"*Pravda?*" Kelly ventured.

"They're more accurate. Listen, let's do her a good deed,"

proposed Lefkowitz. "Rocco's been awfully uncreative lately. We've only pulled down two new accounts since that magazine of Maxi's started. All right, they each bill about twenty-five million a year, but I still think something is bothering him. I wouldn't be surprised if it isn't connected to worrying about the success of B&B—you know what it's like to have an ex-wife who goes into business."

"Tell me. No, don't tell me, I know," Kelly amended quickly.

"Let's be nice to her."

"Rocco said that we weren't to give her any favored-nations treatment."

"I just said nice," Man Ray Lefkowitz said, "nothing extravagant."

They paid their check and rose to leave, passing Maxi's table as they turned toward the door.

"Miss Amberville, I didn't see you there," Kelly said. "Oh, hi, George, how'd you get so lucky? Trying to get the jump on the rest of the space buyers? Naughty boy—but I don't blame you. I hope you're paying for lunch. Miss Amberville, may I say how pleased we are with our buys in B&B? Best deals we ever made."

"Just a minute, Kelly," said Lefkowitz, who saw, not to his surprise, that Kelly had cast him in the role of the bad cop. "Just one tiny minute. I think that B&B owes us a favor. We bought in before the first issue was published. That showed confidence and the willingness to take a risk on a new book. I think that as far as the proposed changes in ad rates are concerned, we should get some sort of break. Something, I don't know what, but something, damn it! I'm not suggesting that we can renew at those start-up giveaway prices . . . but I'll be very unhappy if we don't deserve some kind of favored-nations treatment. After all, Miss Amberville is almost a member of the family."

"Hey, guys, take it easy," Maxi said sweetly. "I'll split the difference . . . on one buy. Tell Rocco that there's no way, no way in the world, that I'm about to give away space in my magazine this time around. I suppose he told you to hit on me?"

"Those weren't his exact words," Kelly said sheepishly.

"No, Rocco always speaks of you with respect. He did say that this was the time to buy, if you were selling, but he wasn't taking

388

anything for granted, just because . . . well, because of old times' sake," Lefkowitz finished delicately.

"Where," asked Maxi, "are the snow jobs of yesteryear?"

"Do you fellows intend to join our table or just stand there?" George asked in irritation. "I'm trying to do a little business here. See you two around, huh?"

"I hope that your auction is coming up soon," Monty said, watching Maxi sign checks toward the end of May. "Tomorrow would be good. Today would be better."

"It isn't exactly tomorrow," Maxi said, carefully casual. "I thought all I had to do was make a phone call and it would happen like that—sort of a superior garage sale. But no, Sotheby's tells me that the jewelry can't be sold until their next jewelry sale in the fall—it's past the season now, there aren't enough rich people in town, it's too soon to be pre-Christmas, all sorts of silly reasons. And my collections are just too varied: the pictures have to wait till exactly the right big picture sale; the boxes won't bring as much until they're included in a major box sale. Boring. Almost the only thing that they can sell in June is my furniture. Auction-arranging is some sort of fine art in itself and they refuse to let me rush them into anything. Apparently I didn't have quite enough of everything to warrant their doing a special auction of all my possessions at the same time; unless I'd dropped dead, which, I gather, would have given everything a certain cachet and brought in more money." Maxi shrugged it off: a petty problem.

"June! You're not getting any more money until then?"

"You heard me. And who knows how much it will be, after they finish taking out their commission? The apartment turns out to have been my major asset and Donald was only able to sell it for almost the six million he gave me. I returned the difference. It had something to do with the overvalued dollar. Almost half of Trump Tower is owned by foreigners and last month they weren't spending dollars. Ah—go figure the economy. It's a waste of time."

"We're in very deep into . . . waste products, Maxi."

"Eighty-five percent—maybe more—of the advertisers have renewed at the new rates."

"Some of them don't go into effect until July, many of them not till August or September."

"Why don't we borrow from a bank against the page rate increases? Our advertisers are all major companies. They're good for the money. No, Monty, don't tell me we can't. I know it already . . . I've tried."

"If it were up to me, I'd lend you anything but I'm not a bank. I wish I were." Monty sighed as if he were about to be embalmed. "Don't you think it's time to ask the staff to take pay cuts?"

"Even if they worked for nothing, their salaries are a drop in the bucket compared to our other costs. And if word of pay cuts got around on Madison Avenue people might think we were in trouble and start to renege on the advertising commitments they've made. No, nothing gets cut, not the free lunch, not the quality of the photographs, not the amounts we pay to get celebrity writers. It would be fatal. We'll go down in glory or continue in glory, but no in-between measures."

Maxi finished signing the checks with a brave flourish and smiled so encouragingly at Monty that he decided not to jump out of the window. The May sunlight seemed to scatter like drops of water off her shiny, dark, messy hair when she moved and although she was down to her very last million she refused to let Monty know how desperate she felt until it was necessary. Each issue of *B&B* that was sold proved to her that she'd been right in her idea about the need for a magazine that didn't count on women's ever-present supply of depression, guilt and anxiety for its subject matter. "Admit it, Monty, don't you get just a tiny kick out of being on the cutting edge?" Maxi asked, laughing, her eyes so green that he blinked.

"Of what?" he asked, almost smiling back.

"Bankruptcy."

A week later, in the first days of June, Maxi sat down by herself to leftovers in Toby's kitchen. Everybody was out with springtime projects, but as worn out as she felt, she hated to find herself alone. During the working day Maxi still managed to present a picture of confident leadership but more and more frequently, when she found herself without an audience, even an audience of one, she felt beset with anxiety. For the first time since her struggle with Cutter began she wondered if she weren't being ridiculously quixotic, if she hadn't started a fight that was impossible to finish, a struggle whose dimensions she had never anticipated when she first went to see Cutter to try to use moral suasion on him. Who, after all, had appointed her trustee of her father's heritage? He had left control to her mother. Could that have possibly meant that he wanted her mother's wishes to be followed strictly, even if they did involve the destruction of Amberville Publications? Why was she, Maxi, the only one in the family who knew— or thought she knew—as absolutely as if she could hear Zachary Amberville talking to her, that nothing must be left undone to keep the magazines together? Oh, she had had a special closeness to her father that not even the boys had felt. He had been the one person in the world who had always believed in her, stood up for her, no matter what escapade she had been involved in, but did that mean that she could know *now* what he would have wanted?

The only person with whom she could share a part of her worries was Pavka and she'd seen him that day for lunch. She made a point of meeting him at least once a week so that she could keep track of what was happening on all the other Amberville publications. The picture he reported grew steadily worse. Every shrewd, ingenious and experienced move he had made to keep up the excellence of the magazines during the last few months since Cutter's edict had been accomplished only by the exercise of utmost cunning and patience. Nevertheless half of the things he had tried to do had been detected and countermanded by Lewis Oxford who was in touch with Cutter every day. Only his promise to Maxi not to resign kept Pavka on a job in which he was no longer in control, and Maxi, who knew how close to the end of the line she was, felt guilty for the struggle he was undergoing. Yet neither of them was acting out of selfish or ambitious motives; they were both doing it for Zachary Amberville, or, to be accurate, for his memory.

It couldn't last much longer, she realized. The sale to UBC, if it were made, would take place at the end of June, when the quarter's profits were known. The struggle couldn't go on for more than another month in any case. By the end of June she might not have the money left to go to press. It all depended on the auction of her furniture that was scheduled for the following week. If that went exceptionally well she could just scrape by, and if she were sure she could publish the next issue she could ask Lily to reconsider.

That afternoon Maxi had decided to take her jewelry and her precious boxes out of the unhurried, deliberately careful hands of Sotheby's and sell them herself to anyone who would buy them. To hock them if she couldn't sell them, although how she'd find the time to do it she didn't know. She didn't begin to know how you hocked things or where. If only she'd bought real estate instead of beautiful playthings. If only she'd worn fake pearls. If only she'd invested in the safest possible bonds instead of buying old furniture with uncertain market value. If only she hadn't put central heating into Castle Dread but had frozen to death without protest. If only she'd acted like the squirrel in the fable and had stored away nuts for winter instead of like the feckless grasshopper. If only. If only she hadn't acted like herself, she thought angrily. Too late now, and a pointless exercise. The doorbell rang and interrupted her fruitless replay of her life.

"Justin? Am I glad to see you! I can offer you pâté, five kinds, all original and still nameless, of Toby's own making. I haven't started to eat yet—come on and I'll put another plate on the kitchen table."

Justin followed her, sat down but only accepted a glass of wine. "How's the news from the front?" he asked.

"We're not taking prisoners."

"So I've heard. That's the word that's around."

"What are people saying?" Maxi asked, frowning.

"Oh, it goes all the way from rumors of the sale, which might have come out of UBC, to outraged denial. You name it, people are saying it. Confusion in the ranks, civil disorder, darkness at noon. Listen. I don't want you to think that I'm avoiding the showdown but I've *got* to get out of New York, New York, it's a hell of a town. And too much for me, Maxi. I can't take all these stones any longer, now that the weather is so beautiful. There are so many other places I want to be. Better places. I'm going to hit the trail, kid, before the monsoon season starts. I like a Gershwin tune, but babe, I *hate* New York in June." He tried to speak lightly but his expression was mordant.

"I know you feel that way and, truly, I understand. At least I know you'll always come back, sooner or later."

"I'm going to miss your birthday."

"So what, darling? You always miss my birthday. But honestly, it doesn't hurt my feelings. Oh, you're worried about my turning thirty, you think I'm going to go into a decline or something. That's it, isn't it? Oh, Justin, what's thirty? What's forty? Betty Friedan is what forty looks like, for God's sake."

"Gloria Steinem," Justin corrected her.

"You see, it doesn't matter. And I've got other things to think about, believe me."

"Well anyway, what the hell, I wanted to give you an advance birthday present to take the pain out of leaving your outrageous, picaresque, lust-filled twenties." Justin casually pulled out a piece of paper and put it down on the table. Maxi didn't reach for it.

"Since when," she asked, "do you give your own sister a check?"

"When she's grown up," Justin answered, "enough to know what to do with it." He took it, and delicately deposited it on her empty plate. She looked down and read the figures. It was enough to keep publishing *B&B* until all the new space she'd sold had been paid for, enough to save the magazine.

"Didn't I tell you I wouldn't borrow from you? Would not, could not and will not," she reminded him somberly, picking up the check and pushing it back across the table. "I have to see this through by myself."

"Don't be too proud, Maxi. We're a proud bunch, you and Toby and I—it must be Mother's influence. I ask you, if Father had been in money trouble with a magazine he believed in, wouldn't he have done anything, short of dishonesty, to save it? Don't get carried away by pride, Maxi. Anyway, this is a present, not a loan. A nonreturnable *gift*. There's nothing you can do about it except say, 'Thank you, Justin.'"

"But why? I don't understand."

"Because this is the only way I can find to join the fight. We're all in this together, we're a family and we're doing this for the family name. I've got to be part of that! Zachary Amberville was my father too, Maxi. You aren't the only one who loved him, you know. If you don't win, at least I won't feel that I didn't do as much as I could have. *Let me help!* It's for all of us. Please, Maxi, take it," he begged, showing more emotion than she had ever seen on his ironic, remote, withdrawn face.

Maxi snatched the check back, as full of expectation and excitement as if she were watching the arrival of a comet.

"Thank you, darling, darling Justin! And while you're in this generous mood, could you possibly let me have ten dollars till payday?"

26

Cutter, can't you really go up to Canada without me?" Lily asked. "We've seen Leonard and Gerry Wilder for dinner at least three times since the two of you met. Isn't that enough courtship, even for a major business transaction? Why is my presence necessary on this trip?"

"I thought you liked Gerry."

"I do, she's a perfectly agreeable woman, but this weekend trip with them up to look over the timberlands that the company owns —don't you realize that it brings up difficult memories for me?"

There was a change in Cutter's expression, below the surface of his polished and almost absolute charm, something seemed to be happening, a tightening of resolution.

"Darling, you're being just a bit self-indulgent, changing your mind at the last minute, aren't you? The fact that Zachary died in Canada shouldn't make the place impossible to visit—you've never even been there. You still live in the house you shared with him all those years, yet that isn't too painful for you. So why should this make any difference? You know I've planned this trip for weeks. Gerry is counting on your company while Leonard and I inspect the stands of timber."

"Oh, really," Lily complained, "this does drag on so."

"It's the kind of weekend that consolidates a relationship in a way that no number of New York dinners ever can," Cutter explained. "When the time comes, two weeks from now, to sit down and talk business at UBC, my personal relationship with Leonard will make a difference. He won't admit it, he won't even be aware of it, but I know it's true. So much hinges on you. You're the star of our little group. You *own* Amberville, I only speak for you. Be a big girl, my darling. You're so important in the end game. Remember, no deal is consummated until the papers are signed."

Lily sighed. She wanted to get this difficult, overdue sale over with and behind her. She was so weary of being looked at and standing in as the symbol of ownership, so tired of constantly having to watch herself in her mind's eye, that most difficult judge of all, ever alert to the position Cutter put her in at the center of the Amberville Publications stage, always the gracious soloist. She knew that Gerry Wilder, pleasant as she was, was still slightly awed by her, as impressed as a member of a *corps de ballet* would feel about the ballerina. Still, she was accustomed to enduring that central role that once she had coveted beyond all else, and Cutter was evidently intent on her being part of this weekend.

"All right, I'll go. Will I need a heavy coat or just lots of sweaters?"

"Bring everything you think you'll need. We're going in the UBC company jet so baggage is no problem."

"Good. That's something. I'll just go and tell my maid what to pack."

The interior of the UBC jet was so arranged that it didn't look like a flying boardroom. Intimate conversations were possible at both ends of the cabin. Cutter and Leonard Wilder sat together talking while their wives chatted up front.

"This timberland, thousands of acres, was one of the last things that my brother bought before he died," Cutter said. "He felt that the more independent Amberville was from paper manufacturers, the better. Hell, he'd have bought a printing plant next, and then a distribution business. That might be something for UBC to consider."

"One thing at a time," Leonard chuckled. Now that he had every intention of buying Amberville Publications his normally brusque manner had mellowed. "Speaking of things to consider, I've been giving a lot of thought to *B&B*. When we first met we only talked about the established books. I didn't give *B&B* another month's life. Since then your offbeat experimental baby has begun to fascinate me. At first I thought it would bring down your profits; then I saw the circulation figures, and lately I've started to ask myself if the first thing we should do is pour money into it or, on the other hand, shut it down. Any suggestions, Cutter?"

"Leonard, I've been going through all of that questioning myself, multiplied by ten. I've been tinkering with the magazine personally, doing all the fine-tuning and I promise you I've managed to get it over the hump. It was a challenge I took personally. But the jury's still out. As I do on any new project, I've let it go just so far and no further. It keeps our people on their toes and it's good for the company."

"I heard Lily's daughter speak at the dinner for Women in Publishing and I was damned impressed. Does she come with the package?"

"Maxi's a wonder. A chip off the old block. You'd have to cut your own deal with her, Leonard. I couldn't speak for her . . . but I'm not convinced that she's necessarily in it for the long haul. Still, who knows?"

"Won't the start-up losses distort your profit picture?"

"Less than you'll ever guess. I've been personally riding herd on Maxi and I think you're going to be pleasantly surprised. I'm satisfied with the Amberville balance sheet. I think you will be too."

"The figures will tell the story, won't they?" He stretched agreeably. "Ah, it's nice to be getting away. I've never been to the wilds of Canada."

"We have flush toilets for VIPs."

"Somehow I'd imagined you would."

"Leonard and I never had any children," Gerry Wilder told Lily, as she did each time they talked. "I envy you so much. And not just three children, even a granddaughter. You must be so proud."

"I am . . . but recently I began to realize something. I can't take the credit for them when they're being wonderful and so I shouldn't blame myself when they're being . . . difficult. It's taken

397

years to even begin to reach that conclusion. I always thought that they had to be perfect or else it meant that I wasn't perfect. Well, I'm not and they're not. We're all just human."

Gerry Wilder tried to hide her astonishment. She'd never heard Lily talk about herself so intimately before. She seized the opportunity to delve further into the character of the woman whose manner and breeding had always caused most of the other women of New York to think of her as set apart from them.

"Are you closer to one of your children than to the others?"

Lily smiled gently at the question. Only a woman without children could imagine that such a question could be answered simply, or even at all. She said the obvious and satisfactory thing. "They're each different and I'm close to each one in a different way."

"It must be wonderful having a daughter," Gerry said wistfully.

"Actually I'm more optimistic about Maxime than I've ever been before," Lily said, surprised at her own words.

"Optimistic?" Gerry Wilder said, puzzled.

"Oh," Lily laughed at her impulsive remark. "She's had three husbands, you know. That's a bit worrying for a mother. She seems to have finally settled down. Happily unmarried."

"Goodness, yes. Leonard took me to the Women in Publishing dinner and I thought she was marvelous. So businesslike. That combination of intelligence and beauty bowled us over. And I do adore that magazine of hers. I even go out to buy it—I can't wait to read it at the hairdresser's. It always makes me feel so—well, pleased with myself. I suppose she shows it to you before it comes out every month?"

"Actually she's quite private about it. I have to go to the newsstand to get it too."

"For heaven's sake," Gerry said, mystified by the world of publishing. After all, Lily Amberville owned the company. You'd think she'd get advance copies of every magazine. It sounded as if she knew as little about her own business as Gerry herself did about next season's pilots. Leonard wouldn't let her look at them because she couldn't conquer her habit of comparing them to "Masterpiece Theatre." But then she didn't own UBC.

Soon the small jet landed on the airstrip that had been carved out of the forest. The passengers left the plane, pulling on the heavy coats they had brought along. It was windy and bright but still very chilly up in this part of Northern Ontario. A tall, obviously young man in spite of his fine red beard stood waiting for them with a new jeep. He approached the group, shyly. "Mr. Amberville?" he asked, looking questioningly at the two men.

"I'm Mr. Amberville," Cutter answered. "You must be Bob Davies. You look like your dad."

"Yes sir. Nice to meet you, sir."

"This is Mrs. Amberville and our guests, Mr. and Mrs. Wilder. Bob's just learning the ropes, Leonard. His father used to be in charge of the camp here but he retired last year, went down to Florida. Just out of college, aren't you, Bob? How's your dad?"

"Fine, sir. Thank you. Why don't you all get into the jeep while I stow those bags? I don't like to keep you waiting in this wind. It's about a half-hour ride to the guest house."

Leonard Wilder entered the enclosed jeep reluctantly. He wanted to drink in the sight of the dark green, towering trees that, like the sea, had the power to awe a city man. Network television had never given him such a heady sense of being in touch with the real world, with growing things. This particular, surprising asset of Amberville Publications, he decided, was going to become his private fiefdom. The next time he flew up here it would be as host, not as a guest. He'd let Gerry redecorate the guest house, whatever shape it was in, so that she'd stop complaining about his never sharing the pilots with her. She refused to realize how lucky she was that he didn't.

On the same Saturday that Cutter and Lily were up north, Toby and India, in New York, were getting dressed for the first night of a Broadway play that had been written by Sam Shepard, India's costar in her last film. They had invited Angelica and Maxi to go with them but Maxi had promised to spend the evening with Julie who was kicking up an alarming fuss, digging in her heels about her growing conviction that a magazine that thought women were fine just the way they were didn't need a fashion editor at all, but rather a resident bag lady. When they found themselves with an extra ticket, they had told Angelica that she could bring a friend so long as the girl was properly dressed for an important theatrical event that was sure to draw a crowd of the usual curious civilians as well as a covey of photographers.

Impatiently India changed her dress at the last minute. She had fallen into the trap of this particular spring and bought a number of the chintz-printed gowns that looked heavenly on the hanger and turned their wearers into walking English country sofas. "Cabbage roses on the body don't work like cabbage roses on cushions," India said out loud to herself, ransacking her closets, and coming up with Nile-green satin Saint-Laurent evening pajamas, sashed at the waist in the palest pink, and a brighter pink satin raincoat that went with it, that must never be worn if it looked at all like rain.

"Angelica's friend is here, I heard the doorbell," Toby said.

"How do I look?" India asked.

"Come closer. Yeah—like the sky in the moment between sunset and sunrise in Norway, on Midsummer's Night."

"How did you know?"

"From the sound of the fabric, from the color I see out of a tiny tunnel, from the sound of your walk, from the way you smell, from the tone of your voice. By the way, when we go downstairs, try not to say the very first thing that comes into your mind about Angelica's friend."

"Toby, don't be mysterious. You've just picked up her voice, haven't you?"

"Right. This bat has super-sensitive hearing. Just keep your head." He touched her lips. "Lipstick. I'm going to kiss you anyway, but I won't smudge—I also specialize in super-sensitive, ultrasonic, laser-beam kissing."

"Go on, smudge," she invited. "Otherwise how will I know you've touched me?"

"You'll know . . . you know, don't you? Oh yes, you know. Come on now, we'll be late." Together they walked down to the living room where Angelica was waiting.

"Oh, what lovely cabbage roses, Angelica," India said automatically. It was true even when spoken out of stunned surprise. On Angelica the slipcovers were like a garden just coming into bloom.

"Thank you, Godmother," Angelica said with the utmost formality. "May I present Henry Eagleson, a friend from school. My godmother, India West, and my Uncle Toby."

"How do you do," the young man said.

"Basketball," India said wildly. "You must play basketball."

"He's the tallest boy in the eighth grade, Godmother," Angelica said, a note of triumph creeping into her tremulous voice.

"Center?" asked Toby.

"Yes sir. But if I stop growing I'll have to give it up."

"How old are you?" India finally ventured to ask.

"Fourteen, ma'am."

"Why should you stop growing at fourteen?" Toby wondered.

"I'm over six feet three already, sir. I have to stop sometime, at least I hope so."

"Not necessarily," Angelica said, grasping this neutral topic with both hands. "He could keep growing until he's twenty-one or -two, couldn't he? What do you think, Uncle Toby?"

"Why don't we wait and see? And why don't you call us India and Toby, Henry?"

"Swell. If you call me Dunk. Chip knows everybody calls me Dunk but tonight she's being proper or something. What's with you, Chip?"

"Nothing, nothing," India rushed into the breach. "Chip's been brought up by a very old-fashioned mother, you know, Dunk, of the old school. *Vieille* New York."

"Punctilious, hum? My mother gets that way too. Tonight I thought she'd have a complete breakdown before I left the house. She made me change my tie three times and my socks twice. Listen, Mom, I said, just because this is my first date doesn't mean that *you* have to get nervous. I don't understand parents at times. In most cases I do, but not always."

"My mother was the same way when I had my first date," Angelica said. "Wasn't she, Godmother?" She looked imploringly at India.

"Oh, indeed she was, Goddaughter. I thought she'd turn

green. Or was it blue? But that was *ever so long ago*, wasn't it, Uncle Toby?"

"Years, must have been years. So far in the past that I can't even seem to remember it. Shall we go? It's getting late."

Toby had borrowed Maxi's limousine for the evening. It had survived her great purge of possessions because it was the only practical way to get around New York. Cabs were never available at lunchtime in the neighborhood of *B&B* and Maxi had to race uptown for lunch and then race back to work. And her blue limo was part of her essential image of unquestioned success.

Elie ushered Angelica and her first date into the big car with not the slightest change of expression. They might have been an aged duke and duchess on their way to church, for all his solemnity. What Miss A. would say about it, he thought, he couldn't say. He supposed that Angelica had to start carrying on sometime, but with a giant? Maybe he was younger than he looked. At least they had chaperones, although Miss West and Mr. A. were too much in love to notice anyone but themselves, in his opinion. What a *terrible* family. He sighed in pure pleasure.

There was a large crowd gathered in front of the theater. "I wouldn't do this for anyone but Sam," India said. "I'm going to withdraw into being oblivious until we're inside the theater. Just don't let go of my arm, Toby, because I'll be walking straight ahead as if there weren't anyone watching me, O.K.?"

"Right. Chip can take your bows. Elie, see if you can let us off right in front of the theater, please."

"Yes, Mr. A.," Elie answered. You could see he wasn't used to a good driver, asking a damn fool thing like that. Where did he think he'd be left off, halfway down the block?

Angelica and Dunk got out of the limousine first, two tall, magnificent, unknown young people who were scanned by the crowd and then ignored as if they didn't exist. Then Toby stepped out and waited for India.

As they crossed to the entrance to the theater, so many flashbulbs went off, combined with the lights of the local television minicam crews, that India was blinded. Voices shouted out greetings to her but she didn't hear them in her condition of willed nonresponse.

402

"India, India, I've got something for you," one voice called, almost lost in the commotion caused by her appearance. She walked on but Toby instantly dropped her arm, whirled toward the voice and threw himself into the crowd like a linebacker, bringing a man crashing down to the street. They fought frantically for an instant, and before people started to scream there was the sound of a pop and a grunt. As if in slow motion Toby continued to struggle with the man on the pavement while the crowd stood milling, hysteria mounting, but directionless and ineffectual. Using all his great strength to hold the man down, Toby forced his fingers open until the gun he held dropped out of his hand. It was only then that India turned and screamed. It had happened so quickly that, like all such attempts, it seemed as if it were over before it had started. Only the bright arterial blood pouring out of Toby's arm was real. And the loaded gun that Dunk picked up carefully and held until a policeman took it away from him.

"How did you know, how did you know?" India wept, holding Toby's hand tightly as the ambulance careened through the streets.

"Recognized his voice—the nut who kept phoning you at the house, knew it right away. Didn't figure you'd want whatever he had for you." Toby was still in shock and seemed not to notice the ambulance attendant who was trying to stop the flow of blood.

"He was going to kill me. I knew he was crazy but I never thought he'd try to shoot me."

"Nobody is ever going to hurt you while I'm around."

"How did you know *where* he was? Oh, Toby, how did you know?"

"Training, orientation training. Comes in handy lots of times . . ."

"Lady, would you stop talking? I'm trying to fix this man up till we can get him to the hospital. Ask questions later. Oh, Oh! India West! Say, do you think I could have an autograph when we get there? It's for my wife . . . otherwise I wouldn't bother you at a time like this but she's a fan, see, a real big fan."

Lily would have been content to spend the morning in the neighborhood of the guest house but Gerry was clearly anxious to see more of the surrounding forest.

"Shall we ride?" Lily proposed.

"Horses terrify me. Don't you think we could ask that nice young man to take us for a tour in his jeep?" Gerry asked.

"Why not? Cutter left him here in case we wanted him for anything."

Soon they were in the jeep with Bob Davies who had overcome his first attack of shyness with the city visitors. Lily soon realized that this particular woodsman was far from silent. He was impossible to shut up without downright rudeness as he regaled them with tales of the towns that existed on the outskirts of the wild lumbering country, where the local workers got pig-drunk every Saturday night and fistfights were the normal end of the evening.

"Goodness," said Gerry, fascinated by this rough aspect of her new domain, "have you ever been involved in a fight, Bob?"

"No, Mrs. Wilder. My father wouldn't let me go near one of those bars when I was in high school. After that I was away at forestry school, and then I came straight here to work. That was when he retired, so suddenly. Out of the blue a relative died, someone he hadn't even known about, and he had enough money to buy a little place in Florida. That was always my mother's dream— she didn't like the cold. They just packed up and left. He's got a little boat-rental business down there now and they're as happy as newlyweds. Mr. Amberville let me take over here without even interviewing me. I really appreciated that, believe me. This is the first time I've had the pleasure of seeing any of the Amberville family. The old owners were always around; bringing friends up with them for the hunting season and the fishing season, using the horses, having big cookouts, just having a great old time. Do you think you'll be back often, now that you've seen the spread, Mrs. Amberville?"

"I have no idea," Lily said distantly.

"It sounds wonderful," Gerry remarked thoughtfully. Lily knew that Gerry was thinking that as soon as the deal went through she and Leonard would immediately begin to entertain their friends up here. She felt a sharp pang of annoyance, as if Gerry's obviously proprietary interest were an attack on her own territory. Yet, when UBC bought Amberville none of this would still belong to her. So why not just accept it? What on earth did it matter?

The jeep drove slowly along the trail, in the shadow of the thickly planted great trees. It was a sunny day and light struck down into every space that the trees would grant its entrance.

"Oh look, Lily, there's a sort of clearing up ahead. Why don't we get out of the jeep and take a little walk in that direction? It seems a shame not to get some exercise," Gerry proposed.

"Bob, could you stop here for a minute? We're going to take a stroll," Lily agreed.

"Will do, Mrs. Amberville." He braked carefully to a halt and slid out of his seat to help them down. "I'd better come with you ladies. There's a ravine on the edge of that clearing."

"That won't be necessary, Bob," Lily said coldly. She wanted to have a little time this morning ungarnished by his life's story. Reluctantly he let them go on without him and the two women walked energetically along the trail for hundreds of feet, breathing deeply of the pine-scented air. When they reached the grassy clearing they found that it was almost hot in the sun trap and they took off their coats and sat on the grass for a few minutes, enjoying the silence and the peace of the moment.

"Let's go look for the ravine," Gerry suggested, her eyes sparkling with interest. She'd never owned a ravine and she wanted to see it for herself. It was a feature of the place, like the horses and the lake that was reputed to be full of fish anxious to be caught. The air itself was part of the deal, the grass, the trails, the guest house. She couldn't be less concerned with the timber except as a background for her future pleasure parties.

"I'd rather not, if you don't mind," Lily answered. She had had enough of Gerry Wilder for the morning. "I'm feeling a bit tired. But you go on. I'll wait for you."

"You're sure?"

"Absolutely."

Gerry wandered off and Lily forgot her, almost falling asleep. Suddenly she heard a sharp cry. "Oh, my God!" She opened her

405

eyes and saw Gerry on the grass at a distance, backing rapidly away. "Lily! There's the most god-awful drop there. You can't imagine. 'Ravine' my eye! It looks like an opening into hell . . . all jagged boulders and a terrible steep drop . . . and you can't even tell it's there until you're almost right on top of it. Those places should be marked, for heaven's sake. They should have railings around them."

"Well, you'll put them there, won't you?" Lily muttered to herself. "Come on back, Gerry. Let's get into that jeep. It must be almost lunchtime."

"Bob," said Gerry, as soon as they were on their way back to the guest house, "I think it's terribly dangerous not to mark that ravine. Why isn't there a fence there?"

"There are so many of them, Mrs. Wilder. There must have been an earthquake here once. There are dozens just like that, but not a one that's nearly as close to the guest house. Everyone who works in these woods knows about them. It's only strangers who are surprised. That's why I warned you. In fact . . . well, it's not a story I should tell you ladies . . . it happened just before the old owners finally sold the place. My dad told me about it, but in confidence . . ."

"Oh, come on, Bob," Gerry said eagerly. She wanted to know everything about this new future toy of hers and if there was a local mystery, so much the better.

"Well . . . I don't know . . ." He was obviously dying to regale them with the story.

"Oh, Bob, what difference can it make? Tell!" Gerry insisted.

"See, my dad, he used to fly a little one-engine plane, like the new pilot who's taking your husbands around. He was up in it one day, on his way to an emergency in a camp all the way on the other edge of the forest—a lumberjack had been injured real bad and had to be picked up and rushed to the hospital. Anyway, he spotted two guys, visitors from the city like you ladies. He never told me who they were but they were on horses. They got off the horses in the clearing back there and they must have had some sort of argument. Not so different from the boys here on Saturday night, because they got into a fistfight. One of them must have thrown a hell of a punch because the other ended up at the bottom of that ravine."

"What did your dad do?" Gerry asked breathlessly.

"He couldn't stop, see, not enough room to land, and he was real worried about that lumberjack I told you about. Anyway he knew that the accident was real close to the guest house and he figured the other guy would ride back as fast as possible and get help. But when he finally got back here, a day later, they still hadn't located that poor fellow in the ravine. There was all sorts of confusion, search parties going out in every direction but the right one. Nobody seemed to be in charge or know what was going on. Dad was fit to be tied. He led them to the ravine right away but it was, well . . . it was too late. The visitor from the city was dead. Nobody ever did know if it was from the fall or from being out all night in the cold. See, it was below zero that night when it happened. Anyway . . ."

"Stop the car!" Gerry screamed. Lily had fainted and slumped sideways, halfway out of the vehicle, and it was taking all of her strength to keep Lily from falling out onto the trail.

Lily sat in the semidarkness in the main bedroom of the guest house. She'd asked Gerry Wilder to draw the curtains and insisted, in a way that permitted nothing but obedience, that she be left alone. She hadn't attempted to explain her brief descent into unconsciousness to the other woman. "Let me rest. I don't want lunch. Please do not come back upstairs to see how I am," she had ordered in a tone so absolute that Gerry Wilder had not dared to ask a single question.

Throughout the afternoon Lily sat by the window in a straight-backed chair while her memory and her vision turned in upon herself. In the passage of a few hours she grew old and bent and drained of pride and beauty. She was desperately cold, as if the flow of blood in her veins had stopped, yet she lacked the will to rouse herself to put on another sweater. At moments she muttered a few words out loud and then fell silent. From time to time she doubled over, her hands cramped painfully over her mouth to silence her spasms of howling grief, her attacks of brutish anger. She had to summon all her strength to quiet those hands. They wanted to rend her, to tear her flesh, to pluck out her hair, to damage her forever.

Eventually, as the afternoon grew to a close, she mastered her emotions and concentrated on the door to the bedroom. Soon, as she knew he must, Cutter opened it quietly, obviously expecting that she would be resting on one of the twin beds. Lily made no sound.

"Lily?" he asked, not seeing her in the gathering darkness. He walked a few steps into the room and then turned to snap on a standing lamp. "Where are . . . Lily, what are you doing there like that?" He approached her and stopped dead at the sight of the ugly woman whose face was contorted in a grimace of some unnameable emotion, an old woman wearing Lily's clothes, a woman with Lily's hair, who glared at him with savage, slashing eyes.

"Good God, Lily, what's happened?" he asked in horror. "Gerry told me about the ravine. What the *hell* kind of stunt was that, Lily, to go and look at it, of all stupid things to do. How could you *do* that to yourself? Just look at you . . ."

"No." Her voice was dry and broken by the tears she had shed, hoarse and ancient. "Don't bother to look at me. It doesn't matter what I look like. Look in the mirror, look at yourself."

"What kind of riddle is that supposed to be?" Cutter asked, disgust and ferocity mixed. "Damn! I should never have brought you to Canada. If I'd known that you were so morbid—"

"You shouldn't have. But you didn't anticipate everything, for once in your life. You didn't know that I'd find out." Lily's voice had faded to a whisper.

"'Find out'? There's nothing here for you to find out. What are you talking about?"

"How . . . how did Zachary die?" she hissed.

"Lily," Cutter said in a reasonable way, "Lily, you have *always* known how Zachary died. Darling, everyone knows. You've had a shock, that's all, from being so near the place where it happened. Come on, let me help you up and get you into a warm bath. You're going to make yourself ill if . . ."

"*Murderer,*" she screamed.

"Lily! Stop that at once! You're hysterical!" In a bound he reached the chair and pulled her to her feet, trapping her flailing arms behind her back with one powerful hand.

"*Murderer!*"

"Shut up! The Wilders are in the next room, they'll hear you . . ."

"*MURDERER!*"

Cutter clapped his other hand over her mouth and she bit deeply into the pad of his thumb. Roughly he pushed her away so that she fell onto one of the beds. "That's enough! That's more than enough out of you. You're out of control, don't you understand that, Lily? It's this place, that's all, it's making you hysterical."

Lily shook her head violently and rose, standing to confront him. "You were there, at the ravine, yes, you were there. *It was you!* You knocked him in and you left him to die." She looked at Cutter in bitter wonder and there was steady accusation in her voice now as she only stated the facts that she had spent the hours facing.

"That's the most . . . the most purely, utterly *insane* thing you've ever said in your life, you've gone mad, completely mad—"

"You can bluster all you like, it's all the same to me." Lily kept looking at him as if she were trying to assemble his separate parts into one human being, looking in bewilderment as if she were trying to persuade herself that he was Cutter Amberville, the man she had loved, trying and failing utterly. Yet she continued to speak firmly, without faltering, and her voice seemed to come from far away, from inside a death's head, primitive, hollow and devoid of life. "Bob Davies told me. He didn't know what he was saying. Now I understand why his father was able to retire at forty-seven. I know who gave him the money to go to Florida. Only one man saw what happened but he was as talkative as his son. We heard it all, Gerry and I. Two men in the clearing, two men who got off their horses, two men who got into a fistfight, one man who was hit—or was he pushed?—into the ravine and one man who came back and *did not* send a rescue party for his brother. In subzero weather. The closest ravine to the house. You must have been terrified when Davies came back the next day and told you he'd seen what happened. But you didn't get him out of the way quickly enough. He told his son and he'd tell any court in the world. I'll make sure of that."

"Lily, you can't believe that story! That kid is full of wild stories, lies—"

"Shall I call his father down in Florida? It's only one little long-distance call. He'll admit everything when I tell him he's an accessory to a murder." Lily reached for the telephone. "I have his number. I asked Bob for it when Gerry wasn't listening. I said I wanted to tell him what a nice, helpful son he had."

"Wait! Put that phone down. I can explain—"

"No, I don't think you can." Lily's voice made Cutter go cold with fear but she put the phone back in its cradle. He drew a deep breath.

"Lily, something did happen that day. I hoped you'd never have to know. I *was* with Zachary when he fell into the ravine. We did have a fight, *but it was an accident,* Lily, an accident!"

"But why didn't you send back a rescue party?" Lily asked relentlessly.

"I still don't understand it. I was in total shock, Lily. I don't remember what happened for hours afterwards. I was out of my head with grief. I looked over the edge and I could tell he was dead just by the way he lay there. Even if he'd been rescued right away it wouldn't have made any difference. I found my way back here somehow and I just blanked out. I couldn't function. My brother was dead . . . my brother . . . I just couldn't believe it. That's why I had to get rid of Davies—sure I bribed him. I knew nobody would believe what had happened. Oh, but Lily, *you* have to believe me! You know I would never have harmed Zachary on purpose. Why should I have done such a thing? *Why?* It doesn't make any sense. Admit that it doesn't make sense. It would have been insane." Cutter stopped, his eyes searching her face pleadingly.

"What did you fight about?" Lily asked.

"You. I don't know what had given him the idea or why he suddenly picked that particular time to bring it up but, Lily, he had suspicions about us. He got violent. Raging mad. He accused me of having been your lover when we were young. He said he was beginning to think that Justin was my son and not his. I can't imagine what might have made him sniff out our secrets so many years after they'd happened but I couldn't take the risk of reacting in any way but as if he were insulting *you*. I swung that first punch for you, Lily. It was so out of character that it was the only way I could think of showing Zachary how wrong he was. I did it to protect you. I did it for your sake, my darling. If I hadn't, who knows what might have happened? How he might have taken it out on you and Justin? I admit I did it, but it was for you, only for you, Lily."

"You can't *stop* lying, can you?" she said, wearily, no surprise left, only contempt.

"Lying?—Lily, what else would have made me fight my own brother?"

"*I told him about us thirteen years ago.* He knew about you and me and Justin all those last years. We made our peace with each other, Zachary and I, but before we did I wanted to start fresh or not at all. So I told him everything. *Everything.* He forgave me completely. He had always loved Justin as his son and he kept right on loving him until the day you killed him. He was hurt, but he hadn't exactly been a saint himself. So we made it up and went on to create a good life together. You're the last person in the world to whom he would have admitted that he knew." As empty and dead as Lily's voice was, her tone was irrefutable. Truth rang through every word. Cutter turned his back to her.

"Whatever your reason for killing my husband, it doesn't matter. Envy and hatred were at the root of it. That's why you made me love you. To take something of his away. I was almost as bad as you, then. But I'm not a murderer. Or a liar. Not anymore."

"Lily . . ."

"Not another word. Never, *never* another lying word. I'm leaving now, back to New York. You can tell the Wilders whatever lie you choose. I'll send the plane back for them as soon as it lands. Zachary Amberville was murdered by his brother. I know the truth. Nobody else will. I won't try to punish you. It would serve no purpose. You're not worth it. Unless . . ."

"Unless?" Cutter said, still unable to believe that she really meant what she was saying.

"Unless you ever try to come into contact with any member of the Amberville family again. If you do, I'll bring you to trial. I swear it, by all that's dear to me."

"Wait, stop—" he cried, but she had already gone.

27

Every other time that Maxi had crossed the lobby of the Amberville Building in the last year it had been at a run. Today she lagged, finding more than enough unwelcome time to inspect the giant ferns that flourished under their special health-giving lights, many minutes to sneer at the lusty condition of the bromeliads, to count with disdain the ranks of huge palms and reflect on the greening of corporate America. What was wrong with the city fathers of her Manhattan who permitted more and more builders to reduce the amount of sunlight that could reach the streets so long as they guaranteed that each new, ever-taller building was to have a mere token indoor green space? Greener lobbies, darker streets, she thought to herself, aware that her mood was generated by the dread with which she approached the summons she had received to talk to Lily, a meeting for which she was early, due to Elie's overly skillful driving. Still, even if she had been precisely on time—even if, unthinkably, she had been late—the outcome of this interview had already been decided, she thought as she took the elevator to the executive floor.

"Mrs. Amberville is waiting for you in Mr. Amberville's office," the receptionist said to her as soon as she appeared. The full treatment, Maxi realized, backed up by the authority of Zachary Amberville. Good news didn't come hedged by such a display of legitimate command, of absolute jurisdiction.

She went in. Here, at least, the prodigal sun could enter and rollick, here the two rivers that clasped Manhattan like the arms of a giant lover could both be perceived, one running darker than the other, but both running to the ocean. She looked around, momentarily dazzled, and could not distinguish her mother's presence until her eyes adjusted to the light. Lily was sitting on the lower step of a library ladder and she held a bound volume of copies of *Seven Days* from the 1960s, open to pages of photographs from the Kennedy-Nixon campaign, taken by the many Amberville photographers who followed every step of the national drama. She put the heavy book down when Maxi approached her and looked up almost unchanged in her still moonlit beauty and intensely studied elegance. Yet there was something battered, something blighted in the flesh around her eyes that Maxi had never seen before, as if a flower had been sucked of its freshness overnight, grown limp, tired, faded.

"Who ran for Vice-President with Nixon?" Lily asked.

"Damn," Maxi said. She couldn't remember, except that it certainly wasn't Spiro Agnew. Or was it?

"I didn't know either, Maxime."

"That's reassuring. . . . How was your weekend?" she added, since small talk seemed to be the first thing on the agenda.

". . . Illuminating. And yours?"

"Horrible. Poor Toby. I think I'm still in shock," Maxi answered.

"I went to see him at his house yesterday but you weren't back with Angelica yet. Thank God he's going to be as good as new as soon as he heals. Tell me, just who is Dunk and what is a Dunk?"

"Angelica's first boyfriend. He's fourteen, very polite, and eats like an army, Napoleon's army. But he has excellent table manners."

"Toby and India spoke highly of him."

"Angelica's not *their* daughter. He'd just better treat her properly," Maxi said in a warlike tone, her fists clenched.

"Or?"

"I'll get Rocco to deal with him. Imagine Angelica sneaking off on her first date when she knew perfectly well I wasn't going to be home. She'd never have dared try that with her father. I'm still fuming."

"The trouble with you, Maxime, is you forget what it's like to be young," Lily said, brushing her objections aside.

"Mother! I'm not even thirty yet! Not for a few weeks. And I didn't start dating until I was . . . sixteen."

"Ah, but when you did . . ."

414

"I remember, that's what I'm worried about."

"Angelica's a very different kind of person than you were. She's sensible and well balanced. If I were you, I wouldn't worry about her."

"Thank you," Maxi said with dignity, refusing to rise to the bait. She had no intention of trying to defend her teenaged self. If Lily still thought of her that way, there was nothing she could do about it.

"Of course," Lily continued, "she'll change, in all sorts of ways as time goes on—we all do, we all have to, don't we? But Angelica's character is pretty well formed. I can imagine her almost as she'll be in ten years' time, unlike you, Maxime. I could never be sure just what was going to happen to you. You were a rather difficult child, you know, but I had no idea that you'd be a late bloomer."

"A late bloomer? Just what is that supposed to mean?"

"Now don't be defensive, Maxime. I simply mean that you hadn't reached your full potential . . . no, you hadn't started to reach your potential . . . until very recently." Lily's voice was as neutral as clear water, and as difficult to read meaning into as a night without stars.

"I suppose that you're leading up to the letdown with these kind words?" Maxi said, barely listening to Lily, burning over the description of herself as a "difficult child" and the implied comparison to Angelica who had managed to escape being judged in any way by her doting grandmother. Not that Angelica wasn't ideal. More or less.

"If you would just sit down, Maxime, we could discuss this more comfortably," Lily remarked, settling in one of the chairs in front of the desk.

Maxi, who had been standing throughout the conversation, went to the desk and automatically sat down in her father's chair, where she had sat when she asked Pavka not to resign. Lily allowed a little silence to fall.

"Do you feel comfortable there?" she finally asked Maxi.

"Oh. I'm sorry!" Maxi stood up abruptly, confused. "I wasn't thinking."

"I know. I'm quite aware of that." Lily smiled at her, an involuntary smile. "That chair's been empty for so long. You almost fit it."

"Mother?" What was this cat-and-mouse game, Maxi asked herself, thrown off balance.

"I told you that you forget what it's like to be young, really young, Maxime. Well, so do I. But sometimes I'm smart enough to remember. Your father was younger than you are now by the time he had founded his first magazines. You're the age he was when I met him. You've already founded one magazine and made a roaring success out of it, if we ignore your untraditional financial methods. Why shouldn't you be able to take over the others . . . with the help of all the people who've been running them since your father died? That is, if you want to."

"Take over the others? But—but I never asked for, never dreamed of—that," Maxi stammered, turning pale.

"But surely you realize that if I don't sell Amberville someone in the family has to take over? And you're the only possible person, aren't you? That's finally, at long last, obvious even to me. Late bloomer that I am."

"You're not going to sell?"

"You didn't think I'd brought you here to tell you that I was? Good God, Maxime, I wouldn't have done anything so unfeeling. I would have told you, but not here, not in your father's office. Sometimes I think you don't understand me at all." Lily sighed with bafflement. "But let's not talk about that . . . it's a problem we may never settle, and it has no bearing on your answer. Do you want to take over? As publisher of all the magazines?"

"But what . . . I don't understand . . . what will Cutter say?" Maxi's normally nimble, skeptical tone had dissolved into the utter disarray of surprise.

"He will never have anything to say about how your father's magazines are to be run, *ever*. He is . . . gone. I have sent him away. I intend to divorce him. His future is no concern of mine. None of us will ever see him again and I trust that we will never discuss him, never mention his name." The liquid surface of Lily's voice, as she spoke these abrupt, curt phrases of absolute banishment, was flawed, for the first time in Maxi's memory, by whirlpools of raw emotion of complex, unpolished pain.

416

Another silence fell. Neither woman looked at the other, but in the dust motes that danced in the sun-striped air, questions were asked, answers were refused, questions were withdrawn and put away for all time.

Of all the rare and desirable luxuries that Zachary Amberville's money had bestowed on her in her lifetime, Lily thought, this power to cast Cutter out of her life was finally the most valuable, the most necessary. The same power enabled her to impose silence on her children, to keep from ever having to explain to them. But one thing money could not buy, the only cessation that no coin could purchase, was freedom from her own knowledge of the kind of man he was. How could she have chosen such a man? Where did her faults begin? For how much of the tangled story had she been responsible? Why had she maintained that wild, irrational connection, unwilling to change her stubborn fantasies about him, no matter how often he had disappointed her? Just how evil had he been? Had he ever really loved her? Worse—*how could it still matter to her?* She was certain of one thing. Somehow she was as much to blame as he except in one vital way: Cutter had not left Zachary to die *because of her,* and in that fact she would have to find her strength, no matter how hard were the questions that tormented her. "Well, Maxime," she asked again, "do you want the job?"

Maxi's head was as light as if she had rapidly scaled a mountain peak and breathed deeply of the light, bright exhilaration of the air of the summit. She saw nothing except the vastness of the shining temptation, the immensity of the horizon, the infinite vistas that opened before her. She stayed there a moment, dazzled, and then she forced herself to return to practical things, coming back to the reality of the office, trying to visualize herself here every day, dealing with all the decisions, demands, problems and responsibilities that would fall to the lot of whoever was the head of Amberville Publications. She understood suddenly that she couldn't possibly know what it would be like in advance. When she had so blithely demanded that Cutter give her a poor old rag called *Trimming Trades Monthly,* had she had any idea of what it would be like to actually publish *B&B* month after month? Publisher? *Head of the company?*

"Oh, yes, Mother! *I want it!*" she exclaimed, out of a whole heart. She wanted it and she knew that her father would have wanted it for her.

"Good. I'm glad, Maxime. Very glad. I wouldn't have offered the job to you if I didn't think you could do it," Lily said calmly, yet with a deep note of tenderness. "The sale was always possible, it is still possible. But I'd like to keep Amberville Publications in the family. I was once told that I'd sacrificed my life to the company, that I'd been deprived of my freedom by all the different ways in which I helped your father while he was running the magazines. I believed that interpretation of my life. I thought that my birthright, whatever that means, had been taken away from me." She paused for a moment, as if pondering the meaning of "birthright."

"Father believed in you," Maxi said, "or he wouldn't have left you control of his business. He would never have done that unless he'd thought you were worthy of the responsibility."

"I don't know about being worthy, Maxime, but I've done a lot of thinking in the last day, enough for years, and I know now that the magazines have enriched my life. Being part of them has become part of my life, a part that is much too meaningful to permit me to sell them to strangers, to see them pass out of Amberville control. I'm proud of the magazines, Maxime, *damn proud* and I want them to be better than they've ever been before—"

"Mother!" Maxi interrupted, "do you have any idea—"

"Indeed I do, more than an idea. I spent the morning with Pavka. I know what's been going on behind my back. That's over, once and for all. All those disgraceful orders have been revoked. But no others have been given. I was waiting to see what you'd decide. Now the only person who will give orders in the future will be you. You'll have Pavka's guidance, but I imagine you'll have to earn the support of the old editorial board. Some of them may very well resent you. I won't interfere—but you can always use me . . . for window dressing. I'm very, very good at it."

"Don't say that!" Maxi protested. "You gave up a great career as a prima ballerina! Oh, Mother . . . you could have had *that.*"

"Not necessarily," Lily murmured, with a small, mysterious, inward smile. "Not necessarily. I'll never know, never *have* to know. Surely that was the *point?*" She shook her head and came back from the past. "However, as window dressing I was the very

418

best and I intend to continue to be. Every window needs dressing, otherwise it's just a bare and naked piece of glass. Never underestimate the power of window dressing." Lily sounded matter-of-fact now, but there was a newly perceptive expression on the perfect oval of her face and a mourning, rueful look in her gray-green-blue eyes, a look that contained all the shrewdness that she had always hidden, the shrewdness that she now shared with this daughter whom she admitted to her confidence for the first time in their lives.

"Angelica once told me that Father said that she was the only one in the family with a head for publishing," Maxi confided.

"He was wrong about that . . . even Zachary Amberville could be wrong. Even I can be wrong on occasion," Lily said with a gossamer smile, in which relief vied with the beginning of self-mockery.

"The trouble with you, Mother, is that you always like to have the final word on any question," Maxi said.

"Like you."

"Like me. Just like me. Come on, Mother, give me a kiss."

"Toby," Maxi asked, "would your feelings be hurt if Angelica and I moved out of your attic? Now that I've got job security and a regular paycheck I can afford to pay rent. Nothing fancy, but just a little bigger. More closet space of course, a bigger room for Angelica, somewhere to put a few bits and pieces."

"A few? You never had 'a few' of anything," Toby retorted.

"Well, I will have," Maxi insisted. "You know that I never did get around to auctioning anything? Even the furniture hasn't been sold yet. I've decided to keep only the very few things I like best. Now that I've gotten used to living without all those objects I'm going to try the pared-down look for a while . . . just a couple of marvelous pieces, each one set off by its relationship to the space around it. Of course I'll need a really top lighting designer . . ."

"Spare me, please spare me your decorating plans," Toby begged. "Don't you have Ludwig and Bizet to discuss this with? I thought they did all your places for you."

"They used to but I feel as if I'm ready for a change."

"Does it make the slightest sense to undertake a job that's going to consume your life and try to redecorate a new apartment at the same time?"

"Put like that, no," Maxi answered. Toby was lying in his favorite Eames chair, his feet up, his arm in an embroidered sling that India had somehow fashioned out of one of her sacred pillowcases, ruthlessly wielding a pair of scissors while Maxi vainly offered any scarf from a drawer full. "Still, we do have to move, now that the emergency is over. Angelica is miserable about it. She loves being here and the Troop really enjoys your pool."

"It would have been nice if they'd brought their own towels, but somehow they never remembered to," Toby said thoughtfully.

Maxi ignored him. "I don't really want to move either. It's so cozy up there and the leftovers are even better than the meals, and, oh Lord, you're right about the job. I won't even have time to do a proper job of apartment hunting. I won't have time to do anything until I get the job under control. I'd better start going in early and staying late and working weekends and . . ."

"Don't be dumb. You're having an attack," Toby cut in. "A stupidity attack. It comes over people when they're faced with enormous changes in their lives, especially people like you who are all-or-nothing people, no compromises, no halfway measures, no doing things a little bit at a time. Now it's your compulsive career. It used to be the compulsive search for fun, so that means that if you work it has to be compulsive work without any time off."

"My compulsive career, as you charmingly call it, also happens to be the most marvelous fun in the world," Maxi sputtered, outraged. "Instant analysis—disgusting."

"May I remind you," Toby said, "that you're only almost thirty—"

"Why does everybody pick this time to remind me of my age all of a sudden?"

"Thirty," Toby continued, "in the prime of life, with, I should imagine, from my memories of your scandalous past, a normal need for male companionship."

"Men," Maxi snorted.

"You sound just like Dad," Angelica piped up from her place

420

on the floor at Maxi's feet. "That's what he says, 'women' in that same contemptuous tone of voice. He isn't even dating anymore. Remember the girl I used to tell him smelled like vanilla? Well, she's been gone for months and actually she wasn't bad if you don't mind funny smells. And that exceptionally pretty one I told him I just instinctively *knew* was a wrong broad, he hasn't called her in ages, and she wasn't really all that bad, just not my type. And there were a whole bunch of others who were after him because he's so successful—at least that was my opinion—or only interested in his looks. Superficial ladies. I always let Dad know my true feelings about them so he wasn't in danger of being taken in—well, he's not seeing anybody at all now. I wonder if I gave him some sort of complex?"

"Adolescence," India ruminated, "was invented by a psychologist named G. Stanley Hall in a book he wrote in 1905. Eighty years ago, Angelica, before we knew about adolescence, somebody would have put you in the corner or made you write things on the blackboard a hundred times, like 'I will not meddle in my father's love life.' Or maybe put you on bread and water. Even the ducking stool. I don't know which you would have hated more."

"I didn't meddle, I just made observations. If he hadn't paid any attention to me, like a regular father, it wouldn't have affected him. And 'love life' is such an old-fashioned expression. He was just seeing them."

"'*Seeing,*'" Toby growled bitterly. "Now it's become a word for all sorts of relationships, from the casual to the engaged-to-be-engaged. Just yesterday one of your gossips told me that Julie Jacobson was 'seeing' that young art director at *B&B*—does that mean nightly, semi-nightly, twice a week? I wonder what damn fool invented that miserable *perverted* usage of a word?"

"Well, whoever did, I don't know about Julie and Brick Greenfield but all *Dad* was doing was casual seeing," Angelica answered him as Maxi and India exchanged worried glances. "It wasn't as if he'd saved one of their lives and he was seriously in love, like you are with India. Anyway, I have to get dressed. Dunk is coming to pick me up in half an hour. We're going to a revival of *Wuthering Heights.*"

"I'll come help you dress," Maxi said hastily, ignoring Angelica's surprised eyebrows. She knew how to dress, for heaven's sake.

"Well, you did, you know," India said after a pause.

"So you've mentioned. Several times. Does saving your life make me your captive?"

"If you were Chinese and you'd saved my life you'd owe me all sorts of things because I'd become your responsibility or something like that."

"I'm not Chinese."

"No, you're a full-fledged member of the Running Wounded," India said angrily. "I'm going to pack. I'm sick of not being appreciated."

"What the hell is that—the 'Running Wounded'—what's that supposed to mean?"

"You know what the walking wounded are—soldiers who've been wounded but don't have to be carried off the battlefield. You're different—you're wounded but you're running away from it, running around in meaningless circles, running so hard that you don't feel the pain or you can pretend that it doesn't exist. I'd thought you were different. You seem to have come to terms with being blind and you can do more than most men who can see. You'll always be able to do more. Blindness is finite . . . it's not going to get worse. But you've decided to cut yourself off from the rest of life. The harder part maybe. The human part. The part where I come in. *I'm not interested in your reasons anymore!* I'm only interested in what it does to me to be in love with you. Without hope. I'm not willing to put up with it. I refuse to become one of the Running Wounded myself."

"Doctor Florsheim?"

"I haven't seen her for months. My analysis is finished. I'm leaving you, Toby. For good."

"Hey, wait a minute."

"Now what?" India said from the doorway.

"Are you taking your sheets?" He looked meditative, with the beginning of concern.

"Of course."

"Pillowcases? And all the little baby pillows with the scalloped edges?"

"What is the point of this?" India snapped. "Just because I finished my analysis doesn't mean that I have to give up my bed linen. One thing has nothing to do with the other."

"I don't think I'd be comfortable sleeping on no-iron, fifty-percent manmade fiber anymore," Toby grinned, as if he'd solved a weighty problem that had bothered him for years.

"Oh?" India's heart started to beat so loudly that she thought that even a man with sight must be able to hear it.

"So let's make a deal. We'll get married and I'll get custody of your hope chest." Under his casual words was the tensile strength of a stubborn man who had finally changed his mind.

"My hope chest? Do you mean my linen?" India asked, approaching him slowly, carefully, so as not to betray her sudden tumult, the wild fluttering of her hands.

"Aren't they the same thing?"

"I don't believe so. Certainly not. Hope chest indeed!" India said, sounding deeply affronted, in the best acting of her short but glorious career.

"Well, let's get married and sleep on your sheets." He spoke with his habitual tone of command but India could detect a tremble in his voice.

"Is that your idea of a proposal?" She almost achieved a sneer but failed, failed utterly.

"Yep."

"You can't do better than that?"

"I saved your life, didn't I?" he said, too impatient to try for courtliness.

"You can't use that line forever, Toby Amberville," she whispered, the sweet wine of her voice denying her words.

Toby got out of his chair and walked over to her and held her tightly against him with his good arm. He gazed at her intently, his amber-brown eyes happier than she'd ever seen them, abandoned to utter tenderness. "If there were a moor nearby, I'd take you up on it and fill your arms with heather and tell you how much I love you, Cathy . . . but there's only Central Park. I love you, Cathy, and I want to live with you forever and ever and have a dozen children and take my chances with life."

"Heathcliff!"

"Does that mean yes?"

"I'll have to call my agent first, but . . . I think we can work something out."

In San Francisco, two weeks later, Jumbo Booker's secretary buzzed him.

"It's Mr. Amberville," she said, "calling from New York. Shall I put him through?"

Jumbo was not surprised by the call. He'd been expecting it ever since the word had reached him that Cutter was out of Amberville Publications. During the two years that had passed since Cutter had left his job with Booker, Smity and Jameston, of which Jumbo was now president, he had all but lost touch with his high-flying former employee. However, the extraordinary news of Cutter's unannounced, abrupt and unexplained departure from the publishing world had reached him through the corporate grapevine, a grapevine just as effective as the one that had passed on the knowledge of Cutter's sexual exploits during his marriage.

Jumbo was perfectly aware that Cutter had not been able to find another job in all of investment banking. Cutter had had a dozen job interviews but nothing had materialized for him and Jumbo knew why even if Cutter did not. A third grapevine had slowly operated on the highest levels of San Francisco society and many influential people had become gradually aware that Candice Amberville had killed herself. A number of them had guessed why, and from that number arrows of gossip had flown to Manhattan; gossip that would always be contained within a small group; gossip that would never leak beyond a certain circle; gossip so shocking, so vile, that it made anyone who heard it unwilling to ever have anything to do with Cutter Amberville again.

It no longer suited Jumbo Booker's needs for superiority to do favors for his former roommate. He wished that he had never laid eyes on the man, that he had never had any association with him.

It was embarrassing, no, worse than embarrassing. It was shameful to be known as his friend.

"Tell him I won't take his call, Miss Johnson," Jumbo said to his secretary.

"When shall I tell him he can reach you?"

"Tell him he can't," Jumbo answered.

"I don't quite understand, Mr. Booker. Do you mean you'll be out all day?"

"No, I mean that I will not speak to him on the phone now or at any time in the future. Not on the phone and not in person. Make it perfectly clear, Miss Johnson."

"Oh," she said blankly, astonished and not sure what to do.

"Don't worry about being rude. Just repeat what I've just said and then hang up the phone. Don't wait for an answer."

"Mr. Booker?"

"And if he ever calls again, under any circumstances, tell him the same thing."

"Yes, Mr. Booker, I'll remember."

"Thank you, Miss Johnson."

Cutter put the phone down slowly. During all the humiliations of the past days he'd prevented himself from calling Jumbo Booker. He'd counted on Jumbo all along. He had felt certain that he would welcome him back to a job, if not his former job, then another, equally good. He'd made money for Booker, Smity and Jameston in his years with them, he'd always had Jumbo in his back pocket, but he'd grown tired of being patronized by someone he'd known too long. After giving the orders and running the show at Amberville Publications he had preferred to deal with strangers than to go to Jumbo with his hat in his hands; Jumbo, that talentless, boring, stuffy man who'd lived through him for so long; Jumbo, who had everything only because he'd been born an heir; Jumbo, who even now lacked the guts to insult him and had made his secretary do it for him.

Cutter lay back on the bed in his hotel room. It was all Zachary's fault, of course, as it always had been. Zachary's fault that he'd gone to San Francisco in the first place; Zachary's fault for marrying Lily; Zachary's fault that he'd had to marry Candice; Zachary's fault

425

for being so unbearably forgiving and smugly understanding, so sickeningly unmoved by the revelations about Lily and Justin. It had been necessary to smash him up, necessary to leave him to die. Yes, to die. Yes, to die finally, because there was no other way to get rid of him, no other way to get even at last. It had been only fair, only just, only what he *deserved.*

Justin. Yesterday, in some gossip column, he had read that Justin had come back to New York to do the pictures for Toby's wedding to that actress. What had the columnist written about him? "An American Lord Snowden shooting the marriage of the year," something like that. Justin. The child Lily adored, Justin who didn't know that his real father wasn't dead, Justin who owed him life.

An hour later Justin answered his doorbell and found Cutter standing there, looking as confident as if he were an eagerly awaited guest at a party. Justin recoiled and Cutter took advantage of his movement to walk into the living room and shut the door behind him.

"Hello, Justin," he said, putting out his hand to be shaken. Justin moved backward another step. "All right, Justin, I understand if you're hostile, believe me I do. I know what's been going on since I had that flare-up with your mother . . . she hasn't wanted to see me, she's probably been saying things about me to all of you children that aren't true, poisoning your minds against me, but it isn't her fault, Justin. She had a bad shock, a serious trauma that was caused by hearing a pack of lies when she went up to Canada."

Justin stood still, not looking at Cutter. "I decided that I should leave her alone long enough for her to realize that nothing she had heard would stand up under the exercise of common sense, or even under any investigation. God knows she was free to make one if she'd chosen. Now listen, Justin, I've come to talk to you because I think you're the most sensible and the most sensitive of all of Lily's children, and I'm worried about her."

Justin retreated farther into his room, speechless.

"O.K., if you don't want to discuss it, I do. I think it's too important to just let matters stay as they are. This separation from your mother is as bad for her as it is for me. She loves me deeply, Justin, and I love her far more than she knows. We have a long, happy future together if only she can be made to see it. I know she said that she doesn't want to lay eyes on me again, but by now, and I know my Lily, she wishes that she hadn't been so hasty. Still she's a proud woman and won't make the first step. That's why I've come to you. You're the one person I think she'd listen to with an open mind."

Justin turned and looked out of the window, his shoulders tense with the effort not to say anything to Cutter, not to dignify his presence in any way.

"Justin, just consider the situation. Isn't your mother going to be a very lonely woman without me? She's never existed without a man to guide her, to be devoted to her happiness, to protect her. As soon as my brother died she turned to me in such need, in such utter loneliness, that it broke my heart. I never failed her, not for an instant." Cutter took a step toward the window and then stopped as he saw the tight control in which Justin's slender, powerful body was clenched, a study in utter rejection.

"Look, Justin, you're never around town for more than a few weeks at a time. Toby is getting married and probably moving to California and Maxi, God knows, is going to be busy with running the company. . . . Who will have time for Lily if I'm not there for her? Justin, I came here to ask you to do something, not for me, but for your mother. I want you to go to her and ask her to talk to me . . . just talk to me."

Justin moved away from the window, picked up a camera, sat down, and began to examine it closely.

"I don't blame you for giving me the silent treatment, Justin. For some reason we've never managed to have a decent, warm relationship, but we should have been friends a long time ago . . . more than friends." Cutter stood over Justin, speaking quietly, as if to gentle down a wild animal.

"I have a *right* to come here and talk to you, Justin. I would never have intruded on your privacy if I didn't have that right. I would never tell you what I'm going to tell you if I didn't think that the time had come for you to know the truth, to know why I feel entitled to ask you to do something for me and for your mother that

427

I wouldn't ask anyone else in the family to do. No, don't shake your head, Justin, don't refuse to listen, don't shut me out."

Cutter's voice took on a pleading tone. Justin sat tensely, only looking at the camera now, using all the fierce concentration of his martial arts training to remain absolutely immobile.

"Justin . . . this is not easy to say. I know how much you love your mother. She's a woman who's impossible not to love. Years ago, when she and I were very young, both of us no more than twenty-four, younger than you are now, we fell in love with each other."

Justin dropped the camera he'd been holding, stood up and turned toward the blank wall, like a prisoner in a cell.

"We fell in love, we loved each other in all the ways a man and woman love each other, and we had a child . . . you, Justin. You're my son."

"I know." Justin spoke quickly, throwing the words away.

"What! Did Lily tell you?"

"I read that letter you wrote to her when you left her to go to California. I figured it out from the date on the letter and my birthday. I was just a kid, sneaking around looking at things in her desk the way kids do and I found it, hidden away. After I read it I put it back. It's probably still there."

"But . . . then, if you *know* . . . if you've *known!* Why did you never . . . how could you have . . . just, just kept it all to yourself?"

Justin turned around and walked toward the door. At last he raised his eyes to Cutter. "*Zachary Amberville was my father.* He was the only father I ever wanted, the only father I've ever *had.* He is still my father and he always will be. Please leave."

"Justin! You know the truth and you don't even deny it! Blood is blood. *I'm* your father, Justin! And I'm *alive* . . . doesn't that mean anything to you, for God's sake?"

"Just get out of here. Go away." Justin opened the door and gestured toward it with a shaking hand. Slowly, reluctantly, Cutter moved toward it and then, when he stood next to Justin, he hesitated. Suddenly, playing his last card, he clasped his arms around his son.

"NO!" With an instinctive movement, swift and powerful,

Justin pulled away and, using all his dangerous strength, chopped the edges of his hands down on the arms that tried to hold him. Cutter staggered backward, his broken forearms dangling uselessly, unable to steady himself or regain his footing.

As he fell backward, screaming in pain, down the long, steep staircase, above him a door was closed and bolted.

28

A few days later, when the excitement over Toby and India's wedding, which was planned for the following weekend, was at its peak, Maxi left Toby's house without being noticed. India, Angelica and Lily were too deep in conversation about what they would wear to see her slip out after dinner and Toby had taken refuge in one of his restaurants to avoid the fuss.

Maxi had put on an old pair of jeans and a plain white T-shirt. Her feet were bare, in flat sandals, and she wore no makeup. A sublime sprite, battle-ready. She made a stop on the way to her destination and finally arrived at Rocco's apartment carefully carrying a large, flat package.

"What's in that box?" Rocco said suspiciously, as he answered the doorbell and she foamed into the room. "And how come you dropped in? New Yorkers don't just drop in. They telephone first."

"I simply had to get away from Toby's . . . they're going loony over there talking about heirloom lace and white satin slippers and all that nonsense . . . weddings seem to drive even sensible women crazy. I thought that since you were home—Angelica told me you were in tonight—you wouldn't mind if I came by and discussed some things. Her relationship to Dunk for instance. I mean, Rocco, he's going to be an usher, for goodness' sakes."

"That's hardly a lifetime commitment." Rocco sniffed deeply. "Is that a pizza?"

"Oh, just a little one. I thought you might be hungry. Shall I go put it in the kitchen?"

"What kind of pizza?" Rocco demanded.

"With everything on it. Would I ever bring you any other kind of pizza, Rocco?" Maxi asked. Her enchantress eyes, her straight dark eyebrows, even her bow-shaped upper lip all expressed innocent reproach.

"No, I guess not. You were always very good at pizza. A consummate artist. By the way, congratulations, sincere congratulations. I think you'll be a great publisher. I mean it. You needed the right outlet for your energies and at last you've got it. I'm happy for you, Maxi. You'll do a terrific job. Just don't try to make another dummy by yourself."

"Thank you," Maxi said modestly. "Should we eat this right away while it's still hot?"

"So we're going to share it, are we?" Rocco shrugged. "In that case I'm not in favor of reheating it. The cheese will get all stringy and the crust will get too dry. Anyway I didn't have any dinner. I've been too busy working to stop to eat." Rocco deftly set the kitchen table and cut large slices out of the enormous pizza for both of them. For a while they ate in the reverent, utterly greedy silence that a really good pizza commands, prudently leaving the crusts for later when there would be nothing else left, for no pizza, however disappointing, had ever remained unfinished by Rocco Cipriani and this was a prime pizza, a definitive pizza. With it they drank beer out of the bottle and the pile of paper napkins in the center of the kitchen table steadily diminished.

"Funny thing about pizza," Rocco said, "you can actually feel your stomach saying 'thank you' to the rest of your body. It's not like regular food, it's more like a transfusion. I guess that's what soul food does . . . although it never does it for me."

"Hot dogs at the track, that's what works for me," Maxi said dreamily. "With tons of icky yellow mustard, those lukewarm white buns and that tepid flabby pink sausage . . . nothing can ever replace them."

"Maybe it's a religious difference."

"Childhood, it all has to do with childhood. Or so I believe," Maxi replied.

"How do you feel about soup?" Rocco asked earnestly.

"Soup? I'm not against soup, by any means, but it's still not my number-one thing."

"If you were sick, or cold, or just needed comforting?" Rocco persisted.

"And there wasn't any alcohol around?"

"Right . . . for some mysterious reason you can't get any booze. Then would you go for soup?"

"Only out of a can," Maxi said decidedly. "It would have to come right out of a can, none of the homemade, it's-good-for-you stuff. That's too European."

"'I'm in the mood for soup,'" Rocco sang off-key to the tune of "I'm in the Mood for Love." "'Only because you're near me, darling, and when you're near me, I'm in the mood for soup.'"

"What's the background?" Maxi asked, sensing the creation of a commercial. Rocco never used to sing in the kitchen.

"Lovers, every kind of lovers, all ages, sizes, shapes, white, black, yellow, brown, red, extraterrestrials, animals, three seconds on each pair, kissing, hugging, caressing, with Julio Iglesias singing the lyric."

"Do you see the product?" Maxi asked.

"Never. It's for the American Soup Canning Association. A full minute. Like it?"

"I think it's brilliant. But not Julio . . . I like him but his English just isn't convincing. What about Kenny Rogers? No, too Western. It's a ballad and Ol' Blue Eyes is too obvious—to say nothing of what he'd charge to do it—I know—Tony Bennett!"

"Perfect! Romantic, warm, familiar—perfect. So you like the concept? You really like it?"

"It would make me go into the kitchen, like a brainwashed zombie, and open a can of any kind of soup and heat it up and drink it before I knew what had happened," Maxi assured him, giving him the last slice of pizza, and all the crusts.

"That's what I've been working on," Rocco said, between bites. "I just wasn't sure if people really liked soup, or if they just thought it was good for them."

"What does that matter to the Soup Canning Association?"

"I have to feel emotional about a commercial before I get it right. And my mother always made her own soup. She'd never let us touch the canned kind, so I couldn't trust my gut on this."

"Your mother did make the most incredibly good soup. She gave me her recipe for chicken soup once but it started with buying a whole chicken and a veal knuckle. I wasn't ready for that. So I went out and bought Campbell's instead," Maxi remembered sadly.

"Well, you were only eighteen, after all. Or were you seventeen? I never was absolutely sure."

"I don't think I was, either. Anyway, I still can't cook."

"My mother can't run a publishing company. To each his own," Rocco said fairly, putting the plates in the sink and finding two more bottles of beer. "But damn it, she made her own wine too—I'm having problems with the Gallo account but I'll get over them. Thank God Mama couldn't make beer, or cars or soap. Let's go in the living room. What about Dunk? I thought he seemed like a good guy when Angelica dragged him over to meet me. You can't really believe that Angelica's in danger of being seduced by him?"

"Probably not. My mother pointed out that she's a different and wiser teenager than I was. I guess I should relax."

"Would you have been seduced by him when you were twelve?" Rocco wondered, standing by the window and looking out at all of Central Park, spread before him from his tall windows.

"Of course not. I was waiting for you." There was great art in her simple statement.

"Wouldn't you even have necked with him? . . . Dunk's pretty attractive."

"I never necked. Not with kids," Maxi answered, gazing at the reflection of the fine, well-lit room that floated in front of the windows, the Isis suspended in midair, timelessly queenly; the majestic croup of Rocco's Han Dynasty horse visible on a table. "You were the first man I ever kissed," she added after a pause. She batted her lashes until they quarreled but avoided looking at him.

"Oh."

"You always knew that."

"No I didn't. I thought you had experience—not real experience since you were a virgin, but something. You were a hot number, as we used to say in the old neighborhood."

"All an act," Maxi confessed, hanging her impertinently frivolous head.

"No, you *were* a hot number," Rocco insisted.

"The experience part—that was an act. The hot part—that

was you." She raised her head and subjected him to her unruly matchless green gaze, the lips of her sorceress's mouth slightly parted, suddenly girlish, mysterious, as if every minute of their mutual past had been abolished, as if they were meeting for the first time.

"Oh. Well, thanks."

"Rocco—"

"*No*, Maxi. Absolutely *not!*"

"No? How do you know what I was going to say?" Maxi said, beautifully indignant. "How can you be so negative when you don't even know if I was going to say something that required an answer?"

"I've gotten smarter over the years. When you pop up on my doorstep in virtually the same clothes you used to wear to my loft the summer we met, looking young enough to be jailbait and so fucking pretty that it's criminal—except to someone who knows you as well as I do—and then you bring me a pizza with *everything* on it, and are so interested and sweet and helpful about my soup commercial, do you honestly think that I wouldn't *have* to know that you're setting me up for something? A major con? Come on, Maxi. Admit it."

"Don't you believe that people can change their characters as they grow up?" she asked reasonably, tugging her white streak. "Don't you think that I might just want to have a better relationship with the father of my child, a friendly interchange between two adults, a laying to rest of all the anger and hostility that has come between us? A new start, Rocco, so that aside from Angelica and our mutual love for her, we could coexist in the same city with some kindness and regard? Do I have to be coming over here with anything else in mind?"

"Maxi, shape up. Who blackmailed me—viciously—into making the dummy for *B&B*? Who got me drunk when I had a head cold and raped me three times? Well—the first time anyway."

"That's absurd!"

"Maybe it can't be proved but I know what I know. You never show up unless you want something. What is it this time? Wait, let me guess. Pavka is going to retire in a few years and you want me to come over and get ready to take over for him. That's it, isn't it?

Actually I'd do it too, except it would mean working for you, no matter how much freedom you gave me. So I won't. No way. What else could it be? Maybe—"

"Rocco! You're absolutely right, I admit it. I am a con artist. It's my nature, it's always been more fun to get places by twisting the odds. I can't seem to stop trying to bend the truth in my favor, and what's more, sometimes I have a bad temper when I don't get what I want."

"That's hard to believe," he grunted.

"But I *have* changed. In this last year I've changed more than in the rest of my whole life put together. I've learned so much, Rocco, I've discovered that if I work very hard and sink my teeth in and don't give up, I can get what I want the honest way, right down the middle—with a lot of help from my friends."

"And you want me to be one of them?" he asked suspiciously.

"No." Maxi faced him, standing squarely but, at last, speaking the unadorned truth, looking him straight in the eye, all determination, all conviction, all fire. "I want you to love me again, Rocco."

"Why?" He didn't move a fraction of an inch toward her. Did she think that all she had to do was ask and he'd fall at her feet?

"You don't have any idea, do you, how I *yearn* for you? Oh, Rocco, it started way back when I first laid eyes on you and now it's a thousand times worse than it ever was when I was seventeen. It's such a yearning, such a *need*—it's unspeakable, impossible to find the right words. It's more than I can stand anymore, Rocco, for you not to love me," Maxi cried out in a voice that concealed no tricks, nothing but her pure emotion. "There's never been another man I've cared about, not deeply, not truly. Oh, if only I'd met you when I was older! I wouldn't have been so impossible, I wouldn't have made all the thoughtless, teenage, rich-girl mistakes I made. I wouldn't have made that one unforgivable mistake—I would have understood you better and realized how proud you were. We could have managed, we'd still be married to each other. Please, Rocco, please at least give me another chance. Just a chance, that's all I'm asking for. Oh, how can you look at me like that, as if you haven't any idea how I'm feeling? I love you so much I can't *endure* it."

Rocco continued to stare at Maxi impassively, brooding darkly

435

down at her with a long, slow look that confirmed everything he already knew about this fantastical creature he had been unable to forget, unable to replace, since the day he had walked out on their marriage. She'd ruined him for other women, deliberately of course. Once you'd been wholly in love with Maxi you were done for, he guessed. He *knew*. She'd always had good stuff. She'd always be trouble, outrageous trouble, sure, but nothing that he couldn't handle. Anyway, who was he kidding, *he adored her*. He worshiped this wonderfully surprising little fiend with her bottomless bag of tricks. He'd *died* each time she'd married those two fruitcakes. There wasn't anyone else for him either. Never had been, never would be.

Rocco was caught up in such a flashflood of disorderly rejoicing that he could barely articulate. "O.K. Fair enough."

"You *will* give me another chance?" Maxi faltered, suddenly unsure. "Where do we start? From scratch, as if we didn't know each other at all?"

"Why do things halfway," Rocco answered munificiently, suddenly finding his voice. "Let's go all out—get married again. It's not as if I don't love you like an absolute madman. It's not as if I've ever stopped—I'm not sure I even tried. We've wasted so many years growing up—or maybe it had to be that way? You're going to move in here with me, you and Angelica, and right away. But no fuss, no big wedding, no heirloom lace this time," he added, taking her into the indisputably jubilant grip he'd made himself hold back for so long, so very long.

"No fuss," Maxi promised. "It's not as if I'm marrying *another* man."

"You're marrying me. For good, damn it, for better, forever! The same man you started with," Rocco stated posessively, abandoning himself to her magic without another backward thought.

"Exactly, that's what I'll tell India . . . not another man," Maxi crooned in her most witching song.

"Tell India?" he muttered in surprise. "Aren't you going to tell Angelica first?"

"Angelica? Oh, her. Of course I'll tell her first," Maxi answered vaguely through the celebration of finding herself back home where she belonged.